LIGHT
OF
DAWN

Center Point
Large Print

Also by Vannetta Chapman and available from Center Point Large Print:

Anna's Healing
Deep Shadows
Joshua's Mission
Raging Storm
Sarah's Orphans

This Large Print Book carries the Seal of Approval of N.A.V.H.

LIGHT
OF
DAWN

VANNETTA
CHAPMAN

CENTER POINT LARGE PRINT
THORNDIKE, MAINE

This Center Point Large Print edition
is published in the year 2017 by arrangement with
Harvest House Publishers.

The text of this Large Print edition is unabridged.
In other aspects, this book may vary
from the original edition.
Printed in the United States of America
on permanent paper.
Set in 16-point Times New Roman type.

ISBN: 978-1-68324-509-4

Library of Congress Cataloging-in-Publication Data

Names: Chapman, Vannetta, author.
Title: Light of dawn / Vannetta Chapman.
Description: Center Point Large Print edition. | Thorndike, Maine :
    Center Point Large Print, 2017.
Identifiers: LCCN 2017023999 | ISBN 9781683245094
    (hardcover : alk. paper)
Subjects: LCSH: Regression (Civilization)—Fiction. | Survival—Fiction.
| Large type books. | BISAC: FICTION / Christian / Suspense. | GSAFD:
Suspense fiction. | Christian fiction. | Dystopias.
Classification: LCC PS3603.H3744 L54 2017b | DDC 813/.6—dc23
LC record available at https://lccn.loc.gov/2017023999

For Dad

ACKNOWLEDGMENTS

This book is dedicated to my dad, who passed from this life to the next twenty years ago. My father loved to debate, to toss ideas back and forth, to challenge me to think outside my box. During my teenage years, we would stay up late into the night discussing "wars and rumors of wars," how to survive in this world, and how *surviving* wasn't enough—unless you had a clear conscience, unless you had helped your neighbor, unless you'd followed that Golden Rule. I love him and miss him and am so grateful to have had him in my life.

Many thanks to the awesome staff of Harvest House for your guidance as we jumped into the dystopian genre together. The fine folks in sales, editorial, and marketing all helped to make this project possible. Kim Moore, you are the best! Thank you to Reagen Reed for providing editorial input, and my agent, Steve Laube, for guiding me through the continually changing publishing world.

My pre-readers, Kristy and Janet, deserve rubies and gold, but this thanks will have to do instead. My family continues to encourage me through every deadline. A special thank you to Dorsey Sparks for inspiring my main character.

Many readers have written to me since the release of Book 1, *Deep Shadows*. You've taken my scenario to heart, spent time in prayer, some have put together go-bags, and others are purchasing generators . . . not necessarily because of what I've written, but rather because the times seem to point to an impending upheaval, a fundamental change in the way we live. I want to remind you to keep the faith. In the end, our faith and God's provision are what will see us through any trouble this world throws at us. I continue to pray the events described in this series never happen, but as Max has said, "We hope for the best, but plan for the worst."

And finally . . . "always giving thanks to God the Father for everything, in the name of our Lord Jesus Christ" (Ephesians 5:20).

LIGHT
OF
DAWN

In that day the Lord will reach out his hand
   a second time
to reclaim the surviving remnant of his
   people.

The Book of Isaiah
Chapter 11, Verse 11

Winter kept us warm, covering
Earth in forgetful snow.

T.S. Eliot
The Waste Land

Excerpts from Shelby's Journal

July 3
11:35 P.M.

"We're going to weather this. Together, we will find a way." I want to believe Georgia's words. I need to believe them. Carter has yet to move. He hasn't opened his eyes or squeezed my hand. We managed to lower his temperature with cold cloths to his head and crushed ibuprofen that we spooned into his mouth. His insulin levels, though—they remain dangerously low.

July 4
8:15 A.M.

Jerry Lambert came by this morning to check on Carter. A retired vet is treating my son, and I am grateful to have him. This says more about the world we live in than anything I could write on the pages of this journal. Jerry thinks the reason for Carter's hyperglycemia is the infection that has set in due to his broken leg. There's no way to know how much or what type of bacteria was in the creek water where he lay for over twelve hours. Jerry gave him an injection of antibiotics. I didn't think to ask how he managed to have that. My every prayer is, "Please, God. Don't take my son."

2:45 P.M.

Every able-bodied person in the area is preparing for battle with the Cavanaghs—a group that has taken over the ranch on the other side of the creek. The group that Carter told Roy about when they first found him. Carter hasn't spoken another word since. Hasn't even opened his eyes. I want to be with them, protecting this place, but I can't leave Carter's side.

10:40 P.M.

I am bargaining with God.

July 5
6:45 A.M.

Carter still hasn't opened his eyes or spoken, but his glucose levels are improving. Max stopped by long enough to tell me they tried reasoning with the Cavanaghs. The result was a shoot-out that left two of our men injured.

July 6
2:15 A.M.

I've been listening to the echo of gunshots for more than an hour. Georgia
says we are to pray, to have faith, to
believe, but my mind and my heart and
even my soul are numb. I sit here and
hold Carter's hand and try to remember
how to pray. I flinch at the sound of the
battle raging less than a mile from here,
and I try to envision life without Max or
Roy or Lanh. I wonder how we'll survive
if Jerry Lambert is killed. Since I've
returned, we've been visited by someone
from every surrounding farm—checking
on Carter, asking how they can help,
bringing food they can't afford to share.
We are suffering and tired and afraid, but
we are also a family.

July 7
3:15 P.M.

Carter woke today. He's weak and still
battling the fever, but Jerry says he's
turned the corner. We don't talk about
what happened to him in the creek or to
us in Austin. I don't know if he's aware
of the battle raging with the Cavanaghs.

How can one group of men hold out for so long in a place they have no legitimate claim to? Why don't they just leave?

July 8
7:15 P.M.

Today has been a good day. I didn't think I'd ever write those six words again. Carter sat up for a full half hour. The heat in his leg has lessened. Jerry says we'll try to put a cast on it once the swelling goes down. I have no idea how he hopes to make one of those with our limited resources, but Georgia says that Jerry Lambert could create a . . .

July 9
4:25 A.M.

The horrors of last night exceed anything I saw in Abney before or after the flare. They even surpass the anarchy of Austin. There I didn't have to unload the bodies of friends and neighbors, worrying with each person I moved that one of them might be the man I love. I shouldn't have written that, but then I am long past worrying about someone finding my journal and sharing the secrets of my heart. I have loved Max for at least twenty-five years of my life. When did it begin? Junior high? Family vacations that my parents took with his, dragging us in their wake? Last week in Austin?

I won't hide those feelings from myself any longer. If nothing else, tonight cemented in my mind the futility of looking toward the future, of imagining a happily-ever-after ending. The battle with the Cavanaghs is over. The toll in human lives is high—too high. Any more death is too much death.

I'm sitting by Carter's bed, looking back over these pages, and I wonder, what is the point? If those we love are going to die, are bound to suffer so grievously, then why should we struggle so mightily to live? But as soon as those thoughts enter my head, I see the faces of those who have sacrificed so much: Patrick and Bianca and Max. And other people I barely know, and yet they risked their lives for me: Lanh and Bill and Clay. Donna. Gabe. My thoughts circle round and round, vacillating wildly between hope and despair as I wonder what the dawn will bring.

17

ONE
High Fields Ranch
March 14

Shelby's head jerked up at the sound of the emergency bell. She dropped the bucket full of slop and ran full speed toward the house, the March wind whipping at her clothes. Carter reached the porch steps at the same time she did. Roy had hurried over from the main barn, and Georgia stood wiping her hands on a kitchen towel.

Max stood next to the bell, an old rusted thing they'd found in the barn and fastened to the front porch as a kind of emergency warning system. There were many things they'd learned this first winter on the ranch with no electricity, no power, and no one to depend on but each other. One of the most important was the need for the bell.

Max grinned and held up both hands, palms out. "I'm sorry. I didn't mean to scare you."

Shelby wanted to scold him, but instead she leaned over, hands on her knees, and tried to pull in deep breaths. She focused on convincing her heart that it was okay to slow into a regular rhythm.

"So what's up?" Carter asked.

"Got a call on the radio from the roadblock crew. Patrick's on his way."

"Patrick? Seriously?" A grin broke across Carter's face.

Roy reached over and circled an arm around Carter's neck, pulling him into a bear hug.

Georgia breathed a sigh of relief and sank onto the porch rocker.

"You're sure?" Shelby raised her gaze to Max. "You're sure it's him? Because he's not due for another—"

"Three months. Yeah, I know."

"But you're certain it is him?"

"Know anyone else who is still driving a red '65 Mustang?"

An ache deep in Shelby's heart eased at those words. Patrick. Alive. Here. It was something she'd prayed for every night since that day in July when he'd sacrificed himself for Carter.

Max walked down the steps and pulled her into his arms. "He's okay. I told you he would be. He's fine."

She pulled away out of habit. Instead of being offended, Max grinned at her.

And then they heard him—the rumble of the V8 engine reaching them well before they could see the red hot rod. That it still worked was a wonder. But then many things they'd expected to work didn't, and a few things they didn't expect to still be functional were. The classic Mustang was one.

20

It made the curve in the caliche road and headed up the hill to the ranch house. Carter let out a whoop when sunlight glinted off the bright red finish. He took off at a lope and reached the car before it made the parking area. Patrick stopped the car in the middle of the road, stepped out, grabbed Carter, and pulled him into a hug.

Shelby's legs began to tremble. She plopped down on the top porch step.

"Easy, Sparks." Max moved so that he was standing in front of her. "This is a good thing."

It was. Certainly it was, but they'd had so much death and tragedy that a part of her wondered.

Why was their dearest friend here three months early?

What had happened in Austin?

Was there more trouble in Abney?

And then the passenger door opened, Bianca stepped out, and Shelby was running, her feet flying over the distance between them.

TWO

Twenty minutes later they were all seated around Georgia's kitchen table. Shelby rubbed her fingertips across the worn oak.

Sunshine streamed through the window over the sink, landing on a jar of honey that they had harvested from the bee boxes they'd traded for last summer. Georgia had reheated their morning coffee on the gas stove top. It was made from acorns that they had gathered, soaked, and then roasted. It wasn't Folgers, didn't have a drop of caffeine in it, but somehow she'd become accustomed to it.

"Tell us everything," Carter said. "How's Abney? And . . . and the capital? We don't get any news out here."

Shelby tried to look at her son objectively, but of course that was impossible. He'd grown an inch since they'd come to High Fields. Georgia had measured him the week before at five feet eleven inches. He'd also dropped twenty pounds, weight he couldn't afford to lose. His black hair curled at the base of his neck, and his dark brown eyes remained glued on Patrick and Bianca. Her son was no longer a child. He'd become a man since they'd moved to High Fields. He'd earned a seat at the table.

"When was the last time you visited Abney?" Patrick asked.

"Late fall," Max said. "November, maybe."

Max was tall and wiry, black hair streaked with gray, and deep-set hazel eyes. He'd celebrated his forty-sixth birthday the month before. Shelby had known him nearly all her life. In truth, she knew him better than any other person in this room, including her son. In many ways Max was more of a father to Carter than his own biological dad had been, but then Alex had died of a drug overdose when Carter was only three years old.

"We've been meaning to get back," Roy admitted. "Something always comes up, though, and we figured they wouldn't have what we needed anyway."

Max's parents had fared the changes since the flare better than anyone else Shelby knew. Roy's daily work had changed very little. He'd been a rancher before and was a rancher and farmer still. Though these days he was doing both of those jobs more like his grandfather had done. Georgia had taken the changes in stride, working diligently to provide them with balanced meals and adequate clothing. Shelby hadn't realized how much she missed her own parents until she moved to High Fields. Georgia and Roy were in their late sixties, hardworking, and pillars of strength both emotionally and spiritually. Her thoughts skipped back to last July, to those dark days when she'd wondered if Carter would survive his accident. She pushed those memories away, determined to focus on the situation at hand. She knew they were getting down to business when Bianca and Patrick exchanged glances, and Patrick cleared his throat.

"Abney doesn't have what you need," Patrick said. "Other than the springs, which provide an unlimited supply of water, they have very little."

"Is your mom okay?" Shelby asked Bianca.

"*Mamá* died. Six weeks ago."

Shelby popped out of her chair, skirted around the table, and pulled Bianca into a hug. "We didn't know."

"How could you?"

"I'm so, so sorry. She was a very special person."

"She was." Bianca brushed at her eyes and pulled in a deep breath.

No one spoke for a moment. Shelby stood there, holding her friend, grateful that they were together. When Bianca stepped back, Shelby fetched a glass of water for her and returned to her seat.

"The doctor thinks it was a heart attack. At least I was there beside her at the end."

"What about your sister?"

"Went back to Mason the week after *Mamá* died."

"I'd guess the population is half what it was

before the flare," Patrick continued. "The winter has been hard."

They all digested the news in silence, Carter glancing at Shelby. She didn't know what to say to him. He had to be thinking about the friends they'd left behind, but there was no way to know how everyone was doing. The days of being able to text someone and check on them were over, maybe forever.

"What about Austin?" Roy asked. "That was a fine thing you did, by the way. Offering to stay at the university so they'd give Shelby the insulin for Carter."

"A fair trade," Patrick said, placing his hand on top of Carter's head. Patrick was a big guy, former linebacker, retired military, large hands. He gave Carter's head a playful shake and said, "But you still owe me a chess game."

"Anytime," Carter murmured, a smile breaking through his worried expression.

Patrick again clasped his coffee mug. "The university fell three weeks ago."

"Steiner?" Max jerked his head up.

"No. Actually, the final attack came from the kids caught in the middle, the ones camping in the stadium. They hooked up with some of the street gangs. Our side managed to escape while they were attacking Steiner's side of the campus. We tried to help at first, but we were outgunned."

"And they would have broken through your side?"

"Maybe. Our barricades were good, but at that point we were out of supplies. There was no real reason to stay, especially if it meant that we might be surrounded by hostiles."

"So you fled the UT grounds? Where did you go? To the state government compound?" Shelby still sometimes had nightmares about the school, the perimeter fence surrounding the capitol buildings, and the great masses of people camped on the outside.

"We did, but three days later their forces attacked the governor's troops. We held them off at first, but in the end Governor Reed had no option but to retreat."

"Retreat?" Shelby shook her head in disbelief. "Retreat to where?"

"Corpus," Bianca said. "Apparently, the governor had a fallback position there, and Corpus Christi fared better than other cities throughout the state."

Max sat back, folding his arms across his chest and scowling at his best friend. "You're telling me that Austin is a loss."

"It is."

"A bunch of students and thugs overpowered the state government?"

"I wouldn't say they overpowered us, but you know Governor Reed. You met her. She wasn't willing to fire into the crowds and kill hundreds or even thousands of citizens. When a show of force didn't stop them, and the water cannons didn't slow them down . . ."

"Using gray water." Shelby shivered at the memory.

"They sure weren't going to use fresh water." Patrick shrugged. "Reed had two options—shoot to kill or retreat. She chose to retreat."

"Wow." Carter drummed his thumbs against the table. "It's hard to imagine that things are that bad."

"They are. Much worse than last July."

"How is that possible?" Shelby asked. "How did things deteriorate to where we are now?"

Instead of answering her, Patrick glanced around the table and said, "That's why I'm here. I agreed to do something for Governor Reed, and I'm going to need your help."

THREE

Max resisted the urge to grab a piece of paper and list the pros and cons to what Patrick described next. He wanted to see it written down and analyze it, hammer it into a form that might make the scenario more palatable.

"I'm in," Carter said.

Shelby and Bianca started talking at once, and Max caught his parents looking at each other with wide eyes. The fact that this surprised his father, that he hadn't expected things to be as drastic as they were, said a lot. His father was a realist, a salt-of-the-earth kind of guy. The flares hadn't slowed him down, but hearing that no one could even locate the federal government seemed to have momentarily stunned him.

"Okay, wait," Max said. "Everybody hold on."

Patrick grinned, and Max knew why. He'd slipped into his lawyer mode.

"To summarize, Abney is holding on by a thread. Austin is gone—"

"For all practical purposes," Patrick clarified. "A few buildings are still relatively unscathed. Some folks are staying, but there's not much to keep them there."

"And the state government is now in Corpus Christi."

"Correct." Patrick snagged a few of the shelled pecans from the dish that Georgia kept on the table and popped them into his mouth.

"Governor Reed hasn't heard from the federal government."

"Not a word."

"And she's sending you to Kansas to look for them."

Patrick folded his arms on the table and leaned forward. "We don't know where the feds are. We can guess where they aren't."

"They wouldn't be on the East Coast, not if what you're describing in urban areas is widespread." It was the first thing Georgia had said since Patrick began to describe what had happened and why he was here.

"Then they also wouldn't be on the West Coast. That's for sure." Roy scrubbed a hand across his face, stood, and walked into the living room. He returned with a national map, which he unfolded and spread across the middle of the table. With his index finger he traced a line south to north, beginning at the Mexican border. "San Diego? Los Angeles? Even San Francisco? No way."

"Portland and Seattle are a possibility," Patrick admitted. "Reed is sending scouts there as well, but she strongly suspects that whoever is in control, whoever is left, would rather set up in the middle of the country."

"But why Kansas?" Shelby asked.

29

"Have you ever been to the Flint Hills?" Patrick asked. "I was stationed in Fort Riley for a time. We drove out there once. Miles and miles of nothing. Fertile in spite of its limited topsoil. There's water but no development. If the government's looking for a place to start over, it's as good as any."

"Wait." Max placed both hands flat on the table. "That could be said of certain areas in almost every state."

"True, and she's sending out scouts to every state."

"Like before," Shelby murmured. "Like she did when she sent Dr. Bhatti—"

"Gabe," Patrick corrected her. "Gabe Thompson."

"Right. I know that, but I still think of him as . . . you know. Dr. Bhatti."

"Hard to believe that guy was a government operative," Carter said. "Or whatever he was."

"You're right, Shelby. It is like before. Reed is a practical woman. She understands we need help, and she's not afraid to ask for it. Plus, it's been almost a year since the flare. We need to know what is or isn't out there."

"Whether the cavalry is coming," Max said.

"Yeah. Pretty much." Patrick hesitated, and then he added, "There's something else. The gasoline we have is degrading . . ."

"That's why we're having trouble with the

Dodge." Carter rubbed his hand across the top of his head, causing his hair to stick up. It was comical, but the look on his face was dead serious. "We keep topping it off, but the engine still knocks something terrible."

"Smart move," Patrick said. "Topping it off leaves less room for condensation to develop."

"Condensation waters it down." Carter sat back, crossed his arms, and looked from Max to Patrick. "We figured that out, and it worked for the first few months. Now it's back to knocking."

"The only other thing you can do to increase the lifespan of gasoline is add a stabilizer."

"Which we don't have."

"No one does, except maybe the survivalists. It was scooped off the shelves pretty fast when the flare hit. Diesel lasts longer, and the reserves we had were already treated for long-term storage—with both stabilizer and algicide."

"But we're still talking about a finite amount," Roy said.

"Exactly. The clock is ticking. If we're going to send out a search party for the feds, now is the time to do it."

"What does she hope to gain?" Georgia asked. She leaned forward and tapped the map. "Say you find the government. What then? What does she hope you'll be able to achieve?"

"Three things." Patrick ticked them off on his fingers. "There are federal storage facilities

31

around the state that include food, medicine, and fuel. We need the exact locations and the codes to get in."

"You think they're still there?"

"It's a possibility." Patrick held up his second finger. "There are some federal units still within the Texas borders. Holdouts that either were left behind, forgotten, or simply didn't disband when the rest did. Reed needs authority over those troops, and it needs to come from the president."

"That would help with her manpower problem." Roy crossed his arms and nodded for Patrick to continue.

"Third, and perhaps the most important, Reed needs information. She needs to know how long it will be before the feds assert their presence, before they return to the state level. What is their long-range plan? And by long-range, I mean three to five years."

Shelby was shaking her head before he finished speaking. "I understand why you're steering clear of the large metropolitan areas, but there's a Presidential Emergency Operations Center right under the East Wing of the White House. What makes her think that they aren't holed up there?"

"For nine months? Doesn't seem likely. Maybe at first, but at some point they would have needed to move."

"There's supposedly more than a hundred underground bases—secret ones." When everyone turned to stare at him, Carter shrugged.

"How do you know that?" Shelby asked.

"Google? Comedy news? The Internet? Surely you all still remember those things."

"He's right," Bianca said. "Some of my colleagues pursued that story once. They tried to make a documentary photographing the underground bases, or at least the communities where they were rumored to be. They didn't get far, though. The places they tried? All off limits."

Bianca had been a freelance photographer and graphic designer before the flare. She'd been good too. But like many other professions, hers had gone the way of the modern world.

"All right," Max conceded. "I'll agree it's possible that the seat of the federal government has moved, and I understand Reed's need to locate it. But why you? No offense, but—"

"I know what you're saying. *Why me?* is a good question, especially since I'm asking for your help." Patrick shook his head. "You can't conceive how much pressure she's under unless you've been with her. Half of the Texas National Guard has gone home. Of those remaining, she lost a few more to injuries in the battle of Austin. The truth is that she doesn't have many trained soldiers left, and the ones she has she needs there in Corpus."

"You're trained," Shelby pointed out.

"But I'm not active military. She actually foresaw that this might happen, and she had a

33

plan laid out already. The idea was to send one military person and one nonmilitary person to each state, looking for the federal government. Get there, look around, request help if we find them, and if not—get back."

"Wait." Shelby cocked her head to the side, trying to make sense of what he was saying. "So . . . who are you paired with?"

"Gabe." He didn't give Shelby a chance to argue with him. "We're to meet up with him tomorrow morning. He had to, uh, pick up some supplies first."

Max could actually feel the anxiety rolling off Shelby now. He knew what was coming. Everyone at the table knew what was coming. Shelby's issues with Gabe Thompson were legendary, though Max had thought most of that had abated when the guy helped to procure a supply of insulin for Carter. Unfortunately, Danny Vail, their former city manager, had stolen their supplies and forced them out of the government compound at gunpoint.

Patrick was the one to face Shelby's attitude head-on. "I know you don't like the guy."

"I like him."

"Or trust him."

"I trust him—sort of. But he did mislead us. We thought he was a doctor—an ear, nose, and throat specialist—who just happened to stumble into Abney."

"When, in fact, Reed sent him as part of Operation Nightshade."

"It's a good thing we had him," Bianca said. "He saved a lot of lives. I understand Shelby's hesitancy, but I believe that Gabe Thompson is a decent man, and of course I want to help Patrick. That's why I'm going."

"I'm in," Carter said, repeating his earlier sentiment.

"Me too," Shelby said quietly.

Max didn't answer. Instead, he turned to his parents, a dozen questions on his lips.

"Go, son. The crops are planted. We can handle things here."

"Are you sure?"

"We're sure," Georgia said. "Patrick needs you. Our state needs you. How could you not go?"

"All right. I'm in."

"There's one more thing," Patrick said. "One more reason that we came here early. There's something we—Bianca and I—need to do."

FOUR

After lunch Carter and Lanh carried their backpacks, each stuffed with two changes of clothes, into the storage room. The last few months had been difficult, and they were fortunate to have anything still on the shelves.

Carter picked up a Nalgene water bottle, a compass, and a set of work gloves.

Lanh reached for duct tape and an emergency first aid kit.

"So they're getting married?" Lanh was Vietnamese. He was shorter than Carter, around five feet six, with black hair that was in constant need of a cut. He was also two and a half years older than Carter, and he didn't have diabetes. Other than those things, they were pretty much the same.

If Carter had gone off to college, if the flare hadn't happened, he would have picked someone like Lanh to share a dorm room with. The guy was laid back most of the time, yet freakishly quick to scope out and assess a dangerous situation. Which was how they'd found him. Carter's mom and Max had needed help when they were in Austin. Lanh provided that help and more. His only request had been a ride out of the *Austin Anarchy*, their favorite term for what had happened in their state capital.

36

"Bianca and Patrick? Married?"

"Yeah. Surprised me. I thought they were like—friends. I never caught them staring longingly at each other."

"So she waited for him while he was staying in Austin, filling his side of the bargain."

"That entire plan was crazy."

"You should have met Agnes Wright. That lady was a poster child for crazy."

Carter crouched in front of a shelf, but he wasn't seeing the supplies stacked there. Not really. He was trying to envision what had happened in Austin. He'd been stuck on the ranch, which was kind of a good thing because he'd learned a lot. It was kind of a bad thing because he'd broken his leg and been bedridden for six weeks.

"She was the lady at the university, right?"

"Professor Agnes Wright. Not a woman you want to cross."

"But don't you think she'd have eventually agreed to give them the insulin? That she was like . . . bluffing?"

"Nope. Patrick saved your skinny butt. You owe him—"

"Big time," they said in unison.

Carter reached for an LED headlamp and a pack of glow sticks. Georgia was packing their food supply, and Max was taking care of weapons and tools.

"No use trying to figure adults," Lanh added.

"Yeah. I try to save my energy and not immerse myself in useless tasks."

They continued putting items into their packs. The trick, Carter thought, was to be sure and take what they might need while leaving enough for Georgia and Roy. That was the problem with breaking up their group.

"Are you worried about leaving Georgia and Roy?" Lanh asked.

"A little."

"But you still want to go."

"Of course."

"It's better here than there. I'll guarantee you that."

"We don't know where there is."

"Exactly."

"But if we can find help—"

"Yeah, I get the reasoning."

Carter reached for a pack of water purification tablets. Little chance that Roy and Georgia would need them since their drinking water came from a well. He stuffed the tablets into an interior compartment of the pack. "I want to see what's out there. What if someone has found a way to resuscitate the grid, and we don't even know it?"

"We would have heard."

"Maybe, if it was somewhere close. But we're going to Kansas. That takes us past Dallas and Oklahoma City. No telling what we'll learn."

"It'll be nice to be anywhere but here," Lanh admitted.

"Really?" Carter had been squatting in front of the shelves, but he dropped onto the floor, crossed his legs Indian style, and studied his friend. "I thought you were the new Asian cowboy, totally into this whole live-off-the-grid scene."

"Yeah. I like it. Plus, I'm good with horses."

He was good with horses. Who would have figured that, since he'd never been within a hundred feet of one before the flare? He had become a sort of veterinarian apprentice. A vet tech in the new age of no tech. Which was why he hadn't been around when Patrick and Bianca had first shown up. He'd left before dawn to walk to Jerry Lambert's place so he could help with a foaling. The mare had done well, and the foal was healthy. Society might fall apart around them, but nature plodded on.

"So you love it here, but you want to leave."

Lanh shrugged. "You appreciate a place more if you get away now and then. And who knows? Maybe we'll meet some girls."

"Thought you'd already found one."

"Yeah, so did I."

"Monica is working through some stuff. Give her time."

Lanh shook his head. "Hopefully we can be

friends someday, but we'll never be more than that. We just weren't . . . right for each other."

"I guess."

They finished combing through the supplies and carried their packs down the hall to the room they would be sharing. Lanh had lived in the house since moving to High Fields, but Carter had stayed in the cottage with his mom. Tonight, it would apparently become the honeymoon suite.

"Boys, great. You appear just when I need help." Georgia pushed two stuffed bags into their arms. No one else called them *boys,* but coming from Georgia it sounded like a compliment.

"What is this stuff?" Carter asked.

"Take it over to your mom. She's helping Bianca get ready."

Georgia hurried back into the kitchen, muttering something about wedding cake.

"No way she can come up with a cake," Lanh said. "When was the last time we had sugar?"

"I wouldn't put it past her." Carter opened his bag. It was filled with candles. More candles than he knew they had. "Why would Patrick and Bianca need these?"

"Adults, dude. They're not to be understood."

They hustled across the yard to the cottage. The wind had turned from the north, which no doubt meant rain. Temperatures were dropping too. Carter hoped it wasn't a true blue norther. Surely, March was too late for that.

Lanh banged on the door.

Carter's mom opened it, but she didn't let them in. "Thank you. Would you see if you could help Patrick and Max in the barn?"

So they tromped over to the barn and helped arrange a ragtag collection of chairs and benches into a semicircle. Everyone was laughing and joking and teasing Patrick, who seemed to be enjoying every minute of it. But when they were finished sweeping and swiping at cobwebs, Patrick pulled the two of them aside.

"I appreciate your offering to go—"

"Don't say it." Carter looked him directly in the eye. He'd known Patrick for practically all of his life, and he could feel what was coming.

"Yeah, we're going," Lanh said. "After all, we're the next generation. We need to know what's out there."

"I know you do. The thing is, I didn't want to alarm Georgia and Roy with the details, but it's pretty grim."

Lanh stuck his thumbs in his pockets. "I was in Austin, remember? I've seen grim."

"Yeah, you saw bodies stacked on the side of the road and hoodlums taking over neighborhoods." Patrick ran a hand over his face and glanced up at the rafters of the barn before returning his gaze to them. "All the petty

41

thieves—they're gone. Killed. The people who weren't quick enough to respond? Also killed. What's left are the hardened criminals who will do anything . . ."

"They'll want our food and supplies," Carter said. "I get it. We're both good shots."

Georgia hustled into the barn carrying a basketful of fabric.

Patrick jerked his head to the left, and they all trooped back near the horse stalls. "They want more than our food or supplies. Some of these people will kill you because they're bored, or because you refuse to join their clan. You're either with them, or you're a threat. If you're a threat, you need to die. If you're not a threat, then you don't deserve to live."

"Why are you telling us this?" Carter asked.

"To ease my own conscience, I guess. You'll be a big help. Both of you will. Going out in twos? That's foolishness because someone has to be on guard all the time. Together we make a group of seven, and that's better. I just want you to know how bad things are. To be prepared for it."

Patrick waited a moment, but when neither Carter nor Lanh replied, he turned to go.

Lanh called after him. "What about the Remnant?"

For his answer, Patrick shrugged and walked away.

FIVE

Shelby and Bianca had been holed up in the cottage for most of the afternoon. They'd placed Georgia's candles all around the small living room, the bathroom, and the bedroom. The other bag had held a variety of items, including some lace, a disposable razor, lotion, and shampoo.

"Real shampoo." Bianca opened the top of the travel-sized bottle and took a deep breath. Then she pushed it under Shelby's nose. "Smell it."

"Honeysuckle."

"Where did she find this stuff?"

"There's no end to the things that Georgia can find. She goes beyond resourceful. She's amazing."

"Tell me about Carter. He looks . . . different."

Shelby had been pulling items from the bag, but she stopped and plopped onto the couch next to her best friend. "That day in July, when we returned from Austin, Roy met me at the door and told me that Carter had been in an accident. He looked terrified. Even Georgia was rattled."

Bianca moved closer so they were sitting on the couch and staring into an empty fireplace, their shoulders touching.

"He'd broken his leg badly and fallen into the river—so there was some hypothermia. His blood sugar levels were all over the place. It took five days to stabilize him."

"You must have been in a panic."

"I was. After all we'd been through, I thought I was going to lose him from a broken leg. Meanwhile, Max, Roy, and every other able-bodied person were dealing with the Cavanaghs."

"Cavanaghs?" Bianca scooted back into the corner of the couch, pulled her knees up into the circle of her arms, and waited.

"Some losers on the far side of the creek. They'd been stealing from the families on this side for a week or so. We hadn't figured out who it was, but Carter . . . he'd heard them talking. If he'd been seen by them, they would have killed him."

"They were that bad?"

"Worse. We'd hoped when we showed up in force that they would leave, but they'd taken over the farmhouse on the far side." Shelby pulled in a deep breath and attempted to explain what had happened with as few details as possible. "The fighting lasted nearly a week. We lost . . . too many."

"And Carter?"

"He healed. Somehow he healed. Not even a limp, but something happened to his metabolism . . ."

"He's painfully thin."

"We feed him everything we can spare, which he doesn't want to take. Jerry Lambert—"

"The vet."

"Yeah. He thinks that the infection was so deep that his body had to use all of its resources to fight. He says to give Carter time."

"I'm surprised you want him to go with us."

"I don't know that I want him to, but Carter . . . he's different now. He's not a child anymore, and he deserves to be able to make his own decisions."

"And the insulin supply?"

"We had to use more than we'd planned when he was sick. What's left should last us through mid-June, barring any other problems."

"Three months."

"Yeah."

"We'll find more. Somewhere between here and Kansas, there has to be more."

They sat there for a moment, thinking of what might lie ahead of them and all that had occurred since they'd parted in July.

"I'm sorry about your mom, Bianca. She was always kind to me."

"We've all lost someone. You lost your parents long before the grid went down. Carter lost Kaitlyn. Georgia and Roy have lost neighbors and friends. We're living in a time of loss. Of grief."

"Tonight we're not." Shelby stood and then pulled Bianca to her feet. "Tonight we're having a wedding."

They spent the next three hours preparing Bianca to be a bride.

She took a long, hot bath in the tub, though they'd stopped using the limited propane supply for baths months before. Shelby heated water on the woodstove in the living room. They both laughed as she poured it into the tub, mixing it with the two inches of cold water and adding a splash of bubbles. When she had the bath half full, Bianca slipped into the old claw-foot tub and sighed.

"A bubble bath. I didn't think I'd be having one of these anytime soon."

"It's your wedding day. I want it to be memorable."

Bianca opened one eye. "Memorable. Yeah, I think we have that covered."

Shelby walked over to the wedding dress, which was draped on a satin hanger they had hooked over the shower door. She shook out the dress, which was unnecessary. The steam from Bianca's bath was already doing its work, the wrinkles in the fabric practically disappearing before her eyes. Plopping onto the floor, her back against the wall, she confessed, "I always dreamed of a lavish wedding—a string quartet, fountain of champagne, and a wedding cake decorated with fresh flowers."

"And the groom? I assume there was a groom in this daydream."

"That part was always a little fuzzy for me." Shelby ran a thumb nail along the grout that separated the pink tiles. The floor must have been laid in the fifties when the cottage was built, when pink tiles were the rage.

"Tell me about you and Max."

"What's there to tell?"

"So you're still dancing around your feelings . . ."

"I have no idea what you're talking about."

"Don't lie to me, *hermana*. I know you."

"Like a sister," Shelby whispered.

"Yes. You are like family." Bianca raised a bubble-covered foot and pointed her toes at Shelby. "But we don't have to talk about it if you don't want to."

"Thank you."

"What do you want to talk about then?"

"Your pedicure." Shelby jumped up and pulled out a drawer in the bottom of the bathroom vanity. "What color do you want?"

"Red."

"Red?"

"Yeah, red. The color of love."

SIX

Georgia had placed lanterns around the barn.

Jerry Lambert showed up a few minutes before sunset. In addition to being a retired veterinarian, he was licensed to perform weddings. "It was my sister's idea. We filled out one of those online forms."

Shelby thought it was a perfect though small assembly—Roy and Georgia, Lanh and Carter, her and Max, Patrick and Bianca, and Jerry.

Max had set the benches and chairs up at one end of the barn.

There was little doubt that Georgia had been in charge of the decorating. Ribbon that Shelby was sure she'd seen at Christmas had been twisted and hung from the hayloft. A table to the side was covered with Georgia's lace tablecloth— something they used on the first Sunday of every month when they had their celebration dinner— an extravagance that Shelby found herself looking forward to more than she would have thought possible.

"Celebrating life is important," Georgia had explained that first month. "It's too easy to take what we have for granted and to focus on what is lacking."

"Give thanks to the Lord," Roy had echoed.

And so it was that every month each member of their group looked for a special treat to squirrel away—a bar of chocolate someone had given Lanh when he tended to their lame horse, beef jerky Max had seasoned with honey and garlic, wild onions Roy had found by the creek. The meals rarely made sense nutritionally speaking, but they always lifted their spirits.

Tonight the table was covered with lace. Georgia had managed to rustle up a single layer sheet cake, baked in the outdoor oven Roy had rigged up. It was sweetened with honey instead of sugar, but it was a luxury nonetheless. Someone had pulled early blooming bluebonnets from the field and placed them in bowls on both sides of the cake.

Georgia's company dishes—a white pattern with light pink flowers—and good silver were stacked at the end of the table.

Everyone had cleaned up. Carter had managed to wrestle down his cowlick, Lanh had changed out of the hoodie he constantly wore, and Max had donned a freshly starched shirt.

"Your mother did that for you?"

"What?"

"Ironed your shirt. You realize she had to use that antique cast iron that weighs about eight pounds."

"She's old fashioned like that."

"I have no idea how she had the time."

"To iron a shirt?"

"To do all of this."

Georgia hurried to the front of the room, handed Jerry their family Bible, and then sat down in the front row. She was wearing a dress Shelby hadn't seen before, a soft blue knit that fell to her ankles.

Max nudged her shoulder and cocked his head toward the open door. "Would you look at that."

Shelby turned and saw Bianca crossing from the cottage to the barn, holding up her dress so that it wouldn't drag in the dirt. She'd insisted on spending the last thirty minutes alone "to pray and think about my parents." The last of the day's light spilled across the fields, catching the pearls on her dress and the shine in her hair.

Roy stood by the door, dressed in his Sunday suit, complete with black tie. He offered Bianca his arm, and that act of kindness caused tears to sting Shelby's eyes.

"You're crying already?"

"I'm not crying."

"It hasn't even started yet." Max snagged her hand and pulled her toward one of the benches, but they all remained standing as Bianca entered the room.

She wore her mother's dress that she'd brought from home. The fabric was aged, and the style was from a bygone time—floor-length, tulle with an A-line design and a princess V-neck.

50

Appliqued lace adorned the shoulders, hips, and hem. Shelby had braided a two-foot length of light blue lace through Bianca's long, black hair that was twisted and piled on top of her head. It wasn't a veil, but it would have to do.

The bouquet she held was more bluebonnets, tied together with the remainder of the lace.

Patrick wore clean jeans, a western shirt, and a look of pure adoration.

Jerry opened with the simplest of prayers, asking for God's provision, protection, and grace. Then he asked, "Who gives this woman to be married?"

"I do," Roy said, his voice deep and steady as he guided Bianca's hand to the crook of Patrick's arm.

"We have gathered in this place tonight to join Patrick Goodnight and Bianca Lopez in holy matrimony." Jerry peered over the top of his reading glasses. "Are we ready?"

"We are," they both murmured.

Patrick and Bianca turned toward one another, and then Bianca realized she was still holding the flowers and there was no flower girl. She laughed and held them up as if to say, *Who wants these?* Georgia darted forward and took them, saying, "I'll press these for you later."

Patrick clasped Bianca's hands in his.

"Do you, Patrick, take Bianca to be your wife, to have and hold from this day on, for better or for worse, for richer, for poorer, in sickness and in health, to love and to cherish, until death do you part?"

"I do."

"And do you, Bianca, take Patrick to be your husband, to have and hold from this day on, for better or for worse, for richer, for poorer, in sickness and in health, to love and to cherish, until death do you part?"

"*Sí*. I do."

Max reached into his pocket, pulled out a handkerchief, and passed it to Shelby. She didn't bother to deny the tears streaming down her face.

"God has promised to never leave you, to follow you. For where you go, he will go, and where you remain, he will remain." Jerry opened the Bible, adjusted his glasses, and said, "The book of First Corinthians, chapter thirteen reminds us of the nature of love. I encourage you both to read it in the days ahead, to commit those words to memory, to let them sink into your heart."

"We will," they said.

Jerry looked down and read, "And now these three remain: faith, hope and love. But the greatest of these is love."

Those words seemed to sink into Shelby's bones. So little remained of what had been. Yet this group—every single person here—loved one another. She tried to fill her heart with that thought. To banish the doubt and fear, and focus, if only for a moment, on that one truth.

There was only one ring, the wedding ring Bianca's father had given her mother. Patrick slid it onto her finger as she gazed up into his eyes.

Then Jerry raised his hands and said, "Forasmuch as Bianca and Patrick have consented together in holy wedlock, and have witnessed the same before God and this company of witnesses, and have given their pledge, each to the other, and have declared the same by giving and receiving a ring, by the power vested in me by the State of Texas, I now pronounce you husband and wife."

When Patrick kissed the bride, the boys let out a holler, and Roy started up a tune on his harmonica.

The next hour passed in a blur. For a little while, the darkness of their reality was pushed away. They ate the honey-flavored cake, celebrated with two of Georgia's remaining bottles of wine, danced to Roy's harmonica music, and laughed. Georgia insisted on wrapping up a piece of the cake for Jerry and his wife. The boys slipped off to hang soda cans on the front door of the cottage and light the candles that had been positioned throughout the little structure.

And then Patrick picked up his bride and carried her across the yard.

Maybe it was the wine that loosened Max's tongue. He walked up behind Shelby, close enough to touch but not touching. "This could have been a double wedding, Sparks."

"Is that what you want?" She didn't turn, didn't look at him. She just continued staring across at the cottage. "To marry me?"

"It's what I've always wanted."

A dozen questions flooded her mind, but she pushed them away. With Max, it was best to keep her questions and her emotions at a distance. She'd nearly knocked down that wall of reserve when they were battling their way through Austin. Then they'd returned to High Fields, and she'd been so focused on Carter that she couldn't think about Max fighting the Cavanaghs day after day, night after night, for almost a week.

The evening that one of their neighbors pulled up to the house, the back of his truck filled with bodies of those killed in the fighting, Shelby had known a terror deeper than any fear for her own life. The driver hadn't known who the deceased were. They'd put the bodies in the barn and laid them out so that families could come and pick them up. With each body that she helped to move, she'd braced herself against seeing Max's face.

Standing in the last of the lantern light, with Max so close to her now that she could feel his breath on the back of her neck, she forced her mind away from that dark day. She couldn't allow herself to love. Not that way. Not now. Maybe when the world settled again. Maybe when she no longer needed to identify bodies or help dig graves.

"Is it what you want, Shelby? Will you marry me?" His voice had turned suddenly serious, and she felt a river of goose bumps trickle down her arms. She fought the emotions and breathed in and out once and then again.

Instead of answering, she turned, stood on her tiptoes, and planted a kiss on his cheek.

"Get some sleep, Max."

And without waiting for an answer, she hurried out into the darkness.

SEVEN

Gabe Thompson had set the prearranged meeting spot for 7:30 A.M. in Langford Cove. Though the rendezvous point was only thirty miles to the north, they had to wind their way through caliche roads and then pass through the roadblock. The drive took an hour and fifteen minutes. Fortunately, they were going north, away from Townsen Mills. Max didn't care to see that devastation again, though he had a hard time imagining how it could be any worse than the last time they'd gone through.

They left High Fields as the sky was lightening but well before sunup.

Goodbyes with his parents were short and heartfelt.

"No more than a month," Max promised.

His father pulled him into a bear hug, as he'd done with each person in their group. "You take the time you need. Whatever it takes to find answers and bring everyone home."

His mom made a valiant attempt not to cry, but he knew she was struggling. She pulled in her bottom lip and stood as close to Max's father as was humanly possible. "Godspeed, son."

"Take care of him, Mom." Max glanced at his dad and winked. "You know how stubborn he is."

"That I do."

And then they were driving down the caliche road, scaring up deer and causing doves to take flight.

Max drove, and Shelby sat next to him in the front seat of the old Dodge. Carter and Lanh were squeezed between supplies in the second seat— items that hadn't fit in the back storage area, which was packed to the roof of the car. Patrick and Bianca followed in the Mustang, which was also full. They'd tried to plan for every scenario, tried to anticipate every need.

They drove at an even speed, but not too slowly, and always keeping a three-car distance between them.

Max constantly scanned the road, left shoulder to right shoulder, and then checked the rearview mirror before returning his eyes to the ribbon of road directly in front of them. There was little to see.

"So many of the power lines have fallen." Shelby's voice was detached, the objective observation of a reporter. She held her journal in her lap, but she'd yet to write anything. She'd told him after the flare and the chaos in Abney that she needed to record what was happening. Some days she struggled with that, but always she picked up her pen and began writing again.

"No maintenance crews." Max glanced at the boys, who had their gaze pinned out the window.

Trees had fallen into some of the power poles, causing them to sag precariously.

"That storm last month could have knocked them down."

"Or the one in November," Carter said. "I thought it was going to rip the roof off the cottage."

"I thought the cottage was going to end up in the creek." Lanh sounded so serious that they all laughed, and it eased some of the tension.

Max knew there was nothing to fear here, no one to threaten them.

It was the desolation that tore at his soul. He'd grown up in this area, and it had been a thriving part of central Texas. Not anymore. What wasn't destroyed was abandoned.

In places where power poles had come down, they'd dragged those around them into a lopsided stance. Brush had grown wild and was now encroaching on the road. Cars that had been abandoned on the shoulder now had thistles, nettles, and dove weed winding through their shattered windows. In the pastures, the weeds fought with the bluebonnets, which had begun to bloom.

"Is this what it looked like before?" Shelby asked.

"Before?"

"Widespread agriculture." She waved toward the fields to the west. "It's a carpet of blue."

"I'd rather see a carpet of food," Carter joked.

By the time they returned, the bluebonnets would be interspersed with Texas paintbrush and Indian blankets. Max vowed to himself that everyone in their group would see that change. He'd lost too many friends in the last nine months. In one way, it had hardened him to the cruelty of life. In another way, though, his insides were raw and bleeding.

The few houses fronting the road appeared to have been abandoned long ago.

Most were burned.

Langford Cove looked even worse.

The first structure on the east side of the road was the 2A school—grades K through 12 held in two connected buildings. School was definitely not in session, and the Langford Lions wouldn't be competing anymore. Max remembered clearly how proud folks were when the new athletic facility had opened. Now it lay in ruins like the rest of the school—windows shattered, doors torn off, the press box and stands burned to the ground.

Where there had been a string of stores on the west side of the road, charred ruins sat like props for an apocalyptic film.

Feed store—gone.

Taxidermist—closed.

Grocery store—looted.

On the east side of the road was the bank. Made

of brick, it had avoided complete destruction, though Max could see that the windows had been busted and the office furniture lay scattered across the lawn. What was the point? What good would any money in that bank do anyone? There was nothing left to purchase.

In front of the bank and bordering the road was a square grassy area. Formerly, it had held park benches and a gazebo. Those were gone, though Max couldn't imagine how or why anyone would want a gazebo.

None of that mattered.

What did matter was that Gabe Thompson was waiting for them, and he'd brought along a very sweet ride.

EIGHT

Carter was out of the Dodge before Max came to a complete stop. "Whoa!"

"Is that our ride?" Lanh hopped out and followed Carter over to the military vehicle.

"Hey, Dr. Bhatti. I mean, I guess I heard your name is . . . uh . . . Gabe Thompson."

"Good to see you, Carter."

"Might take me a while to get used to that name."

"Then I will answer to both . . . for a while."

The man standing in front of Carter looked exactly like the doctor who had lived next door to him in Abney. They'd been neighbors for a week, until the explosion in their neighborhood that had killed his girlfriend, wrecked their house, and sent them scurrying to High Fields.

The doctor looked the same, but he also looked completely different.

He stood straighter, acted more confident, and seemed like what he was . . . a military guy.

While everyone said hello, Carter and Lanh circled the Humvee. Bigger than an SUV, it looked like a tank and was the color of sand.

"That's at least a nine-inch ground clearance," Lanh said.

"Oversized, all-terrain tires."

"Off-road suspension package."

They peered in through the open driver's door.

"Wow."

"Exactly."

"Think he'll let us ride with him?" Lanh asked.

"Only one way to find out."

They made their way back to the group. Everyone had slipped past the pleasantries and begun to plan the trip.

"Unusual ride, Gabe." His mom walked over and pressed a hand against the side of the vehicle. "Are we taking this all the way to Kansas?"

"We are." Gabe stepped closer to her. "Shelby, I want to say I'm sorry about what happened in the capital, with Danny Vail—"

"That wasn't your fault."

"No, but if I had known, I would have stopped him. Unfortunately, we didn't become aware of Danny's duplicity until he led a coup against the governor."

Max let out a long, low whistle. "He was in charge of that?"

"Yes, and he will be tried as a traitor if he's ever caught."

"We still have trials?" Bianca asked.

"We will." Gabe looked absolutely certain. Carter admired that about the guy. "One day we will."

Everyone was quiet for a moment as that thought took root. Could it be that the people who were causing suffering, who were preying on others, would one day pay for their deeds? Carter didn't know. He wasn't sure exactly what the future would look like, only that it would be different.

"I've always wanted to ride in a Humvee," Carter said. He'd seen them pass through Abney a few times on their way from Fort Hood to points unknown.

"This is actually a JLTV, or joint light tactical vehicle. It was designed to replace the Humvee."

"That's a mouthful," Lanh pointed out. "Could we just call it a Hummer? Or a baby Hummer?"

"Whatever works for you."

"The governor gave it to you?" Patrick asked.

"I believe it was a loan." His tone was dead serious, but a smile tugged at the corners of his mouth.

"We definitely need those kinds of friends." Bianca walked up to the vehicle and opened the front passenger door.

Carter leaned in, trying to take in all of the technology he'd glanced at earlier. "Does this stuff work?"

"Anything not satellite based does. As you know, the satellites were fried along with the grid."

"So why does it still run?" Max asked.

"Ruggedized it."

"I realized you could do that to a laptop,"

Shelby said. "Didn't know they had anything big enough to protect a tank."

"They can be armored up. There's a good supply of gasoline in the back, and I managed to get a few weapons and some extra ammo, plus some food and utility packs for everyone."

"Then we're as prepared as we can be." Patrick nodded toward their cars. "We brought more food, tents, and our own handguns and rifles."

Gabe reached into the Hummer and handed Shelby and Bianca a radio that looked to Carter like a SAT phone, only there were no satellites anymore.

"They're preset to the correct frequency. Their radius is supposedly 50 miles, but that's questionable. They should operate fine between vehicles."

"Why are we even taking our vehicles?" Max asked. "We'd all fit in that beast."

"There may be places that a military vehicle won't be welcome. If so, we'll hide it and take yours."

"But there may be places our vehicles can't go," Patrick pointed out. "That thing can go off road and through streams."

"In which case, we'll hide yours and take mine."

When he opened up the payload area, Carter let out a long, low whistle.

"That's a lot of guns."

"M16s. I brought ten." He passed a military-grade backpack to each of them. "It'll feel heavy at first, but everything you need is in there should you get separated—first aid kit, emergency blanket, water purification tablets, and some MREs."

"Why did we take stuff from Georgia's pantry?" Carter asked Patrick.

"Because we don't know how long we'll be out on the road, and we may need to trade some of this stuff. We were trying to plan for every contingency."

There were murmurs of agreement and thanks as they all struggled into their packs. Only Patrick looked comfortable in his. Max barely managed to get his arms in his, and when he did, the waist belt was around his rib cage. While the others laughed, Gabe showed him how to lengthen the straps. Carter's mom and Bianca looked swamped by theirs.

"Those were the smallest I could find," Gabe said, but they waved away his apology and assured him they'd be fine.

"Each pack also has a 9mm pistol. Are you all familiar with how to use a semiautomatic?"

Each person in the group nodded. Carter was suddenly glad that Roy had insisted on training them on every type of weapon they had.

"When we stop tonight, we'll go over how to clean the pistols as well as how to use the

M16s. For now, I want to emphasize that you keep this with you all the time—if you step out of your vehicle, you're wearing your pack. Your backpack is a part of your person. This way if we're ever separated, you have a fighting chance." Gabe turned to Carter, who was already pulling out his insulin supplies. "Split those up between yourself, your mom, and one other person. I want you to be sure you have enough in your pack to last you a week. Clear?"

"Crystal."

"All right." Carter's mom stared at the radio in her hand and then up at Gabe. "I guess you have our route planned."

"I have an ideal route mapped out, but it's important that we stay fluid. There's a good chance that we'll have to stop and turn around a few times."

"With that thing?" Lanh shook his head. "You could go over anything in your path."

"You're correct." Gabe stuck his hands in his pockets, and then he leaned in and lowered his voice, as though he was sharing a state secret. "We could, but our mission is to reach the Flint Hills of Kansas. If it's more expedient to go around a vicinity—to avoid trouble—then that's what we do."

He pulled out a laminated map and spread it across the hood of the Hummer.

Max pushed in closer for a better look. "You want to follow Highway 281 north."

"It's what we came up with last night too," Patrick said.

"Best to avoid the urban areas."

"Like Dallas, sure. But are we certain we want to go the Wichita Falls route?" Shelby traced a different path—Highway 183 north through Goldthwaite, Early, Rising Star, and on up to Seymour, which lay fifty miles southwest of Wichita Falls. "Smaller towns. We could cross the Red River a few miles past Vernon. Less chance of running into big groups."

"We have intelligence that Midland to Lubbock and Amarillo has been taken over."

"By whom?" Patrick crossed his arms and scowled at the map.

"Good question. All we know for certain is that they are not friendly to the Texas government."

"Who would want that area?" Carter asked. "The Panhandle is desolate on a good day."

"There's oil there," Lanh said.

"Exactly. Though we're not sure what they're going to do with it since it still has to be refined. But if they're pushing south, Vernon would be their next stop. Our best bet is this way." He tapped the Wichita Falls route. "Cross the Red River past Burkburnett and then shoot up west of Oklahoma City and straight into the Flint Hills."

Gabe suggested that Max lead, followed by Patrick, and then he'd bring up the rear. Everyone started toward their vehicles—except for Carter and Lanh.

His mom looked at them quizzically, but Max began to laugh.

"They want to ride in the Hummer."

"JLTV," Carter corrected.

Shelby shook her head, but then she waved them on.

Gabe tossed a radio to Carter. "You two can take turns being my radioman."

Then the engines were rumbling, and they were on their way. As they drove north through what was left of Langford Cove, Carter looked out the tinted windows and saw a pickup truck lying on its hood. Spray painted across the side was a symbol—an *X* inside of a circle. He had no idea what it meant, but it seemed menacing somehow. Red spray paint dripped down like blood. Carter understood that whoever had been inside the vehicle hadn't survived. And whoever had killed them? That person was marking their territory.

NINE

Shelby and Max pulled over to the side of the road a few yards shy of the top of the hill. To the west was Hamilton Municipal Airport. Little of it remained other than charred blacktop and some planes that were mere burned-out shells. To the east were uncultivated fields as far as they could see.

The other two vehicles pulled in behind them. Wearing their packs, they jogged the final few yards to the top, Max darting behind a tree and Shelby following. They were less than a mile outside of Hamilton. Though the sun was shining, the wind was picking up from the north, and Shelby could feel it beneath her layers of clothes.

"What can you see?" Shelby asked.

"Cars."

"A blockade?"

"Probably. Someone's approaching and . . ."

Shelby waited impatiently as Max scanned left to right and then left again.

"Well?"

He handed her the binoculars. "It is a blockade. Looks pretty similar to what we had in Abney."

Shelby gazed through it for a minute, the sight causing her stomach to tumble even as her temper spiked. Why did people think they could block public roads? She understood the need, but still it galled her. They turned and jogged back to where the others were waiting.

"Looks like a blockade," Max said. "I saw someone drive up to it from an east-west road and hand over their weapons."

"They're operating the same way we did in Abney," Bianca said.

"Pretty much. Hand over your weapons, do your business in town, and then presumably they return your things to you as you leave."

"I don't like it," Patrick said.

"And obviously I am not handing over all the weapons in the Hummer." Gabe reached into the vehicle and pulled out the map.

Max traced a path through the maze of county roads. "We can circle to the west, though there's no guarantee we won't come across more roadblocks . . . or worse."

"I say we go around," Patrick said.

Carter and Lanh had walked over to a road sign to study it.

Shelby tried to focus on their decision. "I think we should go forward. Hamilton was supposed to be a refugee center. They could know something about where the federal government is. They might even know what kind of trouble we're heading into."

"I doubt you will learn anything, but you're right that we should try." Gabe stood with his hands on his hips, staring at the map and then up at the horizon, no doubt wishing he could see over the hill and into the town of Hamilton. "Patrick and I will go around. Max and Shelby, you drive through. It will cause less alarm if there's only one car, and you can leave your weapons with us so you don't risk losing them."

"We should take them," Max said. When Patrick started to argue, Max stopped him with a raised hand. "We'll only take two handguns. If they don't give them back, all we've lost are two Glocks."

Shelby was surprised to hear herself agreeing with him. "It would look suspicious if we showed up unarmed. They would know that something wasn't right."

Patrick frowned and then nodded. "All right. I don't like the idea of losing any firearm since there's no telling what we'll face between here and Kansas, but you have a point." Patrick walked around behind them and pulled the 9mm pistols out of their packs, handing them to Bianca. "We'll give these military-grade beauties back to you on the other side."

Gabe turned back to the map and pointed to a spot on it. "We'll meet a few miles north of town . . . here. If you have any trouble, use your radio. Otherwise, keep it in your pack."

"They'll see it."

Patrick tossed Shelby his radio. "They'll

assume you're using them to talk to each other."

It was settled. Patrick would be without a radio, but he'd be with Gabe, who had a Hummer and a stash of M16 rifles. In addition, they each had their 9mm pistols, plus the weapons they'd brought.

Shelby resisted the urge to exact a promise from Carter. He'd be careful, but it was obvious that her son's thoughts were not on his own safety. He jogged over to her as she got into the Dodge. "Keep your eyes out for an X with a circle around it."

"Huh?"

Spying a pen on the middle console, he grabbed it, opened her palm and drew the symbol on the inside of her hand. "Look for this. See if you can find out what it means."

He mussed her hair, and she batted his hand away.

Carter grinned at her as Max started the Dodge, and then Shelby and Max were moving away from their group, driving toward the roadblock.

TEN

Max stopped fifty yards from the group of vehicles and armed men.

"Ready?"

"I guess."

They stepped out of the Dodge at the same moment, hands half raised to show they were no threat.

The head of the patrol, a thirtyish-looking man with an overgrown beard, stepped forward, rifle slung across his chest and in the ready position. "We'll need you to put your weapons on the ground."

"We only mean to go through."

"To do that you have to put your weapons on the ground."

"Will we get them back?"

"On the other side."

Max began to reach with his right hand, and the guard said, "With your left. Both of you."

He glanced at Shelby, who rolled her eyes and pulled her Glock out of her hip holster with her left hand. It was an awkward movement, which is what they wanted. Smart. He'd have to remember that and tell the folks in Abney. If he'd begun to draw the weapon with his left, no doubt they would have told him to use his right.

He placed the Glock on the ground and kicked it away with his foot. Shelby did the same.

"Now the packs."

When they'd shrugged out of them, the guard jerked his head to the left, and a kid about Carter's age jumped down off a flatbed truck, darted over, and picked up both packs and both weapons.

"We done here?" Max asked.

"Not quite. Renshaw and Kirby, move the vehicle."

Max glanced at Shelby. They'd both been hoping to hear *Micah 5,* the code word for a group called the Remnant that had helped them in Austin. Apparently, these people were a different sort. Max moved to the left to block the old man's progress—Renshaw or Kirby. Someone on the back of a truck raised a rifle and sighted Max through it. He didn't have to look up to know that. He recognized the motion. He'd done it often enough himself.

He held his ground. "There's still such a thing as private property, last I checked."

"Times have changed."

"Even the Constitution? Has that changed?"

"You don't want to fight me on this."

"Head on down to your library and check out the fifth amendment of the US Constitution. It plainly states that private property shall not be taken for public use without just compensation."

"Got us a smart one this morning." The leader

stepped closer, and Max made out the name "Hardin" sewn above his jacket pocket. Must have worked in a factory because the thing was machine stitched. No doubt part of his uniform. "You want through this town, or you want to go around?"

"We'd rather go through."

"Then we have to move your vehicle."

"Why?"

"Because you might have bombs in there or other people. There's no telling what you're transporting, and I'm not going to risk the safety of my town because you want to tout your constitutional right. Got it?"

"Yeah. I got it."

Hardin motioned them with his rifle to walk toward the right side of the blockade. Two other guards waited there to search them and send them through.

Renshaw and Kirby drove off in the Dodge, turning left and going around the far west side of the blockade.

"I didn't think about them taking our packs," Shelby whispered as they were motioned through and told to wait.

"Makes sense, though."

"We don't have our radios."

"No, we don't."

"Maybe this was a bad idea. What if they take Carter's insulin?"

"Too late to back out. We're in it now." He

gave her his best cowboy smile and resettled the black Stetson that he'd come to think of as his good-luck charm.

A middle-aged woman walked up and offered to escort them through town. She wore a police uniform, complete with the utility belt, handgun, pepper spray, and cuffs. A radio was clipped to her shoulder.

"Sorry about that." She held out a hand to Shelby and then Max. "I'm Edith Fletcher, and I'll be escorting you through Hamilton."

"Is that necessary?" Shelby asked.

"Town council decided it is."

"What's with Hardin?" Max gestured toward the other side of the blockade.

"Lost a brother last month. He was working on the blockade. Since then, security measures have tightened."

Max felt a surge of sympathy for the man. But who hadn't lost someone since the grid collapsed? They were a nation in mourning.

"Where are you folks from?"

Max guessed the length of the town to be close to four miles. Was she going to accompany them the entire way? How many times a day did she do this?

Shelby was staring at some graffiti on the side of a gas station.

"Abney," he said. "We're from Abney."

"I had kinfolk in Abney, but they came here

after the flare. We kind of circled up on my uncle's property."

"There's a lot of that going on."

"Better than being alone."

They walked in silence a few minutes. They passed homes that looked relatively undamaged, and stores that were closed but not looted.

Max could tell that Shelby was ready to pepper the woman with questions, only she hadn't figured out how to start.

Then they reached the town square.

Shelby stopped with her hands on her hips, looking up and down the main road, across at the courthouse, even at the coffee shop on the corner, which looked to be open. In front of the courthouse was a grassy area where older men and women were setting up tables with items to trade. Max could make out canned food, quilts, stacks of MREs, even live chickens.

"Abney looks worse than this," he admitted.

"We heard there was trouble that way, especially after that early battle with Croghan."

"Even Townsen Mills and Langford Cove have been destroyed." Shelby continued to glance around, no doubt trying to grasp what she was seeing. "Buildings burned, people . . . all gone."

"We set up a hard perimeter within twenty-four hours," Edith said. "And any hint of trouble from someone inside earns them a ticket outside. No exceptions. No second chances."

"Harsh." Shelby didn't so much as blink when the woman turned to stare at her.

"You're right. It is harsh, but the result is a town square that's still standing and a coffee shop that's open. You hungry?"

Shelby and Max shook their head as one.

Edith shrugged. "Let's go, then."

ELEVEN

They were near the cemetery on the north side of town and approaching the roadblock when Shelby pretended to have a cramp in her leg. Max knew she was pretending because he'd been with her nearly every day since the flare, and she'd never had a leg cramp before. Plus, they hadn't walked that far.

Shelby hobbled over to a tombstone. The cemetery bordered the road, and graves were placed right up to the property line. She reached the headstone and lowered herself to the ground, still clutching her calf. He fought the urge to laugh at her pitiful acting. He didn't have to call her on it. The cop did.

"Funny thing about cramps. They don't usually travel from one leg to the other." Fletcher looked more curious than irritated.

"I don't know what you mean," Shelby said.

"You initially grabbed your right leg, but now you're holding your left."

"Oh. Well, they both hurt."

"Uh-huh, and I've got land in Colorado I'd like to sell you."

"Fine. I was faking."

"Why?"

"We're nearly to the next roadblock, and I

wanted a chance to ask you some questions."

Now Fletcher was grinning. "In that case, we should have stopped at the coffee shop." She motioned for Max to move closer. "No one will see us here. Why don't you two tell me what you're doing in my town."

"Traveling through, like we said." Max plopped on the ground next to Shelby.

Fletcher leaned against a tree—close enough to hear them, but far enough that they couldn't grab for her gun. Not that they would do anything that stupid, but he admired her carefulness.

"And you have questions."

"We do." Max grabbed Shelby's leg and began to rub it. When she resisted, he said, "In case anyone is watching."

She batted his hand away and began going through a series of stretches while her eyes remained focused on Officer Fletcher. "Wasn't there a refugee center here?"

"That was in June, after you all had the battle with Croghan. We took refugees from there as well as the surrounding area."

"And?"

"Feds pulled out six months ago. Left us with a couple hundred mouths to feed, which we could not do."

"So what happened to them?" Shelby's voice had taken on an indignant tone, and Max knew what would follow that.

"We didn't do what you're thinking." Fletcher's radio beeped, and she said something into it that Max couldn't make out, primarily because she angled away from them. Turning back to them, she said, "Roadblock wants to know if there's trouble. I told them to give us a minute."

"So what did you do with the refugees?"

"Offered them jobs and homes if we had them. Believe it or not, we actually need people around here." She glanced out over the tombstones, and that was when Max saw the area of freshly dug graves with no markers other than wooden crosses. He knew from firsthand experience that the names on them would be hand carved or written with permanent maker—he wasn't close enough to see which.

"Some stayed. Most didn't. Everyone was still optimistic then. Now, why don't you tell me what you're doing here? We have about three more minutes before someone comes to check on us."

Max wasn't sure how much he wanted to share, but he also wanted to know what had happened in Hamilton. He wanted details about what they'd seen and what Edith Fletcher knew. She seemed like a straight shooter, so with a three-minute clock ticking in his head, he explained as succinctly as possible what their mission was and that they'd just begun.

"Wow. First time I've heard that one. I've had all sorts of people come through here on all

81

sorts of missions, but never someone looking specifically for the federal government."

"Why do you think that is?" Shelby asked.

Fletcher almost laughed. "We're in Texas, remember? The less government, the better, and if that means none, then so be it."

"Yeah, we know people like that too." Max again stared out over the freshly dug graves. Though they'd agreed immediately to go with Patrick and Bianca, Max understood that some people wouldn't have. There were men and women even in the ranches around High Fields who had no desire to find the federal government. Some argued it would do more harm than good. For him and for Shelby, it was Carter's need and the fact that their friends were going— with or without them—that had settled the issue. "I can't say I miss the bureaucracy. Still, it would be nice to know what's out there."

"That's why you're traveling on the open road? Out of curiosity?"

Max and Shelby exchanged looks. An unspoken agreement caused Max to hedge. "It's more than curiosity, but we're not at liberty to say."

Fletcher held up her hand. "Fine by me. The less I know, the better."

"You haven't heard anything?"

"Look. The same transports that passed through Abney that first week passed through here. And yes, we had a refugee center operated mainly by the Red Cross. As far as I know, that organization no longer exists. They became a target because they had supplies—food, medicine, you name it. When the government pulled out, there was no one to protect the workers, and the entire operation fell apart pretty quickly."

Shelby and Max stood, and they all began walking back toward the road.

"No rumors about where the troops went?"

"Plenty of rumors. No proof."

"It might help us if we knew what you'd heard."

"Let's see. That DC was nuked. That the president is hunkered down in Cheyenne Mountain. That aliens are responsible for the collapse of the grid, and my personal favorite—that the Chinese hacked into our system and are waiting a year for the population to decline and folks to get real hungry before they invade."

"Wow," Max said.

"Do you believe any of them?"

"Doesn't matter what I believe. Matters what I can prove, and I can't prove any of it. I haven't left Hamilton since the day the grid went down, except for an occasional patrol, and we never go more than three miles out."

"Three—" Shelby glanced at Max.

"That's the reach of our radios."

They'd nearly arrived at the northern roadblock. Shelby dropped to her knees and pretended to mess with her shoelaces. One hand on the laces, the other palm up, she asked, "Do you know what this symbol means?"

Fletcher made no effort to hide her distaste. "Yeah. That's Hugo's, and you don't want to mess with him."

"So he's what? Marking his territory?" Max frowned at the symbol penned on Shelby's hand. "Didn't I see that on a building we passed?"

"You did. Hugo lived in Hamilton. Born and raised here."

"But now?"

"Now he doesn't."

Fletcher began walking again, crossing the final distance to the roadblock. Shelby jogged in front of her and began walking backward. "So . . . what is he? A robber? Killer? What?"

"Worse than any of those things. Hugo is one of those people who sees the failure of the grid as an opportunity, and he'll destroy anyone or anything that gets in his way. He has no moral compass and will not hesitate to kill you or those you care about."

"Any idea where he's operating? We'd rather avoid him."

"No, but he sometimes uses scouts on horses. Once they've identified a target, he comes in behind them with several raggedy pickup trucks that he stole from some locals. If you see two guys on horses scoping you out, change your course, maybe head for the closest town."

"All right. Thanks for the heads-up."

"What route do you plan to take north?"

Max and Shelby both shook their heads. They'd agreed to share as little as possible. There was no point in doing so, and in the worst-case scenario it would make it easier for someone who wanted to ambush them. They'd learned in Austin that you can't trust everyone you meet, even if they appear to be on the right side of things.

"We haven't decided," Max said.

Shelby added, "More like figuring it out as we go."

"Well, you came from Abney and you're headed north. Take my advice. Swing west. Don't attempt to go through Hico."

Max wanted to ask more, but they'd reached the group of folks manning the roadblock. They'd learned all they could from Fletcher. It wasn't much, but it was something. Stay away from Hugo and avoid the town of Hico.

TWELVE

Shelby wasn't too surprised when they reached the prearranged spot before the rest of their group. The Dodge Ramcharger was sitting in the middle of the lane pointed north, pointed away from Hamilton.

"I can't believe they didn't take anything." She'd spent a few minutes digging through their supplies. As she mentally checked off what they'd brought, Max rearranged things now that the second seat was empty, what with the boys riding with Gabe.

He held up her pack and helped her shrug into it. When it nearly tipped her over, he steadied her with his hands on her shoulders. "Did you think they would steal things?"

"I thought they might."

"Who needs a tent when you have a coffee shop?" He laughed as he rearranged things in the back.

"Maybe no one in Hamilton does, but Hugo might decide he wants it, along with our ride, weapons, and food."

"You're worried?"

"You're not?"

Max shrugged, and Shelby had to fight an urge to argue with him. It wasn't that Max didn't take

86

their situation seriously, but he'd learned to save his energy for the fights that actually happened. Shelby, meanwhile, found herself constantly anticipating trouble.

"Relax. We're not going to sit still long enough for Hugo or anyone else to find us."

"That's the plan, I guess."

Max finished repacking, shrugged into his own pack, and pulled out a jug of water from the backseat. He took a swig and then handed it to her.

"Are you glad you came, Sparks?"

"I wasn't about to let you—"

"That's not what I asked."

"I know what you asked." She didn't look at him. Instead, she focused on recapping the jug of water and placing it on the floorboard behind his seat. "You're asking if I'm glad to be off the ranch, and the truth is that I don't know."

"I have mixed feelings too."

"Yeah. But you hide them better."

"So tell me about it."

She felt the smile spread across her face. "You want me to lay bare my feelings right here, sitting in the middle of Highway 281?"

"Good a place as any." Max hopped up onto the hood of the Dodge, patted the spot next to him, and then he leaned back on one elbow.

Shelby wished she could draw. She'd always been good with words. She'd filled three of her notebooks describing what she'd seen and experienced since the aurora borealis spread across the sky as they hiked the trails at Gorman Falls. But what she wanted right in that moment was to be able to sketch what she was seeing—everything she was seeing.

Max, his cowboy hat pulled low to block the morning sun, sitting on the battered Dodge with a half smile on his face. Wildflowers blooming in the pasture behind him, and a mockingbird that had lighted on the barbed wire fence paralleling the road. If she could draw that picture, if she could capture it, she could believe that there were moments of normalcy even in the midst of the tragedy that had become their lives. Looking at the picture, at Max right now, she could almost believe in their future.

She tried to hop onto the hood of the Dodge, forgetting the weight of the pack on her shoulders, and nearly fell off the bumper. Max grabbed her hand and pulled her up. She only did it so she could see the road to the west better. Not so she could sit next to Max in the sunshine. She needed to watch for the rest of their group. At least that's what she told herself.

Sensing that Max wasn't finished with their conversation, she said, "The ranch was safe."

"Relatively."

"Safer than most places."

"But . . ."

"Yeah, I want to know what's going on. I'm curious. I don't want to know badly enough to get shot by some loser named Hugo."

"I wouldn't let that happen."

"*I* won't let that happen." Shelby shook her head, causing curls to drop in front of her eyes. She shoved them back and leaned forward, elbows on her knees. "I've changed, Max. I'm not the little girl who used to live next door, or the single mom who wrote romances. I feel stronger than I've ever been. It's like we've been tested, and our ordeal has stripped away all the fluff."

"Careful, or I'll think you've become an optimist."

"I'd rather be a realist. I want to look at life as it is, not as I want it to be."

"You're still worried about Carter."

"Of course I am." It came out too sharply, as though she blamed him. "It was a good idea for us to come to High Fields. You were right."

"But he needs more insulin."

"He does. Yeah." She didn't want to admit her thoughts to Max or to anyone. But she was so very tired of them circling in her brain. "This isn't like our trip to Austin. It's not enough to find another year's worth because we'll be out here again a year from now . . . searching for supplies that will grow harder and harder to find."

"So why are we here? What do you think you can find?"

89

"Our future?" She looked at him now, allowed herself to meet his gaze directly even if his brown eyes did send her stomach tumbling. How she wished that she didn't feel anything for Max Berkman. He'd claimed her heart when she was a high school kid, and she'd never quite learned how to stop the fluttering when he was close by. She still couldn't control the blush that crept up her neck when he turned those warm eyes in her direction.

She did her best to ignore all of that and focused on Max's question, trying to make sense of her feelings and intuition and hopes and prayers. "I need to find how Carter fits into this world. And I don't mean for twelve months. I mean his future . . . where he belongs. How he can live with certainty for the next five or ten or fifty years."

"I'm not sure any of us have that anymore, Shelby. I'm not sure we ever did."

"You're right." She shrugged, jumped to the ground, and stretched her neck left and then right. On the horizon she could just make out two vehicles headed their way, sunlight glinting off windshields. "You're right, but that isn't going to stop me from trying."

THIRTEEN

Carter jumped out of the Hummer before Gabe brought it to a complete stop. They didn't bother to pull off the road. What was the point? They'd passed no other moving vehicles. The real trick was maneuvering around the broken down cars and places where people had created blockades, only to abandon them.

"You okay?" he asked his mom, glancing over at Max, who gave him a quick nod.

"I'm surprised we beat you," Max said.

"We had to go around a few places." Patrick, Bianca, and Gabe joined the group. The sun was up, but the wind had definitely turned directly from the north. It would be cold by evening.

His mom relayed what they'd seen in Hamilton, which wasn't much.

"They had a coffee shop?" Bianca shook her head in disbelief. "And you didn't stop?"

"I wanted out of there. It was like there were eyes on us the entire time."

"She's not exaggerating." Max glanced back over his shoulder. "They're being very careful, which is probably why they're still standing."

"But you know what we didn't see? Any families or children—maybe some older teenagers working the roadblock, but no little

91

ones. Even the people who were trading goods in the marketplace were older. And the only other people we saw were the ones on patrol."

"Maybe they stay off Main Street," Patrick suggested.

Gabe leaned against the front of the Hummer. "We had an interesting conversation with a farmer back on the county road."

"He just walked out and talked to you?" Max asked.

"Nah. He saw the Hummer," Lanh explained. "We were going nice and slow, watching for any type of trap."

"He was in the middle of the road by the time we reached his place." Gabe smiled. "It was either run over him or talk to him . . . and I figured the five of us could take on one farmer. Plus, he didn't look like much of a robber."

"The guy was old," Carter chimed in.

"Former army. Still flying the Stars and Stripes over his place too. How could I pass that up?" Gabe ran a hand up and down his jawline. "Bad news is, we won't be going through Hico."

Shelby was shaking her head before he'd finished talking. "We heard the same thing, but it's only another twelve miles, and . . ."

"I know, Shelby. I know that was the plan, but we all agreed to stay fluid. According to Mr. Hinojosa, the barricade in Hico is a little different."

"They're requiring a toll." Bianca pulled on a shoulder strap to try to relieve the weight of her pack.

Carter couldn't resist walking behind her and holding the bag up. Everyone laughed, which made Carter feel as if he'd finally done something useful. Yeah, they could be heading into a bad situation, but everyone was so tense it was making him itchy. He didn't mind being the comedian of the group now and then.

"What kind of toll?" Max asked.

"That's the worst part of it." Patrick had been scanning the road, but now he directed his attention to the group. "They decide. Basically, they let you in on one side, take what they want, and let you out the other."

"So that's what Fletcher meant," Shelby said. "I'd hoped she was being overly cautious."

She explained to the others what the officer had told them about avoiding Hico, and then she showed them the symbol Carter had drawn on her palm and told them about Hugo.

"We've been seeing that since Langford Cove," Carter said.

"First one was on a vehicle north of there," Lanh confirmed. "Once on a road sign, another time on a truck, and I spotted another when we were making our western detour."

Patrick glanced at Bianca. Carter still couldn't

get it in his head that the two of them were married.

Stepping closer to her, Patrick said, "Pretty wide territory for a punk with horses and antique trucks."

"He won't be able to outrun us," Gabe assured them. "Maybe he won't even try when he sees the Hummer, but one person in each car needs to remain on lookout at all times."

They pulled out the map and traced a route around Hico.

Though it was only ten thirty in the morning, Patrick suggested that they eat something while they were stopped. Carter was always ready to eat. There was a gnawing hole in his belly that couldn't be satisfied, but he hated taking more than his share.

His mom tossed a couple of looks his way, but she didn't ask about his blood sugar. Carter was relieved about that. He appreciated all she had done, all everyone had done, but he didn't need them watching over him like mother hens. He knew to monitor his blood sugar, knew what to eat and what not to eat. In fact, he'd checked his glucose levels in the Hummer while they were driving toward the meeting spot.

The fact that they trusted him to do that— well, it went a long way to making him feel like a part of the group rather than deadweight they'd been forced to bring along.

In some ways, what they were seeing was worse than anything he had imagined.

How many nights had he and Lanh stayed up, wondering what was going on in the world outside of High Fields, trying to imagine what life for most people had become? A lot. Too many. He'd always regretted it the next morning when he had to be up at sunrise slopping pigs or bringing around the cows.

Which didn't stop him the next night from doing the same thing.

And though the devastation was harder to see than it had been to imagine, in another sense it put many of his nightmares to rest. Yeah, there were bad people who would try to take their things or even kill them. But they weren't invincible. In many respects, they weren't even smart. As long as their group stuck together and planned out each step, they should be able to make it to Kansas. And when they did, he hoped they would find the new world.

FOURTEEN

They drove northwest through Lamkin, Edna Hill, and Dublin, skirting both Hico and Stephenville.

Information would have been nice, but after hearing about Hico, they decided unanimously that it wasn't worth the risk.

The going was slow, as Max had known it would be.

At each hill, they stopped a few yards shy of the top to scope out the area in front of them. Two times there were roadblocks, though they were nothing like the one in Hamilton. Regardless, they backed up and went around.

Everyone tensed as they prepared to cross over Interstate 20. They pulled all three cars over to the side of the road, and Max and Lanh jogged ahead.

"Cars in both lanes," Lanh radioed back as Max looked down on an interstate that was both crowded and deserted. There were cars aplenty, but not a soul in sight. Had people been fleeing the city and run out of gas? Or had they been caught on the highway when the flare first occurred? They were directly west of Fort Worth. Where had they gone when their vehicles had broken down? Where were they now?

Gabe replied, asking for more details, and Lanh

said, "We might be able to push them out of the way."

In the end, it was the Hummer that pushed them out of the way. There were four vehicles in the right-hand lane headed northbound, though they contained no bodies, and Max was grateful for that. Three were trucks, abandoned in the northernmost part of the bridge that crossed over the interstate. They managed to move them by hand. Max put them into neutral. Carter and Lanh and Patrick helped push. Gabe, Shelby, and Bianca waited inside their three vehicles, engines idling, ready to make a fast break if necessary. But they didn't see a single soul. Only the carcasses of abandoned cars.

The last vehicle was a Suburban. The fool who had left it had also locked the thing. Perhaps he'd thought he might be back to get it and didn't want to find anything missing. Patrick busted the window with the end of a military-grade flashlight he found in his pack, but there must have been some type of security installed—LoJack maybe. The wheels seemed to be locked.

Gabe pulled up behind it, nice and slow so that the bumpers were touching and nearly interlocked. The Hummer pushed the Suburban off the bridge without even straining the engine.

By the time night began to fall, they'd reached a curve in the road southeast of Graham, barely a hundred and fifty miles from High Fields.

"At this rate we'll reach Kansas in July," Shelby grumbled.

"Summer in Kansas doesn't sound like such a bad thing. Think of it this way—the weather will be better there in July," Patrick pointed out. "Better than the typical one hundred degrees we have."

"I know you're kidding, so I refuse to answer that."

They'd pulled behind an abandoned gas station, effectively hiding their vehicles from the road.

"I'm going to check the station out," Patrick said.

Lanh and Carter immediately volunteered to go with him.

At the look on Shelby's face, Max picked up his rifle and said, "Wouldn't mind looking around myself." He understood that she was trying to treat both boys like men, but maternal worry ran deep.

"I'm sure it's empty," he whispered to her before turning to follow Patrick, Lanh, and Carter to the front of the store. Bianca was standing guard a few feet shy of the road. She had the radio clipped to the strap of her backpack and her rifle slung over her right shoulder. Gabe had spent the first thirty minutes they were stopped going over both the rifles and handguns and then handing one of the rifles to each person. Extra ammo went in backpacks, which he again emphasized were to stay on or beside you all the time.

They stepped over broken glass into the building, and all four of them stopped, fanning out slightly and covering the entire store.

"Lanh and I will take the back," Patrick said.

Max and Carter walked through the retail area of the store, though it was obvious from the second they stepped into the building that nothing useful remained.

Shelves were empty, displays were knocked over, mud and trash and blood were tracked across the floor.

The significance of the blood hit Max less than a second after he saw it—the time it took something you see to become an electrical signal and travel through the optic nerve to the brain, connecting it with something you know. Which was a fraction of a second too long.

Carter had started around the counter separating customers from workers.

All color left his face, and he backed up into a still-standing display, sending it careening against the wall. What he didn't do was drop the rifle. Max put a hand on his shoulder as he raised the M16 and sighted it in on the bodies.

"They're dead, Carter. It's all right. Put it down."

Carter lowered the rifle, still holding it in his right hand and wiping at the sweat beading down his face with his left. "Better check them." The words were strangled, but they showed he was thinking straight.

Patrick and Lanh burst back into the room.

"It's all right," Carter called out. "Just . . . bodies."

"A man, woman, and child from the looks of it."

Max had moved next to the bodies, but he didn't want to get too close. He had no idea what kind of disease could spread from a corpse, or if that was even possible after so much time. Another question to ask Gabe once they'd settled for the night.

"We going to leave them like that?" Lanh asked.

Max knew that Lanh had seen worse in Austin, but he'd also become accustomed to the way of life at High Fields, basically secluded from the rest of the world. Or maybe death and destruction was something a person never grew used to seeing.

Patrick motioned toward some posters still hanging on the wall. The boys pulled them down and helped Max to cover the bodies, weighting down the corners of the posters with rocks that Carter fetched from outside.

Lanh pointed to the graffiti over the register—an *X* inside a circle. "Hugo did this?"

"Could be." Patrick sounded as disgusted as Max felt.

What type of person killed a family in cold blood? And for what? Three lives ended for no better reason than they were hiding in the wrong place at the wrong time. There was no justice in that, and the anger in Max threatened to explode. It had been simmering in him since the night their neighbor was gunned down for his car, through the hundreds needlessly killed in Austin, and right up to the fight with the Cavanaghs at their ranch. Its roots reached to a prelaw class at the University of Texas and his graduation with a law degree from Baylor. Their current state of anarchy was not something he'd ever be able to simply accept.

"You okay?" Patrick asked.

Max didn't realize that the boys had trudged back outside.

He took in a deep breath.

"Yeah."

"We're going to see worse than this."

"I know we are."

"Doesn't make it any easier, though."

"No. It doesn't." They followed the boys back outside into the waning light and the gale of a frigid wind that threatened to blow them over. The cold front had arrived, and the best they could do was hunker down until it passed.

FIFTEEN

They were able to create a windbreak for the person standing guard using metal and plywood ripped from the back of the store.

"We'll take two-hour shifts," Gabe said. "You notice anything—any movement, light, or sound—and you get on the radio. Don't stop to figure it out. Clear?"

They all nodded. Any doubts Shelby had harbored about Gabe Thompson melted into the night. There was no question in her mind that he would take a bullet for them, and quite possibly he would help them avoid being caught in such a situation at all. The timid, quiet doctor she'd known in Abney, when he was pretending to be Farhan Bhatti, was gone. He was still a doctor—there was no doubt about that. But for the moment, he was a soldier first and foremost, and she was glad he was leading their group.

Patrick took the initial two-hour shift while the rest trooped back behind the building, where they'd made a circle of their vehicles. Camping in the middle, they were spared from the worst of the wind. They'd tossed around sleeping in the store.

"The rate of decomposition, as well as the lack of odor, indicates they've been dead some time," Gabe said after checking out the corpses himself. "Because they didn't die from disease, and they aren't in contact with our drinking water, there's no health risk."

"Doesn't mean I want to sleep in there," Lanh admitted.

"I'd rather be back here where we can't be seen from the road." Patrick leaned against the front bumper of the Mustang.

"Then it's decided." Shelby adjusted her pack so she was lying on it rather than holding it up. The thing was beginning to remind her of a tortoise shell.

The second seat of the Hummer, the backseat of the Mustang, and the second seat of the Dodge had been cleared off. Three of them would sleep inside, and the other three would sleep outside, sheltered by the vehicles.

"You come off duty, you get two hours inside a vehicle."

No one argued, mainly because they were exhausted and cold and didn't have a better idea.

Shelby's watch was from midnight to two. She relieved Patrick, who patted her clumsily on the shoulder and warned her to keep an eye out for snakes.

During the time Shelby had lived at High Fields, she'd only seen two snakes—one in the creek after sliding from a tree into a recess in the bank. The other had been in a woodpile and had taken a year off her life. She'd clobbered it with

103

a piece of wood and kept slamming until Max came outside to see what all the noise was about.

"I think it's dead," was all he had said, but the smile on his face told her he was proud.

Later he'd said, "Smart thinking, using the wood instead of a bullet."

"We need to conserve those."

"Yeah, but Shelby, if you ever encounter another rattler and don't have a piece of wood handy, shoot the thing. Okay?"

It had been a funny moment, though the look in his eyes had been intensely serious. She thought of that now as she stared out at a moonless sky overflowing with stars. It was amazing what you could see and hear in the dark if you sat still long enough, if you paid attention. A coyote called out. A calf bawled for its mother, and a fox passed close enough that she could have reached out a hand and touched it. Which didn't say much for how she must smell if a wild animal would come that close.

Her shift passed quickly. She was surprised when Lanh gave two short whistles.

"Didn't want you to shoot me."

"That makes two of us."

He settled into the scout position. Shelby was supposed to head back and kick someone out of their car bed. Instead, she stayed beside him and listened to the wind beat relentlessly against their blind. "Ever wish you'd stayed in Austin?"

"No."

"And now . . . do you wish you stayed at High Fields?"

"No."

She waited a few beats. When it was obvious he wasn't going to say any more, she called him on it. "I know you have more rattling around in your head than that."

"I thought we were supposed to be quiet out here."

"Like anyone could hear us over the wind."

"Good point."

"So?"

Lanh turned toward her, and though she couldn't exactly see his expression, she knew he was wearing his customary lopsided grin. "You worried about me, Mrs. S?"

"Guilty."

"Well, don't. I'm glad I came to High Fields. I learned a lot of good stuff from Max's parents."

"Yeah, like how to domesticate those wild pigs Carter and Monica trapped."

"Never thought I'd have bacon again."

"It was kind of gamey."

"It was delicious."

Shelby reached out and mussed his hair. Sometime since bringing him to High Fields, Lanh had become the second son she never had.

She gathered up her weapon and backpack and was nearly out of the blind when he called her back.

"Think we'll find them? The feds?"

"Maybe."

"If we do . . . could be that they'd know something about what happened overseas."

"I know you worry about your family."

"Yeah, I do. But there are people with family just a few towns over who don't know how they're doing."

"Doesn't make it any easier."

"We took so much for granted, but I think communication is what we didn't fully appreciate . . . possibly more than any other thing."

She understood what he was saying.

It was one thing to go hungry and learn to eat roots or nuts and berries. That was a problem you could solve with enough knowledge and a little luck. But not knowing . . . it was something that weighed on you constantly.

She squeezed his arm and started toward the camp.

The wind cut through her with a brutality that was startling.

Hadn't they earlier that day passed fields of wildflowers?

But then this was Texas, and the weather always had been capricious.

She opened the door of the Dodge, forgetting who had fallen asleep in it.

Max sat up, rubbing his face.

Gabe had insisted they disable the interior

lights so that they wouldn't inadvertently come on and act like a beacon to their position should anyone be watching. A year ago she would have thought such measures extreme, but now she was glad he'd thought of it.

Max didn't say anything. He yawned, stretched, and grabbed his pack and rifle, but as she stepped aside to let him by, he cupped the back of her neck with his hand, pulled her to him, and kissed her on the lips. He smelled exquisitely like Max, and she understood that she would know him anywhere—regardless of whether she could see or hear or touch him. Her other senses would always tell her the truth. His lips lingered on hers for a moment, and then he brushed past her to fall back asleep in one of the bedrolls on the ground.

Shelby curled onto the warm car seat, waiting for sleep to come, with the wind in her ears and Max's kiss on her lips.

SIXTEEN

They woke to frost on the windshields and clouds obscuring the morning stars, but at least the wind had stopped. Max suspected the temperature was a full twenty degrees cooler than the day before. Springtime in Texas. They were lucky it hadn't snowed.

Breakfast was instant coffee, granola bars, and dried fruit.

They followed the same procedure as the day before—stopping before the rise of each hill, scoping out the area in front of them, and deciding whether to forge on or backtrack. They ran into trouble on State Highway 114 and shots were exchanged. The instigators made only a halfhearted attempt at stopping their caravan, but there was evidence of more trouble ahead. A farmer's wife hanging wash on the line confirmed that the highway between Jacksboro and Loving was basically closed with bandits.

"No one goes there now, not even with the horses. We go around by way of Throckmorton."

The detour cost them most of the day, but they again found an abandoned building and set up camp. Though the temperatures hovered in the upper thirties, the wind had stopped howling. They circled up around a campfire, secure in the knowledge that their cars blocked the flames from sight.

"Someone could smell it, though," Carter argued.

"True, but the smell of a campfire isn't that unusual. Not anymore." Patrick poured hot water into a mug holding instant coffee. "Even if someone was looking, they couldn't find us in the dark. And if they do? We'll hear them before they get within a quarter mile."

Which was apparently what happened, because fifteen minutes later, Patrick returned dragging a guy by the collar of his coat. Max was on his feet, his gun in his hand before he realized he'd reached for it.

"Easy, folks." The man apparently hadn't shaved or bathed in weeks. He offered a lopsided smile as he reached up and pushed his hair out of his eyes. "I meant no harm."

"Found him creeping through the brush to the north, noisy as a toddler at a birthday party."

Gabe moved in front of the man. "Name?"

"Dan. Dan the music man."

Max noticed Shelby was also holding her weapon. It had somehow become second nature to them to reach for their firearm first and ask questions later.

"What's in the guitar case, Dan?"

"Um . . . a guitar?"

"Check it, Patrick."

Dan's hands were still in the air, but he wiggled

out of the strap holding the case to his back. He also carried a backpack, which he dropped to the ground.

Patrick laid the case in front of him on the ground and clicked open the fasteners. "Like the man says—a guitar."

Five minutes later, they'd determined that Dan was exactly who he said he was.

"So you walk around and play music?" Lanh asked. "Aren't you afraid that someone will kill you?"

"My playing isn't that bad."

Max exchanged glances with Shelby.

"When I was writing romance novels, if I'd written stuff this weird, my editor would have made me rewrite it. No one would believe it."

"Where are you from, Dan?" Bianca had offered the man one of their MREs, which he'd eaten with surprisingly good manners.

"Around. Texas, of course. Grew up out west, near San Angelo, but it's gone now."

"Gone?" Gabe leaned forward, suddenly alert to what Dan was saying. "What do you mean, gone?"

"Just that—gone. No water. No reason to stay. No way to stay. Scattered to the wind."

Dan reached for his guitar and began to strum lightly. Max had never been a musician or an artist of any kind, other than some minor doodling. Art was Shelby's territory. But he'd always enjoyed listening. Before the flare, he'd even begun rebuilding his collection of vinyl. The first chord from Dan's guitar sent a shiver through his soul.

Dan apparently had eclectic taste. His voice was soft but stirring as he picked the old Beatles' tune "Hey Jude," Johnny Cash's "Ring of Fire," and Eric Clapton's "Tears in Heaven." He strummed "America the Beautiful." Max attempted to sing along with the rest of their group, but the lyrics stuck in his throat as he was overwhelmed with love for his country, which teetered on the brink of collapse. It was one of the few times Dan looked up from his guitar, as though he sensed the surge of patriotism that had swept through each person sitting around the campfire.

Nodding once, he tapped the body of the guitar three times and began to pick a contemporary country tune that had been popular on the radio the week before the flare, transitioned straight into Dylan's "Knocking on Heaven's Door," and ended with "Amazing Grace," each person in the circle softly singing along. Max reached for Shelby's hand as they whispered the last stanza, the final chord bleeding off into the night.

"*Gracias*," Bianca said softly.

"You're welcome." Without another word, he pulled a thin bedroll out of his backpack, shook it out, and crawled inside, his back to the fire.

The music stayed with Max as he crept into his

own bedroll. Some might think that a gift like that was useless in their apocalyptic world, but Max realized moments before he drifted off to sleep how much he had longed for music. It lifted the heart and fed the soul.

Dan was still asleep when Max woke for his shift, but he was gone before sunrise.

They traveled on, settling into a rhythm.

Their world was the road, their destination, each other, and anything standing in their way.

They made progress.

And maybe they grew a little overconfident.

SEVENTEEN

They were fifty miles south of Wichita Falls and waiting for Patrick and Max to scope out the area when Gabe whistled twice, calling them into a group.

"Someone's following us."

Max immediately popped his head around the Dodge, but Gabe pulled him back down. The afternoon sun was taking on a westerly slant. He glanced at his watch and saw that it was a few minutes past four in the afternoon, which meant they had another two hours of light.

"Two horses, mostly they stay in the brush, but I've caught sight of them three times now."

"We're a long way from Hamilton, but that sounds like Hugo. Should we hold up until tomorrow? Find a place to bed down?"

"Not with them on our tail," Patrick said. "They'd wait until the middle of the night and make their move."

Gabe nodded. "Right now they don't know that we know they're following us."

"What's your plan?" Carter asked, which was pretty much the same thing Max was wondering.

"There's a crossroads a mile and a half from here."

Shelby frowned at her hiking boots. "I don't

know what you're suggesting, but it's bound to slow us down."

"I'm suggesting we take the offensive."

"Though we probably could outrun them if we tried."

"Unless they have people in front of and behind us, which is what I expect." Patrick shrugged. "It's what I would do."

Gabe glanced around the group. "We need to take care of this. Are we agreed?"

Everyone nodded.

"When we reach the crossroads, I'm going to peel off and head west."

"I'm not sure we should go separate directions," Bianca said.

She was no doubt thinking of what had happened in Austin when they broke up. Max and Shelby had to walk six miles in a storm, and Shelby was nearly killed by a lowlife who wanted to rob her. The episode had ended in an old barn, where they'd first come in contact with the Remnant, but Max didn't hold out much hope that they would stumble upon them twice in their moment of need.

"If this is Hugo, and I suspect it is, we know he typically sends his scouts on horses and then follows them in trucks. I suggest we try to take out the two on horseback and to do that . . ." He glanced at Bianca. "We have to separate initially."

"Better that we pick the spot than wait for them to," Patrick said. "And I agree that it's best for us to take the offensive."

"You're sure they're out there?" Shelby corralled her black curls with a rubber band and squashed a hat on top of her head.

"I've caught a glimpse of horses three times now. Each time we stop to scope out the next section, they stop to scope out us."

"All right," Bianca said. "I'm in. Let's meet whoever this is on our terms rather than theirs."

Shelby, Carter, and Lanh nodded in agreement, and Max said, "Tell us what to do."

The plan was simple. They'd divide at the crossroads. Whoever was following them would have to choose which direction to take. Once they were sure, the group not being followed would circle back and come in behind.

"And then what?" Carter asked.

"Depends on what we find."

The Hummer would go west. The Dodge and the Mustang would continue north, toward Wichita Falls.

Everything went according to plan at first.

The Hummer turned left. Within ten minutes, Carter radioed them. "Can't see the horses, but a pickup is behind us now. It's keeping a fair distance."

"We're on our way," Bianca said.

Max navigated a U-turn across cracked asphalt

stuffed with weeds and a crumbling guardrail that stood sentinel over a small creek.

He led the way, with Patrick nearly on his bumper. They didn't bother to slow down and scope out the path. They were only a few miles north of the section where Gabe had turned west.

They followed the road and soon caught sight of the pickup.

"Carter is driving," Gabe said over the radio. "We're going to stop at the top of the rise, and I'll jump out with my weapon pointed toward the truck. I want you a half mile back."

Bianca and Shelby radioed that they understood.

It was a good plan, but Max had a hard time shaking the bad feeling that settled in his gut when he spotted the circled *X* spray painted on the tailgate of the truck trailing the Hummer.

He realized they were in trouble when another vehicle pulled in behind the Mustang, and he could see in the distance, in front of the Hummer, a large flatbed truck stop mere inches from where Gabe was standing.

Lanh was out of the Hummer, back to back with Gabe. He had his weapon pointed at the flatbed, and Gabe kept his weapon pointed at the truck to their rear, which had pulled off the road in a flanking position. Carter remained behind the wheel of the Hummer. No doubt Gabe had told him to stay there and run over anything or anyone who threatened them.

116

Max halted the Dodge at an angle across both lanes of the road, and Patrick did the same, creating a two-sided box of shelter where Max, Patrick, Shelby, and Bianca could spread out in a line, two facing the Hummer and two facing the Volkswagen bus coming to a stop in the road behind them. For a moment, Max thought they'd arrived at a standoff, but then he glimpsed the two men on horses emerging from the brush to the south, rifles raised, and he knew that they had been outmaneuvered.

He was nearly overpowered by the urge to empty the twenty-round magazine in his M16, but as his finger crept to the trigger, Shelby said, "Don't."

She was staring toward Gabe, and Max realized everyone else had already dropped their weapons.

"Pretty smart, Mamma-jamma." This from a boy who didn't yet have facial hair. Short and thin and incredibly dirty, he approached from the truck that had flanked the Hummer. "Wouldn't want a bloodbath. You all look like a nice little family. Very multicultural." He reached out with the muzzle of his gun and scooped up Bianca's hair.

Max dropped his weapon.

They were herded into a circle and told to sit facing outward.

When it was clear they'd been neutralized, Hugo stepped from the passenger seat of the flatbed. There was no questioning who he was. For one thing, he had an *X* inside a circle tattooed on his forehead. His long hair was pulled back with a leather strap. Tattoos snaked up and down his neck and over the backs of his hands. He was tall and gangly, and he had a bad case of acne down both sides of his face.

He silently walked up and down, giving them a quick once-over and focusing most of his attention on the vehicles. One of the men on horseback tossed his reins to the other, and then he confirmed that each vehicle still had the keys in the ignition. When Hugo reached the Hummer, a smile broke out across his face. "Looks like it's my lucky day."

"It will be if you walk away now."

Hugo froze for a moment, hands lifted as if he was about to lay them on the Hummer and bless it. Instead he turned, walked over to their group, and squatted in front of Gabe.

"You talk big for a man who has been disarmed and is now sitting on his hands."

"I thought you deserved a fair warning."

"Oh! My man has nerves of steel." He leaned in closer.

Max could see that Hugo had his face right up to Gabe's, and he was sure that Gabe would head butt him. Adrenaline coursed through his veins, and he focused on his rifle leaning against the front of the Dodge. He was planning how he'd plow through the goon standing in front of him, snatch the rifle, and get off a few rounds when the stillness of the afternoon was broken by a shout and then a clicking that bizarrely reminded him of a camera stuck on automatic.

Gabe shouted a warning and threw himself on top of Bianca, who was seated to his left. Max saw something cross Hugo's face—alarm or irritation or fear. And then a rocket hit the flatbed truck, sending it careening toward the side of the road.

EIGHTEEN

Carter's ears felt plugged with cotton.

He could make out random words, but they wouldn't string together correctly.

AT-4 rocket
Move those . . .
Go. Go. Now!
He's bleeding.

There were other sounds as well. Fire crackling. Vehicles peeling away. Someone screaming his name. A mockingbird calling out.

He pushed up from the ground into a sitting position and tried to take in a scene that made no sense. The flatbed truck was a pile of flames and smoking metal. The Hummer was gone. Lanh was holding his shoulder. Blood was oozing between his fingers running down his arm. Bianca stood and stumbled toward Lanh. Max was checking on Carter's mom. Patrick had jogged down the road and stopped in the middle. He pulled up the rifle, sighted in one of the fleeing vehicles, and pulled the trigger.

The tat-a-tat of the weapon brought Carter back to his senses. Everything came together—the ambush and Hugo and Gabe about to be killed.

He jumped up, vaguely aware that he was

still wearing his pack, and ran toward Lanh.

Bianca didn't turn to look at him, but she said, "Pull the med kit out of my pack, Carter."

"What happened?"

"A piece of the flatbed hit me." Lanh's eyes were open wide, his pupils darting left to right, left to right. His skin had taken on a shiny pallor.

"Not a bullet?"

"Nothing as cool as that."

"Just as dangerous," Bianca said. "Unless we manage to stop this bleeding."

"We need to go," Gabe hollered as he jogged over to where they were.

"I'm bandaging it—"

"No time. Hugo and his goons are going to circle back."

Carter realized that his mom and Max were also hurrying in their direction.

"Are you okay?" she asked.

"I'm fine. It's Lanh who was hurt." He saw then that she had a scrape across her forehead and blood had dripped down the side of her face. Max had wrapped a rag around his left hand, but it was soaked through with blood. He shook his head once quickly when he saw Carter staring.

So they were fine, but bruised and battered.

Off to the side, holding what looked like a shoulder rocket launcher, was a large, burly man with wild red hair and a beard that covered most of his face.

Gabe reached past the med kit, pulled out the duct tape, and wrapped it quickly and tightly around Lanh's left arm.

"Are you hurt anywhere else?"

"No."

"You're sure you can walk?"

"Yeah."

"All right. Carter stay on his right side."

Patrick took Gabe's place on Lanh's left, and they maintained a tight group of three as they all rushed into the woods. Maybe Gabe was afraid Lanh was going to faint from the loss of blood. It was plain that his legs worked fine, but he still had that shiny look to his skin, and his eyes continued to dart back and forth.

Gabe rushed ahead and was saying something to the redheaded man. Carter couldn't make out what it was, though. He could only hear his heart hammering and their feet pounding against the dirt and the sound of branches bending for them and slapping back too quickly as they pushed through. It seemed they'd been running for an eternity, but it had probably only been ten minutes. Gabe stopped, held up his hand, and they all listened. Carter tried to will his heart to beat more quietly, but it was no use. All he could hear was the thundering of his pulse and his own labored breathing.

They were standing in a knot now. Gabe next to the stranger. Carter's mom and Max on his right. Bianca and Patrick to Lanh's left.

Carter's mind had caught up with what happened. They'd been ambushed. Outplayed. Robbed. Rescued? He felt the weight of his pack on his back, saw his mother glance at it and smile tightly. She reached out and squeezed his arm, but she didn't need to say it. He understood well enough.

If it hadn't been for Gabe, that pack would be in the backseat of the Hummer right now, headed to who-knew-where. Carter had thought it kind of stupid, even a tad dramatic, when Gabe insisted they carry their packs with them everywhere. He'd thought maybe the kind old guy he knew as the doctor next door was feeling the effects of too much strain. Now he understood that Gabe was seeing the world as it was. Carter had been looking at the world as he hoped it would be.

And his survival lay in the difference.

"Where are we going?" Gabe asked the big guy.

"Gustav Jacobsen. Folks call me Gus." They shook hands, and Gus nodded at the rest of the group. "We need to keep going. Hugo will be back—sooner rather than later."

"You have a camp near here?"

"A few more miles."

"How'd you happen—"

Gus cut him off. "I understand why you wouldn't trust me, but I did save you back there. Now you can stay here, have a meeting or whatever, and decide what you're going to do. But I'm headed back to the compound."

Carter's mom started to speak, but he held up his hands and stopped her. "Don't mean to be rude, ma'am. We have enough time to make it back before dark if we leave now. Being out here at night with Hugo on our scent? That's not something I care to do. If we survive this, I'd be happy to listen to what you have to say."

With a nod, the giant of a man took off across the open field.

"Not much shelter here," Max said.

"The woods we came through might throw them off . . ." Bianca had her hands on her knees and was pulling in deep breaths.

It made Carter feel better to see that he wasn't the only one winded and struggling to keep up.

"We crashed through those woods like a bear intent on protecting its cub," Patrick said.

"Even a fool like Hugo could follow our trail." Gabe looked directly at Lanh. "Can you keep going?"

"Yeah. I'm good."

Everyone muttered words of agreement. Carter even felt his own head bobbing. Then Gabe led them after the big guy, Gus, toward a compound, into the middle of somewhere else. But away from Hugo, and that was good.

NINETEEN

There was very little light left when they reached the compound. It was a semi-circle of RVs backed up against an embankment that overlooked the Brazos River. The river was broad and surprisingly swollen, owing to recent rains. The cliffs were somewhat steep—another thing Shelby didn't expect south of Wichita Falls, but then the terrain was hilly here, and the river had cut a path. The rust-colored dirt reminded her of the Red River that they were so desperate to find a way across. But first it seemed they would cross the Brazos, headed back the wrong direction.

The RVs were a tan color rather than the sparkling white Shelby had always seen as they traveled through Abney coming down Highway 281. With the way the RVs were positioned against the backdrop of Texas dirt and the little bit of light peeking through the trees, the result was that they were practically invisible.

"How did you get the RVs here?" Shelby asked.

Gus had slowed down and waited for them once they were within sight of the compound. She would never have found it if she'd been looking for it. A stand of trees higher up the bank blocked it from above, and below was only the river, which had no activity on it. At the moment, they were standing across the river from the compound, which brought up a whole other set of questions.

"Surely they weren't here already. How did you . . ."

Gus grinned, revealing dazzling white, perfectly straight teeth. For some reason, Shelby was surprised, and then she was embarrassed that she'd expected him to have tobacco-stained teeth where they weren't missing. In spite of the people she'd met since the flare—the frightening-looking ones who had helped them and the normal-looking ones who had nearly killed them—she was still sorting people into stereotypes by their appearance. Maybe that was just what humans did.

"Everyone in our group is an amateur survivalist."

"Amateur?"

"They didn't build bunkers, but . . ." He waved toward the RVs as though the rest was self-explanatory.

To Shelby, none of what she was seeing made sense. Unfortunately, she didn't have time to ask more questions. Everyone was standing in a group, once again catching their breath, but it was obvious Gus was ready to move on. For a big guy, he hiked across the fields and through the woods with remarkable ease.

He pulled his fingers through his beard and

stepped out from the stand of trees where they were regrouping. Standing in the open with his legs spread apart, he waved his arms back and forth over his head, causing him to look like a giant *X*.

"Tell me Gus has a plan," Max said as he passed her a bottle of water.

She noticed that the rag wrapped around his hand was stained red through and through, but it was dried blood.

"That needs to be disinfected," she said.

"Later."

Two whistles answered Gus's pantomime, and then a long canoe nosed out of a cove filled with reeds as two people began to row toward them.

"Best get going. Boys don't like to wait." Gus stepped back into the trees and began to pick his way down the steep bank.

"Are we actually going over there?" Carter asked.

"Yeah, we are." Gabe had been relatively quiet on the trek to the compound. His eyes were like ice, and his expression was completely unreadable. Shelby assumed he was still fighting his anger. Either that, or he thought they were in serious trouble and didn't want to scare everyone. She was hoping for the former.

Lanh once again assured Bianca he was okay.

Max brought up the rear.

They reached the canoe and found it was two

boys who had paddled over. They were all hands and feet, and Shelby guessed they were sixteen years old—at the most. Obviously, they were experienced with the canoe. They held it steady while Bianca and Shelby climbed on board with their packs. There was enough room for Carter and Lanh as well.

"We'll come back for ya," the taller of the two said to the rest of the group.

They were halfway across the river when the same boy said, "My name's Decker. This here is Jack. I guess we're the welcome committee."

"Thank you for coming to fetch us," Bianca said.

"Oh, well, you know. Gus was pretty clear."

Shelby introduced herself, and the rest in their group did the same.

Decker and Jack were interested in Lanh's wound. It didn't take long to tell the story of their ambush and Gus's rescue.

"He set off the rocket launcher? On Hugo?"

She had the feeling the boys would have high-fived, but they were sitting on opposite ends of the canoe.

"No wonder Gus brought you back," Decker said.

"Gus never brings no one."

Shelby resisted the urge to correct Jack's grammar. Now probably wasn't the time.

"He feels responsible since he saved ya." Decker nodded to Jack. "Tie up."

The boy jumped out of the canoe and tied it to a pier that Shelby hadn't been able to see from across the river. The wooden structure was covered with reeds and painted the same color as the water. Of course it was. It had been built by amateur survivalists. Maybe to Gus they were amateur, but to her they seemed like experts. They'd managed to make their compound practically invisible.

Fifteen minutes later, they'd ferried the rest of the group across.

The first order of business was for Gabe to look at Lanh's arm.

Perhaps having Decker and Jack look on in admiration helped.

Carter joked that at least it was his left arm, and Lanh would still be able to eat fast and shoot straight.

What with all of the attention, Lanh was actually fighting a smile by the time Gabe finished with him.

"Keep it clean, keep it covered, and don't do anything to rip out those stitches."

Gabe actually had small vials of antibiotics in his pack, and he injected one into Lanh's other arm.

"Thanks. Now they both hurt."

"You'll live." But Gabe's tough words were softened by the look he gave the boy.

Only he wasn't a boy. Shelby had to remind

herself that he'd turned twenty-one a few months ago. Both he and Carter were men, so why did she still feel like it was her responsibility to protect them?

Next, Gabe cleaned up Max's hand, which required a butterfly stitch across the outside and below his pinky finger. Last, he poured hydrogen peroxide on a rag and began to wipe Shelby's forehead. "You don't need stitches, but you do need to keep it clean."

She nodded, though she felt incredibly stupid a few minutes later with a Band-Aid across her forehead.

"Is Lanh's arm a problem?" Shelby squatted next to Gabe, helping him repack, and the tops of their heads were almost touching.

Gabe stopped to rub the fingers of his right hand against his forehead.

When he glanced at Shelby, she could practi-0cally see the guilt and weariness rolling off him.

"Shouldn't be doing triage . . . not here, not like this."

"But this is our life." She shrugged as she sat back on her heels. "I would think you would be used to it by now."

"Even in Austin, I mainly worked with the military. I hated to see anyone injured, but we volunteered to serve. We understood the risk. That's not true of civilians. Lanh and Carter, Decker and Jack . . . even you."

"Hey."

"You didn't sign up for this, and it makes me angry." He closed the medical pack with a jerk and stuffed it into his backpack. "Not to mention I put us in harm's way by thinking I could take on Hugo."

"You didn't know for certain who we were taking on."

"But I should have."

"You know, Gabe, it would be nice if you were perfect." She waited until his eyes met hers. "No doubt we'd get there faster and have fewer problems. Unfortunately, last time I checked, we're all human. So how about you give yourself a break?"

Instead of answering, he stood and reached for her hand to pull her up from the ground. Then they walked to where the others were waiting.

TWENTY

It was fortunate they arrived at dinnertime, and the fact that Gus's group shared their beef stew said a lot about what type of people they were.

"Actually, it's squirrel stew," Gus said.

"Tastes great." Bianca scraped the last bit from her bowl. "Nearly as good as my *mamá* cooked."

Max thought a look of longing passed over her face, and he wondered fleetingly how she was dealing with losing both parents so close to one another. But at that moment, Bianca looked up into Patrick's eyes, smiled, and accepted his last bite of stew. Bianca would be fine, and Patrick? He was a good man to have the faith and dedication to take on such a thing as a marriage at this point in their lives.

Or maybe Max had that backward. If there was ever a time to commit to one another, it was now.

He stared down into his empty stew bowl, and then he glanced up at Gus. It was incredibly kind of them to share what food they had. Unless they'd poisoned it.

But why bring them all the way here to kill them?

Gus could have left them back at the ambush site. Hugo would have found them soon enough.

The RVs blocked the worst of the north wind,

and a small campfire blazed in the middle of the group. Max had no doubt that it couldn't be seen from the opposite bank. This group wasn't messing around. They even had mesh stretched over the top of the entire encampment.

"So it can't be seen from above." Gus grinned like a proud father.

"But . . . there aren't any planes."

"No, but we're halfway down this riverbank, and though we're tucked in, if the sun shines at a certain angle, you can make something out from either the top of this bank or the opposite side."

The group consisted of eight RVs and eighteen adults, almost equally split between men and women. There were an unknown number of kids. Unknown because the young ones were passed from lap to lap, making it difficult to count, and the middle-aged ones were playing a raucous but silent game of freeze tag. Other than Decker and Jack, Max didn't see any other teenagers.

Surprisingly, the leader wasn't Gus. It was Hauk.

"H-a-u-k." He shook hands with each of them. "I'm not a bird of prey, but our parents enjoyed the old names."

Hauk and Gus looked enough alike to be kin. They had the same red hair and long sideburns, but there the similarities ended. Hauk was smallish, trim, and a few years older, given the gray in his sideburns.

133

"Cousins," Gus explained when Max asked. "And sometimes cousins can be closer than brothers."

"I still don't understand how you anticipated the flare." Shelby had pulled out her notebook, with the permission of the group, and was taking notes.

"We didn't," Hauk said. "We anticipated something, but we didn't know what."

"We scoped out this place years ago," Laurel said. She was Hauk's wife and petite in a way that reminded Max of a child. She had warm, brown skin and long, black hair. "We even tried to buy some land along the river, but it was either privately owned or government owned, and no one was selling."

"Funny. No one from the federal government has stopped by to ask why we're here." Gus glanced up from the fire, a grin tugging at his face. The man seemed to always be smiling, though Max couldn't imagine why. Or maybe why not. His family was here. He seemed in his element. Whatever he'd done for a living before the flare apparently wasn't something he missed.

"So we appropriated it for our use," Hauk admitted.

"Don't worry, cousin. I have a feeling the taxes I paid for the last twenty years were more than enough to cover it."

Hauk laughed. "Gus was a dentist in our

134

previous life. He's still bitter about the thirty-eight-percent tax he paid."

"Money I could have used to buy more supplies when there were supplies to be bought."

As they had finished eating, most of the adults peeled off into twos and threes. Lanh and Carter walked off with Decker and Jack. Max and the rest of their group were left in the company of Gus, Hauk, and Laurel.

"You've done a good job making a safe place for your families," Patrick said. "Do you plan to stay here?"

A silent look passed between Hauk and Gus. After a moment, Hauk said, "We have several other locations. We start up the RVs every third month and move to a different place."

"You're moving to keep the tires in good condition," Gabe said.

"RVs are designed and built to be moved. We knew that would be one of the most challenging aspects of our plan. While they provide good shelter, if we can't move them, if we become stuck in one spot, chances are that we will be attacked and won't survive."

"It's hard to believe that's what our world has become." Shelby stared at the journal in her lap, but still she didn't write anything.

"Perhaps it has always been that way, only we'd forgotten." Hauk pulled his wife closer to his side, whether because of the cold or for emotional support, Max wasn't sure. "Although we didn't know what the crisis would be, everyone in this group was convinced that the way we were living could suddenly end. Some folks expected a virus, others a domestic uprising. Gus and I were betting on a natural disaster . . ."

"Like a flare," Bianca said softly.

"Yeah. Statistically, some scientists were predicting a one in eight chance that we could have a major solar event that would knock out the power grid, but no one wanted to hear that. The news media did a terrible job of reporting it, and people were preoccupied with living their lives." Gus stood and placed two more pieces of wood on the fire.

"We couldn't guess the exact nature of the crisis. So instead, we decided the best plan was to be somewhat mobile, have a shelter that could be concealed, and have several locations so we wouldn't be depending on the resources in one area."

Shelby nodded and began to jot down notes.

"We start the vehicles once a month to make sure the gas is still good—"

"But it won't be. Not for long."

"We brought enough to top them off and added stabilizer. Should be good for five years. We park the RVs on parking mats made of rubber. They provide a barrier between the wheels and the ground to reduce the chance of rot. We also clean the tires with soap and water and keep them covered."

"You thought this thing out," Shelby said.

"As much as anyone can. Some things we've had to learn as we go."

Max couldn't resist. "Anyone in your group named Micah?"

Gus had taken a sip from his water jug, and he nearly spit it into the fire. "As in Micah five?"

Max glanced at Shelby, then Gabe, and then back at Gus. "Yeah."

"We did have." Hauk's expression turned suddenly grave. "The Remnant spent a few weeks with us back in . . ."

"December," Laurel said. "After the nuke went off to the east."

TWENTY-ONE

"Nuke? As in nuclear bomb?" Patrick hunched forward, though he was still holding Bianca's hand.

"The same." Hauk glanced at Gus.

Everyone began talking at once then, and Max had to hold up his hand to quiet them so he could hear what Gus was trying to say.

"The blast site was in Fort Worth, or maybe Dallas, as near as we can figure. We haven't seen anyone from the east at all, so we're assuming that the blast radius was fairly wide."

"The governor heard rumors of that," Gabe said. "I'd hoped they were exaggerated."

"Nope. We sealed the windows with duct tape and stayed inside for the better part of two weeks. I even have a Geiger counter, and I'd go out to check periodically. Never registered anything, so I guess the fallout went east."

Shelby's pen was frozen above her paper, and Max knew without asking that she wasn't thinking about the buildings in the Fort Worth Stockyard or the Kimball Art Museum. She was thinking of the millions of people who called the area home.

"So the Dallas–Fort Worth metroplex is . . . gone?" Bianca's voice trembled. "They had a combined population of . . ."

"Seven million." Max swallowed the bile that rose in his throat, reached for Shelby's free hand, and prayed that what they were hearing wasn't true.

"We haven't seen or heard of anyone who survived it, and I keep my ear to the ground." Gus leaned forward and ran his gaze over their group. "As far as your asking about the Remnant, they seemed to be good people. Laurel is right. They arrived about three weeks after the blast. They had come from Abilene and were taking some old folks north, hoping to find care for them there."

"I'm not sure those places still exist," Max said.

"Yeah. We told them the same thing, but they'd heard a rumor . . ."

"That's mostly what we get here," Laurel said. "People chasing rumors."

"I know one thing that isn't a rumor." Gabe sat up straighter, and Max knew they were down to the business part of the meeting. "Tell us about Hugo."

"Hugo's a thug. Before the flare, he would have been arrested and imprisoned. But once the municipalities collapsed, he grew bolder. Now folks are scared."

"What folks?" Patrick asked.

"I'm sure you've noticed there are still farmers, especially on the back roads. Anyone on a major highway frontage pulled up and left. But the people with more rural farms, they stayed—or they tried to."

"He's harassing them too?" Max asked.

"He harasses whomever he wants, takes what he finds whether he needs it or not." Hauk scratched at his sideburns.

"Why hasn't someone stopped him?" Gabe leaned forward, elbows on knees. "Why haven't you stopped him?"

"Mainly because of the children." Laurel didn't even blink when Gabe turned his gaze on her. "If it were only us, then perhaps we would have, but we have to think of the children."

"And Hugo doesn't like an armed and organized opponent, so we're fairly safe from him," Gus said. "He prefers the innocent or the unsuspecting. I guess with you all, he simply couldn't resist the shiny toy you were driving."

"I still can't believe you had a Hummer." Hauk patted his wife's hand and stood to stretch his legs. He walked closer to the fire, studied it a moment, and then turned to look at them. "Where were you all headed before your run-in with Hugo?"

Gabe explained about their search for the federal government without supplying too many details.

"And you think they're in Kansas?" Gus's amused smile had returned. "Why would you think that?"

140

Max shrugged, noticed everyone else in his group had done the same, and nearly laughed. It seemed strange to find something funny after hearing about the devastation to the east. But he couldn't change that. All he could do was try to find their way north, try to find help for Carter and answers for Governor Reed.

Gabe cleared his throat. "What about Wichita Falls?"

Max jerked his head left, surprised at the sudden change in topic.

"What about it?" Hauk asked.

"Who's running the place? What's it like?"

"You won't get across into Oklahoma there. The highway is closed and blocked to the north of town."

"We'll find another way across then. What I'm asking is, do they have any type of law in place? What do they do with thieves? With murderers?"

"It's not pretty." Laurel clasped the cross pendant she wore on a long chain. "Hauk and I went there together a month ago, hoping to find supplies, thinking they'd be less wary of a man and woman approaching the town blockade."

"And what did you find?"

"A few supplies—at astronomical prices. We managed to buy some fresh fruit for the children. It had been brought in from the southwest, maybe Arizona."

"Wichita Falls exists both as a town and as a

trading center. They've been able to do that because they use extreme measures to protect their people and their borders."

"What type of extreme measures?" Max asked, his lawyer brain suddenly wide awake.

"You'll see indications if you approach from the west, south, or east. At each point where you can enter the town, signs warn that the penalty for stealing or killing is death."

"You'll also see the bodies." Hauk moved back next to his wife. "They like to leave them hanging as a deterrent to others."

Max dropped his head into his hands. Wild West justice—no trials, no jury. Just swiftly delivered consequences. A lawyer's worst nightmare.

"Can the authorities be trusted?" Gabe asked.

Max had no idea where he was going with this line of questioning. The litigator in him wanted to call out, "Irrelevant," but he held his tongue and waited.

"Trusted?" Hauk shook his head. "They're not in collusion with Hugo, if that's what you're asking."

"And you can show me on a map where Hugo is?"

"I can show you where his camp is. He's not always there."

"Good." Gabe stood. "How many men does he have with him?"

"Six, usually." Hauk stared at the fire. "Hugo

you've met. He has the X in a circle tattooed on his forehead. His top two compatriots have just the X. They haven't achieved full membership in his gang yet."

"What about the other three?" Patrick asked.

"That's where it gets complicated." Hauk looked to Gus, who took up the story.

"Hugo kidnaps kids and forces them to do his dirty work. If they won't do it, he goes back to kill their family. The kids aren't there because they want to be, but over time some of them get addicted to the power."

"The two guys with the X."

"Yeah, there was even a girl a few months back. We only saw her once and from a distance. She either died in one of their skirmishes or ran away. Hard to say."

Hauk ran a hand up and down his face. "I assume you're thinking of some type of retribution, but if so, then you need to fully consider the situation. It's not as black and white as you might think. The three younger kids— the ones with no tattoo at all on their forehead— are being forced to do these things by Hugo. They might still be guilty . . ."

"But they've also been coerced," Max said.

"What are you thinking about doing, Gabe?" Now Bianca stood, walked over to him, and stared up into his face. "What are you suggesting that we do?"

143

"I'm going to get my Hummer back. If you'd rather stay here—"

"No. We'll go with you." Shelby stuffed her pad and pen into her pack. "We can't exactly walk to Kansas."

"I'm in." Patrick was grinning ear to ear. No doubt he would have followed Hugo from the moment of the ambush if it hadn't been for the rest of them.

"Wait." Max wondered if he was the only one thinking straight in this group. "We're going to waltz over to Hugo's and take back our vehicles and go on our merry way?"

"No. We're going to take back our vehicles, and then we're turning Hugo over to the Wichita Falls authorities."

TWENTY-TWO

Carter resisted the urge to grumble when his mom shook him awake the next morning— if morning was what you wanted to call it. His watch said 3:30, and it was still plenty dark.

"Remind me why we're up this early." But even as he said it, he remembered about Hugo and losing their vehicles and Gabe's plan. He remembered Fort Worth. He thought he had adjusted to the way things were. He no longer woke expecting to grab his phone and check Twitter or text a friend. This was an entirely different level of messed up, though. All those people—gone.

"Miles to cover, *amigo*. Miles to cover." Bianca mussed his hair as she walked by on the way to the campfire coffee that Carter could smell from where he lay in his borrowed bedroll—his was still in the Hummer. With Hugo.

"You good?" his mom asked.

"Yeah. Sure."

He struggled out of his bag, checked his glucose levels, and then dialed in the correct dosage of insulin. Crazy that he could do that sitting in the dark and holding a small flashlight between his teeth, but there you had it. Their life was officially bizarre. He let his mind drift back to High Fields and prayed that Georgia and Roy were okay. He guessed it was a prayer. Mostly, he kept it inside his head and aimed it toward the sky, hoping someone was up there.

Carter and God had an on-again, off-again relationship. He clearly remembered praying when he thought he was going to die in the creek running along the east border of High Fields, his leg broken, bad guys on his tail, and his glucose skyrocketing. He'd mumbled the best foxhole prayer ever, and God had heard. Or maybe it wasn't his day to die.

Sometimes he could believe, when he looked up at the stars scattered across the sky or watched a buck with a giant spread and thoughtful eyes. Other times, like when they'd come across the bodies in the gas station, he had a harder time. What kind of God allowed the people who had murdered whole families to continue to exist?

Spiritually, his thoughts were a knot of questions.

He'd mentioned it once to Max, who had assured him that God could handle his doubts and his questions—whatever that meant.

"How's the arm?" he asked Lanh, who had also sat up and was now gingerly moving his shoulder through a few slow rotations Gabe had shown him.

"Worse than yesterday."

"You going to be all right?"

146

"Yeah."

" 'Cause we could leave you here with Decker and Jack."

Lanh grunted and began cramming his bedroll into its stuff bag. "Never met two guys who were so interested in fishing."

"And hunting."

"And cars."

"RVs."

"Whatever." Lanh cinched up the bag and set it to one side, ready to be returned to Hauk. "Besides, I want to be there when we get our vehicles back."

"Yeah. Me too." Carter leaned forward and they bumped fists, which seemed ridiculously childish but still served to make him feel better.

Max had explained the plan to them when they returned to camp the night before. Actually, there wasn't much of a plan. Gus and Hauk had agreed to lead them to within sight of Hugo's camp. After that they were on their own. They'd take the canoes an hour downstream and then hike another three miles, which Gabe hoped they could do in ninety minutes. A thirty-minute mile didn't sound like much, but carrying their packs and stumbling through the woods in the dark was bound to slow them down.

They ate some granola for breakfast. Gabe had a big sack of it, which he swore was high in carbs and protein. He kept passing it around the group, perhaps hoping they could eat enough to spur them into jogging instead of merely hiking.

"Gabe's intense this morning," Lanh noted, helping himself to another handful of the granola mix.

"They shouldn't have taken his Hummer."

"Guess they didn't know who they were messing with."

"Sounds like no one has stood up to Hugo before." Carter stretched out the word *Hugo* as though he were announcing his name over a loudspeaker, maybe introducing the guy at a concert. Huuuu-Goooo. Only he wasn't a rock star. He was a punk, and Carter for one was tired of punks running the show.

"No lights once we're on the water," Hauk reminded them. "We're fairly sure the adjacent banks are clear of other people—"

"Or they were," Gus said.

"They were clear two days ago. We do reconnaissance three times a week, but anyone could have moved in since then. We want to go undetected." Hauk held his hand in front of him and slid it softly through the air. "Like a duck in water."

That image struck Carter as funny.

They should be comparing themselves to a stealth flyer, or a sleek submarine, or a ninja warrior. But a duck? The image didn't fill him with confidence.

Though he had to admit, their team was focused and determined to a degree he hadn't seen before. Everyone was awake, packed, knees jiggling as they scarfed down the cold breakfast.

They walked single file down the bank to the canoes. Carter walked behind Gus, who once again carried his rocket launcher.

"Where did you get that thing?"

"Found it."

"You found it?"

They were practically whispering, and Carter had to crane his head to hear.

"I like to go out, you know . . . beyond where the group normally goes."

"And—"

"And sometimes I come across some weird stuff. Figured this baby might come in handy."

"Saved our butts."

"Yeah, but I wish I'd killed Hugo. Then this mission wouldn't even be necessary."

That was one thing about the post-flare world. People chose sides pretty quickly, and the good guys—like Gus and Hauk—were committed once they teamed up. Not committed enough to go with them, but loyal enough to protect them as far as they could go. Carter understood that family always came first. He got that, and he didn't blame them for not wanting to poke the bear that was Hugo.

Gus, Shelby, Bianca, and Patrick slipped into the first canoe.

Hauk, Max, Gabe, Lanh, and Carter piled into the second.

And then they slid into the Brazos, like a duck through water.

TWENTY-THREE

Shelby would have felt better if they'd had an actual, detailed plan. Gabe had insisted that it was smarter to stay flexible until they could size up Hugo's camp and security. Patrick had agreed, and because they were the two with military experience, no one else voiced any objections.

They rounded a bend in the Brazos, and Shelby was able to glance back at the other canoe. She could just make out Max's silhouette in the starlight. It did something funny to her stomach seeing him there. She was reminded of him sitting on the hood of the Dodge, cowboy hat pulled down against the glare of the sun. Had that been only three days ago? It seemed wherever her memories landed, as far back as she cared to go, there was Max.

Seeing Carter and Lanh back there sent a stab of pain through her heart. How she wished she could spare them this. Why were they forced to creep along a river in the dead of night? Was it too much to ask that they simply drive up the interstate? How many years had she taken the ability to freely travel from one spot to another for granted? All her life. That was how long.

She tried to focus her mind on staying positive. Hauk and Gus knew where Hugo's camp was.

They were willing to ferry them to within a few miles, something that saved them at least a day and maybe more.

They'd shared their food and their camp.

There were still good people in the world.

The canoes slipped through the water, and Shelby lost track of how long they'd been on the river, how many miles they'd covered, what was behind them and in front of them. In places, the overhang of trees blocked out the stars completely. After what seemed hours, but couldn't have been more than one, they paddled the canoes into waist-high reeds.

Bianca jumped up and helped secure their canoe to a half-sunk pier.

Carter was doing the same to his.

Making as little noise as possible, they waded through the foot-deep water and climbed up the riverbank.

When she reached the top, Shelby's heart was hammering against her ribs, and she kept blinking her eyes, trying to put what she was seeing into the context of what she'd been expecting. Maybe she'd been anticipating another ambush or more darkness.

But she was greeted by something so completely normal that it caused an ache to settle deep in her heart. It was another beautiful Texas morning— night, actually, because it was before five and the sky hadn't yet begun to lighten. But the stars

. . . they were riotous. They were the same stars that shone over High Fields. Before that, they had twinkled down on her home in Abney, but she understood that she'd never seen them like this—a dome of millions of lights, the Milky Way evident against the inkiness of the sky, God's wonders holding steady, assuring her that the world would continue to spin as it always had.

He determines the number of the stars and calls them each by name.

The verse rose from her memory, lightening her heart.

Gus led them across the field and into the cover of trees. He pulled out a flashlight and a topographical map. "We're here. Hugo's camp is nearly three miles to the northwest."

"I wish we could go with you," Hauk said.

"We understand. This isn't your fight, and you've already saved us once." Max studied the map as if he needed to memorize the details, apparently hoping its contours and roads could save them.

Gabe stared off toward the northwest. "You're sure no one has tried this before?"

"I would have heard about it." Gus ran his fingers through his beard. "That may work to your advantage. He won't be expecting you to be so bold."

Patrick warned Gus to be careful with the rocket launcher.

There were handshakes, whispers of Godspeed, and then they were again on their own, headed toward trouble this time instead of away from it.

And though it might be foolish, Shelby was suddenly filled with confidence in their ability to handle whatever they found.

TWENTY-FOUR

Gabe set a fast pace, but no one had trouble keeping up.

Max understood why everyone had extra energy. They'd rested a full night without having to stand patrol. Gus had insisted that it was their camp and their responsibility. The uninterrupted sleep had helped. Plus Hugo's arrogance was working into their collective psyche. When Gabe had said he was going to take back his Hummer, it had been like a battle cry, and they'd all responded.

The sky was barely beginning to lighten when Gabe halted them by holding up his right hand in a closed fist.

He waited until they had all circled up, and then he whispered, "Should be in the next mile. Everyone, get your weapons out. We don't know what kind of guard rotation he has out, and we want to be prepared."

Patrick added, "One shot and the entire camp will be awake. From that point . . . the battle is on until the last man—"

"Or group," Lanh mumbled.

"Or group is standing."

"Listen." Gabe made eye contact with each of them. "I know this is intimidating, but guys like Hugo aren't usually the smartest."

"You don't have to be smart to pull a trigger," Carter pointed out.

"That's right, and that is exactly what he's been doing the last nine months. At this point, he's used to people cowering anytime he shows his face. But we're smarter than he is. We can outthink and outmaneuver him. Five minutes and then we move closer. Check your weapons, grab a drink of water, use the facilities if you need to."

The last won some smiles and groans from the group.

Everyone began pulling out their weapons and checking them.

Shelby stepped closer to Max under the pretext of needing to use his flashlight.

"Should we attempt to keep Carter and Lanh near the back?"

"They're not boys, Shelby. They're men. And we're going to need everyone." He reached out and touched her face, trying to ease the harshness of his words. They must have mirrored her own thoughts because, though her shoulders slumped, she didn't argue. Instead, she sighted something along her 9mm and said, "All right. Then let's get this over with."

One weakness in their plan was that they had no rifles. The pistols had been stored in their backpacks, so they still had those. Gus had attacked with the rocket launcher before Hugo had a chance to demand they hand them over. But a handgun was only good at close range, and from what Gabe had said, Max suspected he'd rather use the knife on his belt to defend them. Quieter. More efficient. Lethal.

Once everyone indicated they were ready, Patrick led them forward.

Coming to the top of the hill, Gabe motioned for them to spread out right and left. But they encountered no guards, and from what they could see of the scene in front of them, Hugo's group wasn't used to needing to defend their territory.

Every pack had binoculars in it. Once they were sure they weren't going to stumble over a guard, they each pulled out their binoculars and studied Hugo's camp.

Max figured there was only one way to explain what he was seeing. Arrogance.

Hugo's group had taken over an old hunting camp. Three rickety trailers straggled out from left to right, and no one had bothered to move them into a circle or tried to conceal them in any way. A campfire smoldered in front of the trailers, and around the campfire five lawn chairs formed a lopsided ring. Max focused to the far left of the trailers and could make out three horses grazing in a field with a dilapidated fence that wouldn't hold the animals if they were spooked.

At the other end of the trailers sat a porta potty that had clearly been stolen from a highway construction site. It had "Property of State of Texas" stamped over the door.

Beer cans littered the ground, and a pile of suitcases had been thrown haphazardly on top of one another—spoils of war.

Patrick touched his shoulder and pointed to a stand of trees to the far right. Targets had been tacked up, and used casings littered the ground. They weren't worried about saving ammo, not based on what he was seeing. They also weren't particularly good shots. Very few hits in the kill zone. Of course, it only took one.

The things Max was seeing were important, but what he wasn't seeing? That was even more telling.

No guards.

No dogs.

No easy exit.

No attempt to conceal who they were or what they were doing there.

In front of the trailers and the campfire and chairs was a makeshift parking area, which was basically hard-packed dirt. Sitting there side by side with Hugo's vehicles were the Hummer, Mustang, and Dodge.

All three vehicles looked to be in good shape, though the blast seemed to have done minimal damage to the Mustang.

"Why couldn't it have hit your ride?" Patrick grumbled. "No one would have been able to tell the difference."

Gabe motioned them back the way they had come.

Time to decide on a plan.

TWENTY-FIVE

Carter admired the strategy, which was a product of Gabe's determination.

The man was getting his Hummer back.

He was willing to use everything at his disposal. Of course, this was rather a life-or-death situation. The thought of traveling on to Kansas by foot made Carter's head hurt. And returning home without ever making it out of the state? That didn't sound any better.

Gabe handed the stun gun to Carter. "Remember, I've put it into touch stun mode."

"And you're sure it's charged?"

"Yes."

"But . . . how?"

"Generators, Carter. The governor has generators. I charged it before leaving Corpus."

"Okay. If you're sure."

"It's not like we have the time or desire to test it on someone. See this green light? Means it's ready. If it turns yellow, the charge has dropped too low to give an adequate voltage. And red means it's dead. We don't have a way to recharge it, so you get the juice that's in it, and that's all."

"It'll be enough," Patrick assured him.

Carter glanced up. Everyone in the group was watching him with an amused expression, except for his mom, who was chewing on her thumbnail, something he hadn't seen her do in years.

"You don't have to worry about aiming," Gabe said. "But the device does have to come into contact with skin, and you need to leave it there for four seconds. Otherwise, it will only startle him. We want him incapacitated."

"Got it."

Carter glanced at Lanh, who was holding a small hand mirror, several lengths of rope, a tree branch, and a roll of duct tape.

"See you in a few," Lanh said, and then they took off to the south.

Once they had taken up their position behind the porta potty, Lanh flashed the mirror in the direction of their group and received the same in return. They could have used the radios, which had also been stored in their packs, but they wanted to be able to communicate even when one of Hugo's goons was nearby.

A moment later, he saw a flash from the north. His mom, Max, and Bianca were in position.

"I feel like I'm in a James Bond movie," Carter admitted quietly.

"A very low budget James Bond movie."

"Low budget, low tech."

And then they stopped talking, though Carter's heart continued to thump against his chest.

Gus had estimated anywhere from three to six henchmen in Hugo's group. The chairs in a circle seemed to indicate five, including Hugo, but they wouldn't count on that. There could be more people than chairs—maybe someone came in late or stayed in the trailer or sat in the dirt.

He probably didn't have enough charge in the stun gun for six. The idea was to reduce their number before the battle began.

The day started to warm, and Carter could actually feel his eyes growing heavy when Lanh nudged his shoulder. Wordlessly, he indicated that someone was coming, and then Carter heard it: the sound of shoes scuffing against dirt.

Gabe had said to wait until they heard the door open on the toilet. "The guy will be focused on getting in and doing his business. Hit him while he's unzipping."

The door scraped open, sounding incredibly loud in the still morning.

Lanh held his hand in front of them and signaled *one, two,* and *three.*

Henchman number one had stopped inside the door and paused to spit into the toilet before unzipping his trousers.

Carter hit him with one hundred thousand volts. He counted to four and wondered if he should do it again, but the guy's face went suddenly slack, as though he were surprised, only not able to understand what had surprised him. Then he collapsed to the ground, which was when Carter noticed it was a young kid—

younger than him. He didn't even have facial hair yet.

The tricky part was moving him because Lanh's left arm and shoulder weren't exactly in tip-top shape.

Carter made sure the stun gun was turned off before handing it to Lanh. Grabbing the guy's arms, he pulled him into the tall grass behind the porta potty and kept pulling him until they'd reached the closest tree line. Lanh stayed back long enough to brush their footsteps clean with the tree branch. He caught up quickly and, with his good arm, grabbed one of the guy's legs.

They positioned him sitting up against a tree, facing away from the compound.

Lanh slapped a strip of duct tape across his mouth, covering the drool that had run down his chin. Carter was already tying his legs together, and Lanh wound a longer coil of rope around the guy's torso, effectively securing him to the tree. By now his eyes were starting to focus, but Carter and Lanh didn't stay around to answer any questions.

The next two were older, but not by much. Maybe Carter's age. Maybe not.

He and Lanh nabbed them with the same process, though there was a long wait—at least a half hour—between the first and the second. The third guy came out quickly on the heels of the second, and they had to crouch and run back from the woods to get to him in time. When they were finished with henchman number three, the power light on the stun gun was a solid yellow.

"Better not risk it," Lanh said.

So they flashed the mirror back toward Gabe one more time. Next they flashed it toward where his mom and Max and Bianca were waiting.

And then things got real interesting.

TWENTY-SIX

Shelby gnawed on her thumbnail and stared out across the camp. "You think the keys are in the vehicles?"

"Why wouldn't they be?" Max flicked his eyes toward her, but he kept his entire body pointed toward Hugo and crew, ready to launch himself across the camp.

"Because someone might steal them . . . someone like us."

"Relax, Shelby. Hugo thinks he's king of the mountain. No one would dare steal from him."

"We're up," Bianca said, though she didn't give her opinion on where the keys might be. Could be Max was right. Could be they were about to make a terrible mistake.

Two short whistles from Gabe, and then they were running, and Shelby was praying that the keys were in the vehicles. She slid into the Hummer, cranked the keys to the right and rammed it into reverse. She could already hear Bianca peeling away in the Mustang, and Max was gunning the engine of the Dodge.

She wanted to shout in relief as the Hummer shot down the dirt road.

But then she looked in her rearview mirror and saw the doors of the trailers thrown open.

Three men came out with their rifles raised. They were already too far away, but that didn't stop the idiots from shooting.

Shelby rounded a corner, threw the transmission into park, turned off the engine, pocketed the keys, and jumped out of the Hummer. Bianca and Max had done the same and were already on the ground, running back the way they had come.

Which was the crazy part.

Instead of taking what was theirs and hightailing it to Kansas, they were going back to ensure that Hugo's reign of terror ended once and for all.

"But why?" she had argued. "Why can't we take our vehicles and skedaddle?"

It was Patrick who convinced her they had to finish this. "As long as Hugo is alive, he'll come after us."

So they ran back toward the hunters' camp. She spied Carter and Lanh in position behind the trailers, waiting in case anyone tried to escape that direction.

The morning's beauty was destroyed by the sound of multiple shots, though what they could be shooting at she wasn't sure. You couldn't even see the vehicles from where they stood. Shelby and Max and Bianca joined the boys at the back of the trailers and then peeled off three to the left and two to the right. As they moved toward the side of the trailers, she caught a glimpse of Patrick climbing on top of the roof, as agile as an alley cat.

Gabe had positioned himself behind the tree nearest to the front of the trailers. Up to this point, Hugo and his two remaining goons had been focused on the fleeing vehicles, but when Gabe started shouting at them, they fired indiscriminately at the tree, using up all of their ammo. The first goon turned to go back inside, but Patrick was already standing there and hit him with the end of his rifle.

He dropped to the ground without so much as a sound.

The second goon turned toward Shelby and Max and Lanh but stopped, confused to find three pistols pointed directly at him. Hugo didn't realize Bianca and Carter were behind him until he felt the cold muzzle of Bianca's gun pressed against his neck.

The entire battle had lasted less than four minutes.

As Gabe had said, guys like Hugo weren't usually the smartest.

Gabe, Bianca, and Patrick held the three men at gunpoint while the rest of their group went through the trailers—making sure no one else was in there and looking for any items that might have been taken out of their vehicles. They didn't find much. In each trailer, trash was a foot deep throughout. The only furniture consisted of a couple of old mattresses, and the entire place was filthy.

"Nice supply of food," Carter said.

"Should we take it?" Shelby asked.

"Couldn't hurt." Max squatted in front of a towering stack of MREs. "We don't need it, but we might come across someone we could share it with."

"What do we do with the horses?" Lanh asked.

Shelby remembered then how close Lanh had become to Jerry Lambert. How he'd enjoyed working with all of the animals, but especially the horses.

"What do you think we should do?" she asked.

"Can't leave them here with no one to look after them. That would be cruel."

"Agreed." Max rubbed a muscle at the back of his neck. "What will happen if we let them go?"

"They'll probably hang around for a little while, a few days at the most. Then they'll go in search of water and food."

"To a nearby farm."

"Probably."

"All right. We can't take them with us, and we don't have time to find them a new home. Open the gate and try to spook them out. Maybe that will send them looking for greener pastures."

While Lanh and Carter went to free the horses, the rest of the group stacked the cases of food into the payload area of the Hummer, where their backpacks had originally been. The backpacks stayed on them. Shelby was to the point that she was happy to sleep in hers. Until they were back at High Fields, she was thinking of it as her outer shield.

Once everything was loaded, they returned to Patrick and Bianca and Gabe. Hugo and his two sidekicks were handcuffed.

"Other guys still in the woods?" Shelby asked.

"They are." Gabe squatted down in front of Hugo and pulled the duct tape off his mouth. "You should have been more careful, Hugo. You got arrogant."

"Leave now." Hugo grinned, revealing a mouth full of crooked teeth. Almost like he had double the amount a person needed.

Anyone else would have had braces, had a bunch of teeth removed, but Shelby guessed Hugo's childhood hadn't included such things as dental care. Not that parental neglect was an excuse for his actions. He'd stolen and plundered and killed. Now he was about to pay for those deeds.

"Leave the cars, and I won't kill you."

"You're negotiating?"

"You have no idea who you're messing with."

Gabe reached out with the end of his handgun and traced the circle surrounding the X on his forehead. "We've seen your mark, Hugo. Seen your handiwork."

"Yeah?"

"Yeah. Burned-out buildings, shot-up vehicles, even a family of three murdered in a gas station southeast of Graham."

"They were in the wrong place at the wrong time. Not my fault, man."

Gabe's face darkened, and Shelby thought he would kill the man right there. Just pull the trigger and be done with it. Instead, he stood and walked over to their group.

"We can't take them all," he said. "I'm not even sure we should take them all."

"Hugo and these two seem to be the worst of the lot, and they all have the—" Patrick reached up and touched his forehead. Shrugging, he leaned back to run his gaze over the three men who sat in the dirt, hands cuffed behind their back. Bianca remained in front of them with her pistol raised and ready.

"So what do we do with them?" Shelby asked. "What do we do with the guys in the woods?"

It was Max who said what she was thinking. "We can't take care of every bad guy in the new world, and the ones in the woods—they're kids. I'm not suggesting they're innocent, but like Gus and Hauk told us, they were more than likely coerced."

"So we let them go?" Gabe asked.

"I think so." Max holstered his weapon. "But not Hugo. He needs to be off the street. Maybe even those two imbeciles sitting with him. I say we loosen the ropes that Lanh and Carter used to secure the other three. By the time they work their way free, we'll be long gone."

TWENTY-SEVEN

Once Hugo figured out what was happening, he started to holler, sliding from threats to negotiation to begging almost within the same breath. Max was surprised Gabe didn't slap the duct tape back on the guy's mouth, but then it occurred to him that Gabe wanted the other two to hear how panicked their leader was. He wanted Hugo to have the chance to mouth off.

As Patrick hauled him to his feet, Hugo made a last attempt. "I have stuff, man. It's yours. Take it all."

"We already did."

"But there's more . . . I'll show you."

"Big-hearted all of a sudden." Patrick looked across at Max, who shrugged. He didn't much care what Hugo had hidden. He cared about getting to Kansas. Plus, Hugo's stash felt a little like tainted goods. Who had he killed to get the stuff? Food was one thing. The MREs could go a long way toward helping families, but anything else he had Max wasn't interested in. No, he didn't think they'd be taking Hugo up on his suddenly generous offer.

One of Hugo's sidekicks was loaded into the front of the Mustang, with Carter driving and Bianca riding in the back, gun on the thug.

The other guy was loaded into the Dodge, with Shelby driving and Lanh keeping a weapon pointed on him.

Those two didn't appear to be much of a threat. They'd stayed pretty quiet, even when Gabe had pulled off their duct tape. Maybe they understood the end was near, or maybe they were waiting for a chance to run, which wasn't going to happen. Either way, they were quiet, cuffed, and guarded. And they only had a half hour drive ahead of them.

But Hugo was another matter.

He bucked when they put him in the Hummer.

He attempted to head butt Patrick, which earned him a crack across the skull with Patrick's pistol. He begged and threatened. The guy was not going quietly "into that good night." The line from Dylan Thomas's poem jumped unbidden into Max's mind. Strange how something he learned thirty years earlier could catapult to the front of his thoughts.

Gabe would drive the Hummer, with no one beside him in the front seat. Max and Patrick sat on either side of Hugo in the second seat. Both had their weapons drawn and trained on the guy, though he was still handcuffed. Seemed a bit of overkill, but all Max had to do was remember the family at the gas station, and he decided that erring on the side of caution was probably a good thing.

172

Hugo tried one last time. "You gonna sell me to somebody? If you were going to kill me, you'd do it here, so I know you're planning something. Whatever they're going to give you, I'll give double. I'm not bluffing. I've got it—gold, silver, and even batteries and generators."

"Put the duct tape back on him." Gabe started the Hummer and pulled out in the last spot. Carter led in the Mustang, and Shelby took the middle slot in the Dodge.

"This was just getting interesting." Patrick was sitting with his back against the door, facing Hugo, loosely and confidently holding his 9mm.

"Yea, he's got gold," Max said. "Never mind who he killed to get it."

"You think you're better than me?" Hugo's voice rose as he realized that he was leaving his camp forever. "What's the difference between your killing me and what I did to those people? They didn't have the sense to protect themselves. That's not my fault."

Spittle flew from his mouth, and his face turned a dark shade of red. Max sincerely hoped that the guy didn't seize, because then they'd have to make the choice whether to save his sorry life. Max couldn't dredge up even a speck of sympathy for the despicable person sitting beside him. It made him sad to think of the destruction Hugo had left in his wake, but he had no illusions about being able to rehabilitate someone who had no remorse for what he'd done. Given the circumstances of their society, he wasn't sure that such rehabilitation would exist for quite some time.

"You can't just kill me."

"We're not planning on it." Gabe's voice was calm, cool.

He'd entered that zone that Max had heard Patrick talk about. Max knew that what they were doing wasn't about getting the vehicles back. They could have "requisitioned" other rides. Gabe was on special assignment from the governor.

No, the vehicles were only the catalyst.

This was about the murdered family in the gas station, the shot-out cars on the road, the businesses and homes that had been marked by Hugo. This was about finding some semblance of justice, regardless of the condition the world was in.

Gabe glanced up and met Max's gaze in the rearview mirror.

Patrick kept his eyes locked on Hugo.

"Then where are we going?" Hugo sounded young then. He sounded almost hopeful. He sounded more like the very ignorant man he was.

"Wichita Falls," Max said.

Hugo's head swiveled right, forward, and left—looking at each of them to confirm what he'd heard. His eyes widened, and his ears turned pink. His mouth gaped open.

It was Gabe who explained it to him. "We're turning you over to the authorities, Hugo. Maybe you can explain your innocence to them."

All color left Hugo's face. Seething with anger only a few minutes ago, he now looked deathly pale.

"I never said I was innocent." The words were mumbled. No doubt he realized that anything he said at this point would not matter at all.

Gabe shrugged and returned his attention to the road. "Then I wouldn't pin my hopes on receiving any sort of mercy."

TWENTY-EIGHT

Carter was kind of glad that they'd left the three younger thugs in the woods. He didn't care if the authorities hung Hugo from a noose on the town square. Hugo was a lunatic with no remorse. God might have mercy on his soul, but the people in Wichita Falls wouldn't. The top two guys in his organization or gang or whatever it was were no better. They all deserved whatever justice the good people of Wichita Falls decided to hand out.

But the other three guys—they'd had tears running down their faces as Gabe had explained what was happening. That he was loosening the ropes so that they could work their way free. hat Hugo wouldn't be a problem for them anymore. That they had one more chance.

There had been more. Gabe and Patrick had promised to come back and personally hunt them down if they heard even a whisper of future misdeeds.

But it was Bianca who had the final word. "Go home. Be farmers. Learn to live in the new world. Take care of your *familia*. *Cuidado con la ira de Dios*."

Carter didn't understand the last part, but Lanh had leaned closer and explained, "Something about watching out for the wrath of God."

And then they had all walked away and loaded into the vehicles, which still had all of their stuff in them.

Now he was driving the Mustang, which should have made him ridiculously happy. Only this wasn't the way he'd imagined it. There wasn't a cool chick sitting beside him riding shotgun. His mind flashed back on Kaitlyn, but he pushed that memory away. He still thought of her, still missed her, but he'd accepted that she had died on the streets of Abney. Her life, his life with her, was over.

He'd never imagined this, though.

A thug riding beside him, handcuffed, bound, soon to pay for his deeds.

Bianca riding in the back, holding a pistol on their prisoner.

And the guy hadn't said a word. Hadn't even tried to talk them into letting him go. He sat there, staring out the window, as though he knew it was probably the last ride he'd ever take.

"You're doing well, Carter. We'll be in Wichita Falls in twenty minutes, and we can be done with these people."

"They'll kill us, you know." The man didn't bother to look at Carter or Bianca.

"What's your name?" Bianca asked.

"Stoney."

"No, what's your real name? What name did your mother give you?"

"Stephen. My name is Stephen."

"Well, Stephen. You made the choice to hook up with Hugo. You made the choice to kill and plunder and rob—"

"You don't understand what it's like."

"Oh, I don't? Because I've lived in a bubble the last nine months. I didn't hold my *papá*'s hand as he died or sit beside my *mamá* as she breathed her last. I haven't been cold or hungry or afraid."

Carter had never heard Bianca talk with so much passion and anger. He glanced in the rearview mirror. Her gaze met his, but she continued addressing Stephen or Stoney or whoever this guy was.

"How many people have you killed?"

"I don't know."

"Sure you do. You pull the trigger. You remember."

"It wasn't like that."

"How many?" Bianca's voice had dropped to a hush, but it had the force and power of an army of angels.

"Fourteen." Stephen was sobbing now. Snot and tears were running down his face. "I killed fourteen, but this won't bring them back."

The last was a plea, a final effort.

"You're right, Stephen. We can't bring them back, but we can make sure you won't kill any more."

And then no one spoke.

Carter glanced in the rearview mirror at his mom, who was driving the Dodge.

Behind her, he could see Gabe driving the Hummer.

They'd made the highway, and the signs ticked off the miles to Wichita Falls—ten, then eight, then five. Two miles out, the bodies began to appear.

TWENTY-NINE

Max had seen many terrible, truly tragic things since the flare, and he'd imagined even worse. He'd struggled through nights when he couldn't sleep and been paralyzed by moments when the sheer helplessness of their situation had overwhelmed him. Days when his love and concern for those in his family, which included Shelby and Carter, had driven him to his knees.

But he hadn't imagined what he was seeing now.

The first body they passed was hanging from a traffic signal. *Justice will prevail.*

The second had been strung up on a telephone pole. *An eye for an eye.*

The third was tied to a tree with a bullet hole in the middle of his forehead. *Beware.*

The signs were crudely made, but the messages were clear.

Justice had never been particularly pretty when a person was found guilty, but a year ago such justice would have been delivered away from the public eye. No one really wanted to know what the day-to-day life in prison was like. No one wanted to see an execution up close. It was easier to rest in the comfortable knowledge that things were being taken care of and go about

180

your day. They'd become somewhat immune to the concepts of justice and punishment.

Justice had always been harsh—it was just that they had managed to move it out of the public eye, out of the town square. Perhaps that had been a mistake.

Gabe toggled the radio twice. They'd decided to maintain radio silence in case anyone happened upon their frequency. The two beeps, like a private Morse code, signaled for them to tighten their formation and stop.

Their group stepped out of the vehicles— all seven of them. Hugo and his men remained handcuffed within.

"We're actually going to do this?" Shelby asked.

"We are." Gabe's voice sounded rock solid. It brought Max back to his senses. This wasn't an apocalyptic movie or a Western novel. There was nothing exciting or romantic or remotely heroic about leaving three thugs outside the gates of this town. And there was no question as to what would happen to them once they were found by the authorities.

Max understood that Hugo and his men had murdered and robbed. There were no longer any courts to hear their case, or appeals to be filed, or lawyers to hire. There was this desolate stretch of road, their nightmarish reality, and the guarded gates farther ahead.

"And we don't want to walk them in? To explain to the authorities why . . ." Shelby pushed black curls away from her face. "Why we're leaving them."

"Trust me, that won't be necessary. The only question is why someone from Wichita Falls hasn't taken care of them before now."

"Probably they knew enough to stay away from the town," Patrick said. "Instead, they preyed on those making their way to and from."

Bianca turned in a circle. "But where do we leave them?"

Patrick nodded toward a four-plank wooden fence that bordered the highway. On the far side in the distance, Max could make out horses grazing. Bluebonnets lay across the field like patches on a faded pair of blue jeans.

"That will do," Gabe said. "Let's get them out and be on our way."

Hugo began shrieking when they pulled him out of the Hummer, kicking his feet and twisting back and forth.

Patrick came within an inch of his face as Gabe and Max held his arms. "We still have the stun gun, and there's just enough juice in it to give you a good buzz. Is that what you want?"

Hugo went slack, all of the fight sucked out of him.

Not that he helped them in any way.

His body hung like deadweight between them.

They dragged him to the fence, cuffed him around a post, and went after his buddies. When they were done, all three men sat facing the road, their arms pulled behind them and cuffed to the fence, their legs secured together with a rope, a space of eight feet between them.

It was Bianca who stopped, turned to face them, and said, "If you believe in God, now is the time for you to make your peace with him. It may be the only chance you have left."

They all turned and walked back to the vehicles, resuming their original places. Gabe in the Hummer with Lanh and Carter. Bianca and Patrick in the Mustang. Max and Shelby leading in the Dodge.

As a lawyer, Max would have preferred a trial with a judge and jury. But some time in the last nine months, he had accepted that trials were a thing of the past—for now, not forever. They were a land, a people, based on laws. He prayed he would see the day when they returned to those laws, to a place of justice and fairness, where a person was innocent until proven guilty.

There was no doubt that Hugo was guilty. They'd seen it with their own eyes. They'd heard it with their own ears.

Still, it was a relief to drive away. Max didn't speak. Shelby wrote furiously in her journal, as if she couldn't get the words on the paper quickly enough.

He spared one last glance in the rearview mirror at the men who would soon pay for their deeds, and then he turned his attention to the road ahead.

THIRTY

"What if we can't find a way to cross the border?" Shelby clutched her journal in her lap.

"We'll find a way."

She'd been writing in the journal since they'd left Hugo handcuffed to the fence. She was writing down every detail, and that was good. Max didn't want to forget the things they'd seen or the things they'd done. He didn't want anyone to forget what life had become, because if they forgot? Then they could lose sight of what society had been, of what a civilized justice system looked like.

"If we can't find a road across, an open road across, then what?"

"We'll leave the Dodge and the Mustang and continue on in the Hummer. Gabe could drive that thing through any roadblock, and maybe . . . if we found a shallow enough spot . . . even across the river itself without the help of a road."

"Sounds like a bad idea."

"Which is why we won't do that unless we have to."

Shelby nodded and stuffed her journal into her pack. Max was aware that she already knew the answers to her questions, but sometimes asking them aloud helped.

The Red River ran for more than 1300 miles, and more than 600 miles of that was in Texas. He couldn't remember the exact numbers. It was a tributary of the Mississippi and Atchafalaya rivers. Originating at the Minnesota and North Dakota borders, it flowed east across the Texas Panhandle and through Palo Duro Canyon. His parents and Shelby's parents had taken them on vacation there once—to hike the trails and camp for five nights.

He glanced over at Shelby, and in his mind he could see that younger girl, the one who had tagged along until he'd realized she wasn't a girl any longer but was becoming a young woman. He'd fallen head over heels for Shelby Sparks his senior year of high school, and his biggest regret in life was that he hadn't held on to her when he'd had the chance.

After leaving the panhandle, the river formed the border between Texas and Oklahoma. Strange that now so much depended on their being able to cross it. They had to cross it to travel into Oklahoma, to make it to the Flint Hills of Kansas. The Hummer might have been able to descend the nearly vertical bank, but the Dodge and Mustang didn't stand a chance. Yet once down, could the Hummer cross water? Max had no idea. He understood that the better option was to find a bridge that still allowed access.

The most direct route across the river was I-44.

They didn't hold out much hope that it would be open, but all other routes were a substantial detour. They'd voted to give it a try.

"Looks like another roadblock," Shelby said.

Max immediately braked. They were still a good distance back. In fact, he wouldn't have seen the barricade if it hadn't been for sun glinting off windshields.

He picked up the radio and keyed up Gabe and Patrick. "Go around?"

"We need to know what we're up against here." The Hummer was in the middle of their small caravan. Max could look in his rearview mirror and see Gabe scratching his jaw.

He glanced at Shelby, who was still staring through her binoculars. "I'll volunteer," he said.

"Take someone with you."

"I need to stretch my legs." Bianca was out of the Mustang and walking toward them before Max could argue.

"Looks like you get to ride with Patrick."

"Never turn down a ride in a Mustang." Shelby unbuckled her seat belt, opened the door, and then turned back to him. "Be careful."

"You worried about me, Sparks?"

"Always."

Bianca took her place.

"Why are you so eager to head into trouble?"

"You might need my translation skills."

"Actually, that's a good point."

"*Gracias.*"

"*De nada.*"

She rolled her eyes at his terrible accent.

"We're going to follow you until you're fifty yards out," Gabe said. "Just as a sign of support."

Bianca pulled the radio from Max's hand. "Please don't start a gun battle with us in the middle."

"Wouldn't think of it, sweetheart." Patrick's voice was smooth and confident, but Max wondered how much of that was for show. It didn't matter how many times they faced danger. His own reaction was the same—pulse racing, heartbeat thumping in his ears, sweat running down the back of his neck. It wasn't something you got used to—at least he hadn't.

He, Patrick, and Gabe were all progressively minded and wouldn't have thought of suggesting the girls stay back while the men took care of the bad guys. How could they? Bianca and Shelby had earned their spots on this trip. They were each as good a shot as Max, calm and steady when pressured, and quick to assess a situation. Carter and Lanh had also matured in the last year. They were a solid team, and that was the way they would cross into Oklahoma—as a team.

Which might be easier said than done by the look of the barricade in front of them. Max and Bianca stopped well back from the guards standing directly in front of the roadblock.

Unlike most of the other blockades they'd come across, this one wasn't a straight line across the road. Cars had been pushed into position so that the way through was a zigzag, and there were sentries at every turn. Even if they made it past the front guards, which they wouldn't, they would have to deal with a new threat at each zig and zag.

"Don't come any closer." This from a man in his thirties with an enormous belly, bald head, no neck to speak of, and large ears. In spite of the fact that he was holding what looked like an AK-47, he reminded Max of Shrek. Paint him green, and you'd have an identical match.

"Fair enough." Max held up his hands to show that he wasn't holding a weapon, though it was plain there was one in his holster, and he wore his pack, which had his rifle. Bianca was similarly armed.

"We'd like to cross here," Bianca said.

"Sure." Shrek nodded toward the maze behind him. "We'd be happy to open it up."

Bianca glanced at Max, and he knew what she was thinking. It couldn't be that easy.

"All you have to do is pay the toll."

The two goons beside Shrek snickered, and Max's temper began to spike. "You do realize this is a public road."

"Was. Isn't no more."

"And I guess you decided that."

189

"Me and my rifle. Which would you rather argue with?"

Bianca took a step forward. "What's the toll?"

"Both your packs, and whatever is in them, plus your weapons. Give us that, and we'll let you and your friends through."

Max was considering shooting the guy. He knew it would be a stupid move, but the temptation was just so strong. His hand actually twitched in an urge to touch the butt of his gun when a jeep traveled through the maze, pulled to a stop next to Shrek, and a Hispanic man stepped out.

"Do we have a problem here?"

"They don't want to pay the toll, boss."

"Is that so?" Then in a low voice he said, "*Está bien. No te preocupes.*" He half turned to his goons and continued speaking in Spanish, causing the men to laugh and catcall.

Max's Spanish was rudimentary at best, but he caught the words for *momma* and *babe* and *good time*. It didn't take someone fluent in the language to catch their meaning—that and the way they were ogling Bianca, which probably explained why she lost her temper.

Stepping forward, she shouted, "It *is* a problem. *Queremos cruzar por aqui.*"

"*Pagar el peaje?*"

"*No hay necesidad.* It's a public road!"

Max reached out to pull her back at the same time Shrek raised his rifle.

190

"We need to talk to our friends," Max said. "We'll see what we can work out."

"*Bien por mi.* And take that hot tamale with you before she gets you killed."

"They're likely to shoot us in the back." Bianca's face was a dangerous shade of red, and her body was rigid, ready to fight.

"Why would we do that?" The leader cocked his head and studied her as if she were a curiosity, though no doubt he'd done this a dozen times before. "If we shoot you, then your friends would feel the need to shoot my men, and we'd have more bodies to clean up. In case you haven't figured it out, this is the only road across for many miles. Go and talk to your friends. *No se preocupe.* You'll be back."

But Max knew they wouldn't be. One way or another, they would find another way across.

THIRTY-ONE

Carter and Lanh rode in the Hummer. Lanh sat up front, holding the radio and monitoring the right side of the road. Carter was scanning the left side, while Gabe kept his eyes straight ahead, attuned to anything out of the ordinary. Capturing and leaving Hugo had been intense. Carter hadn't felt pity for the guy. Letting him go would only result in more innocent folks being killed or injured, but he did feel a stab of regret at what the world had become. Or perhaps it had always been that way, and he just hadn't been paying attention.

Twice they'd stopped to leave Hugo's boxes of food with families—farmers working in the fields, women hanging laundry, kids peering out at them from barns and garages and once from a tree fort. When they asked about a road to Oklahoma, no one had a good answer. The next hour passed in a haze of frustration. Every road they tried, every road that might possibly lead to a bridge crossing the Red River, was blocked.

"Why do they want people to stay in Texas so badly?" Lanh asked.

"There are a limited number of access points, so it's a naturally good place to set up a toll booth."

192

"Is that how you think of it? A toll booth?"

Gabe shrugged as he met Carter's eyes in the rearview mirror. "People will take advantage of a situation."

"Drastic times . . ." Carter said.

"And drastic measures." Lanh scanned the map in his lap. "We've tried just about every road except this one, which takes us too far east."

"If it's the only way north, that's the way we go."

But it too was blocked. The Hummer might have been able to ram its way through the ragtag pile of sedans, but not without a firefight.

"Not worth it," Patrick had said the last time they'd stopped to discuss it. No one wanted to see more bloodshed.

There had to be another way.

They backtracked again, the day growing darker around them, the air heavy with the promise of rain. They were driving through a wooded area now. At last, the trees parted. They came to a crossroads of sorts and pulled into a parking lot in front of a long-abandoned, burned-out gas station. In fact, there was little of the original structure remaining—mostly charred counters and shelves, plus a small section of one wall.

No roof.

No shelter at all.

Gabe slapped the map on the hood of the Hummer, and everyone circled up. "At this rate, it might be a good idea to drive west, cross along the New Mexico border, and then wind our way north and east back to Kansas."

His mother kicked at the dirt with her hiking boot. When she noticed Carter watching her, she smiled weakly and said, "What?"

He rolled his eyes and laughed, but then he turned to look for Lanh and caught sight of the western sky.

"Uh, guys. That doesn't look so good."

Everyone was still talking about their route and discussing different options, though they all sounded the same because there were only two options: force their way through or keep searching for an alternate route.

But what Carter saw scared him more than anything they were saying, so he put two fingers to his lips and let out a shrill whistle. When everyone turned to stare at him, he pointed west.

"We have a problem."

"Sweet Jesus," Bianca murmured, moving forward to stand beside him. The wall of clouds was massive, and there was a distinctive line between the darker clouds to the front and the greenish ones behind it. "*Que Dios nos ayude.*"

"Could be only a hailstorm if we're lucky," Shelby said.

"It came up all of a sudden." Patrick's voice was grave, worried.

But it was Max who got them all moving. "We need to go . . . now!"

Gabe grabbed the map and tossed it at Lanh, who began folding it up. "Tight formation. Looks like we have ten, maybe fifteen minutes before it reaches us."

"There was an abandoned farmhouse two miles back." Max was jogging to the Dodge. They were all running as the day turned eerily dark, though it was only one in the afternoon. The massive wall cloud barreling toward them had blocked all remnants of the setting sun.

"How did we not notice that?" Lanh asked.

"Trees kept us from seeing it." Gabe clutched the wheel so hard his knuckles turned white. "And we were distracted. We should have been paying attention."

The pecan and oak trees lining the road began to sway back and forth, nearly meeting in the middle of the road.

Carter leaned forward, sticking his head into the space between the front seats.

"You're not from here, are you? From Texas?"

Gabe and Lanh both shook their heads.

"I've seen this before—in San Antonio a couple of times," Gabe admitted. "I grew up in New York, though. Give me a blizzard over a tornado any day."

"Happened a couple of times in Austin too." Lanh finished folding the map and stuffed it into his pack. "But we had . . . you know. Tornado sirens and stuff. I got into the tub with my phone and my laptop."

"We saw this sort of thing a couple of times a year in Abney, but they were usually small or just skipped over us. The last big one to touch down there was in the '70s—we had to study about it in school, which I thought was pretty lame."

A deer darted toward the road, and then it pivoted and dashed back into the woods. Gabe didn't even slow. They were following Max, and he was going seventy, maybe eighty miles an hour.

Gabe accelerated even faster, as if they were being chased. "Any words of wisdom?"

"Yeah. If the rain and wind stop suddenly, seek shelter immediately."

Two more minutes, and then they made a hard left, swinging around the corner after Max, Patrick hot on their bumper.

"He wants us to shelter here?" Lanh's voice actually shook.

Carter felt sorry for him. Yeah, the weather was scary, but he'd been through this before. It was only a storm. He used to sit on the front porch with his grandpa watching them, his grandmother calling them fools and insisting they come inside.

"We'd be better off in the vehicle," Lanh said.

"Nope. Never stay in a vehicle during a tornado."

Somewhere in his mind, Carter understood that this was the remains of someone's home, but it had been several years since anyone lived there. The window frames were painted a bright pink, though they didn't seem to actually hold any glass. The front door hung at an awkward angle, and the house seemed to groan and shift in the wind. Beside the house sat a rotten trampoline, and a tire swing still hung from an adjacent tree. Behind all of that ran a small creek. Those details all registered in the space of a breath before Carter jumped out of the Hummer and ran between the first of the raindrops. They struck his skin with the force of pellets from a BB gun. He reached the dilapidated front porch as lightning split the sky and the drops became a downpour.

THIRTY-TWO

Max jerked Shelby back a split second before her foot crashed through a rotten board on the front porch. She nodded her thanks, met his gaze for a fleeting second, and then dashed through the doorway. The inside of the structure didn't look any better than the outside. A good breeze would blow it over. There was no telling what tornado-force winds would do.

Max wanted to kick something the way he'd seen Shelby kicking the dirt, but it wouldn't help, and he needed to save his energy.

"Everyone have their packs?" Gabe asked.

They all nodded in unison.

"Check the rooms," Patrick said. "See if you can find any mattresses to place over our heads."

"You think there'll be a tornado?" Shelby asked.

"Looked like rotation to the northwest." Bianca walked past her into the kitchen.

Had they been standing in sunshine just an hour ago? Max glanced through a paneless window. The sky was like night. He reached for his flashlight, turned it on, and shone it outside. The rain was coming down sideways, from the northwest.

Bianca called out from the kitchen. "There's a small dinette table in here."

Patrick and Max moved the table for two into the bathroom, and they all huddled under it, or tried to. Their heads, at least, were protected.

Max had lived in Texas all of his life. He knew the basics of tornado disaster preparedness by heart.

Pick a safe, interior room for shelter.

Put something over your head to protect yourself from falling objects.

Don't panic.

Don't go outside.

The storm intensified. Rain pelted through the roof, the wind howled, and the temperature continued to drop.

Shelby put her arm through Carter's. They were all crammed shoulder to shoulder. They were all wet and shivering. Rain fell through the holes in the roof and splattered against the tabletop. Lightning lit up the single window over the tub, followed by a crash of rolling thunder. Seven people huddled under a two-person dinette table. If the roof fell, it wouldn't do much more than delay the inevitable by a microsecond.

The downpour worsened until it was impossible for Max to tell the difference between the thudding of his heart and the incessant clatter of rain. The wind had increased as well, and they heard a limb crash onto another part of the roof. Then the hail started, popping against the roof, landing on the floor and bouncing, creating a cacophony impenetrable even by thunder.

They were all soaked, even though they were inside. Shelby had begun to shake. Max inched closer until they were pasted against each other like two sides of a cardboard sign. Another peal of thunder, sensed more than heard, rumbling for ten, twenty, thirty seconds. It felt as if they were inside a drum.

It felt as if God were angry and intent on cleaning the earth.

Max had no sooner had that thought when everything stopped.

No rain.

No thunder.

No wind.

Had the storm passed, or was this simply the calm before the tornado?

"We better go see how bad it is," Patrick said.

"Never go outside!" Bianca's hand was trembling as she reached out to stop him, but Patrick only smiled, kissed her fingers, and strode out of the bathroom.

Everyone else quickly followed, looking like they were attached by an unbreakable string.

The living room they walked through looked more derelict than when they'd arrived.

The front porch sagged. A portion of the roof had caved in, blocking their exit. They skirted around it and hopped off the side as they picked their way across the front yard. Rain dripped from trees. The sky had lightened. Fallen limbs lay everywhere, along with pockets of hail amidst a river of mud. Not a hint of wind, not so much as a breeze, stirred the air. They looked around, looked up, looked at each other.

"We're alive."

"We made it."

"Never been through a storm like that before."

"It was so sudden."

"How long were we in there?"

"Felt like hours."

"Felt like five minutes."

They continued toward their vehicles. The Mustang, Dodge, and Hummer all had limbs on top of them, but nothing large. No trees. Just dead wood that had been blown down and green leaves stripped from branches that had recently begun to leaf out.

Max heard a slurp sound each time he raised a foot as his boot pulled free from the mud. He was thinking of that, looking down and wondering if he'd ever be clean again, when he heard Shelby gasp. She reached out, gripped his arm, pushed, and turned him toward the west.

The sky's greenish cast looked like something from a horror movie.

A cloud of dust moved toward them, but then he realized it couldn't be dust. Everything was wet. What he was seeing was a giant wall of debris, and it was twirling, spinning through the air.

And within that cloud, stretching from the tips of the clouds to the ground, was a large, black funnel.

THIRTY-THREE

Shelby felt a giant fist close around her throat. She couldn't pull in a good breath. Opening her mouth, she tried to scream, tried to yell, *Run!* but nothing came out.

The funnel, which dipped down from hideously black clouds, branched and formed two separate tornadoes.

One turned south. The other continued straight toward them.

The pressure began to build, and she clapped her hands over her ears, willing it to stop. She turned, trying to locate her son. She had to protect him. She had to get him to safety.

There was a screech, like the train passing through Abney late at night—a horrifying, painful roar.

It matched the cry of her heart.

Carter pointed toward the house and hollered, but she shook her head. She tried again to speak, but the wind pulled the unformed words from her mouth. She had to make them see, had to speak loud enough for them to hear, and she had to do it now.

Everyone was holding their hands over their ears except Patrick, who had grabbed hold of Bianca with both hands, as though he intended to pick her up and carry her to safety.

Carter and Lanh were on either side of Gabe, and Gabe was staring at the sky like he'd seen the four horsemen of the apocalypse. And maybe he had. Maybe this was the final trial that would whisk them from their earthly lives.

Max was pulling on her arm, trying to coax her back toward the house.

She yanked hard once, and then she fell into the mud. Carter turned to help her. She struggled to her feet, grabbed his hand, and pulled him toward the side of the house, toward the creek.

Max put his mouth right against her ear, cupped his hands, and yelled, "We have to get inside."

"It won't stand!" And with those terrible words, she turned and dashed toward the creek, pulling Carter in her wake. Max stumbled to catch up with them. Patrick was half carrying, half pulling Bianca. He plodded after them, his head down as he pushed into the gale-force winds that had replaced the eerie calm. Gabe seemed torn between the house and their direction. His eyes met Shelby's, and she could feel him drop his own instincts and fear. He ran flat out, caught up with them, and pushed them with both hands—or perhaps that was the tornado itself pushing them forward.

And then they were tumbling down the rain-drenched bank.

They huddled in a circle, in the two inches of water that had accumulated at the bottom of the creek bed. Heads together, hands clasped. Over and over, Shelby prayed, "Please don't take my son. Please, God. Do not take my son from me." She studied their hands, their fingers intertwined, and her fear for Carter made her heart ache. She was aware of Max beside her, his arm over her shoulders, every inch of him intent on protecting her from whatever was about to happen.

The most deafening sound Shelby had ever heard filled the air. She couldn't take a breath, couldn't focus on a coherent thought. She squeezed her eyes shut, unable to form even the simplest of prayers. She knew in that moment that she would die.

Trees crashed around them. Something slammed into Gabe. She glanced up in time to see blood pouring down his face. Patrick was trying to surround Bianca with his body. Max and Carter had their arms around her back, pulling her closer into the circle. Their heads were touching now. Lanh still covered his ears with his hands, his head so low that his forehead was touching the water. The deafening roar above them literally shook the earth.

And then, as quickly as the tempest had arrived, everything stopped.

THIRTY-FOUR

They waited one minute, and then two.

They waited until they were sure the funnel cloud had passed by.

Carter had looked up at one point. He'd seen . . . he'd seen the funnel from directly below it. But how was that possible? He'd be dead. Was he dead?

His mother was running her hands over his face, his shoulders, his arms.

"I'm okay. Mom, I'm okay."

She stopped, her hands frozen at his elbows, and then she threw her arms around him.

Any other time he would have ducked away, but he stood there, allowed her to hold him, and waited for his heart rate to return to normal.

Gabe had ripped the bottom inch of fabric off his shirt and was holding it to the cut on his head.

Around them, trees were twisted and torn. Looking down the creek bed in one direction, he saw a bicycle, part of a windmill, and a watering trough. He heard the bleat of a goat, turned the other direction, and saw not one but three adult-sized goats standing in the middle of the stream. How had they ended up there? If the tornado had picked them up . . . shouldn't they be dead?

Carter turned his attention back to their group,

counted people, assuring himself they had all survived, trying to calm the erratic rhythm of his heart.

They were all alive.

Everyone was present and accounted for.

Miraculously, no one had been killed or maimed or taken.

They all started talking at once. What they'd seen. What they'd heard. How frightened they'd been.

Carter looked over at Lanh, who nodded toward the muddy bank.

Yeah. They needed to go up there. They needed to see what had happened.

Side by side, they began to climb, and quickly the others joined them.

It was difficult at first because of the mud and the debris and their own shaking limbs. They pushed on, reaching the top at the same instant.

And what they saw, Carter knew he would never forget if he lived to be a hundred and ten.

"The house is gone," he mumbled, though saying it didn't make what he was seeing more believable.

"It didn't collapse," Bianca said.

Patrick bent over, his hands on his knees. "There's . . . there's nothing left of it."

No shattered glass or planks of wood or cabinets or fixtures.

No porch or tire swing or trampoline.

The entire structure and everything near it had been lifted up and carried away.

"If we had been in it . . ." Max's voice cracked. He sank to his knees in the mud. Carter couldn't tell if he was praying or crying. If his tears were from fear or joy. His mom went over to Max, squatted in front of him, rubbed his back in circles, and spoke to him in a quiet voice. The two of them there, like that, completely vulnerable, caused something in Carter's heart to tighten. His mom, Max, Max's parents, even Patrick and Bianca and Gabe—until that moment, they had all been superheroes in his eyes. He'd thought they were capable of anything. He'd believed that they were invincible.

He saw now that they were all merely human, and though they might pray and cry and struggle and fight, there were times when their lives teetered in the hands of God, when the decision to live or die wasn't theirs to make.

Carter took a deep, steadying breath. They needed to assess their situation, which was what Gabe seemed to be doing. He walked forward a few steps, just past their group, and stopped. Carter joined him.

Beyond the house, where their vehicles were supposed to be, was a tangle of trees two stories high.

The cars must be buried there. Had they been crushed? Would their group be walking to

Kansas? Or worse still, would they be walking back to Abney?

Beyond the cars, leading away from the homestead, was a path cut through the woods as though a road crew had been by. It was easily wide enough for a two-lane highway, and it stretched as far as Carter could see.

Though every fiber of his being resisted, he forced himself to turn, to look back the way they had come.

Patrick was holding Bianca, talking to her, assuring himself that she was okay.

His mother continued to kneel in front of Max.

Gabe, Lanh, and Carter turned as one, staring with their mouths gaped open. They glanced at each other and then back at the devastation in front of them. The tornado had dipped down fifty yards on the other side of the creek and taken absolutely everything in its path. There wasn't even debris—just twisted trunks of trees on both sides.

It had skipped directly over the creek, over where they had taken shelter.

It had passed them by, leaving goats and a bicycle and a windmill and a water trough in its wake. Leaving seven people from central Texas shaking and trembling and wondering at the reality that they were still alive.

THIRTY-FIVE

Max didn't know whether to weep or laugh or shout or pray. He knelt in the mud, with Shelby squatting in front of him, and was overwhelmed by the miracle of their survival.

Exhilaration flooded through his heart, mind, and body.

They had survived.

For some reason that he didn't yet understand, God had spared them.

"How did you know, Shelby?" Bianca walked over to her, pulled her to her feet, and put a hand on each shoulder. "How did you know we shouldn't go back into the house?"

"Something . . . something I researched for a Texas romance."

"I'm going to have to start reading those," Patrick said.

"My story took place in 1896. There was an actual storm—a tornado in Denton County in May of that year. Killed . . . killed seventy-six."

"I guess that was before sirens?" Lanh was watching her closely, caught up in a tragedy worse than their own.

"Sirens didn't become commonplace until after World War II. My characters took shelter in a barn, but it was . . ." She licked her lips, and

Max realized she must be in shock. They were all in shock. "It wasn't well built. At the last possible minute, they ran into a creek bed. I had found interviews in newspaper clippings of people who survived that 1896 tornado. That's why I included it in my story."

"I will never mock your profession again." Patrick enfolded her in a bear hug, smiling over the top of her head at Max and adding, "Writers rock!"

"I'm not a writer anymore."

"You still rock."

"Do you think . . ." She turned and looked at Max and then Gabe, who had been silently watching them. "Do you think our vehicles are in that pile of debris? Or did they . . . did they get swept away like the house?"

"Won't know until we pull off the trees." In that moment, Max felt he could do it singlehandedly. He felt there was nothing he couldn't do.

Gabe had pulled the scrap of his shirt away from his head, stared at the blood-stained cloth, and then pressed it back to the wound. "Shelter first. It's only two in the afternoon, but night will be falling before we know it. Inventory what we have as far as food and water. Make a plan. Tomorrow we can start digging out."

"The others can do those things while I look at your wound." Bianca shrugged out of her backpack, and that was when Max realized they all had their packs. He hadn't even been aware he was wearing his because doing so had become second nature, and maybe . . . possibly that habit had saved their lives. They had supplies—food, water, an extra set of clothes, their weapons and ammunition, Carter's insulin.

Everyone inventoried their packs while Bianca got ready to clean and stitch up the gash on Gabe's head with a medical kit she pulled from his pack.

"Have you ever done that before?" Max asked.

"Nope. Good thing the doctor is alert enough to give me step-by-step directions."

Max noticed that her hands were shaking, but her voice was steady.

"Tell me she's not going to faint," Gabe said.

"Doubtful. But if you move, you're going to have a jagged-looking scar." Gabe raised his eyebrows in mock horror, and Max assured him, "You're in good hands."

They decided to make their camp in the middle of a stand of oak trees.

"Can you explain this to me?" Shelby asked. "These trees are not damaged at all, but fifty feet away, everything is . . . it's . . . everything is gone."

"Hey." Max stood directly in front of her, waiting until she looked up into his eyes. "Are you okay?"

"Yes. I am. I think I am, which means yes."

"We're bound to be in shock, all of us."

"We don't have time for shock."

"Doesn't matter if we have time for it." He jerked his hat off his head, surprised to find it was still there, dusted it against his pants, and put it back on. What he wanted to do was pull Shelby into his arms again, but the look on her face told him that would be a very bad idea.

"I don't understand why these trees are still standing and those are gone. It's a simple question."

"If you need to take a minute, Shelby, then do that. Take a minute. Don't push yourself."

"I'm fine, Max. Let's just . . . figure this out." Her eyes jumped to the left and the right, passed quickly over his face, and then focused on something past his shoulder.

He didn't need a paramedic to tell him what was going on here. They'd had a near-death experience mere moments ago. When the adrenaline left their systems, they were going to be exhausted, hungry, and bewildered.

But he didn't try to explain any of that.

Instead, he followed his initial instinct—wrapped his arms around her, pulled her tight against his chest, and held her.

At first it was like holding a surfboard. Her arms remained at her sides, her posture rigidly perfect, her breathing tight. But inch by inch she relaxed, until at long last he felt her arms encircle his waist. Her words were muffled as she pressed her face into his shirt, but he could still make them out.

"We're going to be okay, Max. I don't know how, but we're going to be okay."

THIRTY-SIX

Shelby pulled herself together.

She stepped away from Max, carried her pack to their makeshift campground, and helped Patrick to determine where the two best locations would be for lookout shifts—basically, to the right and left along the road.

Lanh and Carter found firewood that was only marginally wet and broke it into small pieces. Then they proceeded to make a pit of sorts with rocks that they gathered from the lane leading into the property.

Bianca had finished wrapping a bandage around Gabe's head.

Gabe and Max stood in front of the pile of tangled trees, trying to determine their plan of action.

"I think we should scout the road," Bianca said, looking at her friend.

"Agreed."

The women told the rest of the group where they were going.

"We can take the south," Carter said, motioning toward Lanh.

"All right. We'll go north."

Max and Gabe and Patrick were pulling on a giant oak tree lying across the front corner of the debris pile.

"Should we stay and help?" Shelby asked.

"No. Go before we lose the light." Patrick grunted as they dropped the tree, which they'd managed to move less than an inch. "We won't make any real progress on this until tomorrow."

"Fifteen minutes and then we turn around. Agreed?"

Carter muttered, "Aye, aye, Captain," and Lanh saluted.

"Their sarcasm is comforting," Bianca said.

Shelby stared after them. "Do you think they'll be all right?"

"I think that what we just survived is something they'll tell their grandchildren about."

"Assuming they have grandchildren, or children, or a spouse."

"This isn't the end of the world, Shelby. It just feels like it."

They hiked north on the two-lane road, which was the direction they'd come from. Shelby thought she'd been paying attention at the time, but she didn't remember passing through so much nothingness. The area was dense with trees and cedar bushes. No roads intersected theirs, though an occasional dirt track cut through the brush. The road rose gently, so that they didn't actually realize they were increasing elevation until they stopped at the top and looked out over the surrounding area.

"I didn't imagine it." Shelby could feel her

pulse accelerating, and it wasn't from the hike. It was from the destruction all around them. "The funnel cloud did split into two."

"Looks like the larger one went in a straight line—"

"Over us."

"And the smaller one crossed the larger. Turned back south. It almost looks like it—"

"Hopscotched."

Which described what they were seeing perfectly. Pockets of destruction. The sun had come out to the west, piercing through the clouds, bathing them in warm light. How was that even possible? She was standing on the top of a hill, in a patch of sunshine with blue skies to the west, and thirty minutes ago she'd nearly perished in a tornado.

She put her hand over her eyes and stared west, straining to see where the tornado had first touched down, but she couldn't. She could only see the path of destruction left behind.

A farmer's barn reduced to a pile of sticks, his house next to it untouched.

A windmill dangling from a tree.

A semi's tractor-trailer sitting in the middle of a pond.

Spring crops that were knee high, yet in places that reminded Shelby of a pebble skipping across a pond, there were patches of bare ground where the crops had been ripped away.

"You know what we don't see?" Bianca gathered up her hair and pulled it through the back of her baseball cap.

"People. We don't see any people."

They turned and began walking back toward camp.

"I was terrified," Shelby admitted. "I couldn't even pray. All I could do was think, *God, please don't take my son.* My mind was in a loop, and it was the only clear thought I had, so I just clung to it."

"I thought Patrick was going to crush me."

"He was protecting you."

"He was trying to, but how do you protect someone else against . . . nature? No, that's not possible. All we have is our faith, Shelby."

"But probably someone died today. Died in this storm."

"Then it was their time."

Bianca reached out and squeezed her hand, causing tears to prick Shelby's eyes. She felt raw. Maybe it was the shock that Max was talking about, or maybe it was adrenaline. Maybe it was just the exhaustion of dealing with so many life-and-death situations over the last nine months.

They were nearly back at the camp when Bianca nodded toward the tower of debris covering their vehicles. "God will show us a way through this, I'm sure. We didn't survive that kind of tornado just so we could die trying to walk to Kansas."

It was with that reasoning in her ears that Shelby turned and walked back into camp.

THIRTY-SEVEN

Carter was relieved to walk away, to put a little distance between them and the scene of their near death.

"That was intense." Lanh kicked a fist-sized rock that had landed in the middle of the road.

"I thought we were dead."

"I thought my eardrums were going to burst."

"Guess that would have been the least of our problems."

"Yeah, if we'd been in that house . . ." Lanh glanced sideways at him. "Dude, your mom totally saved us."

Carter didn't know how to answer that, so he didn't try.

They walked for fifteen minutes and were just about to turn back when they came around a bend in the road and stopped short.

"Am I imagining this?" Carter felt his mouth sag open, his eyes widen, and still he couldn't believe what was in front of them. "I've got to be imagining this."

"Not if you're seeing what I'm seeing."

In front of them was the house that they'd first taken shelter in, sitting in the middle of the road. Most of the roof was gone, but there was no question it was the same house. The window frames were the same Pepto-Bismol shade of pink.

Carter and Lanh looked at each other, nodded in unison, and then they walked over to the house, hopped up into the front room because there was no longer a front porch, and stood there, staring, turning in a circle.

"This is freaking me out," Carter admitted.

"Me too."

"How did it . . . how could a tornado pick up this house and set it back down?"

"I don't know, but it happens. I used to watch that show . . . what was it called? *Storm Chasers*."

"Anyone who chases a storm like we just went through is out of their mind."

"Exactly, and there was always a camera guy right behind them. A couple of times they would show houses that had been picked up and set back down again. One episode showed a house that had been moved, and there were still dishes in the kitchen cabinets."

But this house hadn't had dishes. It had been dilapidated to begin with, and dilapidated it remained. The only difference was that now it sat in the middle of a two-lane highway.

It took only a moment to walk through the rooms, which were as empty and decrepit as before. They walked back outside and around the house.

"Hey." Lanh jogged to the side of the road,

221

reached up, and pulled down a shoe. "This yours?"

"It is not."

They walked a little farther, found more items that had been whisked out of someone's possession to land along the road: a skateboard, an old person's walker, a leather jacket.

Lanh tucked the skateboard under his arm.

Carter held the leather jacket up in front of him. One sleeve was missing entirely. He tossed it onto a red wagon that had no wheels. "Too small anyway."

They pawed through another quarter mile of wreckage and came away with a six-pack of Coke, a bucket, a single leather work glove, and a shovel that had been embedded into a tree but came away when they both pulled.

"Not bad for a short walk," Lanh said.

"Think someone will be looking for this stuff?"

"Dude. I think whoever lost this stuff is probably dead."

It was a sobering thought.

As they walked into camp, Lanh looked particularly pleased about the sodas. He'd been craving sugar ever since Carter had known him. When he was younger, Carter would have dialed in a little extra insulin and enjoyed one of the Cokes, but he wouldn't be doing that tonight. He understood all too well that the insulin they had was probably all they were going to get.

Still, as Lanh had pointed out, there was a good chance that whoever had purchased the sodas was now dead. He or she had walked into a store and bought them a year ago, or traded for them more recently. They'd taken their drinks home, only to be killed by a random freak of nature before they could enjoy their spoils.

The way Carter saw it, he could live one of two ways.

He could spend his days worried about his diminishing supply of medication—something he could do absolutely nothing about. Or he could appreciate the evening around the campfire with his friends and family, grateful that he had survived what had to have been an F4 tornado. He hadn't watched *Storm Chasers*, but he'd been subjected to enough of the Weather Channel over the years. In fact, he remembered quizzing his mom about the difference between an F4 that caused devastating damage, and an F4 that caused incredible damage.

His mom had said something like, "Let's hope we never find out."

They had sort of found out, and they'd lived to tell about it. Which just reaffirmed in his mind that rather than worrying about insulin and next month or next year, he'd be better off being grateful that they were still alive tonight.

But he still passed on the soda. No sense being foolish about it.

THIRTY-EIGHT

Things looked worse to Max in the morning light.

The pile of debris on top of the vehicles was unbelievably tall and heavy. How would they move trees with trunks as big around as a man? They needed equipment and pulleys and people—lots more people.

"We're not going to be able to move those larger trees." Max sat down beside Patrick and accepted a hot cup of coffee from Bianca.

"Maybe we should walk out." Shelby sat up, patted down her black curls, and looked imploringly at his coffee.

"You have to get out of bed if you want this."

"You're such a taskmaster."

"I have a badge in that . . . taskmastering."

"The two of you are very strange." Lanh tipped the Coca-Cola can up, hoping to find one more drop in it. Shrugging, he stood, flattened it with his foot, and stuffed it into his pack.

"Souvenir?" Gabe asked.

"Absolutely. The day I survived an F4 and found a Coke. Mrs. S, be sure and write that in your journal."

Shelby gave him a thumbs-up as she breathed deeply of the mug of coffee Max had passed to her.

"Do you think she's addicted to that?" Patrick asked.

"It's a good possibility." Max poured himself another cup from the pot sitting on top of the makeshift grill.

Gabe chimed in. "I've seen her without coffee—once. It was frightening." He shuddered, and everyone, including Shelby, laughed.

No one spoke for a few minutes as the sun rose properly and bathed the area around them in a soft light. The sky was partly cloudy, but there didn't seem to be any impending weather approaching.

"I don't like sitting in one place," Max said. "I feel like a duck in a barrel here."

Shelby glanced up quickly. "We didn't see any signs of people when we went north."

"No one to the south either." Carter pulled a granola bar out of his pack.

"Max is right, though." Gabe fingered the bandage on his head. "We need to move out of here as quickly as we can. People will come— that's one thing you can always count on. They'll come to see what the storm has dumped, what they can find of use, and they'll take whatever they can."

"Not everyone is a criminal." Bianca crossed her arms. "It's possible that someone would come to help us."

"It's possible," Gabe conceded. "But not

225

likely. The good folks? They'll be helping their neighbors or taking care of family. This is a pretty isolated stretch of road. Anyone coming this way will be looking for trouble."

"So we station guards on the main road to the north and south." Max tilted his head toward Bianca and then Shelby. "The rest of us will work on freeing the vehicles."

"Wait. Why are we the guards?" Shelby asked. "Because we're women? Are you saying that we're not strong enough to be of any help . . ."

"Don't go there, *mi amiga*." Bianca stood and stretched. "I've seen you stuck in a store because you couldn't push the door open."

"That hasn't happened in a long time."

"Western Wear . . . the week before the flare."

"I swear that door was locked."

"It opened for me."

"Which still seems very strange."

Everyone began moving at once—ready to jump into the day, ready to leave this place of destruction behind them. Shelby and Bianca checked their water supplies and their weapons.

Honestly, Max did not want them out on the road, but they were both fairly good shots, and Shelby had an uncanny ability to whistle loud and long. They were the right choice for guards.

"One more thing," Gabe said as the two women started toward the road.

They turned back, waited.

"We give this four hours. If we're not making any progress, we change plans and walk out. Might be the best way across the Red River anyway. Might be the only way."

They began working at the back of the debris pile—the side facing the road and what should have been the back of the vehicles. The shovel the boys had found actually came in handy. They were able to use it as a lever, and once they freed some of the smaller tree trunks, they created a kind of ramp. Then it was a matter of rolling the trees down, which was much easier than trying to pick them up. It made for a large pile of logs, but if they could get the weight off the top, there was a chance they could drive forward.

The first vehicle they found was the front bumper of the Mustang.

"Come to Papa," Patrick crooned.

The paint was scraped and the driver's side mirror was missing, but the main body was in remarkably good shape.

"Now if it'll just start."

He wedged himself in through some remaining branches, hauled the door open, slid in, and put the key in the ignition. Miraculously, the engine turned over on the first try.

A shout of victory went up, but that was all the celebration they allowed themselves. They had two more vehicles to uncover. They pulled the Mustang around so that it was free of any

227

falling limbs and also so it was facing the road. They probably couldn't all fit inside it, but it was best to be ready in case they needed to make a quick getaway. Or as Patrick was fond of pointing out, "A bad plan is better than no plan at all."

THIRTY-NINE

Carter had worked hard before. He'd always worked diligently at school, and then after the flare, he'd learned what real work was. Digging a latrine had tested him in ways he couldn't have imagined. Central Texas wasn't known for its abundance of topsoil. Instead, there was a thin layer of dirt covering white rock. They'd hammered their way through. Building the outdoor toilet had taken time and teamwork, which was exactly what they needed now.

They ate lunch standing beside the giant pile of debris. He and Lanh relieved his mom and Bianca so they could grab some lunch and rest for thirty minutes before resuming their posts.

No one had passed by. No vehicles on the road. No sign of life along the tornado's corridor—at least not that they saw.

Maybe they were lucky, or maybe Gabe's predictions had been a bit dire, or possibly God was watching over them.

Carter decided it didn't matter.

What mattered was they now had the Dodge uncovered, and it too still ran. It had taken a few harder hits than the Mustang. The back windshield was spidered, and the tailgate was bashed in so that it no longer opened. But the engine was good.

He glanced up at the sky, surprised to see the sun was past its zenith. He guessed it was tending toward two in the afternoon. No one wanted to spend another night in this same spot. It seemed unnecessarily risky. They needed to free the Hummer, which they could now see.

Unfortunately, it was under a pile of trees that they were having no luck budging.

They each had a small hatchet in their packs. Working in pairs, they hacked away at the giant trunks. Carter's palms turned red, then sore as blisters formed, and finally those burst open and he couldn't feel anything at all. Max caught him staring down at the open blisters, which oozed water mixed with blood.

Max walked over to his pack, opened it, and pulled out a roll of gauze. "Clean them with water and wrap them," he said, tossing the gauze to him.

"Shouldn't we save it for . . . for something worse?"

"If your hands become infected, you'll have to take antibiotics, and last I checked, Gabe only has a limited supply of medication."

"Why aren't yours blistered?"

"Because I'm old, and my skin is like leather."

They both laughed at that. Max had been a lawyer in the pre-flare world. When they'd moved to High Fields, he'd joked about ruining his baby-soft palms. But they'd all become tougher. They weren't the people they'd been before the flare. It aggravated Carter all the more that his palms had betrayed him. He wanted to be tougher. Then again, he didn't want to be old like Max. His forties sounded like a lifetime away, but he wouldn't have minded leathery skin.

He poured water from his bottle over the open blisters, dried them with a clean T-shirt from his pack, and wrapped his hands. Finished, he offered the gauze to Lanh, who had blisters that hadn't burst but would soon, and then they went back to work.

By the time the sun had reached the tops of the trees to the west, the front of the Hummer was free.

"It's going to take another day to remove the rest of it," Max said.

"Unless we drive it out." Patrick chugged the rest of his water, swiped his hand across his mouth, and asked Gabe, "Keys in it?"

"Should be."

"Big engine, right?"

"Much bigger than what you have in that Mustang. Are you thinking what I think you're thinking?"

"I am."

"Not sure it will work."

"We'll never know until we try."

Gabe nodded his assent.

Carter's mom and Bianca walked back into

camp as Patrick shimmied his way through the tree branches obstructing the driver's door. They'd agreed to meet up at four to make a decision about whether to stay another night or walk out. Of course, now they had the option of leaving in the Mustang and Dodge, but no one wanted to leave the Hummer.

"Not this way," Patrick said from inside the tangle of limbs. "Too tight. Can't open the door at all."

Bianca stood with her hands on her hips. "You're too big," she said.

"It doesn't matter how big I am. The door is blocked."

"Uh-huh."

"Honey, I know you want to help, but . . ."

Bianca turned to Gabe. "Keys are in it?"

"They are."

Patrick was trying to scramble back out from under the limbs. He managed to get free at the same time that Bianca handed Shelby her pack, dropped to her belly, and crawled through the mud to the passenger door.

"What's she doing?"

"Rescuing us," Carter said with a grin.

His mom looked miffed that she hadn't thought of ducking in there, but then Bianca was shorter. If anyone could get through, she could.

"I'm in," she called out. They were all standing around the front passenger side of the Hummer. "I'm going to need a hatchet."

"Not happening." Patrick was shaking his head. His amused look had morphed to frustration.

Max stepped closer and peered through the branches. "If you cut the wrong thing, the rest could come down on your head. Think of it like a Jenga game."

"But the stakes are higher." Shelby stepped back, moving right and then left, obviously trying for a better view. With a shrug, she said, "Can you open the door at all?"

"An inch maybe."

"All right. Can you see what's blocking you?"

"Yeah, but I can't move it."

"Try giving it a shake."

The end of a branch moved, slightly, barely.

"Give it all you've got, sweetheart." Patrick grabbed hold of the end of the branch.

This time when Bianca shook it, they were sure.

After that things moved quickly.

Bianca would shake a branch, they would chop it from the outside, and then she'd move to the next.

Carter thought it was like hacking a cave through a mythical forest.

The groan of metal against timber split the quiet of the afternoon.

"I'm in," Bianca hollered.

They all held their breath as she scooted over to the driver's side and started the massive engine.

FORTY

Max didn't like what was happening. He understood that the Hummer was built to handle extreme conditions, but this was going above and beyond the manufacturer's recommendations. What was the weight of the trees crisscrossing the top of the vehicle? How did they know the entire pile wouldn't crush in the top of the Hummer when the load shifted? Why were they taking such a risk?

He'd have preferred approaching the problem slowly, making calculated moves, being cautious.

But, of course, there were risks associated with that as well.

Spending another night in the same spot could be dangerous.

Twice in the last few hours, Shelby had spotted people in a vehicle, moving in and out of the path left by the twin tornadoes, searching through the debris for items that they crammed into the back of their old pickup. Two people went through the wreckage. Another stood guard holding what looked like a semiautomatic military-style weapon. Shelby had only been able to see them through binoculars, and they were moving slowly. Still, there was little doubt that they represented a threat.

Someone would find them soon. The only question was whether it was someone who would help them or someone who would try to take what little they had.

All of that flashed through his mind in an instant—the same instant that Bianca gunned the engine of the Hummer before slipping it into drive.

"Get back," Gabe said.

They all hopped out of the path as Bianca floored the accelerator.

The Hummer shot out of the debris like an arrow from a bow.

Bianca slammed on the brakes as the trees collapsed—groaning, crashing, breaking, popping, and in the end settling into a heap where she had been.

As she exited the Hummer, everyone began talking at once, but it was Gabe who gave a loud whistle and quieted everyone down. "Listen."

No one spoke, Max hardly dared to breathe, and then he heard it—the rumble of an engine followed immediately by the rat-a-tat-tat of a semiautomatic rifle. Someone was coming all right, and it didn't sound like the good guys.

"We need to go now," Gabe said.

"Which direction . . ."

"South. They're south of here." Gabe ran to the driver's side of the Hummer. "We need to head north."

Everyone scattered, grabbing their packs. Max ran to the Dodge, Shelby right behind him. Lanh and Carter passed in front of them, headed toward the Hummer.

"Was Lanh carrying a skateboard?" Shelby asked.

But there was no time to answer, no time to question anyone. There wasn't even time to argue the merits of staying and fighting versus fleeing. They were tired, their energy levels depleted from both the close call with the tornado and the day of arduous work on the debris pile. What they needed was a safe place to rest, a shelter or reprieve of some kind.

Glancing to his right, Max saw Bianca and Patrick slide into the Mustang. Patrick jammed the transmission into first gear and shot around the front of the other two vehicles and out of the drive, turning left, turning north. Max followed, and Gabe brought up the rear.

"I can't see anything out of my rearview." The back window's spidered glass created a prism of color. He split his attention between watching Patrick through the front windshield and monitoring what he could see out of his side-view mirror, which was mostly just the Hummer.

Shelby craned her neck, trying to see more out of her side-view mirror. Finally, she rolled the window down and hung out so that she could better see what was behind them.

Max reached over, grabbed her by the waistband of her pants, and hauled her back into the car.

"Are you crazy?"

"They're still back there." She buckled her seat belt. "It looks like they're gaining on the Hummer."

He knew what she was thinking without having to look at her. He heard the tremble in her voice. Felt the tension in the way she clutched the seat belt.

"We'll make it," he said, pushing the gas pedal until it hit the floor.

Patrick must have seen the same thing they had. The Mustang leapt forward, easily outpacing the Dodge.

Which meant they were holding up the Hummer. If he got out of the way, the Hummer could race past them.

He never had a chance to implement the plan forming in his mind.

He looked in his side-view mirror at the same instant that Shelby looked in hers.

"What are they thinking?" he muttered.

"No. No, no, no, no . . ."

"Hang on." He slammed on his brakes, throwing the Dodge into a spin. Wrestling with the wheel, he tried to work with the deceleration, tapping the brakes, hoping and praying that they would stop facing the threat that Lanh and Carter were about to shoot at.

The Hummer shot past them at the same moment that both Lanh and Carter fired on their aggressor. The Dodge slammed to a squealing, smoking stop in the oncoming lane, facing back the direction they'd just come.

Shelby leaned out the window, her rifle raised. She took aim at the windshield and fired four consecutive shots. Max jumped out of the vehicle, the door shielding him, and fired six more rounds.

The Chevy truck that had been pursuing them swerved crazily, barely clinging to the road as it choked to a halt, front tires shot out, engine billowing smoke.

He saw a stain of red on the front windshield.

The doors didn't open.

"Should we go and—"

"No, we shouldn't." He glanced over at her, saw indecision and doubt and regret flicker across her face. "They were willing to kill us with no provocation, and whoever was in there didn't survive because of the choices they made."

She nodded once, climbed back into the Dodge, her rifle upright between her knees, her hands still clasping the barrel.

He put his own rifle in the backseat where he could easily reach it, prayed that he hadn't thrown a rod or a gasket or any number of things he couldn't name. Prayed that the vehicle would start and that they would find a place to rest.

Sweat ran down his back, and when he looked at his hands on the steering wheel, he saw they were shaking.

That was okay.

In all likelihood, they had just killed someone, possibly several people.

Self-defense? Absolutely. But it still wasn't easy. He hoped it never would be.

Starting the Dodge, he turned them once again so that they were facing north.

FORTY-ONE

Shelby wanted to put her head down and fall asleep. Had she ever been so exhausted? Her arms felt as though they were weighted to her sides. She blinked her eyes constantly, resisting the urge to close them for a few seconds. Her stomach pitched and rolled, and she tried to remember the last time they'd eaten. But she didn't want food. She wanted sleep.

Max reached over and squeezed her hand. Working his way up, he massaged her arm, then her shoulder, then her neck.

"Eyes on the road, cowboy."

"Yeah, but I woke you up. Right?"

"Thanks for that."

"You wanted to be awake, though. I saw you trying to hold your eyelids open with your fingertips."

"I was stretching."

"Your eyelids?"

She peered out into the gathering dusk. They hadn't stopped since shooting out the truck. She kept replaying what had happened in her mind. The horror of seeing Carter lean out the window with his rifle, the truck spinning like a Tilt-A-Whirl at the county fair, Max slamming on the brakes. She hadn't realized she'd reached for her rifle until she was raising it and sighting in the truck's engine block.

Had she killed someone? Or had Max? And what difference did it make? They were literally fighting for their lives. What else could they have done?

"Where are we?"

"Middle of nowhere." Max flexed his fingers on the steering wheel and yawned.

Was he as tired as she was? When would they rest? How much had they even slept the night before?

For the last half hour they'd been traveling on a county road that was barely two lanes. Shelby couldn't even remember which direction they were going. North? Or farther east?

"There has to be a way across the Red River."

"Or through it."

"Not funny. This Dodge doesn't float."

"Indeed it doesn't."

"What if we can't get across? What if every road is blocked?"

She squared herself in the corner between her seat and the door and stared across at Max. It was nearly dark. They were traveling with their low beams on, afraid to go with no headlights, afraid of slamming into an abandoned vehicle. She could barely make out his expression in the glow from the dashboard lights. Watching Max, she thought of him kneeling in the mud, staring at where the house they'd sheltered in had once been. She'd seen fear and relief and joy on his face all at once, and she understood that. She understood how a person could feel so many conflicting emotions at the same time.

"What if we can't get across?" she asked again.

"We'll go around."

"Around?"

"We'll . . . skirt it. West and then north."

"It'll add days, maybe weeks to our trip."

"We knew this wouldn't be easy."

"And it hasn't been." She finger-combed her hair down, wondering when she'd last showered, when she'd even looked in a mirror. It didn't matter, though. All that mattered was finding out if anyone was out there—anyone who could and would help them.

"He's slowing down."

Gabe had taken the lead more than an hour ago. They took turns, like a flock of geese, hoping that the person in the lead could remain a little more vigilant than the other two.

The distance between the three vehicles shrank as Gabe decelerated and tapped his brakes.

They had radios. They could communicate through them, but doing so exposed them to the risk of someone else chancing upon their frequency. The radio in Shelby's lap remained silent.

Their county road had broadened, and they

were now passing through a small town. It was bigger than Langford Cove, but not by much. They passed a church, an elementary school, a library.

"I wonder if there are still any books in there."

"Want to stop and check some out?"

"I want sleep."

"We'll find some somewhere."

He shot her his *I've got this* smile, and she didn't know whether she wanted to sock him or hug him. His confidence could be so irritating and so comforting. She did need sleep. Her emotions were all over the place.

Gabe turned left. Shelby understood why when she saw the road sign that simply read *Grace Chapel*. The road quickly turned to gravel and then dirt. All around them were fields, unplanted, wildflowers reclaiming the soil. And then she saw it—a small white chapel a hundred yards off the road, surrounded on all four sides by fields, with a narrow dirt lane leading to the front steps.

"A place of refuge," Max murmured.

There was no concrete parking area or marquee sign.

They pulled the vehicles side by side, cut off the lights, and killed the engines. A heavenly quiet permeated the evening. Slowly, Shelby became aware of a cardinal's song, the music of crickets, the croak of a frog. Their entire group stepped out of their vehicles, quietly closing the doors and meeting in front of the humble clapboard building.

Shelby leaned her head back, stared up at the steeple, and wondered if she might be dreaming this. The pinpricks of a million stars adorned the heavens. A three-quarter moon had begun to rise in the east.

"We'll check the back," Patrick said. Bianca and Lanh followed at his side.

"Max, stay with the cars until we've cleared the area." Gabe stepped toward the building. Shelby and Carter were practically on his heels.

Inside the church was unscathed.

They walked through the foyer and into the rectangular sanctuary, which had beveled glass windows placed evenly down each side.

No one was here.

Gabe stepped out the door and motioned Max inside.

Patrick and crew entered from the back. "Doors were unlocked," he said.

"Looks like folks stepped away for a moment, like they expected to return the next Sunday." Shelby ran her hand across the back of an old wooden pew. They extended up both sides of the room with an aisle down the middle. The church might have held fifty if they packed in tight. In the beam of Gabe's flashlight, she could make out an altar, piano, lectern, and choir loft. Behind the choir loft was a baptismal and above that, rising to the height of the ceiling, a plain wooden cross.

It only took seconds to clear the room. There was no place for anyone to hide.

"We'll bed down here," Gabe said.

"Being in the middle of a field, no one will sneak up on us." Patrick stretched his neck left and then right. "I like it."

"We'll only need one guard at a time." Gabe checked his watch. "It's eight o'clock. That gives us ten hours. Each person takes a ninety-minute shift on guard duty. Keep your radio with you, and don't hesitate to wake everyone if you see anything at all."

"Eight and a half hours of sleep?" Bianca collapsed onto one of the pews. "I must be dreaming."

"It gets better." Lanh had been wandering around the single room, looking behind things, opening doors that led to closets, rummaging through cabinets. "There's a bathroom back here, and you're not going to believe this . . . there's water."

"Must come from a well," Max said.

"Can't be," Bianca argued. "Wells still need a pump, and I don't see or hear a generator."

"Low flow." Shelby thought of the Amish series she'd written several years ago, what now seemed like a hundred years ago. "You see it in Amish homes all the time. You might not get a lot of pressure, but you'll get water."

Max sat down on the ground with his back against the wall. "Ladies first."

Bianca made a beeline for the bathroom, but Shelby stood in the middle of the aisle scowling. "Why isn't anyone staying here?"

"Are you complaining?" Carter asked.

"I'm just saying, if it seems too good to be true . . ."

"It's good to be cautious, Shelby." Gabe offered a crooked smile as he picked up his pack and wound his arms through the straps, apparently taking the first guard shift. "But sometimes a gift is just a gift. Try to enjoy it."

She wanted to. She thought she would.

It felt heavenly to spend ten minutes in the bathroom, pulling a comb through her hair, washing her arms and face, enjoying a little time alone. She changed into a clean shirt, washed out the one she'd been wearing, and hung it on the towel rack to dry next to Bianca's. The room was small. The guys would have to take their shirts outside to hang, if they bothered to wash them at all. Somehow, she didn't think cleanliness was the first thing on everyone's mind.

She walked back into the main room, spoke with Carter for a moment, and then stumbled over to her bedroll.

One by one she heard everyone in their group fall asleep. Bianca and Patrick snuggled like two pups in a litter. Carter and Lanh both dropped off as soon as their heads hit their sleeping bag.

But Shelby lay there in the dark staring up at the ceiling.

"Problem?" Max asked softly.

"Are you waiting on me to fall asleep?"

"No."

"You are too. I know you are because normally you're like Carter. You fall asleep as soon as your body goes horizontal."

"Can you blame a guy for worrying?"

She couldn't. She didn't.

Max moved his bedroll closer. Shelby turned on her side and studied him in the dark.

"Caramel macchiato for your thoughts."

"Cruel, Max." But she reached out, ran her fingertips down his arm, wondered at the roughness of his palm, and laced her fingers with his. "I was thinking of Saint Mary's."

"Reverend Hernandez."

Shelby was powerless to stop the shiver that crept down her spine. Their trip to Austin had been a nightmare in many ways. Had that really been last summer? She'd left Abney thinking things were desperate, only to arrive in their state capital and find that Abney was actually doing pretty well. Austin? Well, it teetered on anarchy, and they had found themselves caught up in the desperation. They had been forced to do desperate things. She had done desperate things.

Max scooted closer, wrapped his arms around her.

"I've played that night over and over in my mind," she admitted.

"You'd do better to forget it."

"We thought it was a refuge."

"Hey." He cupped her face in his hands, thumbed away the tears that had started to fall. "You did what you had to do, Shelby. When you killed that guard, you were defending yourself, and by doing so, you probably saved all of us."

"I don't regret it."

"You shouldn't."

She sighed, allowed her eyes to drift shut.

She had prayed for weeks after pulling the trigger, crying out to God for his mercy and grace. And she believed she had received that, but then tonight . . . seeing Carter in danger, instinctively raising her own rifle, intuitively protecting her son . . . those things had brought back all of the memories she'd tried to bury.

"We needed a place to rest, and we found this place. Perhaps God is watching over us still."

"This is so different from our modern-day churches. I can imagine . . ." She didn't try to stifle a yawn. "A service here."

Max wrapped his arm around her and began to hum softly—a tune that she should have been able to place, but her mind was shutting down. Too much had happened in too short a time. Too much was riding on the outcome of this trip. She needed rest. She yearned for a long, dreamless sleep. And then she remembered the name of the song—"Precious Lord"—and with that, she let go and tumbled into a deep slumber.

FORTY-TWO

Shelby woke to the sound of voices and the smell of bacon.

Bacon?

She sat up, patted down her hair, and stared around. Where was everyone? Bedrolls had been stuffed into bags and set next to the packs lined against the front altar. Morning sunlight pierced the beveled glass, creating a prism on the floor.

Maybe she was dreaming.

No, she definitely smelled bacon and coffee.

Pulling on her shoes, she stuffed her bedroll into its bag, placed it and her pack beside the others, and made a quick stop in the church's bathroom. As she walked back down the aisle, something caused her to stop, turn, and look toward the front of the room. The sun's rays were higher now, just skimming the backpacks that sat in front of the altar rail. The rainbow of color slipped across each one, and it seemed to her that the prism of light indicated a special kind of blessing, a promise of good things to come.

Could it be that God was telling her, *I've got this?*

Could faith and believing and trusting be that simple?

"I was coming to find you."

She turned to see her son standing in the doorway of the church. It was a marvel to her that they were still alive. Better than that, they were healthy and rested. Would she ever take such basic things for granted again? She didn't think so. She couldn't imagine doing so.

"Breakfast is ready."

"I thought I smelled—"

"You did."

"Why didn't you wake me earlier?"

"Are you kidding?" Carter bumped his shoulder against hers. "You were out. You were snoring. Sounded like Roy when he falls asleep in his rocker."

"I was not snoring like Max's dad."

"Were too."

Carter reached out and tussled her hair, and Shelby batted his hand away. Why did everyone have an urge to mess with her hair? Patrick had put both hands on her head and proclaimed it a Chia pet the day before. It was embarrassing. Then again, if she could provide entertainment—

All thoughts about her hair stopped as they came around the corner of the building.

The other members of their group were sitting around a picnic table she hadn't noticed the night before. Beside the table was a grill you might find at a park or camping area. Probably it was a place for the small congregation to hold Sunday picnics. Where had the people who attended

Grace Chapel gone? Where was the pastor? Why was the church untouched, like an oasis in a raging storm?

Standing in front of the grill was a lady who looked to be ninety. She wore her long, white hair braided down her back, faded jeans, and a red-checked flannel shirt. She glanced up at Shelby and offered a gap-toothed smile.

"Come on over, honey. Your friends told me that you're a real coffee lover, and I make some of the best in the county. Don't I, Stu?"

"You sure do, Mary Jane."

Stu looked even older than Mary Jane. He was sitting at the picnic table, Bianca on one side, Patrick on the other. Carter joined Lanh and Gabe sitting across from them. Max stood to the side, holding a mug of coffee, content to watch the scene unfold.

"Can I interest you in a cup?" Mary Jane held up a chipped blue enamel coffeepot.

"Um, sure. That would be great, but . . . could you give me a minute?"

"Take as long as you want. I can see you have something to say to that young man. Best say it before I serve up breakfast."

Max raised an eyebrow as she walked closer, but he didn't put up much resistance when she tugged his arm and pulled him away from the group.

"Who are those people?" she hissed. "Didn't

you have the last shift of guard duty? Did you just let them walk up to the church?"

"Stu and Mary Jane Faulkner. Yes, and I didn't see any reason not to."

"What kind of answer is that?"

"Hey. Relax, Sparks."

"Relax? What if they'd meant to kill us in our sleep?"

"Mary Jane is ninety-two."

"She looks it."

"And Stu there, he's eighty-nine. Seems Mary Jane caught her a younger man when they married in 1949."

Shelby stared up at him in disbelief. Maybe she was still sleeping, but that coffee . . . it smelled real enough.

"Why did we leave our packs inside? I thought we were supposed—"

"To wear them all the time. Yeah, I know. Look around you, Shelby. We'll see anyone coming from a mile away. The church is a few steps from us. What are you afraid might happen?"

Instead of answering, she pulled his coffee mug from his hand and took a long sip.

"Help yourself."

"You should have woken me up."

"Really?"

All teasing was now gone from his tone, and she had to glance away from his look of sincere concern. Somehow she could handle danger and anger and fear well enough, but when someone was especially kind, it pricked her heart.

"You were exhausted, so I let you sleep in a few minutes. I wasn't going to let you snooze all day. I sent Carter in to wake you up so you could eat."

"It does smell good."

"Because it's real coffee, not instant. You know you want a cup."

He seemed unperturbed by her scowl, as usual.

"More important than the coffee is what they have to say."

"About what?"

"I don't know, but don't you think they're here for a reason?"

Shelby took one more sip of his coffee, pushed the mug into his hands, and turned back toward the breakfast picnic that was happening outside of Grace Chapel.

Why was she surprised to find an elderly couple bringing them breakfast on a beautiful March morning as the world around them continued to crumble? If anything, she should have learned that life was unpredictable. She thought of Gabe's words the night before. *It's good to be cautious, Shelby. But sometimes a gift is just a gift.*

She didn't believe that a couple had shown up simply to bring them coffee and bacon and eggs. Mary Jane and Stu might be old, but there was a shrewdness in the old woman's eyes that spoke of hard times and need—that was what she'd sensed. They needed something. Well, their group had nothing to give.

The breakfast might be a gift, and she was hungry enough to accept it. Then they would be on their way because there was nothing in their packs or vehicles that they were willing to part with. They'd given away all of Hugo's supplies, though they hadn't received a single piece of good information for it. No, they needed to keep what was left. Their very survival depended on the few things they had.

FORTY-THREE

Max watched Shelby walk back to the group, accept a cup of coffee from Mary Jane with a smile, and then bump Carter over so she could sit on the picnic table next to him.

He'd have to tell her the whole story sometime. How he'd watched her sleep for an hour when they'd first arrived. That she'd cried out twice in her sleep, mumbling about a *truck* and *they're coming* and *we need to hide*. He'd fallen asleep beside her, and they'd lain there, huddled together for comfort more than warmth, until Bianca had awakened Shelby for her shift.

When his turn came, he watched the stars go out one by one in the darkness before dawn. The morning sky was just beginning to lighten when he'd pulled the binoculars from his pack and focused on the two forms coming through what had once been a farmer's field. They hadn't bothered to use the dirt lane. Maybe they'd even purposely avoided it. The rusty red wagon they'd pulled held cooking supplies and food—fresh eggs, salted bacon, real coffee.

It wasn't a trap of any sort, of that much he was sure.

Shelby, on the other hand, often had to be convinced.

Max walked back to the table and scooted in beside Bianca. It was crowded with four people to a side, and that left nowhere for Mary Jane to sit. Gabe stood, went into the church, and came back out with a stool, which he placed at the end and sat on, indicating Mary Jane should take his seat.

She pulled an old iron skillet off the grill. Carter jumped up to take it from her.

"You're a good boy—young man, I should say. Good manners. Now see if you can pass that around the table while I unwrap this loaf of bread."

Shelby met Max's gaze across the table. Max understood that she might not want to trust these two strangers, but if there was one thing Shelby loved more than coffee, it was bread. Mary Jane had paved a path straight to her heart.

"Good thing you all carry your own plates and utensils with you. There wasn't much more that Stu and I could fit in that old wagon."

Mary Jane sat after making sure everyone's coffee cup was full, and Max was about to dig in when Stu cleared his throat and reached for Bianca's hand beside him. One by one they formed a circle, and then Stu uttered the blessing.

"Bless us, O Lord, and these thy gifts, which we are about to receive, from thy bounty, through Christ, our Lord. Amen."

Amens echoed around the table, and then they

began to pass the food. There were scrambled eggs, crisp bacon, potato pancakes, which Mary Jane must have made at home and heated on the grill, and coffee with fresh cream.

They spoke of the weather, the coming of spring, and Mary Jane's fine cooking. When he was done, Patrick pushed away his plate and asked, "So do you feed everyone who stops for a night at Grace Chapel?"

Max thought they would laugh off the question, but Stu stared at the church as if he were trying to think exactly how to answer.

"Not all. No. We watch to make sure it isn't someone who would harm us."

"We're old and not that hard to get a jump on," Mary Jane chimed in.

"But if the folks look like good, decent people, then yes. We try to bring them some food." Stu slurped his coffee and then smacked his lips together. "We bring what we can."

"We reckon it's hard, being on the road and having to eat those meals out of pouches."

"How did you know we were good folks?" Lanh asked.

"Good question, son. Mary Jane and I have been around a long time. We know how to look for the little things. You folks came in quiet, bedded down real early, and didn't appear to be robbing the place or tearing it up. *Just looking for shelter,* that's what we thought."

"Sheltering in God's house." Mary Jane leaned forward to she could level a steady gaze at Shelby. "Helps a person sleep even when they're scared. That altar back there is a fine place to lay your burdens down."

"So you live close?" Bianca asked.

"To the west of here. There was a time"—Stu raised his hand, weathered and covered with age spots, to indicate the surrounding pastures—"all of this was cultivated. But then in the last year, folks found out they couldn't plant but a small parcel if they had to do so by the sweat of their brow."

Patrick crossed his arms on the table and leaned forward. "How have you managed to get by?"

"Same way as folks have always done. Same as my parents and their parents. We work hard, Mary Jane and I. We depend on each other, and we have neighbors—not many now, but a few. The Lord's been good. Chickens have survived the winter, wild pigs are good for eating, and Mary Jane can make bread out of anything I give her."

"Like what?" Carter asked. "I mean, what did you use to grind the wheat? A mortar and pestle?"

"How do you know about that?" Shelby asked.

"Science class, Mom. Coach Parish made sure we knew all sorts of obscure stuff."

"Not so obscure now, though." Stu drained his coffee cup. "Also have me an old hand grinder that my grandpa used. Still works. Lots of the old things still work, and they may be what saves us."

There was silence around the table as they all considered the implications of those words. Max resisted the urge to laugh at Shelby. She was fairly bristling with questions, but the protein and carbs and caffeine had hit her system, and she seemed incapable of being her normally confrontational self. Which might explain why the first question she threw out was no question at all.

"I still don't understand why you'd share what little you have . . . with strangers, no less."

"Wouldn't we want someone to share with us?" Mary Jane asked. "We would, and hopefully you people would do so if we were in real need. What you want to know is what do we want in return, and the truth is that you've already given it. Life has become a lonely affair indeed, though Stu is good company."

"As are you, dear."

"Still, a person longs to see a new face, have some questions answered. What would we like in return for our hospitality? Answers. And you can start with where you came from and where you're headed."

FORTY-FOUR

Everyone turned to look at Gabe, including Carter.

He wasn't sure how much of their situation was supposed to be a secret. Actually, what did it matter if these people knew? Stu and Mary Jane might not be as feeble as they looked, but they were awfully old. They didn't pose a threat. That much was obvious, even to him.

Gabe glanced around the table, maybe waiting for someone to object. When no one did, he admitted that he was a doctor in the military, and that he'd enlisted the help of the rest of the group to find the federal government. Then he gave a brief summary of their journey. It was surprising to hear it all at once like that. Finding Langford Cove empty and looted, splitting up at Hamilton, coming across signs of Hugo and then being nearly killed by him, being rescued by Gus and helped by Hauk.

Surrounding Hugo and his goons.

Leaving them handcuffed to a fence outside of Wichita Falls.

The tornado.

The people chasing them as they fled the area.

The shoot-out.

Driving aimlessly through the night.

261

"You're a doctor?" Mary Jane asked.

"Yes, ma'am."

Stu reached for the coffeepot in the middle of the table and poured a little more of the now tepid liquid into his cup. "It's a miracle indeed that you found this little county road."

"There was a sign," Bianca pointed out.

"True. The odds of you seeing it, though—those are pretty slim. And actually turning down the road, slimmer still."

"What's the point of trying to find the federal government?" Mary Jane asked. "Do you actually think they're going to help you and send supplies and people to protect your town? If they were planning to do that, you wouldn't need to search for them."

Gabe had left out the part about being sent by Governor Reed. Now he shrugged and said, "Sometimes you just want answers."

"And you're willing to risk your life for that?" Mary Jane cackled. She reminded Carter of the wicked witch in *The Wizard of Oz*, but one that cooked well and might not be on the dark side of things. "There's something you're not telling us, young man. And that's fine. We don't expect you to share all of your secrets."

"What about you?" Shelby leaned forward and tapped the table between her and Mary Jane. "What are your secrets?"

Carter thought Mary Jane wouldn't answer.

262

After all, she didn't owe them anything, and his mom—well, she wasn't exactly polite about it.

"Our secrets? Hmm . . . that's something we'd have to show you. Can't be told. Not that simple."

Mary Jane glanced at Stu. He nodded once and pushed his way into a standing position. "We can show you, but it's a bit of a walk."

A raucous discussion broke out between the members of their group, half saying they needed to be going and that they should have already left. The other half—Bianca and Lanh and Max—insisted that they weren't in such a big hurry and that maybe what Mary Jane and Stu had to show them was important.

Gabe took a vote, and Carter landed on the side of going to the old folks' place. Mostly because they hadn't tried to influence the discussion in any way. They'd sat back and watched, a bemused look on their faces, giving the distinct impression that it didn't much matter to them one way or the other. If they were up to something, they would have been pushing their agenda.

He didn't try to explain all of that. Instead, when his mom tromped along beside him and gave him *the look,* he laughed and said, "A little curiosity doesn't hurt."

"Tell that to the cat."

They trudged across the fields, leaving Patrick and Lanh to watch over their vehicles. The morning was quiet. The only sounds were natural ones—no vehicles or rifle shots to mar the peace.

"I don't like it," his mom admitted.

They were walking at the back of the group, with Mary Jane and Stu leading the way.

"Are you worried about taking the time to do it? Or about what we might find?"

"Both."

"As long as you have all the bases covered."

Shelby rolled her eyes and reached out to give him a playful nudge. Yeah, his mom was apparently feeling better. It was amazing what a good night's sleep and a decent meal could do.

As for Carter, he'd insisted on coming on this trip. He'd left High Fields because he wanted to see other places. He wanted to find out how others were living and what things they were using to survive. He didn't see an extra hour off the road as a waste of time at all.

Google had failed him.

Wikipedia was a thing of the past.

If they were going to learn, they were going to have to learn from one another.

The walk took less than ten minutes.

"They're spry for old people," Carter muttered.

The home was pretty much what Carter had pictured, though busier than he'd expected. Cows grazed in the pasture next to a brown, shaggy donkey. He could hear pigs rooting around in an enclosure to the south. A vegetable garden had already been planted on the west side. Laundry hung on the line, flapping in the early morning breeze.

Mary Jane didn't take them to see any of those things.

Instead, she and Stu led everyone up the porch steps and into the sitting room.

Carter was diagnosed with diabetes when he was only four years old. He didn't remember much about that time, but over the years there had been the occasional emergency that landed him in the ER—sometimes diabetes related, but more often just the usual mishaps of growing up. You could say he knew his way around a hospital.

He'd barely stepped through the front door when he caught the smell of antiseptic, bleach, medicine, and sickness. Some things were the same whether you were in a technological world or not. When someone was dying, it seemed to him that there was a certain odor in the air. Maybe it was just helplessness that he thought of as a smell rather than a state of mind. Regardless, Mary Jane's house was full of that odor—the scent of a life about to end.

FORTY-FIVE

It took Shelby's eyes a minute to adjust to the darkened interior of Mary Jane and Stu's home. Five from their group had come along to see whatever it was the couple wanted to show them. Surely, it couldn't be this, though.

What would this sad but all-too-common situation have to do with them?

And what could Mary Jane and Stu possibly want?

"I'd like y'all to meet my twin sister, Mary Jo." Mary Jane walked over to the daybed and peered down into her sister's face. "We have company, Mary Jo."

"I can hear, Mary Jane. I'm not deaf, only dying."

"As you can see, she's a real spitfire," Mary Jane said.

Stu seemed used to their bantering. He shuffled to the front window and pulled back the curtains, flooding the room with light.

Mary Jane made quick introductions, and everyone said hello.

Shelby's heart softened when she took the woman's hand in hers and said, "It's nice to meet you."

"You're all the way from Abney?"

"Yes, ma'am."

"My granddad had an old dry goods store in Abney once. This was before my sister and I were born. But he often talked fondly of the area and how kind the people were."

"They are that."

The skin of Mary Jo's hand was paper thin, and Shelby could clearly see the pattern of veins running beneath. Unlike Mary Jane, she had very little hair on her head—a few white wisps. A faded quilt draped her frail body. The sheets and her clothing were crisp and clean. Her eyes seemed to say that she understood what was happening, and that she was at peace with it. Shelby stayed by the bed, talking with her, remembering her time working at the nursing home in Abney. Those dear people had tugged at her heartstrings with their need, their gratitude, and their resilience. She saw the first two in Mary Jo's eyes, but she wasn't so sure about the resilience. The woman seemed to almost fade into the freshly laundered pillowcase.

They'd only been in the living room a few minutes when Stu suggested they go outside to see the chickens.

Gabe and Bianca held back, speaking to Mary Jo in a soft voice.

Stu took his slow, sweet time leading them through the house.

He insisted they stop and admire Mary Jane's

windowsill herb garden. "There's even aloe vera, which is good for many things, including indigestion."

"You can put a spoonful of the jelly into your tea." Mary Jane stuck a finger in the soil and then added a small amount of water from a watering can.

"Also works as a salve for burns," Shelby said.

"Indeed," Mary Jane agreed.

Stu pointed out several other plants—some that Shelby knew about and had growing at High Fields, and a few that she didn't. She'd have to put those names into her journal as soon as they were on their way.

They meandered through the kitchen and across a screened-in porch, walked back out into the sunshine, and trooped over to the nearby chicken coop.

Stu picked up one of his prize roosters to show off. He told them how well the hens were laying, how good the roosters tasted in a stew, what they fed them, and how particular they were to keep their coop clean. "Chickens can be a real help in these dark times. Protein—that's what most people need more of."

"Lots of vitamins too," Mary Jane added.

"And they make an affectionate pet." Stu gently placed the rooster on the ground, and it strutted off. "Not that you want to get too attached."

Shelby was beginning to wonder if they'd come

to the elderly couple's home only to receive a lesson on poultry, when Bianca and Gabe caught up with them, and Mary Jane jumped right to the point.

"We didn't actually bring you here to talk chickens or show you my window box garden. We brought you here because we wanted you to meet Mary Jo."

"She's dying," Gabe said.

Mary Jane and Stu nodded, waiting for Gabe to go on.

"Please understand that oncology isn't my specialty. Mary Jo told me that she first noticed the lump in her breast last summer."

"After the flares," Mary Jane said. "After the hospital closed."

"And the ones in her lymph nodes?"

"Three months ago."

"So you realize she's in stage four."

"Yes, of course we realize that." Stu picked up a smooth, polished walking stick that had been leaning against the fence. He thumped it on the ground and said, "That's why we brought you here. We know she doesn't have much longer until she goes to meet our Lord face-to-face."

"I'm very sorry. I wish there was something we could do, but we don't have any medicine that can help her."

"They don't want medicine." Shelby stepped closer to Mary Jane, finally understanding the calculated look she'd seen in the woman's eyes from the first moment. "You've been trying to decide if you could trust us . . . with your sister."

Steel blue eyes met hers. Mary Jane didn't waver. She didn't look apologetic about what she was about to ask. If anything, she had a more determined look in her eyes. Love could do that to a person, Shelby realized. She was seeing in this woman the same fierceness that she'd felt since the evening she first saw the flares, the same desperate need to care for someone in a world that made doing that very difficult.

"Her dying wish is to see her son. I want you all to take her to him."

FORTY-SIX

Max couldn't believe what he was hearing. "We're not an ambulance service," he said, but no one was listening. Carter was asking Gabe how difficult it would be to transport her. Bianca and Shelby were actually arguing for it, and Mary Jane was simply standing there, letting them voice all of their objections.

After a moment, she raised a hand to silence them. "I made Mary Jo a promise that I would find a way to take her to see her son—"

"Why would you promise such a thing?" Max asked.

"Because it's her wish. Her dying wish. I'd promise her anything, and believe me, I'll find a way to do it. Right now, you're our best option." She waved toward the small, white clapboard church. "Been taking food to people for the last month. You don't think you're the first to stop at our chapel, do you? But most groups . . . well, I wouldn't trust them with one of Stu's roosters. You folks are different. I can tell."

"We know we're asking a big thing," Stu added.

"Yes, it's a big thing." Max pulled off his cowboy hat, ran his fingers through his hair, and resettled it. "Chances are she wouldn't survive the ride."

"Actually, she's stable," Gabe interjected.

Max gave him a *whose side are you on* look, and continued to tick off objections on the fingers of his right hand.

"We need to be on our way, headed to Kansas."

"Won't take you far out of your way."

"This isn't our problem. No offense."

"None taken," Mary Jane said evenly.

"Our vehicles aren't in the best condition, and we don't even know if her son is still alive." He glanced down at his hand, surprised to see he'd reached his thumb. Five reasons. Five good reasons not to do this thing.

Surprisingly, it was Shelby who walked over, took ahold of his hand, and said, "Sometimes you do a thing because it's the right thing to do. Not because it makes sense."

He stared at her dumbfounded.

She did not sound like herself.

"You were the one questioning why these people showed up in the first place."

"I know I did."

"And now you, what . . . trust them?"

"I do."

"But, Shelby, honey. You're talking about taking a stage-four cancer patient in a broken-down vehicle to a place where her son might not even be."

"Actually, that's not a problem." Mary Jane

pulled a piece of paper from her pocket. She handed it to Max, who unfolded it.

There was a simple map to a rural neighborhood twenty miles north of their location, which was at least in the right direction. Names had been jotted down to the right and left of the road, and a star penned by the name of Mary Jo's son.

"Now, this isn't your typical neighborhood. It's folks living way back in the woods where no one can bother them." She pointed at the penciled lines off the main road. "Those are all dirt. You'll be able to get through. We didn't even see that tornado you talked about, though we had the rain. But it wasn't enough to affect the roads. If something's happened and Christopher isn't there, then you leave her with one of his neighbors."

"And Mary Jo is okay with this?"

"She knows the risk. We've talked about it often enough, but this is what she wants. Now if I have to, I'll put her in that wagon and pull her there myself, but that's—"

"Twenty miles." Carter was reading over Max's shoulder.

"Yeah. It's at least twenty miles. Hard walk for someone my and Stu's age."

"I don't see that an extra twenty miles will make any difference to us." Carter stretched and tried to cover a yawn. "We've been traveling in circles for days."

Gabe nodded in agreement. "I could monitor

273

her condition in the backseat of the Hummer while Patrick drives."

"If you think . . ." Max felt his resolve caving.

"We'll do it," Shelby said. "But we should check with Patrick and Lanh first. This has to be a unanimous decision."

"They'll agree," Stu said with confidence. "See, we haven't got to the good part yet. How we're going to thank you."

"But you already fed us," Bianca pointed out. "From supplies I'm sure you needed."

Stu thumped his walking stick against the ground again, a mischievous grin spreading across his face. "That was nothing. I was listening when you told us what you've been through and where you're going. What you need is a way across the Red River—a way that no one else knows about, a way that won't be blocked."

"And you know of one?" Max didn't even attempt to keep the skepticism out of his voice.

"Sure do. I'll even draw it on the map."

FORTY-SEVEN

An hour later, Shelby embraced Stu, who had tears running down his weathered cheeks.

"I know Mary Jane can be hard to get along with, but she loves her sister and would do anything for her." He added as an afterthought, "Or me. She'd do anything for me."

"I understand that. I do. We'll take good care of Mary Jo."

All three vehicles had been moved over to the small clapboard house. Shelby wanted to continue straight to the Dodge, but instead she walked over to the Hummer. Mary Jo had been loaded so that she was lying down in the backseat. Pillows were stacked under her head and tucked around her body. The same quilt that had covered her in the daybed now rested across her in the Hummer.

There was enough room, even with her lying down, for Gabe to sit beside her. "I'll monitor her condition. We'll do our best to ensure she makes it to her son's."

"I trust she will." Mary Jane bent over, kissed her sister on the cheek, and whispered something in her ear. Then she turned and began to walk away from the Hummer, nearly bumping into Shelby.

What could Shelby say to this woman? That

275

everything would turn out fine? Not to worry? That she was doing the right thing? The first two she couldn't guarantee, and the last she didn't know. What she did know was that she saw much of herself in this woman's eyes.

The bond between twins was strong—she'd always heard that. Was it as strong as the bond between a mother and child? Maybe. The love and pain shining in this woman's eyes reflected Shelby's own every time she wondered how Carter would survive in this world turned upside down. She'd always hated empty platitudes, so instead of offering false condolences, she said, "Thank you for allowing us to be a part of this. For having a hand in granting her last wish."

The tears didn't spill from Mary Jane's eyes, but she stared at the ground for a moment, pulling her bottom lip in between her teeth. When she looked up, a steely resolve had returned. "I knew you were good people the moment I laid eyes on you. Knew you didn't trust me, and that was okay because you shouldn't trust just anyone these days. You have to watch and discern. You have to listen to the voice inside your head and your heart. I knew you were good people, and I'm sure that you will do the best you can to transport Mary Jo."

"That's all anyone can ask," Stu added. He'd hobbled over to stand with them.

Shelby clasped Mary Jane's hand in her own.

Max started the Dodge's engine.

She didn't say anything else to the elderly couple. What words were there? The kind of sacrifice they were making—to give up sharing Mary Jo's final days so that she might have her last wish—it was the stuff of novels.

Shelby jogged over to the Dodge and climbed in, glancing in her side-view mirror as they drove away and Mary Jane and Stu became two dots in the distance.

Bianca led this time, with Carter reading Stu's map beside her in the front seat. Patrick drove the Hummer, and Lanh rode shotgun. The Hummer was now positioned in the middle, as if they suddenly needed protection given its precious cargo: one old lady with a short time left to live and a dream in her heart.

Max was the last to drive out of the gate and down the dirt track.

The backseat of the Dodge was still filled with supplies, as was the cargo hold of the Hummer. They made it back to town in a few minutes, a place that was as deserted as the first time they'd seen it.

"You did a good thing back there, Sparks." Max kept his eyes on the road. It was a few minutes past ten in the morning, and they would have rather been on the road hours ago, but some-times life changed your plans.

"I did?"

Max reached up and tipped his hat against the morning sun. "I was skeptical."

"Probably the attorney in you."

"Probably so."

"Hard to change old habits."

"I thought I'd dropped them, to tell you the truth, but every time I think I've banished the lawyerly voice in my head, it asserts itself loud and clear."

"What were you afraid might happen? That they might sue us if we didn't get Mary Jo to her son's?" She had pulled out her notebook and pen, but she sat there rubbing the end of the pen against her bottom lip, trying to understand the ways of Max Berkman's mental process.

"Not exactly." He shifted in his seat and shot a glance her way. "The old me would have worried about that—liability and litigation and charges of negligence if she died on the way to see someone we're not sure is alive."

"And the new you?"

"The new me worried that she should stay where she was, that Stu and Mary Jane shouldn't have trusted us."

"But they did trust us, and that changed everything."

"For them maybe."

"For Mary Jo."

"I guess," he conceded.

"And what about for us? Did you believe Stu's

story about a mysterious bridge that can't be found on any map?"

"Our government wanted to spend nearly four hundred million dollars to construct a bridge to nowhere."

"Wasn't that in Alaska?"

"It was, and the funding was eventually removed, but how many more projects like that existed that we never heard about?"

"And this is the same federal government we're risking our lives to find. Thanks for the pep talk, Berkman."

"Do I believe they might have built a secret road across the Red River? I guess it's possible, but why would they?"

"Good question. Maybe we can ask someone when we get there."

Shelby thought the conversation was over. She pulled the cap off her pen, opened her tablet, and began to write a description of Grace Chapel rising up from pitch-black darkness as a band of refugees made their way toward it.

"The thing is . . ." Max cleared his throat. "The thing is I would hate for you to get your hopes up."

"Me?"

"We might be looking for the federal government, but I know what you're looking for."

"I don't expect to find boxes of insulin on the side of a mysterious bridge."

279

"No, but you do expect to find them when we locate the government."

She didn't say anything to that. She hadn't spoken of those thoughts to anyone, but then her hopes and dreams and fears had always been obvious to Max. He read her as easily as she had once read romance novels.

"I understand what you're looking for, and maybe even why you're not talking about it. But . . . you know . . . try not to get your hopes up. Just in case."

"You're a good man. You know that, Max?"

He tipped up his hat and searched her face for some secret meaning behind her words. The concern and love in that look were almost more than Shelby could bear to see.

She swallowed past the lump in her throat. "Eyes on the road, cowboy."

"Yes, ma'am."

FORTY-EIGHT

Carter kept his eyes on the road, scanning out the right side of the car. It was good to be in the Mustang again. He still thought it was the coolest ride he'd ever seen. But the Hummer was a close second, and it afforded a better view when monitoring for bandits and creeps. He was beginning to understand the appeal of the vehicle's design over a civilian vehicle, and especially over a vintage Mustang.

"This is the road," he said as he checked the map.

They turned right, continued another ten minutes, and pulled onto a dirt lane which ran through a tangle of trees. An even smaller dirt track appeared on the left, and Bianca took it.

"Hope the Hummer and Dodge can make it down here," she said.

"The Hummer could go straight through the woods if it had to."

Bianca glanced in her rearview mirror and nodded.

Carter turned to see the Hummer pull in behind them, followed by the Dodge.

"That Dodge probably should have quit a long time ago," Carter said.

"Max's determination is holding it together."

Carter again consulted the map. "One more turn on the right, and we should be there."

"These people are pretty far back in here," Bianca said.

"Which could be a good thing. They are too far off the beaten path for anyone to mess with them."

Bianca pulled the Mustang to a stop in front of a mobile home that had obviously seen better days. Surely it hadn't come off the factory floor looking that way. The underpinning was torn loose in places. Several windows had duct tape across cracks. The front storm door hung crookedly off its hinges. The yard was a tangle of weeds, bushes, and mud.

Carter had wondered why Mary Jo was having to hitch a ride to see her son on her deathbed. Shouldn't her son be looking for her? But when he saw the mobile home and the passel of kids scattered across the yard, he understood. Whoever lived here wouldn't be going anywhere. The only vehicle was a broken-down sedan covered in leaves, its windshields completely obscured with dirt.

"No one's driven that car in a while," he said.

"Maybe not since before the flare." Bianca leaned forward to peer out the front windshield. "Maybe longer than that."

The Hummer and the Dodge pulled in next to them.

Every child in the yard—Carter counted seven—was staring at them.

And then the front door opened, and out stepped a bear of a man. He was easily taller than Max—way over six feet—and he had the stockiness of Patrick. His hair was mostly gray, as was his beard, and he was holding a Browning rifle that looked like a toy in his hands. Carter briefly thought they were at the wrong place. There was no way this guy was related to Mary Jo.

Bianca stepped out of the car.

They had talked about this beforehand, how they would approach Mary Jo's son without being shot. The obvious solution was Bianca. She was the smallest of them and the least intimidating—though if you knew her, you might not feel that way. Bianca was tough. Carter didn't want to be on her bad side. She'd always treated him like a little brother, but he'd seen her riled up. Kind of a scary sight.

Bianca crossed half the distance between the vehicles and the front door.

Carter rolled down his window. He couldn't hear everything Bianca said, but he made out the words *Grace Chapel, Mary Jane, Stu,* and *your mother*.

The man lowered his rifle, stepped closer, and asked her, "Momma? She's here?"

And then the large man was running to the Hummer.

After that, everything happened fast. They

283

moved Mary Jo into the trailer, which looked dramatically better on the inside than it did on the outside. Food was stacked in crates along the wall. Bedrolls were tucked on top of the crates. Everything was clean, remarkably so given the condition of things outside. But Christopher's wife reigned inside. That much was obvious. From the look of things, and the bows and rifles and even a slingshot hung on the wall, Christopher spent a lot of his time scavenging the woods for protein for their brood of children.

Gabe spent a few minutes in the back room, giving instructions to Aubrey, who was a normal-sized woman. She looked petite up against Christopher. Carter and Lanh walked back outside as soon as they could because there wasn't enough room in that house for the adults.

"How do all the kids fit in?" Lanh asked.

"I have no idea, and I don't want to find out."

The kids gathered around them, apparently hoping they might be Santa Claus about to hand out gifts. But they didn't have anything to give to them. Eventually, the oldest, who looked to be maybe ten, shrugged and walked away. All of the rest followed.

What would their childhood be like?

No school. No field trips. No Saturday movies or texting or video games.

All of the adults except for Mary Jo and Aubrey walked out onto the porch.

"I don't know how to thank you folks. I don't even know why you'd do such a thing." Christopher stared out over the ramshackle yard. "I tried to get to her a couple of times, but there were too many people on the road, people milling about in big groups, attacking anyone they could. I stayed . . . stayed in the woods and watched, looked for a way. There wasn't one."

"The first month was difficult everywhere," Max assured him.

"Then my son and his wife were killed by someone who wanted the deer he'd harvested. After that, I didn't dare leave Aubrey or the grandkids." He looked slowly from one person to the next, his gaze finally coming to rest on Gabe. "I don't know how to thank you. Being able to see my mother again . . . well, it's something I'd given up on hoping for. Being able to care for her, to bury her here on this land, is a real gift."

Tears slipped down his cheeks, landing in his bushy gray beard. He didn't attempt to wipe them away. Instead, he ducked his head again and said, "Thank you. Truly. If there's anything I can do for you—"

"We're looking for a way across the Red River," Gabe said.

Bianca showed him the map that Stu had drawn. "Stu said he'd heard about a secret government project. He seemed to think it might include a bridge."

"Uncle Stu always was one for conspiracy theories." Christopher studied the map.

"So there was no secret project?" Shelby asked. "He made that up?"

"Well. Something was going on. He's right about that. Lots of supply trucks, construction trucks, even road crews. Funny thing was, they didn't build a road."

"I don't understand." Max rubbed the muscles on the back of his neck.

"The trucks went in . . . to a private property right . . . here." Christopher's finger stabbed the map.

"That's not the spot Stu marked."

"My uncle's getting on up in years. He had the right area, which as you can see isn't that far from here . . . maybe another twelve miles."

"How would you not know for certain if something that big was happening only twelve miles away?" Carter asked. Maybe the question sounded rude, but he couldn't help himself. He'd known everything that was happening in their hometown, and he'd only been seventeen at the time.

"Mainly because that's not on the way to anywhere. As you can see, the road ends back here. There have been plenty of rumors, but I didn't have time to chase fairy tales even before the flare."

He stared off into the distance, as if he could see the area he was talking about.

"I've driven past the main gate once or twice when I took the grandkids to the river to fish. We had to park at the end of the road and walk in. The gate itself is right here. Can't see anything from downriver, I can tell you that for certain. Whoever owns it purchased a big tract of land."

"Or several tracts." Gabe looked as if he wanted to add more. He settled for, "You're certain that's the place Stu was referring to?"

"Yeah, I'm sure. I haven't actually thought about what was going on there in quite a while. Why would I? I'm not looking for a way across. Don't expect things are any better on the Oklahoma side, and I've had my hands full since the flare. I guess you know how that is."

They all nodded, even Carter. He felt his head bobbing up and down. It seemed they'd been dealing with one emergency after another since the flare.

"It was winter before last when the trucks started showing up, one or two at a time. They'd turn down this dirt road. You'll be able to find it clearly enough. There are 'No Trespassing' signs all along the road there."

"Folks like their privacy," Gabe said.

"Yeah, but there's not a lot of high fencing around here, and the gate? Eye scanners, fingerprint boards, stuff like that."

"You saw that?" Gabe asked, now watching him sharply.

287

"I didn't, but a guy I worked with—a guy I trust—he did."

"All right." Patrick crossed his arms and frowned at the piece of paper Stu had drawn on. "High fence, no trespassing, super high-tech gate. Paved road?"

"That's the thing. The stuff went in, but they never built the road. It's still a dirt lane. I don't know what happened. Strange, I'll give you that."

Carter glanced at Lanh, motioned to the Mustang, and they both walked away toward it.

"Is that guy making any sense to you?"

"He makes sense. He's coherent, and he hasn't contradicted himself. Plus, why would he lie to us?"

"I don't know."

"What he's saying, though . . . that's a different story. That makes no sense at all."

"Think we'll go check it out?"

"Are you kidding me? Did you see Gabe's reaction? He was like a homing pigeon zeroed in. We're going there. The only question is what we're going to find."

With a shrug and a sigh, they turned and walked back toward the group.

FORTY-NINE

Gabe took the lead this time, which was fine with Max.

Carter and Lanh rode with him in the Hummer, Carter holding the modified map, and Lanh sitting in the backseat watching for trouble. Shelby was once again riding in the Dodge Ram with Max.

"I don't like it," Shelby said.

"Told you not to get your hopes up."

"Yeah, there's that. But this is beyond strange."

They were behind the Hummer, and Bianca drove the Mustang behind them, Patrick riding shotgun with his rifle out and ready.

The high fence appeared suddenly, along with large "No Trespassing" signs spaced at regular intervals. It went on for miles—5.3, to be exact.

"If this doesn't work, we're going to have to locate one of Gabe's fuel dumps."

"Are we low?"

"I'm at a quarter tank."

"We have some left in the fuel cans."

"We do, but I'd rather not use it if we don't have to."

"It feels as though we've been driving in circles for days."

Suddenly, the fence was interrupted by a large,

metal gate. The entrance was wide enough to hold all three of their vehicles beside one another.

"Can you think of a reason to make an entrance that wide?" "Eighteen-wheelers? Concrete trucks? Who knows?"

Max didn't like it. He felt certain they were walking into a trap. Everyone got out of their vehicles, car doors slamming in tandem. Lanh, Carter, and Shelby immediately took up position behind them, facing the road.

Gabe, Patrick, Max, and Bianca walked up to the gate.

First they checked out the electronic pad.

"Fried?" Max asked.

"Yeah, but this model . . ." Gabe tapped the bottom of the screen. "Same kind that you'll find on military bases all over the world."

"Can we break through?" Bianca asked.

Gabe walked up to the wrought iron gates and gave them a rattle. "Maybe. If I'm willing to smash the Hummer into it. But for what? We have no idea what's on the other side."

"Can't climb it." Bianca pointed up. Curled razor wire adorned the top.

"And it runs the entire length of the fence," Max said. "Probably on all three sides—assuming the fourth side is the river."

"Looks like this was a pointless side trip." Bianca whistled. Shelby, Lanh, and Carter started their way.

"No sign of people around here," Shelby said. "No tracks on the dirt road except ours."

"I imagine whoever owns this, owns a lot of the surrounding land as well." Gabe stepped closer to the gate, peering past it. "Look up there."

He pointed first to one tree, then another, and another.

"Surveillance cameras?" Lanh asked.

"Yeah. They'll be fried too, but the thing is that everything about this place is overdone. The gate. The security. The surveillance." Gabe shook his head as he turned and faced the group. "My recommendation is to walk away from this. I don't know what it is, but there's little chance it's what we need."

"How can we know that?" Shelby asked.

"We can't, but I do know that trying to bust through here and then following that road . . ." He pointed to where the dirt track disappeared around a bend. "Well, it could take some time. Chances are there will be more obstacles farther in."

"What do you think this place is?" Carter scuffed his foot against the mud. "You're military. Is it like an Area 51 or something?"

"There are black ops projects," Gabe admitted. "Of necessity, some work the government does isn't shared on the morning news."

"Of the people, by the people, and for the people," Max murmured.

"I heard you, Max, and I even agree with you." Gabe leaned against the fence. "You've probably heard about the Utah Data Center, Cheyenne Mountain in Colorado, even supposed UFO listening centers. The first two are examples of legitimate government facilities, though their actual purpose is far less exciting than the conspiracy theorists would want you to believe."

"I guess the government isn't listening anymore," Patrick said. "As to Cheyenne Mountain, that may be where the feds are hiding."

"Do we actually listen for UFOs?" Lanh asked. "Er, I guess the question is, *did* we listen for UFOs?"

"That one I can't answer. If we did, it would be on the top of a mountain, or somewhere that you wouldn't have other electronic clutter."

"No clutter now," Shelby pointed out.

"True. But as for this place? I don't know what it is. Might be government. Might be government working with private business. Whatever it is, seems to me that it's deserted. Why would anyone stay in there? How would they stay in there?"

"They'd have to come out for food," Bianca said.

"Exactly. So maybe it was something our government started and never finished."

"An incomplete black op." Carter clamped his cowboy hat down on his head. The thing looked more ragged every day, but he liked the way it felt and even how it looked. "I'm starting to get hungry."

"Everyone grab a granola bar and drink some water. It's half past noon." Gabe stood with his hands on his hips, staring at the ground. "If we go now, we can get back to the main road and stop to fill up the vehicles with the gas in our cans."

"Why not do it here?" Bianca asked.

"I don't like the fact that we have little line of sight. Let's get out in the open, fill up, and then proceed to the nearest fuel cache."

They all nodded in agreement, disappointed but ready to move on.

"Did you quote the Gettysburg Address back there?" Shelby asked Max.

"I did."

"This . . ." Her hand came out to encompass the gate, the cameras, the razor wire. "It bothers you."

"Mysteries have always bugged me," Max said as he and Shelby headed back toward the Dodge.

"Bugged you?"

"Like an itch you can't reach."

"You've never read mysteries or watched the television shows. Remember the time I tried to get you to sit through one episode of *Sherlock*?"

"I don't like them. I want things to be laid out—"

"You want forensic evidence and testimony."

"What I want is things laid out in an orderly, logical manner."

"That's exactly what Holmes would say. You're more alike than you realize."

"Take away all the mystery shows ever created, and the world would be a better place."

"Wish granted, unfortunately, for those of us who enjoyed them."

Gabe pulled out onto the road, followed by Patrick.

Max started the Dodge and was pulling away when he glanced into his side-view mirror. At first he thought he was imagining things, that he couldn't actually be seeing a group of people running toward them, running toward the gate from the other side.

And then he heard them begin to scream.

FIFTY

Shelby was buckling her seat belt when Max slammed on his brakes, sending her sprawling into the dashboard.

"What?"

But Max had already thrown the Dodge into park, killed the engine, and leaped out.

She pulled out her handgun, thumbed off the safety, and jumped out after him.

And that was when she saw the five people on the other side of the fence.

She darted after Max, gun drawn, but if she was worried that he was being reckless, she wasn't considering how he had changed over the last nine months. He might still think like a lawyer, but his instincts were those of a papa bear. His hand was on the butt of his holstered weapon, and he didn't venture any farther than the back of the Dodge.

The five people stopped short of the gate, their hands raised as they stared at Max and Shelby as though they'd sprouted wings.

"Why are you pointing that gun at us?" This from a woman who was probably in her thirties. She was black, with a butchered haircut, and thin as a reed.

"Maybe you should tell us what you're doing

on that side of the fence," Max said. "Tell us what this fence is even about."

"Look." The woman raised her hands higher in a sign of submission. "Don't shoot us, okay? All we need is to use your cell phone."

Shelby had been studying the rest of the group. Including the woman talking, they were an odd collection of two men and three women, ages ranging from twenties to thirties, she'd guess, and of different ethnic backgrounds. At the mention of a cell phone, she whipped her head around to stare at the leader.

"My name is Paige. Paige Wakefield." She stepped closer to the gate. "All we want is to make a call. Our . . ." She motioned to the group behind her. "All of our phones are out, and we need to call someone to pick us up."

At this point, the Mustang and the Hummer pulled back in behind them. Shelby didn't have to turn around. She knew the sounds of their vehicles at this point. She heard the crunch of five folks walking toward them, and immediately her danger radar dropped a degree. They were solid. Whatever was happening with these people, they wouldn't hurt anyone on her side of the fence. Her friends—her family—had her back.

Gabe walked past Max.

"What's going on here?" he asked Paige.

"They want to borrow our cell phones." Max

296

said it quietly, flatly, as if they had asked for a ride to the moon.

Paige's group was growing restless. How long had they been stuck inside the enclosure? How could they not know what had happened on June 10 last year? Was this a trick of some kind?

Gabe recovered more quickly than the rest of them, perhaps because he recognized a kindred spirit, a brother-in-arms.

"Name, service, and rank?"

Paige didn't even hesitate. "Paige Wakefield. US Air Force. Major."

"Air Force?"

"Yes. Currently I'm on assignment for . . . that is, we all work for NASA."

FIFTY-ONE

Carter had thought things couldn't get any weirder. These people worked for NASA? He wanted to laugh, but when he looked over at Lanh, he noticed his friend had a deadly serious look on his face. They stepped closer to one another.

Lanh was practically whispering. "Watch the guys in the back."

"Do you think they're going to try something?"

"Nah. But they're like . . . irritated. Restless even."

"Guess they were expecting someone else."

"Yeah, like maybe the cavalry. One keeps fiddling with his phone like he expects it to suddenly work. And they're surprised that we're armed. Who would be surprised about that?"

"Someone who . . ."

"Doesn't know."

"How can they *not* know? Everybody knows. They've been on planet Earth, haven't they?"

Gabe had backed up to confer with the rest of the group. "Thoughts?"

"I don't know exactly what's going on here." Patrick's eyes continued to scan the other side. "But there's one thing I'm sure of, and that is they are more confused than we are."

No one else had anything to add, so Gabe

stepped back to the fence and said, "I'm going to need to see your identification."

Paige bristled, but she pulled off a chain with dog tags, walked up to the gate, reached through, and dropped them into Gabe's hand. "That's all they let us keep."

Which Carter thought was a pretty strange thing to say.

Gabe glanced down at them and passed them to Patrick, who handed them back to Paige.

"I guess she is who she says she is," Patrick muttered.

"Who else would I be? Can you tell me what's going on here? Because I don't understand why your weapons are still pointed at us or what the problem is. A single phone call. That's all we need to make."

"One minute."

They all walked back to their vehicles.

"Those tags are legit," Patrick said.

"She could have stolen them." Max looked from Patrick to Gabe. "Can you make sense of what she's saying? Why wouldn't they know—"

"Because they've been inside there . . . whatever this place is . . . since before the flare." Shelby holstered her weapon. "It's the only thing that makes sense."

"Which makes no sense at all," Lanh said.

"So what do we do?" Bianca nodded toward the group. "They can't get out if we can't get in.

Give me a scenario where this is dangerous to us."

"Maybe they want our vehicles," Carter said.

"Possibly, but they look kind of . . . anemic." Patrick shrugged when they all stared at him. "Pale and soft. They're not a physical threat, that's for sure."

"And they don't appear to have any weapons." Carter could tell where this was leading, and he struggled with competing emotions. On the one hand, he was curious about what was on the other side of the fence. On the other hand, he wondered if they could have even one day where things went as planned. All they wanted was a bridge—a way out of Texas. Was that really too much to ask for?

"All right," Gabe said. "If we're agreed, then we hear their story and try to figure out what's going on."

"Are we going to stand here, talking through a gate?" Lanh switched his revolver to his left hand, clenched and unclenched his fist, which was when Carter realized that he had a death grip on his weapon as well.

"No, we're not. Patrick, Lanh, and Bianca, you're our best shots, so I want you standing left, right, and a little to the left of center and keeping a bead on our new friends. You see anything suspicious, you shoot. We didn't come this far to fall into a trap now. On the other hand, the thought that folks are stuck inside an enclosure . . . well, it doesn't sit well with me."

Patrick, Lanh, and Bianca moved into position.

"Max and Shelby, I want you two at the road, making sure no one approaches from that direction. Carter, you're with me."

"What are we going to do?"

"Break down that fence."

Once everyone was ready, Carter walked with Gabe up to the fence, where Paige Wakefield was still waiting.

"We're going to crash the gate," Gabe said.

"That's a military vehicle, and you're going to crash it through our gate?"

"Do you have another way for us to get you out of here?"

"No, but if you'll let us make a call maybe we can clear this all up." When Gabe shook his head, she added, "Who are you? And how did you get that Hummer?"

"Gabe Thompson, lieutenant colonel. I'm a doctor serving in the US Air Force."

"Okay. So if you weren't sent here to pick us up, why are you here?"

"That answer is complicated."

Paige glanced over at Patrick, Lanh, and Bianca, who were now holding their rifles in the ready position.

"Then what . . ."

"Look. We're a little vulnerable here."

"Vulnerable?"

"We'll answer all of your questions, but we

301

need to do this now and then pull back to a more concealed location."

Paige studied Gabe for less than ten seconds, glanced at Carter, and apparently made the decision to trust them.

She seemed to realize that the situation was much direr than she had thought. "What do you need us to do?"

"Move your group back away from the gate."

"All right."

"Once I'm through, my team will hold their position, and I'll remain in the Hummer. Carter is going to check each of you for weapons."

"We don't have any weapons."

"We need to check."

Paige crossed her arms and nodded. Then she rejoined her group and directed them to move away.

Gabe turned to Carter. "We've gone over this. You know how to check someone."

"Yeah."

"And, hopefully, they'd be less likely to shoot you if they are up to something."

"You sure about that?"

"Not entirely. Look, my gut tells me that they're exactly what they appear to be. Folks who for some reason have no idea what has happened in the last year. But we need to be sure and do this carefully. We need to do it by the book."

Carter looked at Patrick, Lanh, and Bianca.

They would have his back. "All right. How are you going to get through the gate?"

"The Hummer can handle the job, but I'd like to do it with a minimal amount of damage to the vehicle. I want you to line me up so that the grill is against the gate, and let's find something to put over the headlights so they won't be crushed."

"There's the grill."

"If one of the metal bars pop through, it could shatter a headlight. Let's not take the chance."

Carter ran to the cargo hold of the Hummer and pulled out two bedrolls.

"This good enough?"

"Better than nothing. Grab some bungee cords."

Together they fastened them around the front grill.

Gabe climbed into the Hummer and nudged the front bumper right up against the gate. When Carter gave him the go-ahead signal, he slowly accelerated. The gate groaned. The tires on the Hummer dug into the dirt road. Gabe gave the vehicle more gas, and the gates began to bend. Metal screeched against metal as the hinges twisted, and then the gates bulged open and the Hummer shot forward.

Carter ran through the opening. Paige had instructed her group to spread out in a line, facing Carter, hands raised. Slowly and methodically, he began to check them one by one for weapons.

FIFTY-TWO

Shelby and Max didn't move when they heard the gates cave in. Gabe had been clear that they were to hold their position until he whistled.

"This day keeps getting weirder and weirder," she said.

"I have a feeling that trend isn't going to change in the near future."

They were standing back-to-back, facing opposite directions.

No one had come down the road, but then there had been several turns on their way to this location. Anyone coming back this far would be lucky to find their way out. Max hadn't actually realized there were places in Texas still this remote—places all over the country, probably. Before the flare, those isolated locations had been connected via cell phones and computers if the people living there wanted to be. Now? Now secluded sections could easily be forgotten.

Gabe's whistle pulled Max from his thoughts. He and Shelby turned and jogged back to the group. Max glanced at her and realized there was no one else he'd rather go through an apocalyptic world with than Shelby Sparks. Then they came into sight of their group, and all other thoughts fled.

The gates were hanging on their hinges, the barbed wire at the top popped and drooping.

Gabe was out of the Hummer.

Bianca and Patrick and Lanh had put their rifles back in their pack, and Carter was standing with Paige's group.

"What now?" Max asked.

"We're heading to their camp." Gabe turned to Paige. "Right?"

"If that's what you want."

"How far is it?"

"A mile and a half."

Max and Shelby exchanged looks. "How big is this place?" he said, only loud enough for her to hear.

"Yeah, and why is it here?"

"Your group can fit in our vehicles," Gabe said.

"Thanks."

Everyone climbed in.

One of the group, a Caucasian man who looked way too young to be a doctor as he claimed, rode in the back of the Dodge, seated between Bianca and Carter.

"What were you all doing at the gate?" Shelby asked, turning toward the backseat to study him.

"Trying to get out. My name's Otis, by the way."

"Nice to meet you, Otis." Shelby introduced herself, as did everyone else.

"We'd walked down before," Otis continued.

"Yesterday morning. We were hoping to get out, but the access pad wasn't working. So we went back to camp and tried to assess the situation. It doesn't make sense, though. Why weren't we picked up? Where are the newspaper people? And why doesn't our vehicle work?"

When no one answered, he added, "I was looking forward to going home, to seeing my wife again."

"Where's home?" Bianca asked.

"Katy, west of Houston."

And then nobody spoke, because how do you explain to someone that home might not be there anymore?

They followed the dirt road through the trees, exactly one and a half miles as Paige had said. Max didn't know what he was expecting, but when the road curved and they pulled into a clearing, all he could do was stare, his mouth open and his mind trying to make sense of what he was seeing.

Otis leaned forward, staring with them at the two-story structure. "Welcome to the HAB."

Max had a dozen questions, but everyone else in their two groups was already approaching the structure, so he cut the engine, and they hurried to catch up.

They arrived as Gabe was asking, "You want to do this in there or out here?"

"Out here." Paige jabbed a thumb at the HAB.

"We've been in that thing a year, and I personally don't care if I never go in it again."

"All right."

They walked over to a clearing where workmen had apparently made seats out of the stumps of trees—trees that had probably been downed to make room for the HAB. Max wished for a legal pad to keep track of his growing list of questions. What was this place? Why was it here? Was what they were seeing the explanation for what Stu had heard about? Did it explain the trucks and construction and road crews?

But there was no road here, only the clearing and the domelike structure.

They each took a seat on the tree stumps. The March wind was light but pleasant. It was a perfect spring day, other than the fact that Max felt like he'd landed inside an Agatha Christie novel. All that was missing was the dead body.

Evidence of a campfire sat in the middle of the circle. Everyone took a seat, Paige's group on one side, Gabe's on the other. Together they made a motley group of twelve.

"As I said, I'm Paige Wakefield, the pilot and commander of this group." She pointed around the group. "That's Otis Marley, our physician."

Otis gave a small wave.

"Carol Donnally is our mechanical engineer." Carol was blond, petite, and didn't look old enough to have a college degree. She had a bracelet tattoo on her wrist inscribed with a guy's name.

"Kwan Lee is our aerospace engineer."

"And the old man of the group at thirty-eight."
Kwan bowed his head slightly.

"Janet Barnum is our psychologist."

Janet studied them behind designer glasses. She wore her long hair twisted into a knot with a pencil stabbed through it.

Max glanced at Shelby and knew that she was trying to piece this together as hard as he was. A pilot, physician, mechanical engineer, aerospace engineer, and psychologist. What could these five people possibly have been doing in that HAB for a year?

Paige sat down and waited. Max made the introductions on their side, keeping it to first names and no descriptions. Then he locked eyes with Gabe.

As though by silent agreement, Gabe broke the news. "On June 10, a solar flare knocked out the electrical grid."

There was silence for a good ten seconds. They were educated people. A thousand possibilities and probabilities would be spinning through their minds as they processed Gabe's information.

Paige recovered first. "How much of it?"

"All of it."

Everyone began hurtling questions at once. Gabe glanced at Max and shrugged. There was no easy way to do this.

"But . . . are you sure? Wait. That's a stupid question." Otis ran his hand through hair badly in need of a cut. "So you're saying the power is down, and that sections of it aren't operable even after nine months?"

"It's all down."

"All . . . over Texas?"

"According to the limited data we've managed to receive . . . all over the world." Gabe laced his fingers together, his elbows propped on his knees. "This is going to be hard for you to hear. Most of the urban centers across the country collapsed in the first few weeks. The Texas government put up a fight, backed by the Texas National Guard, but they lost Austin and have retreated to Corpus Christi. We think the federal government is still in existence, but our governor hasn't heard from them in months. Some cities . . ."

Gabe pulled in a deep breath, stared at the ground a moment, and Max realized how hard this must be for him. There were things that they didn't dwell on, that they avoided talking about. Now they were having to relive the last year in all its horrific entirety.

"We have it on good authority that some cities have been nuked. We do not have confirmation of that. What we do know is that there have been mass casualties from illness, starvation, and violence."

He stopped and waited.

And then Paige's group all started talking at once.

FIFTY-THREE

Carter couldn't imagine being slammed with end-of-the-world news all at once. Of course, it wasn't the end of the world, but for Paige and Otis's group, it must feel like it.

Paige held up a hand for quiet, and everyone settled down, which told Carter they were used to following her orders.

"Why should we believe you?"

"Why would I lie?"

She turned to Carol, the mechanical engineer. "What they're saying . . . would we have seen it in the HAB?"

"We only saw what they wanted us to see."

"Who is *they?*" Max asked.

Carter didn't think she would answer, but Paige said, "NASA. We were here on a special mission—" She broke off, staring at the HAB and then at her hands, trying to piece together what had happened, trying to come to terms with their new reality.

"That's a biodome. It's a Mars habitation unit. You were here to, like . . . practice." Carter couldn't resist. It was so cool that he was sitting in front of an actual habitation unit, a Mars simulation facility. He'd only read about such things and seen a few in movies.

"Yeah, it is. Our mission began on March nineteenth . . ."

"A year ago yesterday." Bianca shook her head in disbelief.

Lanh leaned forward, like he couldn't believe what he was hearing. "You were in that thing for a year?"

"Yes. We didn't step out of it until yesterday. Normally, there would be people to greet us when the mission ended. People from our research team, news reporters, maybe even family members."

Carter tried to imagine the disappointment they must have felt, but he couldn't. Everyone in his group, everyone he knew, had learned to live with disappointment in the last nine months. It had become a way of life, but these people were optimistic a few hours ago, thinking there had been a simple glitch in their schedule. They couldn't have imagined how the world had changed.

"No one contacted you?" Shelby asked, and then she pressed her palm against her forehead. "Stupid question. How would they have called you? Of course they didn't."

"But you knew." Bianca turned to Gabe. "I mean, the government knew. That's what you told us back in Austin, right?"

"Our task group knew. The entire military didn't, and you have to imagine what those hours preceding the flare were like. It was complete chaos, with people scrambling to back up data and take systems off-line before they fried." He nodded toward Paige. "It's entirely possible that NASA forgot about you."

"Forgot about us?" Kwan asked. "This would not happen. My family would be here. They would come looking for me."

"Except the exact location was a secret," Otis reminded him.

"And there isn't any transportation to speak of. Some of the cars work, but it's hard to find fuel." Carter regretted the words as soon as they left his mouth. These people didn't need any more bad news. But then again, they'd already been shielded from it for too long.

Paige jumped up and began pacing back and forth. "They would not forget us. My crew gave up a year of their life to sit inside that sophisticated tent so they could study us like lab rats."

She threw an accusing look at Janet.

"Hey. I was in there too. I was forgotten too. Don't blame me."

Paige was on a roll now. "Why did we do it? So they could read our vitals and our journals and our video logs. So they could assess whether crew members would kill each other if they were forced to live together in a tight space for a year. So we could see if it's even possible . . .

psychologically . . . to send a person to Mars. Now you're telling me that while we were in there, the entire world has—"

She stopped, unable to find a word to encompass what she'd learned.

"Changed," Shelby said. "The entire world has changed."

"What about our families?" Otis asked.

Carter noticed that Carol stared at her wrist and ran her finger over the tattoo while blinking back tears.

He suddenly felt bad—that gut-wrenching type of remorse you experienced when someone else was hurting but you couldn't do a thing to help them.

"They might be fine," Patrick said. "Lots of folks managed to escape the cities. As for rural towns . . . there has been trouble, but we've also learned to pull together."

Kwan Lee jumped up. "I need to check something." Without another word, he hurried into the HAB.

Gabe nodded toward the man's receding back. "Aerospace engineer, right?"

"Yeah." Paige glared at the HAB. "He's sort of our diagnostician."

The group continued to pepper Gabe with questions.

After five minutes, Kwan came back out, holding a notebook in his hand, which he dropped into Paige's lap. "There. June 10, just like he said. We lost all power for the night . . ."

"We thought it was a test," Carol said. "We assumed NASA was putting us through the wringer."

"But it was real." Kwan walked slowly back to where he'd been sitting.

"You climbed to the top of the HAB and replaced the solar cells." Otis ran a hand up and over the top of his head. "I thought you'd fall, and then I'd be setting broken bones. That was the worst thing I could imagine happening to us."

"Why didn't it fry everything?" Patrick asked. "Not just solar cells, but all of your circuitry boards—they should have been toast. Everything out here was."

"This thing is like a giant Faraday cage. It's built to withstand solar storms from space. The better question is, why did those solar cells fry? They weren't supposed to."

"You replaced them." Paige was reading through the logbook, turning the page, and then closing it. "You replaced them, and we thought it was a test."

"You couldn't have known," Gabe assured her. "How could you if no one told you? There were plenty of people in high positions who were caught unaware. Some because they didn't want to believe what they were being told. Others because they had incomplete information. You

314

had incomplete information. How could you have come to the right conclusion?"

Which seemed to sum things up.

Paige stood and said, "We need a few minutes. Time to digest this and . . . decide what we do next."

"Fair enough," Gabe said. "But it'll be dark in a couple of hours. We either need to leave now or camp here for the night. We try not to travel after dark."

"Because?"

And Carter knew in that moment that they still didn't understand what the world was like now. How could they? He wouldn't have believed it if he hadn't seen it with his own eyes.

Gabe's voice, when he answered, was softer—gentle almost. "Because it's not safe."

FIFTY-FOUR

They spent what remained of the afternoon repacking their vehicles so that they could fit five extra passengers. Paige's group shut down the HAB and pulled what they needed into go bags. Dinner was MREs—some from the HAB and others from Gabe's supply—shared between the groups so they at least had some variety while eating around the campfire.

As they ate, Paige's group would occasionally throw out a question.

What was Austin like?

Where were they going to look for the federal government?

Did they know anyone personally who had died?

Shelby glanced at Carter, saw a sadness creep into his eyes.

But then someone else asked what they'd eaten, which led to stories of squirrel stew and fried nutria. Soon everyone was proclaiming what they wouldn't eat and what tasted like chicken.

Paige didn't participate much in the discussion, and Shelby felt herself wondering what she was worrying about most. Did she have children? A husband? Elderly parents? The commander stood, excused herself, and walked away from the group.

"I'm going to talk to her."

"Maybe you should give her some time," Max said.

"Yeah. The problem is, we don't have time . . . none of us do. They've pulled their stuff together, but I don't think she's convinced they should go with us."

"They could try to walk south."

"To NASA? How far do you think that is?"

Max scraped one last spoonful of spaghetti out of his MRE. "Four, maybe five hundred miles, depending if they went through Houston or around it."

"They have no idea what it's like out there."

"Probably not."

"So we have to convince them. I don't know where they need to go, but they do not need to be on the open road walking across the state of Texas."

"What are you going to say to her?"

"I don't know. I have a feeling that the rest of the group will follow her lead. One thing is for certain. She's going to have to make a decision by sunrise."

She gave Max's shoulder a squeeze and then followed Paige to the banks of the Red River. The bridge—the thing they'd been looking for high and low, far and wide—gleamed in the moonlight. It was imperative that the location be secret so that the group wouldn't be bothered by news columnists or bloggers or conspiracy theorists. Land had been purchased years before, but they needed a back way in. Most of the supplies had come from manufacturing centers in the north. They didn't want to go through Wichita Falls or any town that size or larger. So the persons in charge of this project had built a bridge in the middle of nowhere, with a dirt road stretching out from both ends, installed a fence and security cameras around the perimeter, tucked their guinea pigs into the HAB unit, and walked away.

Shelby had a hard time conceiving a secret government project big enough to move the HAB unit, all of its high-tech equipment, and everything five people would need to survive for a year. But she couldn't deny the fact of the giant dome behind her, the group of five, or the bridge gleaming in the moonlight. As bizarre as this situation was, she wasn't dreaming it. Shelby stared at the bridge a minute, and then she walked toward Paige, picking her way carefully across the overgrown bank.

"If you want to be alone, I'll go."

She thought Paige would take her up on that, but then she motioned to the rock next to where she was sitting. "Suit yourself."

They sat in the quiet for a moment.

Shelby said, "I can't imagine how they built that bridge without anyone knowing."

"The government can do a lot of things in secret if they set their mind to it."

"Apparently."

"There's no telling how many secret bridges have been built, or underground shelters, or domes . . ." She turned to study Shelby in the moonlight. "We might not have been the only Mars HAB."

"I hadn't thought of that."

"Other mission teams might have started earlier than us, or later. They might step out of their dome in a week or a month and, like us, have no idea they're walking into a completely different world."

Shelby considered that a minute and tried to imagine it in light of all she'd seen since that fateful day in June. "In some ways, you're right, of course. It is a different world, but in other ways, a lot of things are the same."

"Like what?"

"There are still good people and bad people." Shelby told her briefly about Hugo and his crew, and then about Mary Jane and Stu.

"If you hadn't helped them, you wouldn't have stumbled upon us."

"That's true. We'd be driving to New Mexico instead, looking for a route around the Red River."

"And if we hadn't walked up to the gate as your boyfriend . . ."

Shelby thought about correcting her but let it slide.

"Was driving away, if he hadn't looked up and seen us, if he hadn't stopped . . ."

"Don't spend too much time on the what-ifs. That can make you crazy."

"Sounds like you speak from experience."

"I do." Shelby started to explain about Carter but decided it wouldn't help the woman sitting in front of her one bit. "Look. You're a pilot, and I'm a novelist. Well, I was a novelist before this happened. So we're two very different people, but in other ways I think we must be a lot alike."

"Such as?"

"I suspect there's someone back home you're worried about."

"Yeah, I am."

"And I imagine you'd do anything to get to them, to make sure they're okay."

"That's true. But the thing is, those people back there sitting around the fire are my crew. I have an allegiance to them too. My world has tilted, and I'm being pulled in two opposite directions."

Shelby took in a deep breath, glanced again at the bridge, and then crossed her arms. "You sort of learn to live with that feeling. Our group is very . . . tight, but we aren't always able to be together. Gabe had to leave for a while, and to tell you the truth, I didn't think I'd miss him."

Shelby laughed at that memory, of her worries

over what he'd buried in Max's backyard, of her insistence he wasn't who he seemed to be. Well, she'd been right, but she hadn't considered that maybe *what*—no, *who*—he actually was might be even better than she'd imagined.

"Patrick stayed back in Austin. He stayed there because he sacrificed himself for my son, for Carter. I thought having to leave him would tear my heart in two. I thought the agony I felt would never mend, but it did. And when he came back? Well, that was a joy I can't begin to describe."

"But some didn't come back, right?"

Shelby thought of Kaitlyn, Bianca's parents, her neighbor who had been killed in the first week by a carjacker. "Yeah, some didn't come back."

They sat together in silence, the moon rising over the bridge that would take them to Oklahoma, which would lead them to Kansas and maybe the federal government. Ultimately, it was the road that would lead them home, one way or the other. And they'd found it because they'd transported Mary Jo to her son, because they'd helped fulfill a dying woman's last wish. Fate or luck or God's hand? Shelby wasn't sure, but she was willing to start believing in the latter.

She stood and turned to go, but then she turned back, walked over to Paige, and said what had been on her heart since she'd left the campfire.

"In this world, your first allegiance is to your

family. Maybe that's the way life has always been, but we forgot. Then friends, and at the end of the line those institutions you still believe in."

Paige shook her head. "I'm a scientist. I don't know how to live in a world without computers or jets or space programs."

"I'm a writer. I doubt any publishing contracts are going to be coming my way anytime soon." She thought of the journal in her backpack, and the ones she'd filled that were stored back at home. She thought of her tub of blank paper. What would she do when that was gone? How would she record their story then?

"Being a scientist or writer, that's what we did. It isn't who we were, and it's sure not who we are."

She walked back to the campfire and settled into her place between Max and Bianca. Carter and Lanh were walking toward the HAB with Otis. She'd heard the doctor say that the dome was twenty feet tall and thirty-six feet wide. It was difficult to imagine five people living in it for a year. The top secret project wasn't top secret anymore. Carter glanced back once, and the look on his face was pure joy.

"Let him enjoy this moment, Mom." Max reached over and entwined his fingers with hers, pulling her hand into his lap. "Both Carter and Lanh are such a mixture of the old world and the new."

Which stirred a hidden ache in her heart. One of the many worries she tried not to dwell on was whether Carter's generation fit in anywhere. Would they ever know happiness like she had known—living in their little house in Abney, writing romance stories, and living her life day by day? Then she looked around her, at Bianca sitting in the circle of Patrick's arms, Gabe playing chess with Janet, the boys entering the HAB, and her hand clasped inside of Max's. And she realized in that moment that she was probably happier than she had been before, more content, more in the moment than maybe she had ever been in her entire life.

The flare had taken so much from them, but it had also shown them a new way of living.

FIFTY-FIVE

With some creative packing, they managed to fit everyone into the three vehicles. Max couldn't even open the tailgate of the Dodge, which had been crumpled by one of the falling trees during the tornado. The cargo area, fortunately, was undamaged. They were able to stack most of the supplies from his second seat and Patrick's backseat there, which left room for extra passengers.

Patrick had spent a good hour the day before looking at the HAB team's one Suburban. "Nah. This isn't going to work. All the circuits are fried."

They had siphoned the fuel out of the vehicle and put it into one of their cans. They'd only use it in an emergency because it had been sitting in the Suburban's tank for a year.

One last look around the HAB, and Paige had declared them ready to go.

"I can't believe we're actually driving across a bridge," Shelby said as they pulled away from the clearing.

"And no one's shooting at us or demanding a toll." Max meant it as a joke, but glancing into the backseat, he saw Carol, Otis, and Kwan exchanging concerned looks.

"Don't worry, guys."

"You've been shot at?"

"Several times," Shelby admitted. "But mostly we try to avoid those situations."

Max could tell they weren't convinced, so he added, "We've been on the road a few times. Nothing's foolproof, but we've developed procedures to scope out an area before we enter it."

"What did you do . . . before?" Carol asked. "For a living, I mean."

"Lawyer."

No one answered that for a few minutes, and then Kwan said, "You are unemployed too, Max. Same as me. In this new world, no need for lawyers or aerospace engineers."

He had a point. Carol would be valuable in any community. A mechanical engineer could be a real asset. Otis would have more work than he could handle, no matter where he ended up. Probably he didn't realize that many people were seen by veterinarians rather than actual MDs. But Kwan would have to find a new way to contribute.

"You're a bright guy. I'm sure that wherever you end up, they will be glad you're there. That's one thing about this new world. Good workers are hard to come by and highly valued."

They reached a perimeter fence like the one on the Texas side, and once again Gabe busted it open with the Hummer. After that, the Oklahoma countryside looked exactly like what they'd left behind them in Texas. The primary difference was that once they'd made their way to the main road, it was clear.

No barricades.

No makeshift tollbooths.

No goons with guns—at least not that they could see.

"Looks pretty deserted," Max said.

"Because no one can get across," Shelby murmured.

They stayed on the interstate as long as they dared, skirting Lawton and only changing to secondary roads ten miles south of Interstate 40. There were plenty of abandoned cars and looted stores, but they saw very few people and then only from a distance.

"Shame we can't go into Oklahoma City," Otis said. "There's bound to be people there—people we could help as well as people who can help us."

"It's best to avoid the downtown areas. In Austin, the gangs took over pretty quickly. Plus, it's easy to get boxed in, and then you can land in real trouble." Max glanced at Shelby, who was staring out the window. "We've done it before, and it didn't end well."

Ten minutes later they passed the scene of a gunfight—three vehicles riddled with bullets straddling across the median. No one suggested stopping after that.

By midmorning, they had found the fuel dump on Gabe's map. They pulled up to a gate, and Gabe thumbed in a combination on an old-fashioned lock. After all three vehicles drove inside, Gabe relocked the gate. The fuel was stored a quarter mile back, hidden behind a stand of cedar trees.

They quickly filled up all three vehicles.

"Tell me again how the government happens to have fuel dumps." Janet frowned at the large tanks.

Max had never spent much time around psychologists, other than the few that had testified in trials he'd been involved in. He kept expecting her to ask someone, "How do you feel?" but Janet seemed to realize that those questions were moot. Feelings came second to survival, and survival took every ounce of energy and all of their attention.

"If you can store fuel, surely you can store food and medicine and anything else people would need," she said.

If Max had to guess, he'd say the tanks held three thousand gallons each, and there were twenty of them. It wouldn't last until the refineries came back online, if they ever came back online, but given how few people were actually on the road and how few had access to the tanks, they would last a while.

"I'm sure the government has stored food and medicine someplace. Supplies didn't disappear the day after the flare hit."

"Then why store it? Why keep it . . ." She ran a hand through her hair in frustration. "Why keep it here when people out there need it?"

"There's not enough for the entire population," Gabe said, walking over to join the two of them. "But the goal, as far as I understand it, is to provide continuity of government."

"Explain that to me."

"They have to keep some corridors of transportation open, and the only way to do that was with strategic fuel dumps."

Max watched her struggle with the difference between her ideas of what was right and the reality of the world around her. He knew from experience the new way of things was something that would take time to accept.

When the refueling was finished, Paige's people bunched together, watching their group as they lined up in front of their vehicles. It was strange, but to Max it seemed he'd known them for years rather than twenty-four hours.

For an awkward moment, no one knew what to say.

"You're just going to wait here?" Carter peered left then right, comically searching for the travel bus that would pop out of a clump of trees, causing several in Paige's group to laugh.

"Good to see the younger generation is worried about us." Otis clasped him on the shoulder. "We'll be fine. We have a week's worth of food, and we can hunt nutria if we run out."

Lanh groaned and held his stomach. "The stew was seriously gross. You don't want to eat that."

"You told my mom you liked it," Max teased.

"Well, yeah. I said that, but it was terrible."

Patrick walked up to Paige. "Keep a guard near the gate, and set up your camp back behind those trees."

"Have you always been this cautious?"

"He has." Bianca tucked her arm into his. "He was this way before the flare, and being married to me for a week hasn't changed a thing."

Patrick wasn't having any of the bantering. "Better careful than dead."

Which pretty much sucked any humor out of the situation.

"Someone will be by. Someone who is headed south," Gabe assured her. "Once you're sure they are military or government, come out with your hands up and no weapons. Show them your tags, and give their commander this."

He handed her a sheet of paper.

"You wrote them a reference letter?" Max asked.

"Yeah, and I had to beg Shelby to tear a sheet of paper out of her journal."

"Scarce commodity." Shelby shrugged. "But given the situation, I was happy to do it."

Max was once again the last in line as they pulled out. He glanced in his side-view mirror, as he had before, and saw the five standing in a line, waving goodbye.

"Good people," he murmured.

"What makes you so sure?" Shelby held up her hand to stop his argument. "I agree with you, but I was wondering if your reasons are the same as mine."

"They sacrificed a year of their lives to advance our scientific knowledge."

"True, though they were probably compensated handsomely."

"Probably they were supposed to be, but I doubt they'll have a check waiting at home—if they make it home."

"Maybe they received some up front, sort of like an advance on a novel. Hopefully, it was something their families used to buy supplies while there still were supplies."

It still amazed Max that currency had lost all value so quickly. But when there was nothing to purchase, then money, especially paper money, was only worth . . . well, it was only worth paper.

"What else?" she asked, warming to her topic.

More details for her journal no doubt, or perhaps it was simply good to speak freely again. Max was suddenly aware that he'd monitored what he was saying so as not to panic the group, not give them more information than they could handle, not give them more information than they needed. No one had mentioned the Remnant. Should they have?

"No one panicked," he said. "When Gabe first busted through the gate, no one tried to run or overpower us and take our vehicles . . ."

"No one in that group weighed more than one hundred and forty. Shows you the effect of a year of MREs."

"Complaining about the food again, Sparks?"

"We seriously need to get back to your mother's cooking."

It was good to hear her talk about High Fields as though it were her home. It was her home, and Max couldn't get back there fast enough.

They wound their way back to the highway. Their plan was to continue on the small highways west of I-35, detouring where necessary to skirt places like Hennessey and Enid. Even allowing for their ongoing caution and the occasional roadblock, it was conceivable that they could be in Kansas by nightfall.

"What about you?" he asked. "Why did you decide they were good people?"

She finger combed her hair back behind her ears and stared out the window. He didn't think she would answer, and then she turned to him and said, "It was the way they treated one another. Did you see the way that Otis sat with Carol

331

when she started crying? Obviously, she had a boyfriend or husband back home . . ."

"I noticed the tattoo."

"He was more concerned about her than how they would travel back to NASA."

"He put the health of his crew first."

"Exactly." Shelby's head bobbed in agreement. "And Kwan. He was great with the boys."

"Carter and Lanh are going to be talking about the HAB for weeks."

"Carol took the blame for not noticing the flare when clearly it wasn't her fault."

"You're right. It was obvious that they had formed a supportive group."

Shelby sighed. "They would have made a good Martian crew."

"That's on hold for a while." He added as an afterthought, "Even Janet seemed to loosen up last night, which I didn't think was possible for a psychologist."

"But it was Paige that convinced me. The way she led her team. The way they followed her." Shelby found the lever under the seat and pushed it back, then propped her feet up on the dash.

He started to warn her that it wasn't a safe position, but she suddenly reminded him of the Shelby who had ridden in his truck when he was seventeen. She'd been every bit as beautiful then, every inch as smart and caring and dear to him, but he hadn't known it. He'd been a kid trying to become a man, and he hadn't realized what he walked away from when he moved to Austin and never called her.

"Teams are made up of good people who care about one another."

He felt a lump in his throat, swallowed, and tried to focus on what she was saying. "Like us."

"Exactly."

FIFTY-SIX

They crossed into Kansas an hour before sunset and slowed a couple miles past the border at Caldwell. Their road went straight through a small downtown area. Max braked slightly as they passed under a large metal sign that arched over the street, proudly proclaiming the town's name and population.

"What do they do if someone is born or dies?" Shelby asked.

"Maybe the metal sign supplier is the mayor's brother."

The place seemed deserted at first glance. A banner hung across the chamber office: "A great place to visit . . . an even better place to call home."

"Seems friendly enough."

"Most places were."

Shelby saw another flyer posted to several of the buildings—a large group of people posing under the arched sign, dressed in western costume. "I guess they had some sort of western show."

"Chances are it's closed." He smiled when she gave him a reproving look. "Sorry. Long day."

"Seems deserted now, but it's strange that none of the buildings look looted. No smashed windows. No graffiti. It's more like everyone simply left." As she said that, Shelby caught movement behind a curtain on the second floor of the bank.

"Someone's home," she said. She picked up her radio and alerted the others.

Patrick responded first. "It would be nice to ask someone the lay of the land."

Carter relayed Gabe's response. "Continue up to the next crossroad. If you notice anything suspicious, keep going. Otherwise, we'll stop there and see if they come to us."

The crossroad was a good idea. They'd have escape routes in four directions.

But their paranoia was unfounded. They parked in the middle of the intersection, their cars bumper to bumper. Each person of their group stepped out of their vehicle wearing their pack, but no one reached for a weapon. No need to scare the locals. It was plain enough that they were well supplied and could defend themselves if they needed to.

Shelby raised her face to the sun, which was dipping toward the western horizon. White clouds scudded across the sky, and the day was pleasantly warm—more so than she had expected it to be.

"Someone's coming," Gabe said.

He took the point position, and the rest of the group divided into pairs and covered the other three directions.

The welcome committee consisted of a woman and a man. Shelby tried to keep her attention on the road in front of them, the one heading west, but she had to stifle a laugh when she caught a closer look at the couple walking toward Gabe.

She nudged Max, jerked her head toward them, and was rewarded with a smile and a tip of his hat.

"Annie, get your gun," he murmured.

The woman was a dead ringer for Annie Oakley. Her long, wavy hair spilled over her shoulders. She wore a fringed suede jacket, leather chaps, and brown boots with more fringe. The only thing missing, quite conspicuously, was a shotgun or rifle. The man was wearing a black suit and a black cowboy hat. Both looked to be in their early fifties—gray sprinkled throughout their brown hair, but they seemed physically fit.

"We are unarmed," the woman said. "But our best shooter is watching you through a scope on the second floor of that building."

She nodded toward the town library, which was small but two stories.

"We're only passing through," Gabe assured her.

"Don't see many folks nowadays, and none driving a Hummer." This from the man, who fiddled with a chain that appeared to be attached to a pocket watch.

"What are they usually driving?"

The woman took over the conversation. "Pickups,

336

Volkswagens, four-wheelers, even horses. Never had a Hummer come through before. Where y'all from?"

"Texas."

"Long way." The man stepped to the right and closer to their vehicles.

Patrick immediately blocked his path.

"No offense, mister. Just checking out your rides."

"Have you seen any military vehicles pass through here?"

"We have not. Most folks take the I-35 route, same as before the flare."

"It's open?"

The woman shrugged. "Haven't seen it myself."

The man reached into a small front pocket on his pants, snapping his hands up, palms out when Patrick pulled his firearm. "I was only reaching for my watch, young man. No need to get twitchy."

Patrick nodded for him to go ahead. Shelby had walked a few feet away from Max now and was directly watching the man and woman. There was something odd about them. What they were wearing—their clothes looked like one of the costumes from the flyer taped to the shop windows.

The man pulled out a pocket watch. Sunlight glinted off gold. He thumbed it open. "It'll be dark in forty-five minutes. Wouldn't advise continuing north once the sun has set."

"Do you know of any specific threats, places we should avoid?"

"Every place is a threat," the woman said. "You could be a threat."

"But we're not."

Shelby was still focused on the couple, and then movement across the street caught her eye. Behind a window, she briefly saw a woman in a red velvet dress. A man in a starched white shirt and black vest—that was all she saw of him—pulled the woman back from view.

"We'll be on our way if you'd rather." Gabe took a step back toward their vehicles. "We only wanted information."

"Information isn't free." This from the woman. "You have something to trade?"

"We don't," Gabe said.

The woman's lips formed a thin red line, which was when Shelby realized she was wearing lipstick. When was the last time she'd seen that? Probably the day before the flare.

The man seemed less hostile than the woman. "Kansas has its share of bandits, if that's what you're asking. Some were born mean, and others became that way after the flare."

"Your town seems to have held up pretty well. The buildings are still intact."

"Because we don't abide outlaws or strangers." The man returned his watch to his pocket.

"We'll be on our way, then."

Gabe whistled once, and they all moved back toward their vehicles. Shelby was opening the door to the Dodge when the man in the suit called out to Gabe. "There's a place just out of town, a mile and a half on the right. Used to be an RV park back when we had tourists here. Had us a Wild West show and everything . . ."

"They don't need the chamber speech, Ryder."

He shrugged. "It's a good place to stop for a night. Thought they might want to know."

The two turned to walk away, not bothering to look back at them.

Shelby buckled up as Max started the engine. "Something about those two doesn't seem right."

"Was it their clothing that tipped you off?"

"They didn't ask where we were going or if we had information. Everyone wants information, but they didn't. Though she did say . . . what was it? *Information isn't free.*"

"They seemed interested in our supplies. Other than that, they just wanted us gone."

"Wish granted." Shelby paused, wondering if it was silly to mention it, and finally told him about the other two people she'd seen in the window.

"Red velvet? You're sure?"

"Yeah. I'm sure. The sun was popping through that window, and I could see her plain as day."

"You couldn't have seen that the man's shirt was starched. Unless you've developed eagle eyes in the last hour."

"Starched shirts look different, Max. They look—more stiff. Anyway, that's not the point. Why were they dressed like that? Why were they watching us? And where was the rest of the Wild West crew?"

But Max didn't have any answers to those questions.

They ended up passing the RV park in case it was a trap and stopping a few miles down the road where there was a pullout into a rest area. There were no facilities, but a half dozen picnic tables and grills were spread across the area.

"Good as anywhere," Patrick said. "And we're on a hilltop, so we can see if that couple comes after us."

Everyone laughed, but they were all uneasy.

The sooner they put Caldwell behind them, the better.

FIFTY-SEVEN

The temperature didn't drop that much overnight, but the wind turned and was now blowing from the north. Carter hated a north wind. It caused the fillings in his teeth to ache, and he wasn't old enough to have those kinds of complaints. Plus, there was the fact that they were headed north, so their gas mileage would be lower.

"The direction of the wind?" Bianca smiled as she stuffed her bedroll into its bag. "Out of our hands, *hijo*. Completely out of our hands."

No one had slept well. Before calling it a night, they'd joked about the creepy couple, but no one could say exactly what had bothered them. It was more a sense—a sixth sense they'd developed since the flare. Patrick called it survival instinct. They'd decided on two guards who would swap off every three hours. Gabe would act as a third the last hour of every shift.

"We've been traumatized," Lanh muttered as they stored their bedrolls in the back of the Hummer. "We jump at shadows now, but yeah . . . those people bothered me too. Why even come down to talk to us? And those clothes were not normal. They were making a statement or something. Not cool whatever they were up to."

"Maybe they just had strange tastes."

"And what was with that pocket watch? I think it was a signal of some sort, when he took the watch out."

"Maybe you've read too many spy novels," Shelby suggested.

"Or maybe he has a point." Gabe added his bedroll next to the others. "Let's not stick around long enough to find out."

The sky had barely lightened at all, and the sun wouldn't be fully up for another hour. As they pulled out of the rest area, Gabe led, Max followed, and Patrick brought up the rear.

They kept their lights off and turned back onto the main road. Carter wasn't sure exactly where the Flint Hills started, but he could tell they were close. The landscape rose slightly before falling away. There were very few crossroads and no gas stations or convenience stores. It was as though they'd left real civilization at the Oklahoma state line.

The road continued north, curving slightly to the east and then back north as they headed toward the Chikaskia River.

They were veering left, out of the curve, when spotlights in front of them lit up everything in the Hummer, effectively blinding them.

"Hang on," Gabe hollered, gunning the Hummer's engine. He didn't veer from the lights, but rather accelerated toward them.

"We're going to hit them," Lanh screamed.

Carter turned in his seat and glanced back in time to see a monster truck broadside the Dodge. Metal grated against metal and the truck slammed on its brakes as the Dodge flipped into a roll and slid off the road. His heart leapt into his throat, his pulse rate spiked, and he shouted, "They're hit! Mom and Max—"

The Hummer headed full speed toward the lights—toward something and someone who wanted to hurt them. It was an ambush, and his mom . . .

The engine roared, and Gabe shouted, "Brace yourself."

But at the last second, the lights veered away, taking off across the hills.

Gabe hit the brakes hard, sending the Hummer into a spin.

Carter lunged for the grab bar, his seat belt locking and pinning him back. He glimpsed the hills and the lightening sky and the fleeing Suburban as they turned round and round, and he smelled burning rubber. Gabe was still working the wheel, pumping the brakes, trying to keep them on the road. They came to a stop facing slightly east. Gabe wrenched the wheel to the right and tapped the accelerator. They were now pointed back the way they'd come.

"Get your weapons," he muttered and flipped on the headlights.

Carter felt like a knife had been plunged into

his chest. The monster truck had come to a stop by the Dodge, which had rolled but was now right side up.

"I can't see my mom or Max."

Another vehicle's engine screeched, and Lanh twisted around in his seat. "It's a tanker, headed straight for Patrick and Bianca."

But Carter saw immediately that Patrick and Bianca were no longer in the Mustang. They'd left the vehicle and had taken up a position on the side of the road, their rifles raised. The Mustang idled in the middle of the road, the passenger door open.

As the tanker truck accelerated—its occupants apparently unaware that their target was now empty—both Bianca and Patrick fired on it.

Meanwhile, Gabe accelerated toward the monster truck.

The tanker veered off course, sideswiped the Mustang, and came to rest ten yards down the road.

By this time the driver of the monster truck had figured out what was happening. He was big—Carter had a good view of how big as they hurtled toward him, and he was wearing a white shirt and a black vest. Not exactly normal attire for a carjacking or whatever this was.

The pickup looked like it had been modified to compete in a truck rally. It was at least twelve feet tall. The wheels were huge off-road things.

Sitting next to the Dodge, it looked like a giant beside a matchbox car.

Carter made out another person in the vehicle as they sped toward it.

"It's her. The lady we saw yesterday." His anger spiked, even as he wondered if his mom and Max were hurt. How could these people do this? Why would they do it?

The driver slammed the truck into reverse and floored it, eventually spinning toward the opposite direction, and speeding south toward Caldwell, staying off road. The last thing Carter saw of the passenger was a fringed leather jacket.

"We can catch them," Lanh said.

"We have to check on my mom and Max."

Gabe jerked the Hummer to a stop beside the Dodge, and they all tumbled out.

FIFTY-EIGHT

Max's mind flashed back over the previous three minutes, trying to make sense of what had happened. He'd thought they were going to die.

Somehow they'd survived the initial hit and the roll, but then he'd seen the monster truck trundling toward them. He'd tried to reach for his pistol, but the seat belt had locked and was pinning him to the seat. Not to mention the top of the Dodge was now mere inches from his head. At least they were sitting right side up.

"You okay?" Shelby asked.

When he turned toward her, he very nearly panicked. There was blood running down her face, glass sprinkled in her hair, and her eyes were wide with shock.

"We need our guns." She was able to squirm out of her seat belt, reach into her pack, and pull out her knife. "What is happening?"

"Ambush." His tongue felt swollen, and he thought a tooth might be loose. He turned his head left and spit out blood.

Shelby's hand shook as she opened the blade, slipped it under his seat belt, and yanked up.

"Get your weapon and get down." He had little chance of fitting into the floorboard area himself, but Shelby was small. There was a chance

346

that crouching in front of her seat could save her.

He looked right and saw the enormous wheels of the Monster truck. It was the perfect off-road vehicle—perfect for an ambush, other than the fact that it must guzzle gas worse than a Cadillac. The truck screeched to a stop, but the driver kept the engine running.

Max heard rifle shots, the scream of metal against metal, and then the engine of the Hummer.

"Get down now!"

Someone in the Monster truck fired one shot down and through the front windshield. It pierced the glass, went through the back of Shelby's seat, and lodged somewhere in the back of the Dodge. The driver of the truck threw it into reverse and sped away.

Then Carter and Lanh and Gabe were surrounding the vehicle and wrenching open the doors.

"Are you okay? You're bleeding." Carter pulled Shelby from the passenger's side, held her at arm's length, and wiped the blood out of her eyes with the palm of his hand. "I was so scared. I thought . . . I thought . . ."

"I'm okay, Carter. It's just a cut."

"Max?" Gabe asked.

"Bruised shoulder, maybe a sprained wrist. I'm fine. Patrick and Bianca?"

Max looked up to see them jogging toward them. "You two okay?"

"We look better than you do," Bianca said.

Patrick continued to scan left and right as he spoke to them. "Area seems to be clear, but I suggest we put as much distance as we can between us and them."

"See if it will start," Gabe said. Miraculously, it did, but Max wouldn't be able to see out of the front windshield, which had spidered badly.

"Stand back." Patrick took the butt of his pistol and slammed it into the middle of the wind-shield. It shattered into a thousand pieces. "Carter and Lanh, put on your gloves and clean out as much of that as you can."

Gabe had already run to the Hummer and returned with a roll of gauze. He wrapped it around Shelby's head. "This will stop the bleeding. We'll clean it when we're in a safe location."

"Mustang?" Lanh asked.

"It'll take more than a glancing blow from a tanker to stop her."

"All right." Gabe turned slowly in a circle, spied the tanker across the road. "Anyone alive in there?"

One jerk of Bianca's head said it all.

"Let's go then. Tight formation. We don't stop for twenty miles for any reason."

"Be careful." Carter squeezed Shelby's arms, nodded at Max, and then jogged after Gabe.

Max and Shelby got back into the Dodge.

They were silent the first few miles, the wind whistling through the front windshield.

"Were you scared?" Shelby asked.

"Terrified."

"Me too."

He almost let it slide, let her believe that he was talking about what she was talking about. But they'd had too many close calls, too many brushes with death. Something whispered to his heart, *Tell her now while you can.*

He cleared his throat. "Not of the truck, though I can't imagine where they got that thing."

"They were . . . they acted like they were in a Wild West show, like the posters." She put her head back against the headrest and closed her eyes. Even with the trail of blood down her cheek, the gauze wrapped around her head, and her black curls resembling Medusa, Shelby Sparks was the most beautiful woman he'd ever seen, ever known, ever would know.

"They played us," she continued. "They knew we'd have to stop close by even if we didn't take their suggestion about the RV park. They traveled past us, or around, in the night. And then they waited until we were in that turn— the perfect ambush spot. A gunfight would have been more honorable, but instead they waylaid us. Yeah, it was terrifying."

Max cleared his throat. "It was, but that wasn't

what I meant. I wasn't . . . didn't have time to be afraid of *them*."

She cocked her head, waited.

"We can stand our ground against most people. Maybe I'm numb, but it's just another . . . another obstacle to overcome. Outthink them. Outplay them. But when I lost control of the car? When we were rolling over, and I couldn't . . ."

Tears welled up in his eyes, and he brushed them away with his sleeve and forced himself to look at this precious, marvelous woman sitting next to him. "When I realized that I might lose you, that this might be the last day we spent together . . . I've never known fear like that."

Shelby didn't have an answer to his confession. She locked eyes with him, hers large and impossible to read, and then she reached out, pulled his hand into her lap, and interlaced her fingers with his.

FIFTY-NINE

They were a ragtag lot.

The Mustang had taken a beating when it was hit by the tanker. They'd managed to close the passenger door, but it wouldn't latch. They'd had to fasten it to the body of the car using duct tape and bungee cords. The taillights no longer worked, and the windshield was cracked. Patrick's prize ride was held together with ingenuity and desperation.

The Dodge wasn't in much better shape. The rollover had dented in the roof so that Max couldn't have worn his cowboy hat if he'd wanted to. Their front windshield was gone. They'd managed to knock out enough of the glass so that it didn't present a physical hazard, though riding in the front seat reminded Shelby of the two times she'd been on a motorcycle.

Only the Hummer looked as it had when they'd first met up on the square in Langford Cove, Texas.

The area they were passing through was a marked contrast to their dilapidated group. Rolling hills stretched out in all directions like a sea of green, spotted here and there with clusters of white wildflowers. There were no ranches, no farms, no other roads—only the Flint Hills, their road, and on both sides the seemingly endless prairie. Shelby was able to make out switch grass, bluestem, and Indian grass. Occasionally, she saw a stream but no trees.

"This countryside looks so foreign to me. If I've ever been here before, I don't remember it."

They'd slowed their speed to thirty miles an hour so Shelby didn't have to shout to be heard over the wind coming through the front of the car where the windshield had been.

Max gave her his arrogant smile. How he could still have that after all they'd been through was a wonder she couldn't quite understand. She thought of his declaration of how much he cared for her, and she looked away. Now wasn't the time for that. Or maybe it was. They could have died today. They might still.

"Then you probably haven't been here," Max said. "Hard to forget this much . . . nothingness."

"Why is there no farming?"

"Too little topsoil."

"How do you know that?"

"I quizzed Gabe about it our first night out."

And indeed, there was nothing on either side of the four-lane road. They'd passed very few cars and seen no houses. Within the first few miles, they passed one combination gas station/convenience store situated in the middle of the highway between the northbound and southbound lanes. It had obviously been looted. By whom? Where did the people come from, and where did they go? No one suggested stopping. They were still too close to Caldwell. Hills green with spring grasses stretched to the right and left and disappeared in the distance as far as they could see.

Shelby watched the unremarkable scene outside the car for several more minutes. Finally, she turned to Max and asked, "Why would the government set up out here?" The question had been tumbling around in her head, repeating itself like a stuck recording.

She thought Max wouldn't answer her. He wore that thoughtful, analytical expression that she'd seen so often when he was in the middle of a case. Maybe he was trying to figure it all out too. Why would she think that Max Berkman would hold the answers to her questions? Why had she always been so sure that he grasped things more quickly and more thoroughly than she did? There was an appeal in that fantasy—a strength she found immensely attractive. Which proved that she still harbored a little of the teenage crush she'd agonized over so many years ago— agonized over until they'd become a couple, and then they weren't. The memories seemed to belong to another millennium, and they seemed to spring up from yesterday.

Max turned to her, reached out, and cradled her face in the palm of his hand. Something in her heart tightened. She wanted to run far away as fast as she could and put an immediate and immense distance between them. She wanted to melt into his arms and let him whisper that everything was going to be all right.

She did neither.

Instead, she squeezed his hand and pulled back into her seat, adjusting the seat belt as she did so. Not that it would protect her much if they crashed. But that seemed like a remote possibility here. They would see anyone coming toward them from miles away.

Max gave her a knowing smile, and then he returned his attention to the road. "Sometimes the best place to start over is where there's no one and nothing to remind you of the past."

"You think our government was running from the past?"

"I think they needed space." He nodded toward the surrounding hills. "Plenty of that here."

They were too committed to turn around and look somewhere else. Plus, Gabe's assignment had been the Flint Hills of Kansas. Other personnel would have been sent to the South Dakota Badlands, the vast plains of Wyoming, the remote Cascade Mountains crossing from Washington through Oregon and into northern California. Their group had made it here against tremendous odds, and now they merely had to confirm that the government had or hadn't established a presence in the area.

They drove three car lengths apart. Gabe was at the rear of their convoy, with Lanh and Carter helping him to maintain a lookout behind them. No use being surprised by someone who had decided to follow them. Max and Shelby were in the middle because the Dodge seemed to be in the worst shape of the three vehicles. Patrick and Bianca were in the front, setting a slow pace that the Mustang could handle given its damaged condition.

Patrick signaled, and then he pulled over at the next gas station.

He popped the hood on the Mustang before they'd come to a stop on either side of them. Steam poured out from the car, and Shelby could hear a hissing sound from where she stood. Gabe and Max joined Patrick staring down into the engine.

"They're making manly grunting sounds under there," Bianca said.

"Always a cause for alarm."

Lanh and Carter trooped into the convenience store. They returned shaking their heads, hands empty.

"Nothing," Carter said.

"At least there weren't bodies this time." Lanh stretched, arching his back and reaching his hands high up over his head. Suddenly, remembering his stitches, he dropped his arm, stared at it a minute, and then shrugged.

"He reminds me of a cat," Shelby said, laughing at the scowl he sent her way. "A masculine, brave cat, of course."

"More like a lion," Lanh said.

"If you say so." Bianca reached up and tussled his hair. "Lanh the Lion."

He shook his head in exasperation, but Shelby could tell he was pleased. It was good to feel normal and tease, if only for a minute.

Patrick slammed down the hood, and they all met together on the south side of the building. The day wasn't hot or cold. It was a pleasant March afternoon. But the wind from the north had a bite to it. Shelby wouldn't be surprised if they saw snow in the morning, though there was no sign of clouds. But that northern wind worried her. She had the overwhelming feeling that something was headed their way.

"What happened back there?" Carter asked. "And do you think they're going to follow us?"

"No reason for them to. Easier for them to stay near their base and ambush the next person who drives through." Gabe stared back toward Caldwell. "They're bold. I'll give them that."

Shelby had an urge to drive back to Caldwell, arrest every one of them, and leave them for the authorities the way they had Hugo. Only where were the authorities in Kansas, and could they afford to sacrifice the time?

"They were bold," Bianca agreed. "But they

356

were also insane. Think about the way they dressed, like they were in an old movie. Those people were not right in the head."

"Regardless, we keep going," Gabe said. "If we find anyone in a position of authority, we tell them what is going on in Caldwell and let them take care of it."

"We're going to have to leave the Mustang," Patrick said. "The engine's sputtering, and I have very little power. I probably couldn't outrun your old, beat-up Dodge."

"Hey. I think you just dissed my ride." Max tried to look offended.

"Looks like the manifold is cracked, and there's no telling what else broke loose in there."

"Sorry, Patrick." Max leaned against the building and crossed his arms. "I know what she meant to you."

"My first love . . ." Patrick pretended to be wounded when Bianca slugged him in the arm. "She *was* my first love. I have a new first love now, and she has a mean right hook."

He pulled Bianca into his arms so that her back was to him and his chin was resting on the top of her head. They looked so natural together, so comfortable, and for some reason it amplified the ache deep inside of Shelby.

"So we pile into the other two vehicles." Carter glanced around the circle. "What am I missing?"

"The Dodge isn't safe," Max admitted.

357

"Driving thirty miles per hour, it isn't a real problem, but if we had to outrun anyone?"

Lanh nodded. "God forbid someone starts shooting at you."

"You'd be like ducks in the shooting gallery at the fair." Bianca looked puzzled when they all started laughing.

Gabe let them get it out of their system, and then he turned their attention to more serious matters.

"We go in the Hummer. All of us. Take what we can as far as supplies. Siphon the gasoline out of your vehicles."

"How are we going to find the government even if they are here? I doubt they set up on the side of the road. At least there doesn't seem to be any indication of that." Shelby repositioned her backpack. "There's so much nothing. There aren't even many crossroads."

"Which won't be a problem with the Hummer." Patrick nodded at the map Gabe was holding. "We set up a grid and crisscross the entire Flint Hills until we've checked it all."

"Exactly. Probably they wouldn't be on a major road anyway—not if they want to keep their presence something of a secret." Gabe hesitated, and then he added, "There's one more thing we can do to increase our odds of finding them."

Shelby waited, sure she wasn't going to like what he was about to say.

"We travel at night. It'll be more dangerous. We'll have to run with our lights off . . ."

"But any government facility is bound to have lights, and we'd see them from a long way off." Carter pulled off his battered cowboy hat and rubbed the top of his head. "They're bound to have lights."

"Nothing like what we knew before," Gabe said. "I wouldn't expect to see streetlights or blinking marquees, but yes, there will be something. There would have to be if the government is here. Given the state of the country, we can assume they're going to be working in shifts, working twenty-four hours a day. Which means there have to be some lights unless they've gone underground, and I don't see how they would have had the time or resources to do that."

"So that's our plan?" Bianca squirmed out of Patrick's arms, squatted down, and retied her hiking boots, as if she needed to be ready for whatever came next. They all needed to be ready.

"That's our plan." Gabe waited for each of them to nod in agreement. "First thing: I want to clean the cut on Shelby's head and have a look at Max's shoulder. Anyone who has a previous injury that needs attention, don't hold back. Infection is my worst fear at this point, so let's address anything that needs to be done medically now."

No one dared argue.

"Afterward we get to work. Lanh and Carter, you're on dinner duty. Make it a high-calorie meal because we're going to be driving all night. Patrick and Max, siphon the gasoline out of your vehicles and into the containers we have. Shelby and Bianca, I want you to both go through the gas station, the fast-food joint, and the store. Look for anything we can use. Check storerooms, behind counters, and inside freezers. Whistle if you need help. I'll work on the map—mark a grid over the area and determine the best way to explore it."

They broke up then.

Headed to their assigned tasks.

Each person praying that this, their ninth night since leaving High Fields, would be their last night on the road.

SIXTY

They ate, attempted to rest on the south side of the building, and waited for night to fall. Carter had thought that High Fields was as remote a place as he could imagine, but it didn't hold a candle to the Flint Hills of Kansas. Starlight spilled across the sky. The only sound was the wind whipping around the building. He was willing to bet there wasn't another soul for a hundred miles. They were truly alone.

"Worried?" Max asked.

Carter hadn't even heard him walk up. "Yes. No. I don't even know anymore."

"Which is exactly the way the rest of us feel."

Maybe it was the cascade of stars above him, or being so far from home, or what they'd been through, but suddenly all the questions that had been nagging at Carter—the questions he could push away when they were moving—spilled out into the cowboy-shaped silhouette that was Max standing above him.

"Why did this happen? If God knows everything, if he can control everything, then why couldn't he move the flare to the right or left, so that it missed us altogether? Why does it seem the good guys don't make it, but the bad guys get stronger and smarter?"

"Hey. We're still here." Max squatted, coming close enough that Carter could see his face dimly in the starlight.

Frustrated, Carter sat up in his bedroll and wrapped his arms around his knees, turning his gaze out to the dark horizon. "I thought I believed in God when I was lying in the creek, sure I was going to die. I knew that my leg was broken and my glucose levels were bottoming out. I cried out to God—like that song we used to sing. And I thought maybe he heard me and saved me."

"He did."

"For what?" Carter turned to stare at Max now, half expecting that Max could and would answer all of his questions.

"I don't know, Carter. But God will show you your purpose. He has a plan for you."

Carter tried not to sigh or let his shoulders sag or do anything to let Max know how disappointing his answer was. Max was, after all, doing his best. He was also very observant.

"You're right. I don't have the answers, and sometimes I struggle with the same questions you have. But there's one thing I'm sure of." He paused, setting one knee on the ground and bowing his head as though it were very important to him that he choose the correct words. Looking up, he said, "When you're completely lost, when you have no idea what comes next or why things are happening, faith is what gets you through. Even if you're not sure what you believe, you keep doing the things you know in your heart are the right things. That is faith, Carter. It's not the absence of questions. It's continuing, day in and day out, in spite of those questions."

Max left him alone then, to stare at the stars and wonder.

He must have drifted off to sleep because, suddenly, Gabe was giving the signal, and they all stowed their bedrolls and threw their packs in the back of the Hummer. No one had slept much, but Carter felt surprisingly awake, especially with all seven of them crammed into one vehicle. Gabe drove and Patrick rode shotgun. Max sat directly behind Gabe, and Bianca sat behind Patrick. Which meant that Shelby, Carter, and Lanh were squished in the middle.

In some ways, it was comforting.

It reminded him of a litter of puppies he'd found when he was in middle school. His mother had let him bring them home, feed them, and together they'd found homes for each one. He'd spent hours watching them crawl over and tumble across each other. They'd seemed perfectly content and had eventually fallen asleep, crammed into a corner of their box, sleeping on top of each other.

That was how he felt with Lanh's elbow continually poking into his right side and his mom pushing into his left as she leaned forward and tried to peer through the front windshield.

They were doing what Max had said—continuing, doing what was right—and suddenly, it was enough.

The ride was bumpier than he'd expected.

The Hummer didn't have any problems with the hills and valleys, but they still felt every drop and climb.

It reminded Carter of the Texas Giant roller coaster he'd ridden at Six Flags. His stomach was literally jostling around, and his hands began to sweat as he wondered if they'd eventually topple end over end. But the Hummer wasn't going to roll. It was, after all, built like a tank.

"There." His mom pushed her way in front of him, practically kneeling on the floorboard so that she could poke her head over the front seat. "There! Northwest."

They'd been following Gabe's grid for three hours, back and forth, up and down. Carter didn't know how she could tell which direction was northwest, but then he caught sight of the compass dial on the dashboard.

"Northwest," she whispered, and then she sank back into the seat and covered her face with her hands.

Gabe braked and turned off the ignition. "Quietly," he warned.

They slipped out of the vehicle like water across stones and stood in a line, facing northwest.

Carter had seen electric lights before. He'd grown up in the modern world. He hadn't forgotten a single thing about it, or so he told himself as he stared at the wonder in front of him. It wasn't a blaze of fluorescent light. No football stadium preparing for Friday night's game. No lighthouse casting out a beacon.

What he saw instead was starlight twinkling across the landscape.

Pinpricks of light—hundreds of them.

And the sight was so stunning, so over-whelming, that he understood his mom's need to put her hands over her face, to hide from the hope that sparkled in front of them.

Only Bianca had thought to bring her binoculars from the Hummer. She gazed through them for the space of three breaths and then handed them to Patrick. Each person peered through them, accepted that what they were seeing wasn't an illusion, and passed them to the next person—like a canteen passed down a line of thirsty, weary travelers.

Carter didn't know how long they stood there or why. Maybe they were afraid that the lights would disappear. Possibly, they simply needed to drink in the sight of them. He didn't under-stand the why or the how, but he did know that this changed everything.

They turned and made their way back to the Hummer.

Gabe led them to the far side, the dark side, and they naturally formed a circle.

"This is it," Bianca said. "It has to be."

"It's more than I expected," Patrick admitted. "It's . . . wider."

Gabe had pulled a collapsible lantern out of his pack and set it on the ground. It cast a low beam of light. Enough for them to see each other by, but barely. "We can't know exactly what it is until morning. I don't want anyone getting their hopes up that we've found the New Jerusalem."

"What else could it be, though?" Max stuffed his hands into his back pockets. "Those weren't lanterns. I've stared at enough lantern light in the last nine months to know the difference. That was electricity—or something like it."

"Could be a town." Patrick stood as if he were in a military lineup—feet inches apart, knees locked, posture perfect, hands clasped behind his back. "We don't know how widespread the grid breakdown was. At the beginning, they told us that some places might have been hit more directly than others."

"That's true, but our grid system is completely interdependent, or rather it was. Once it started going down, it all went down." Gabe stared at the ground, his hands on his hips. "And a town wouldn't be out here in the middle of the Flint Hills with no access road. It's not remotely possible."

"So we agree." Carter couldn't keep silent any longer. "We agree it's them. It's the government, big brother, Uncle Sam, whatever."

Lanh was practically bouncing on the balls of his feet. "If it is the feds, what are we waiting for? Why don't we walk up and knock on the door, or the fence, or . . . whatever."

Gabe glanced around the group, and Carter knew he was weighing a dozen different things— their safety, their need to know, Governor Reed waiting back in Texas, people dying due to lack of supplies. "We wait until morning, and then we run a reconnaissance mission. We do not get sloppy now, not when we're this close."

It made sense. It wasn't the easiest thing to do. Carter thought he could probably walk toward those lights and be on their front doorstep in a few hours. But walking across the Flint Hills in the dark wasn't the smartest idea. It would be impulsive and foolish. The thing was, Carter wanted to be impulsive right now.

What he didn't want was to be bitten by a snake. Or sprain his ankle from stepping in a hole. Or come across a band of marauders.

We do not get sloppy now.

Patrick took the first watch. The Hummer shielded them from the worst of the wind, so everyone else made their beds behind the vehicle on the ground, with countless stars above them and man-made light to the northwest.

SIXTY-ONE

Max drew the last shift. He didn't mind. He'd actually slept pretty well in his bedroll underneath the Kansas night sky. Once he'd heard Shelby's breathing even out, he was able to stop worrying about her, and sleep came immediately.

Now he was wide awake and eager to find out what the day would bring.

He watched the lights on the horizon fade away as the morning sky lightened. He prayed, as the pinpricks of hope disappeared, that they represented what they'd been searching for. He had no illusions that the US government could or would sweep in and fix everything, but in that moment between night and dawn, he understood how weary his group was. And if they felt this way when they had each other, transportation, and a reasonable amount of food . . . how did the majority of Americans feel?

He hadn't spent too much time thinking beyond what was needed for the next day. They'd been thrust into a moment-by-moment existence. But as he gazed northwest at the few remaining lights, he knew that they needed more than their daily needs met. They needed hope for their future. What was that verse his mother had attempted to hammer into his head? Something from the Old

Testament. "I know the plans I have for you . . . plans to give you hope and a future."

Did he still believe that?

He wanted to. He desperately wanted to.

He was trudging back toward the group, anticipating the taste of a granola bar and instant coffee, when something whizzed by his head.

He ducked, swiped at it, and stumbled into the campground.

"There's some kind of psycho bird or buzzard or . . ."

"Drone." Carter was sitting up, staring at the device that was hovering at eye level in front of him. He offered a small wave, and the drone darted away.

Shelby pulled out her Glock.

"You don't want to do that," Patrick said.

Gabe strode toward the middle of the group and waited. The drone paused before each person, and then it circled, rose, dove, and settled directly in front of Gabe.

"Authentication number 7478463291. Thompson, Gabriel. US Air Force. MD. Rank O-5."

"What's O-5?" Shelby whispered.

"Lieutenant colonel." Patrick never took his eyes off the drone.

The drone hovered there, no doubt waiting on a command from someone higher up the military food chain. Max was slightly embarrassed that he hadn't realized what it was. But then he'd been living without technology for nearly a year. The thing could have probably bumped into him, and he'd have thought it was a bat.

Without any warning or explanation, it darted into the sky and was gone.

"What now?" Lanh asked.

Gabe glanced around at them, a smile tugging at the corners of his mouth. "Now we wait."

They didn't have to wait long. By the time they'd finished their campground breakfast and replaced their bedrolls into the Hummer, the sound of vehicles approaching filled the air.

"Leave the weapons," Gabe muttered.

They stood in front of the Hummer, lined up and watching two jeeps approach.

By the time they came to a halt, Gabe had stepped forward.

The jeeps' occupants dispersed around their group in a semicircle, rifles up and ready.

As one, each person in their group raised their hands.

"We've left our weapons in the vehicle," Gabe said.

"We require confirmation that you are who you say you are." The leader of the group was female, tall, thin, and probably thirty years old. She had an obvious no-nonsense air about her.

Gabe slowly rolled up his left sleeve and held out his arm.

The leader nodded once to the person on her right, who stepped forward, pulled out what looked like a stun gun, walked directly up to Gabe, and pointed it at his arm.

A light flashed, the man stared at the small screen, and then said, "Confirmed," before returning to his place in the formation.

"I'm Captain Jenny MacRae. Welcome to New Town, home of the US government."

SIXTY-TWO

Carter didn't know what to think. One part of him—probably the kid part of him—had expected a warmer welcome. The older, more cynical part of him had half figured that they'd be threatened or even shot. Questions twirled in his head as the captain motioned for them to get back into the Hummer.

When did the US government get into the business of founding cities?

How long had New Town been there?

Was that name some kind of joke?

And what was on Gabe's arm that had confirmed he was who he said he was?

MacRae led the way in one of the jeeps, and the other jeep followed behind them.

"Guess they don't want us to make a break for it across the hills." Lanh rolled his eyes and attempted a laugh.

Carter could tell he was on edge. Lanh had been living with them for eight months. They knew each other's quirks. "It'll be fine, man. We're headed into civilization."

"We're headed into something," his mom said.

But the road to New Town was no smoother than what they'd been traveling on across the Flint Hills. In fact, there was no road as far as

372

Carter could tell. That was the first thing that was odd. Carter had expected to see at least a caliche road or dirt track, but instead, the grassland went right up to the wall.

And the wall . . . well, it wasn't much of a wall. There was no wire, no brick or concrete structure at all. But there was definitely a perimeter. MacRae's jeep slowed down, and a green light flashed once. Carter caught it out of the corner of his eye and swiveled his head left and then right.

Patrick pointed to what looked like deer stands, only they were taller and set at regular intervals. "Guard towers. Probably that green flash was a security beam as well. Even if you managed to stumble in here in the middle of the night, you'd trip the perimeter wire."

"But there is no wire," Bianca said.

"Underground. We passed one, and there's another." They trundled past a marker hammered into the ground. It looked no bigger than a stake that Max might have set out to measure off a garden. As they passed it, Carter saw the green light flash again. "A double perimeter—smart."

"Captain MacRae apparently called ahead, or we would have been stopped," Gabe said.

"How big is this place?" Bianca asked.

"And how many people are there?" His mom was leaning over Max, her nose practically smashed against the side window.

They passed hundreds of rows of tents. "Similar to what we had in the Middle East," Gabe said. "They can withstand heat or cold."

And then they moved toward structures that seemed more permanent, but Carter had no idea what materials they could be made from.

"It's not brick," he said to Lanh. "Looks more like canopies stretched over . . . something."

"Can't be concrete or wood. There's none of that around here, so whatever it is . . . they brought it in with them."

"Or they made it here."

But he didn't see anything that looked like a manufacturing plant, and besides, running any type of plant would take a lot of energy, and he didn't get the sense that they had anything near that kind of output capacity. Had they actually even seen electricity the night before? There were no power lines and no substations. There was a good-sized stream they passed over, and Carter realized that would have been another way to find them—follow the streams. Every civilization needed water, regardless what other technology they had.

There were also strange-looking trees in front of some buildings. Some were obviously artificial. Others had what looked like chimes hanging from them. Still more buildings had several windmills close by. "Always slightly taller than the structure," Lanh noted.

And there were solar panels. Lots of solar panels. The March sun glinted off rows of them on the tops of roofs, positioned to the sides of buildings, and one entire field of them that looked like crops, shimmering in the morning light.

They came to a stop, interrupting the dozens of questions popping up into Carter's head.

Stepping out of the Hummer, they found themselves in front of what looked like an old ranch house. It had a porch with three steps and columns positioned regularly across the length of it, which was half the length of the house. The place looked like something he might see in Abney, and that thought stirred a sudden homesickness in him.

"This way," Captain MacRae said. But she was only talking to Gabe. That much was evident.

"We stay together," Gabe said.

"Of course, but perhaps your friends would be more comfortable in the mess hall while you meet with General Massey."

"My friends will stay with me, Captain."

Carter wanted to hug the good doctor then, but instead he pulled himself up to his full five feet eleven and attempted to scowl at her.

She shook her head in mock desperation and said, "Fine. Have it your way, sir. But they're serving pancakes this morning."

Carter and Lanh jogged up the porch steps

behind his mom and Max, who were following Patrick and Bianca and Gabe.

"Did she say *pancakes?*" Lanh asked.

"Pancakes, syrup, real milk . . ." The army grunt behind them cracked a smile. "Welcome to the new world."

SIXTY-THREE

Shelby had the absurd notion that they were following the yellow brick road, heading to see the great and mighty wizard. She stepped inside the home and stopped, staring at a light switch on the wall. Walking over to it, she placed her hand on the switch. Carter had stopped beside her, and the army guy at the back was watching them with an amused look on his face.

She couldn't resist.

She'd dreamed of this moment, wondered if it would ever happen, prayed it might.

She pushed the switch up, and the light in the hallway came on.

"Like old times, right? Except we don't use them during the day. Saves on power." The army guy grinned and then motioned toward the rest of their group, who were now waiting at the end of the hall.

They were ushered into a room where a general with snow-white hair and crow's-feet around his eyes sat behind a large, wooden desk. His skin was a dark black, and he sported four stars on his uniform, which was crisply pressed.

How had anyone ironed a uniform?

At High Fields, they were lucky to be able to wash their clothes, and they didn't do that very often. Georgia had managed to iron the men's shirts for the wedding, but day-to-day hygiene had changed. In fact, Shelby was suddenly aware that she had dirt smeared across her shirt, blood on her hiking pants, and when she reached up and touched her hair, she found it was frizzed out to an alarming height. None of that mattered, though. All that mattered was the man sitting in front of them and what he might or might not say.

The general was frowning at a report as they entered the room, but he quickly tossed it aside and walked around the desk to greet them. "I'm General Massey, and you have arrived all the way from Texas. I can't tell you what a pleasure this is."

Gabe stepped forward, saluted, and introduced himself and then everyone else in the group. "It's a pleasure, sir, and a relief for us as well. We had no idea if you were actually here."

The general shook hands with everyone, and then he motioned them toward seats positioned in a semicircle in front of the desk—seven seats, so MacRae must have called ahead. She must have known they would all insist on staying together despite her attempt to lure them away with talk of pancakes. Shelby's stomach growled at the mere mention of anything that didn't sprout from an MRE bag.

Massey sat down heavily in the large leather chair behind the desk.

"We're here all right. This—" He waved toward the window, encompassing all of New Town with the gesture. "This isn't a figment of your imagination. And I'll be happy to answer your questions if I can, but first tell me about Governor Reed. The last we heard she was attempting to hold the capital."

"Not anymore," Patrick said. "Austin fell on February 25."

Gabe took up the story. "Reed is in Corpus Christi, trying to maintain some semblance of a state government."

"I'm sorry to hear that. We haven't had any reports in . . . well, in months."

Shelby couldn't keep quiet a moment longer. This man was tucked away in a utopia compared to Austin. Didn't he understand what was happening in the small and large towns of America? "Why haven't you sent someone to help? Was your plan to sit here and wait until each state comes to you?"

If Massey was surprised at her boldness, he didn't show it. Instead, he leaned back in his chair and studied her for a moment. "We decided, and it was a unanimous consensus, that a weak federal government would be worse than no government at all."

"What does that mean?" Lanh asked.

"It means they're biding their time here until they can be effective." Max's right ankle was propped over his left knee. He pulled off his hat and balanced it there on his boot.

"That's part of it, yes. We haven't forgotten that we exist for the people. We represent the people, and those same people are our responsibility."

"But they're starving." Bianca sat forward, her hands clasped together. "They need medicine, doctors, food, supplies. Do you have those things here?"

"We have some, but not enough."

"Any amount would help," Patrick said.

"Would it? Or would it create more chaos, panic, looting, and killing?" Massey shook his head. "We tried it—Baltimore, Philadelphia, Columbus. At least half a dozen more. We tried to go in, establish a presence, and ration out supplies. In each and every situation, we lost men, and we didn't improve the conditions one bit."

"Thugs overpowered the US military?" Bianca sat back. "I don't believe it."

"The military exists at the discretion of the people. Once the general populace loses faith in it, once they lose respect for it, we don't stand a chance unless we're willing to shoot everyone in our path. Which we were not willing to do, so we withdrew and moved to Plan B."

"And what was Plan B?" Gabe asked.

"To come up with a prototype."

"A prototype?" Lanh and Carter's words rang out in unison.

Shelby thought of the work Carter had done in Abney in Coach Parish's lab. What had their group been called? The Brainiacs, and they'd created a solar oven that had actually worked. Another team had attempted to make a windmill out of old bicycle parts. They were building prototypes—models—that others could copy.

"You're building a model?" she asked.

"What did you think we've been doing tucked away in a remote location?" When no one answered, Massey added, "We've been building the prototype for the new American town."

SIXTY-FOUR

A young woman dressed in army camouflage escorted them from General Massey's building to their barracks. The room was longer than a football field. The structure seemed to be made of some sort of canvas material, and cots were set up in half a dozen rows that stretched the entire length of the room.

"We were able to put you in the same section. Showers are at the far end, and Captain MacRae has ordered the mess hall to remain open for you."

"Did she say *showers?*" Bianca stared after the young woman as she walked away.

Their packs had been placed at the foot of their beds.

"Firearms are gone," Patrick said.

"I'll make sure they're returned before we leave." Gabe gave their group a good, long visual examination. He didn't try to hide his smile when he said, "You all look terrible. Showers, grub, and then stop by medical."

"You ordering us around, Gabe?" Max had stretched out on his cot and didn't seem inclined to move.

"As a matter of fact, I am."

When Shelby stepped under the spray, all of

her worries and questions and anxiety melted away. She'd forgotten what a hot shower felt like. How long had it been? Nine months? Of course, they'd bathed at High Fields, but those baths had been hurried things in a tub with an inch of water that had been heated on the stove. This? The water cascading over her felt as if it had arrived straight from heaven. She opened her eyes and squinted at a message that had been inked in permanent marker on the wall. "Shower will stop after 90 seconds." Okay, not heaven, she decided as she reached for the shampoo. But for today? It was close enough.

Breakfast was oatmeal with raisins and nuts, and real coffee.

Oatmeal, basically warm granola, and nearly as good as the meal that Stu and Mary Jane had served them. Shelby reveled in it.

The nurse on duty in medical tsked as she redressed their various wounds, but she declared them fit to walk about. Which was when they decided to go different directions.

Shelby wasn't sure that breaking up was a good idea, but after the general's talk, they had a lot of questions they wanted answered. Captain MacRae offered guides, but she also said that they were free to move about New Town unescorted. They agreed to find lunch on their own and meet back at the main mess hall for dinner.

It seemed too easy.

"Is this entire place run by the air force?" Shelby asked. They were standing in a small circle, having had a full breakfast, which made her a little sleepy. She noticed Max stifling a yawn and Patrick rolling his shoulders. Only Carter and Lanh seemed completely awake.

"General Massey is air force. Four stars if you didn't notice." Gabe scanned left and right. "I've seen army as well. I wouldn't be surprised if all the branches are represented."

Lanh and Carter took off to view the research center.

Patrick and Bianca chose to visit the school as well as the medical facility.

Gabe left for a debriefing.

"What would you like to see, Shelby?" Max linked his arm through hers and led her down the street.

"I have a million questions, and I'd like to ask them of some normal people—not a lieutenant or captain or general. Normal people."

"Got it. Our quest is to find the little people. Lilliputians. Normal folk."

"You're mocking me."

"Watch for signs that say 'Island of Lilliput, next right.'"

She socked him in the shoulder, and he pretended that it hurt.

"What would Jonathan Swift think of this? Of our new world?"

"He knew something of political upheaval."

"But this . . ." Shelby shook her head. "This is starting over."

"Do you have your notebook?"

"Of course."

"Then let's go."

Excerpts from Shelby's Journal

Marna Blaylock and her twin daughters, Sylvia and Sheridan, have been in New Town since November.

"We were driving north out of Wichita when we stopped at one of those gas stations in the center of the road. I took the girls to use the facilities. We knew there wouldn't be water or plumbing, but Sylvia and Sheridan liked to pretend that they were washing their hands after they took care of their bathroom needs. We were there in the bathroom when we heard gunshots. I told the girls to hide, to crawl under the counter, and I took off running. My husband was already dead when I reached him, and his murderers? They had taken the car. Nothing left for us. I couldn't bury him, but I stayed by his side, prayed for him, and then I found an old, tattered blanket in the trash bin to cover him with.

"We stayed there—in that bathroom with no food and only the water I could catch from the rain—for eight days. And we were rescued when one of the patrols came through. I was afraid . . . afraid to trust them. But by that time, my little girls were lying on the floor in the bathroom, listless, unable to even raise their heads. My little girls, they were dying, starving to death right in front of my eyes. So it was either trust the men in that patrol or allow my children to die. I chose to trust."

Marna now works in the educational center—she was a fifth grade teacher before the flare. Her daughters attend school in the same building. They are in the third grade.

• • •

Johnny Henderson is a retired civil engineer, who is now working for New Town.

"I worked in Oklahoma City for twenty-two years. Metro area had grown to a million and a half people. And yeah, I was there during the bombing of the federal building. Thought that was the worst I'd ever see. Turns out I was wrong. Here's the thing that haunts me. We had an emergency response plan, and we activated it immediately after the grid failed. At first it seemed to be working—

we set up food banks, neighborhood watch groups, even emergency medical stations. But within the first forty-eight hours, people panicked. Not just that, but the criminal portion of our population grew bold. Those two things alone sealed our fate.

"After my wife died from the flu, if you can believe that . . . well, after that I knew I had to leave. I had a dirt bike I kept in the back of the garage. Hadn't used it in a year or so, but the tires were still good. I crammed some supplies in a backpack kind of like yours, and I headed north. Made it all the way to Topeka, which was a bitter place to be in December. Even then there were rumors of the government setting up centers. Some said that they were for the elite. Others swore that the central government had a plan and a list of people they would take—like so many doctors, scientists, even engineers.

"I didn't believe the details, but the fact that the rumor kept resurfacing told me there was some truth to it. And it couldn't be too far north. The weather in Topeka was brutal. Can you imagine the areas north of there? So I turned around, found a map in an abandoned car, decided the Flint Hills were as good a place as any to start over. Took me three weeks of crisscrossing the place to find them. By then, I'd used all my supplies and weighed less than I had in high school.

"But if the rumors were true, I thought they might let an engineer in. I don't know why I even cared, why I wanted to live . . . maybe to honor Amelia's life, to fulfill the promises I'd made her near the end.

"As far as New Town . . . well, I don't know if it's the future of America, but it's a lot better than what's out there. From an engineering standpoint, if we are going to survive, this is the only way that will work."

• • •

Ryan Dane was a homeless teen, living in Omaha, Nebraska, when the flare hit.

"I might have been living on the streets, but I wasn't stupid. Overnight the shelters had to close because they couldn't handle the number of people demanding rooms, which was crazy. It isn't like there was less housing or hotels. Maybe there were a few extra folks traveling through or stranded or whatever. I don't know where all those people came from. Omaha only has half a million. The downtown area is nothing to brag about. But suddenly, the streets were flooded with people looking for a place to stay.

"When the shelters couldn't take in even a fraction of the folks looking for help, then people grew violent. I saw an older guy who was in charge of the Sixth Street Mission shot because he refused to hand over what little food they had in storage. The group who shot him climbed over the gate, took the keys from the dead guy's pocket, and then stole everything they could find. After that there wasn't any reason left to stay.

"So I walked south. I sure didn't plan to spend the winter in Nebraska. A family picked me up. They were traveling in a pickup that looked like something out of The Grapes of Wrath. Lots of kids and even two dogs. We circled west of Kansas City. They'd set up some pretty serious roadblocks, and they didn't seem any too friendly to new folks. So we headed west. Maybe that was a mistake. We ran out of gas a few miles southwest of Topeka. They were determined to go back into town to try their luck there. I didn't want to have anything to do with densely populated places—and yeah, at that point even Topeka qualified. Mostly, I wanted to be out on my own. To try and scrounge up enough to eat, find a cave, and hide out for a few years.

"And I did find some caves. They're actually all over the hills. General Massey says they're hard to locate. He says I have an uncanny knack. So I go out with patrols twice a week. We've found a hundred and twelve so far. I know— you're wondering, so what? What good is a cave? But they're an excellent place to store provisions. Keeping everything here in New Town? Not smart. We might be well guarded, but these days anything can happen.

"I think about that family—the one that gave me a ride. I hope they're okay. One thing is for sure—they saved my life. As far as New Town, it's all right. There are a few folks who are on power trips, but aren't there always? There aren't any homeless, though. If you live in New

Town, you get a place to live and three squares. You have to work, or you're booted out. Wanna eat? You gotta work."

• • •

Sissy Jones is a doctor at the medical facility, twenty-eight years old with beautiful, black skin and hair cut so short I could see her scalp.

"I worked in the FEMA camps at first. We thought we could make a difference, but when the military pulled out, we were easy targets. After we were attacked the second time, we packed up our camp . . . left what supplies remained with local people we trusted. Left the patients too. I was in New Mexico then. You can imagine the heat in June. No A/C. No fans. My parents used to say that it was tolerable because of the low humidity, but that's with modern conveniences. Without it, that city was unbearable. Lots of folks were walking out of Albuquerque, headed north to the mountains or west to the coast. I went home, picked up my parents, and drove them to Santa Fe. We had some terrible nights, but we made it. I pray every night that they are still all right.

"Once they were settled, though, my parents insisted that I get back to work, that I go and help people. I was assigned to a mercy mission with a group of medics trying to care for the people who hadn't made it into Santa Fe. We were out on Interstate 25, which no one would try now. But we were naive then. Still thought the world was operating under the old rules. We'd nearly made it to Raton when we were ambushed. Everyone but myself and Garrett . . . Have you met Garrett? We were the only two who survived. We tried to make our way back to Santa Fe, but it was impossible going on foot. Eventually, we caught a ride on a military vehicle, and they brought us here.

"I can't say that I agree with the administration's decision to build a prototype town before going out to help the general population. I've heard there are at least a dozen of them in different states. Personally, I think they're waiting for the population to die down to a manageable number."

• • •

Joe Hunter recently celebrated his one hundredth birthday. He's an adviser to several different departments for everything from how to make candle wax to what indigenous plants are edible. Joe's age and experience are considered a huge asset in New Town.

"The days immediately following the flare were bad, but the worst I've ever seen? Probably not. The worst I've ever seen was Dachau, a concentration camp in the southern part of Germany. US forces liberated prisoners from there in 1945. Yes, that was the worst I've ever seen. Inhumane doesn't begin to describe it. And yet in the midst of such tragedy, there are also signs of God's grace . . . The world has changed before. This is another change. The one thing you can be sure of is that there will be more changes. You can count on that. Change is the only constant."

• • •

Kinsley Storm works with the horses in New Town. She's from Garden City, Texas, where she received a four-year scholarship to the university of her choice for her participation in and success with the Wild Horse and Burro Program. She's twenty-four years old.

"My family and I suspected that something was going on in the Flint Hills. There were rumors, people claiming to have seen lights, that sort of thing. Still, we probably wouldn't have come if it hadn't been for the lightning that struck our place and burned it to the ground. There was no water to battle the blaze.

"I thought that was a real tragedy at the time. Now I realize we probably wouldn't have survived the winter. New Town has been good for us. Mom works in the kitchen, and Pop's skills have been in high demand . . . he was a retired dentist. I say "was retired" because he's working full-time now. There's plenty of work for him here, and he's needed. He really is. Did you know folks can die from a tooth infection? He's also training a dozen other dentists. Mostly, they were beginning their medical degree, but there's no way to finish that now. Pop says hands-on is going to be good enough. He says it's better than folks suffering, waiting for the universities to crank back up and spit out a new supply of dentists.

"You could say I'm happier than I've ever been. I work with the horses every day. I don't have to worry about paying rent or living too far from my family. I love it here, and I think the general is absolutely correct that we need to make sure this works before offering it as a beacon of hope. My friend Micah used to say that five minutes of preparation was worth an entire day of frantic labor."

SIXTY-FIVE

Lunch had been another MRE. They were available at various kiosks around New Town. You walked up and received one. There was no money exchanged, no need to produce identification. If you were in New Town, then you were supposed to be there, you were doing a job, and you'd earned your lunch.

Max peered into the MRE pouch—Captain Country Chicken. "There's no chicken in this. I can guarantee you that."

"This Cheese Tortellini is great." Shelby grinned as she scooped out another spoonful.

"So what's your opinion of New Town now?"

"Conflicted. On the one hand, I admire what they're trying to do. Creating a prototype for the great American city—"

"Town. No big cities are on the planning board from what I've heard."

"Town then. Creating a prototype is a laudable goal, but I keep thinking of all the people we've seen on the outside. People who need help from their government."

"What would you have them do?" They were sitting on a park bench. People passed back and forth around them . . . all sorts of people. Different ages and ethnicities, both genders, all busy fulfilling their portion of the social contract in New Town.

"There are two things that bother me the most about what's going on out there." Shelby pointed her fork at him. "The lawlessness and the lack of supplies. What is the point of a federal government if it can't address those needs?"

"And yet when our government was originally founded, it did not provide supplies, and legal matters were left in the hands of the local communities. Think about your average family in the early 1700s. They weren't protected by soldiers or police."

"I don't need a history lesson, Max."

But Max was warming up to the comparison. Shelby had always been good at that, pushing him to see things in a new light. They often butted heads, but it was a process that he found helpful. "Neither did the government provide basic necessities for families."

Shelby finished her meal and tossed the package into a trash receptacle. A label affixed to the front of the box assured her any trash would be recycled and used to produce more supplies for New Town. "We don't live in the 1700s, Max. I realize the flare has changed things, but we're not the society we were then. We're a society that has grown accustomed to law and order and to basic necessities."

"How could what's left of the government possibly provide those things?"

"Not my problem. They have plenty of smart people working for them."

"Even smart people can't create manna from nothing."

"Excuses."

"Manufacturing and distribution have to be reestablished—"

"You should be on my side. On the side of people outside of New Town."

"And it would have to be reestablished on a much smaller scale because of the lack of power."

"Are you even listening?"

Shelby's face was beginning to turn red, a clear indication that she'd lost all patience with him. It should have aggravated him because he was right on this. She didn't want to admit it, and who could blame her? Carter's life was hanging by a somewhat fragile thread.

Still, the amount of energy she put into arguing made him smile.

"Stop that," she said, jumping to her feet.

"Stop what?"

"Getting that dreamy look."

"I was dreaming?"

"And smiling."

"You don't want me to smile?"

"You are infuriating." She turned and stomped away.

He almost went after her. He wanted to follow her, pull her into his arms, and kiss her senseless.

Maybe it was being in New Town, but the heavy press of despair had lifted from his heart—at least for a time.

Everything they'd seen that morning, every person Shelby had interviewed, had confirmed what he'd suspected since the moment they'd crossed New Town's border. This was the prototype for the future. It might take five years to roll out and another ten years to implement. Time during which the people Shelby was concerned about, the people he was concerned about, would suffer.

But that wasn't the point he saw this fine spring day in the Flint Hills of Kansas. The point was that they did indeed have a future, and it looked surprisingly brighter than he had expected it would. It looked like the dawning of a new world.

Max spent the afternoon nosing around the New Town security center. At first they didn't want to let him see past the front office, but a call to Captain MacRae settled that.

"Name's Gavin—Gavin Blake." The middle-aged man escorting him through the facility was of average height and stocky build, and he had bright red hair, including a well-trimmed beard. "Looks like you, Max Berkman, get the gold star tour."

"Lucky me."

"So you're a lawyer?"

"I was."

"I worked in a jail over in Dodge City." Gavin pulled on his beard, trying to suppress a smile. "Learned a lot of good lawyer jokes."

"Jokes about lawyers?" Max deadpanned. "You're kidding."

"What do you get when you run an honest lawyer contest? No winners."

Max groaned.

"How many lawyers does it take to change a lightbulb?"

"As many as you can afford," they said in unison.

Gavin led him down a hall and into a room lined with computer monitors. For a moment, Max stood frozen, staring at them, wondering if he was seeing things that weren't actually there. But then something beeped, a man walked over to turn off an alarm, and Max realized the monitors were not a hallucination.

"Where did . . ." Max needed to swallow, but his throat had gone completely dry. "Where did this stuff come from?"

"Different places." Gavin gave him a minute to walk about the room and grow accustomed again to the presence of technology, but Max wasn't sure he'd ever get used to the sight of bright screens or the sound of a mouse clicking. It was all so familiar, and at the same time so foreign.

"But I thought . . ."

"That it had all been destroyed. Yeah, most of

us assumed that as well, at least during the first few weeks, but of course the flare had varying degrees of intensity. If you were in one of the areas that received less than the full effect and you had your equipment sheltered underground, then it still worked."

"Worked how? There was nothing to hook it up to."

"There were generators, but you're basically correct. When people tried to log on, they found that the World Wide Web was gone. The broad public network ceased to exist the moment the satellites went off-line. In other words, you could boot up a computer, but there was no way to communicate with . . . well, anything."

"And a computer without anyone receiving on the other end—"

"Without the ability to send or receive information? It's a box, a large calculator, basically useless. What you're seeing here is an intranet system."

"You don't have communication with the other prototypes?"

"There's no way to do that short of sending up another satellite, and as you can imagine, we're a long way from having that capability. But as with most things, the old technology can be adapted. In this instance, we use it to monitor the electronic wall that surrounds New Town."

"And direct the drones."

"Yes." Gavin stuck his hands in his pockets, but he looked Max directly in the eye, which said something about the man's integrity. "This is why we don't need a jail in New Town. No one's here we don't know about. No one's here who isn't an asset to the community. You break the laws in New Town, and you're placed outside the wall."

"Which laws?"

"There are only three. Don't take what isn't yours. Don't grievously injure another person. Contribute to the success of New Town."

"Who's the judge and jury?"

"There isn't one."

"So you decide?" Max realized he was moving from casual questioning to interrogating, but this was important. What kind of new world were they building if it wasn't based on the tenets of justice?

"No, I don't decide."

"Then who does?"

"I only enforce the three laws, which are fairly black and white."

"But you put people outside the walls . . . based on your criteria."

"I didn't create them."

"Then who did?"

"POTUS."

"Excuse me?"

"The president of the United States was the

one who issued the directives to each prototype town."

"The president? And you're sure that he still exists? That the three branches of government continue to function, which of course must not be so if there are no courts for the Supreme Court to oversee . . ."

"Look, Max. This is a lot to digest at once. I understand that."

"I'm not sure you understand it at all." Max's temper was rising. He knew he needed to tamp it down, that Gavin wasn't the one who literally decided who lived and who died, but in a way he did—without due process or representation.

Max combed his fingers through the hair that lay too long on his neck. He was no longer the lawyer that he once was, but he would stand up for the institutions he believed in. "Out there? I understand. I've lived in it for almost a year, and I have finally accepted that you can't arrest every thief, that you can't have a nice tidy trial for every accused murderer."

Gavin waited, allowed him to work through his thoughts. Allowed him to vent his cry for justice.

"But in here? In this place that is supposed to represent a new beginning for our country? You'd better find a way to incorporate justice and due process into the prototype. Otherwise, what you're building is really just a house of cards."

SIXTY-SIX

Carter thought dinner was surprisingly good—some type of meat that had been stewed and cooked with fresh vegetables. He knew they were fresh because they had some taste to them. They must have come from the greenhouses they'd passed. Otherwise, how could they have fresh vegetables in March? In addition to the stew, there was cornbread and butter.

"The butter comes from the cows," Bianca said. "They have quite the agricultural center here."

"I thought you were looking at the hospital." His mom reached for an extra piece of cornbread.

"One thing led to another."

"She heard a moo." Patrick finished his glass of iced tea—something none of them had had since the lights went out. "All it took was a moo, and she was snooping right and left."

"They said we could look at anything."

"And you took them at their word, dear."

Patrick leaned over and kissed her on the lips, which Carter found a little embarrassing but also cool. It was good seeing Patrick and Bianca together. Now if only his mom and Max would come to their senses, he could stop worrying about the adults in their group.

He didn't have any concern about Gabe, who, quite obviously, could take care of himself.

True to her word, Captain MacRae had assigned them a first lieutenant who seemed willing to answer all of their questions. Isaiah Perez didn't look that much older than Carter— maybe twenty-five. He had a military haircut, which meant it was buzzed, and a friendly smile. He seemed pretty at home in New Town, pretty relaxed. Carter couldn't remember feeling relaxed anywhere, except maybe at High Fields. But even there he'd spent most of his time trying to prepare for the next emergency.

"How many people are in New Town?" Lanh asked.

"At this point the population is 2840. Well, 2847 if we include you all."

"One of the people we interviewed suggested there are other prototypes like this." Max pushed away his empty plate and crossed his arms on the table. "Is that true?"

"It is, though I can't tell you how many or where they are. Both of those answers are above my pay grade—not that we get paid anymore. But yeah. New Town isn't the only pro-town."

"That's what you call it?" Lanh glanced at Carter, as if to say, *Can you believe this guy?*

"Prototypical Municipal Structure is the exact name. Some folks shorten it to *prototypes*. Others, *pro-towns*."

"So this isn't the only one. Why is that?" Patrick asked.

"Several reasons. If we are attacked by foreign or domestic entities, we don't want all of our resources in one place."

"Is there intel to suggest that might happen?"

"As you can imagine, information between the pro-towns as well as what remains of the central government is sparse. We aren't aware of a specific threat, but if anyone wanted to hit us, if they had the ability, then now would be the perfect time."

"You said there were several reasons for creating multiple pro-towns." Max tapped his fingers against the table. "Defending our resources is one. What are the others?"

"There's always the possibility of another natural disaster."

"More flares?" Lanh asked.

"That, or a flood, a blizzard, a lightning strike that starts a fire that spreads. There are a lot of scenarios, and June 10 proved that we're not good at preparing for everything. The best answer is to divide your resources, which increases the odds that one of us will survive. If we're lucky, more than one will make it."

"How do the prototypes differ?" Carter waved away Bianca's offer of more tea. It wasn't sweetened, but he still knew he needed to check his glucose levels again before eating or drinking anything else. He felt good, but that wasn't always an accurate barometer. Mostly, at the moment, what he felt was curious. He'd been so preoccupied with making it from day to day that he hadn't given much thought to considering the future. Or maybe it had seemed so bleak he hadn't wanted to think about it.

"The towns are created to capitalize on the resources of the region. Take coastal towns, for example. There are at least three, though I've only been assigned to one personally and don't know the location of the other two. But any pro-town established in a coastal region will have a natural food source, fish; salt water, which can be desalinated if fresh water is an issue; and tides to power new technology."

"Where else have prototype towns been established?" Shelby asked. "Not specifically, like the Flint Hills, but in general. Is it always a remote location?"

"By necessity, it has to be. Otherwise we'd be overrun with displaced folks before we could establish a presence. As far as the different regions, we have coastal, desert, plains, and mountains—there are even rain forests in Washington. The towns need to have local sources of food and water. The Science Team's goal, the way I understand it, is to take advantage of those various eco systems and use them to power towns with renewable energy. Those are the basic components."

"Can you give us an example of renewable energy?" Lanh was leaning forward now, glancing at Carter again before turning his attention back to Perez.

They'd seen a lot today. Stuff Carter had never expected to see again. Actually, when he thought about it, they'd seen the future.

"Sure. On both the East and West Coasts we've been able to establish towns that receive thirty-two percent of their energy from tidal power."

"Tidal power." His mom looked as skeptical as Carter felt, but something was tickling the back of his mind, some memory from Coach Parish's class.

"Wave energy." He could practically see the drawing in the textbook. At the time, he'd laughed because no waves were anywhere near Abney.

"Exactly. In one instance, we used buoys tethered underwater. In another, we used a tall, oscillating structure. Both capture and convert the wave energy into electricity."

"You've seen this?" Patrick asked. "Or you've heard about it?"

"I've been assigned to three different pro-towns so far. One was on the West Coast, and yes—I saw it. This isn't tomorrow's technology. It's today's."

"Or yesterday's." Carter sat back and crossed his arms when everyone turned to stare at him.

"I remember something similar in my science textbook."

Gabe had been fairly silent, taking in the information and processing it. "So we won't try to reestablish the electrical grid."

"We couldn't do it even if we wanted to. We don't have the resources to build the equipment, and the substations are not plug and play—each is unique. If there's a way to reestablish manufacturing, I haven't heard of it."

"So you're focusing on alternate energy."

"Absolutely. It's critical after the flare that those systems be independent of one another. Our biggest failure may have been developing and depending on a grid system that we knew would fall like a line of dominoes."

"It didn't have to be a flare," Patrick pointed out. "It could have been a terrorist attack."

"Exactly. And we knew that, but we kept telling ourselves that we couldn't afford to restructure, redesign it. In truth, we couldn't afford not to."

"We met a wide variety of people today," Max said. "Do you let anyone in?"

"We do not, and believe me, that doesn't sit well with a lot of folks—sort of goes against our grain as Americans. But we don't want to spend the resources to police this town. We need people who can police themselves."

"What does that mean?" Lanh asked.

"It means that if someone is caught stealing,

they're put outside the perimeter. If they attack another person for any reason, they're put outside the perimeter. And if they arrive at our gates in a violent or threatening matter, they're shot."

"That's a little harsh, don't you think?" Bianca stabbed a fork into her apple cobbler. "No trial? No jury?"

"We don't have a court system or a jail. How would we hold a trial? And we can't afford to have people spend hours on a jury when we need them at their jobs. We do understand that people out there are dying, that they need us. This town and others like it are the hope for the citizens of America. We can't let some entitled punk holding an Uzi stand in the way of that."

"What's the timeline?" Shelby asked. "When are the people inside this community going to leave and help the people on the outside?"

"Some of us want to go now. The administration recently released a guideline for new communities based on the pro-towns. They're not going to start one unless they're reasonably sure it can survive." Perez paused, glanced around, and then he admitted, "Phase One does not include going back into the metro areas. Instead, we'll focus on creating new communities, and trust that the people will find us—hopefully, that will happen in the next twelve to twenty-four months. Phase Two will involve expanding to rural areas. During Phase Three, we'll go into the urban areas."

"When is that supposed to happen?" Max asked. "When will you return to the cities?"

"Three to five years, and that's an optimistic target. It could be more like ten."

SIXTY-SEVEN

The next two days were busy for their entire group.

Gabe spent most of his days attending military debriefings. He did confirm that he had the location and codes for the supplies scattered across the state of Texas. He had what Governor Reed needed. In that sense, their mission was a success. He shared what he could with them, but most of the information was classified. No one held that against him. Gabe had proved time and again that he was on their side, and he would tell them what they needed to know.

Bianca was training with some doctor, learning more first aid so she could help out at the hospital in Abney.

Shelby continued interviewing people for her journal.

Max and Patrick rode outside the perimeter of New Town and observed new planting techniques that required less water and no technology. Max thought it was a hoot that the methods had been learned from an Amish community, but Shelby had nodded absentmindedly and said, "There are four communities in Kansas." Carter remembered she'd learned that while researching a book set in the 1800s and focusing on Kansas settlers. It

413

had coincided with an American history project he was working on, so he'd been able to use some of her research.

"Your mom knows a lot of trivia," Lanh said to Carter the morning of the second day as they made their way across the center green of New Town.

"Yeah. Only when she's deep into a story, it's not trivia. It's like she's found something hugely important. She would storm into my room, holding up her phone and saying something like, 'You're not going to believe this.'" Carter attempted a laugh. "I haven't seen her that excited or that happy since the flare."

"When are you going to tell her?"

"I don't know."

"But you're sure?"

"Yeah. Aren't you?"

"Oh, I'm sure."

Carter and Lanh were free to explore. They'd spent the day before walking around randomly, asking questions when they popped into their heads, stopping and staring at things they never thought they'd see again: small, college-sized refrigerators, bathrooms, hot showers, laboratories, a library.

They'd made a list at breakfast of things they wanted to confirm and places they needed to see before they shared their plans with the group. First up, they wanted to know more about the technology. How did it actually work? They found out that some of the trees they'd seen on that first drive in were actually 3D printed solar energy trees.

Ashley Campbell, who had been pursuing a career in additive manufacturing before the flare, didn't mind answering their questions, and Carter was happy to stand around talking to her. She was super cute—a couple years older than him and a couple of inches shorter. Her blond hair was cut shorter than his, and her brown eyes practically danced as the young men stood there with their mouths gaping open at the information she shared. Maybe she was used to that response from newcomers.

"How did you print them?" Lanh asked, staring up at the leaves, which were actually flexible organic solar cells. "Or did you have them before the grid went down?"

"Both. We had some at various government installations, and some we have printed since then."

"How?" Carter reached out to touch the tiny leaves, which were colored pink and maroon.

"Generators were hooked up to 3D printers stored inside underground government facilities, and, of course, many of the commercial labs were built underground as well." Ashley explained that the leaves were able to gather and store energy. Not a lot, but enough to power small appliances.

"Imagine the day when every home has one of these in their yard," she said, the pride obvious on her face. You'd have thought she'd grown the trees herself. To be fair, she had overseen their installation and maintenance.

"Then if the grid went down, it wouldn't matter." Lanh stuck his hands in his pockets, his forehead creased in concentration. "Why didn't we do this before?"

The answer was simple enough. "Because we didn't have to."

She led them over to a parklike area across the dirt road, filled with ten trees evenly spaced apart.

"What are these things?" Carter asked. "Wind or solar? And what are they made of?"

"This is actually a wind turbine. Each tree holds seventy-two turbines, which are made of a treated plastic so that the humidity, sun, or any other type of weather won't damage them. Each tree has a power output of 3.1 kilowatts."

"Not much."

"True. It produces approximately 3100 watts. There are ten trees here, so that equals 31,000 watts. Not much in the pre-flare world. But now? Pretty helpful. Remember, a ceiling fan only uses 35 watts. We might not be cranking up the A/C anytime soon, but I bet many people in the South would give their eyeteeth for a fan."

"And the turbines are silent," Lanh said.

"Another plus, because much of the complaint with the giant wind turbines was their noise."

"Not to mention how many birds they killed."

"Exactly. These trees have been sprayed with a substance that repels animals."

"I can't smell it," Carter said, leaning in and taking a big whiff.

Ashley laughed. "Humans can't, but animals can. The turbines are able to spin with the wind blowing as low as 7 kilometers per hour, which here in the Flint Hills is nearly every day."

Carter could have stayed there talking to Ashley the rest of the day, but Lanh pulled their list from his pocket and checked off the trees. Next up were the large, tentlike structures they'd glimpsed the day before.

The canopied buildings were actually a type of biodome. Daylon Walters, a black man in his mid-twenties, explained the concept to them. "Google actually designed their new headquarters from something similar."

"Before the flare . . ." Carter reached out and touched the translucent canvas.

They'd walked inside, and Carter was staring up at the twenty-foot ceiling. Sunlight pierced through, negating the need for lights, though he noticed there were lights installed along tracks. He supposed they were for nighttime or cloudy days.

"A couple of years before. Their intention

was to build mobile structures that allowed for flexibility rather than permanent structures with a single purpose. The canopies replace what would have been permanent walls."

"And ceilings." Lanh sounded as impressed as Carter was feeling.

"And ceilings," Daylon agreed. "These block structures you see can be rearranged, repurposed, even recycled."

He proceeded to give them a tour through the building, pointing out the different areas, what people were working on, what they hoped to accomplish, and an abbreviated timeline of their goals.

Carter's thoughts jumped from idea to idea, revelation to revelation. He forgot about his diabetes, stopped worrying about their next meal, and didn't once question whether they were safe. They were safe. Their next meal was guaranteed, and his insulin levels had been fine that morning. He was starting to feel like his old self, his pre-flare self. Maybe that was because of everything they were seeing. It helped to dispel the sense of gloom that had pervaded their life since the flare tripped their collective breaker.

SIXTY-EIGHT

Carter and Lanh met up with their group for lunch. Shelby had conducted another dozen interviews. "I'd like to develop some pamphlets and send them out with people as they travel through Abney."

Gabe stopped eating, his fork halfway to his mouth. "Without divulging the location of New Town."

"Yeah. Of course. But it's not the *where* that matters. It's that there's hope, that there's something in our future other than darkness and hunger."

That quieted everyone, and they all focused on their lunches, which were MREs. The real food was provided at breakfast and dinner.

Lanh kicked Carter's foot.

When he glanced up, Lanh nodded toward Shelby and arched his eyebrows, but Carter shook his head and returned his attention to his food. He wasn't ready. He had to do it, and he knew it was the right decision, but he wasn't ready yet.

Captain MacRae appeared beside their table. "Your supplies are ready over at loading dock nine."

"We appreciate it." Max stood and shook the

captain's hand. "The people of Abney appreciate it. The medication is desperately needed. Thank you."

"We're not against helping people." MacRae had the straightest posture of anyone Carter had ever known, even straighter than Gabe's. But she seemed to relax slightly as she stepped closer and added, "We want to help, especially if we can trust it will actually arrive at the intended location."

"We'll do our best," Patrick said.

Max and Patrick left to pack the supplies into the back of the Hummer.

Gabe left for yet another meeting. "Some things about the military haven't changed one bit," he grumbled as he gulped down his coffee and followed a second lieutenant out of the mess hall.

"I'm headed over to the grade school to interview a class of third graders." Shelby made it sound like a trip to the beach. "Anyone want to go with me?"

"Can't," Bianca said. "I have more medical training."

"And, we—" Carter gave Lanh his best *help me* look. The last thing he wanted to do was spend an afternoon in grade school.

"Oh, yeah. We were wanting to see this uh . . . thing . . . place."

Shelby rolled her eyes. "Fine. I don't mind

going alone," she said, and then she smiled before leaving—a small thing, but it settled some of the nerves in Carter's stomach.

Bianca looked at them. "Tell me what you two are up to."

"Nothing," Carter said, maybe too quickly.

"We don't know what you mean."

"We're just . . . hanging out."

She stared at them a minute before shaking her finger and saying, "Come with me. Triage training is important stuff, regardless of what plan you guys have up your sleeves."

As they hustled over to the medical center, Bianca gave them a rundown of her morning. "I learned to separate people into groups if we have another disaster."

"What kind of disaster?" Lanh asked.

"You name it: attacks from an outlaw group, some type of explosion, fires like we had on the square last summer, even a flu epidemic."

Carter didn't want to think of any of those things, but not thinking of them didn't make them any less possible. So he asked, "How do you separate them?"

"Immediate, which is life-threatening. Delayed, which can wait to be treated if need be. Minor, which is exactly what it sounds like. And dead."

"Good grief. I hope there won't be a need for that in Abney."

"We could have used someone taking care of

those things in Austin," Lanh said. "It was pretty much utter chaos, and a lot of people . . . well, let's say the bodies started to pile up. Those days in Austin seem like a nightmare now. Like something that happened to somebody else."

"Think about it, though. If our group hadn't run into you, we probably would have never made it out of Austin, and we sure wouldn't have found the insulin Carter has been using this last year."

"I owe you, man." Carter bumped his shoulder against Lanh's.

"No problem."

And that was the way it was between them, the way it had been since Lanh had joined them at High Fields. In every way, he was like the brother that Carter had never had.

"So where are we going now?" Carter asked.

"To meet the man in charge of homeopathy."

"Home what?"

But they were already entering what looked like a combination laboratory, medical clinic, and produce department. Carter's mind slipped back to his days working in the grocery store in Abney. There was no longer a store to work in. It had been looted, then burned, and finally abandoned.

"High tech meets homeopathic," Bianca muttered.

Carter wasn't sure what that meant, but it sounded good to him.

Dr. Aiyanna Charley introduced herself.

"Charley is your last name?" Lanh asked.

"It is."

"And your first name is A . . ." Carter tried to pronounce it the way the doctor had, which caused everyone to laugh, including himself.

"I'm Native American, and yes—my name is difficult to pronounce. You can call me Doc Charley, like everyone else does."

Doc Charley had skin that reminded Carter of a road map. Her hair was white, pulled back in a leather band, and reached her waist. But if he thought she was too old to know what she was doing, she quickly altered that opinion. The woman was sharp, energetic, and had a great sense of humor. If they still had such a thing as television, she would have made a great central character in a medical drama.

She walked them through the room that was filled with herbs and other plants he couldn't identify, down a hall where they could view workers learning acupressure, and lastly to a courtyard filled with bee boxes.

"Honey?" Bianca asked.

"Actually, what we're after here is the bee pollen, which has been used for hundreds of years by herbalists." Doc Charley smiled, and her eyes nearly disappeared in a myriad of lines. "My grandmother insisted we have some twice a week—sort of like a vitamin. We're only now discovering the science behind many of the traditional treatments. For example, samples of bee pollen have been proven to contain nearly two hundred kinds of fungi and almost thirty types of bacteria."

"What good is that?" Bianca asked. "What I mean is . . . what could it be used for?"

"Health supplements, vitamins, and treatments for certain ailments. As you all know, it will be many years before factories are running again. In the meantime, we need to learn to use all that nature offers us, all that God has provided."

It surprised Carter to hear an old Indian doctor talk about God, but he realized that was closed-minded of him. Anyone could read the Bible and believe, or have a conversion, or grow in the faith. Hadn't he grown since he was a high school senior playing video games and waiting to traipse off to college? Sure, he had been expressing his doubts to Max only two days ago, but what was it he had asked? What was the one question he'd mulled over the most since leaving High Fields? Even before that, since they'd left Abney? What was his purpose? Why was he still alive? What was he supposed to do with his life?

And Max's answer, which had made no sense at the time, had been, *God will show you your purpose*. Perhaps God had. Maybe his purpose was here in New Town.

SIXTY-NINE

When they were nearly finished with the tour, Doc Charley pulled him aside and offered suggestions for ways to stretch what insulin he had left. "We do understand what medications are most critical, and we're working to start producing those again as soon as possible."

"But—"

"It's going to be a while. We obviously don't have a pharmaceutical plant, the ability to build one, or the resources to power one."

"But it doesn't have to be a plant on the scale that you're thinking," Carter argued. "You're building a prototype here. You've included power, communication, and security using new technology in your plans, but you're content to address medical issues with bees and plants."

He held his hands up and shook his head. "I didn't mean that as disrespectfully as it sounded."

Doc Charley cocked her head and studied him. "How can we do what you're suggesting? Our resources are severely limited."

"Instead of rebuilding the huge pharmaceutical plants of the past, think about local apothecaries—ones that use new technology for discovery, testing, and distribution."

"On a small scale."

"Exactly. So each town doesn't have to depend on a truck from a factory hundreds of miles away."

"It wouldn't be cost efficient."

"It would, because you wouldn't have huge companies with billion-dollar marketing campaigns." Carter hadn't realized how passionate he felt about this, but he'd spent his entire life immersed in the medical world because of his condition. It didn't have to be as convoluted as it had become. He didn't know how to explain that, how to explain how simple it was in his mind. He settled for, "We have to think differently. Forget how it was done before and think . . . forward."

Doc Charley stared at a spot in the distance for a moment, and Carter wondered if he'd sounded like a naive eighteen-year-old. He felt older than that, but that didn't mean the doctor would take him seriously.

"Here's the thing, Carter. We can try our best to anticipate the needs out there, but you've seen what they are firsthand. You've lived through them. Someone my age has experience and knowledge, and we can try to envision the future, but your generation is the future. You should have a voice in what it looks like."

"I don't know what you're saying."

"I'm saying we could use someone with your perspective and talents. I'm saying you should think about staying."

426

Carter didn't know how to answer that. He'd already decided he was staying. He and Lanh had made that decision the first night. But he hadn't been able to see how he might fit in. Was this it? Could he have a hand in creating the next generation of medicinal supplies?

"Promise me you'll think about it."

Carter nodded, and then Bianca and Lanh rejoined them, talking about the therapeutic properties of cactus.

When they'd come out of Doc Charley's building—that was how Carter thought of it now and probably how he always would—Bianca caught sight of Patrick across the town green.

"Later, guys." A smile and a wave and she was gone.

"They're such dorks," Lanh said.

"Now they're kissing in public."

"I'd be happy to find a woman like Bianca."

"That's kind of gross . . . she's like my aunt."

"Sorry."

"Forgiven."

They walked over to a bench, sat down, and watched people walk back and forth. Lanh broke the silence.

"So you're cool with this being our new home? Because if you're having second thoughts, I wouldn't hold it against you."

"I'm not having second thoughts. I'm trying to process all we've seen."

"Same here." Lanh crossed his arms and frowned at something he was remembering. "Their thinking is limited by how things were."

Carter nodded but still said, "Give me an example."

"Robotics. Other than the drones, they consider the field a lost cause. That's not necessarily the case, though, and with reduced resources, we need that type of advancement more than ever."

"I had a similar discussion with the doctor." Carter cleared his throat, sat forward with his elbows on his knees, and glanced over at his friend. "Doc Charley asked me to stay."

"She wants your talents in the medical field, huh?"

Carter shrugged.

"When we were touring the cactus lab, my tour guide mentioned the same thing. She said it when Bianca was out of earshot. Said they need people our age."

"Because we are the future."

"Exactly. Think it's a line they give to everyone?"

"No. In general, I think they probably have more people than they need here in New Town."

"Then why ask us to stay? It's not as if we're engineers or scientists, and they could be rid of us tomorrow morning."

Carter pulled off his cowboy hat—Max's old hat—and studied it for a moment. He'd wondered the very same thing Lanh was asking. Why would the powers that be in New Town want a diabetic eighteen-year-old and an Asian guy? What did they have to offer?

But he knew deep inside that the answer didn't much matter. Here they could make a difference. Back at High Fields, they were able to lend a hand, but they also used up precious resources. It made perfect sense for them to stay. All that was left was to figure out how to tell his mom.

SEVENTY

Max was amazed at how quickly they'd fallen into a routine. Their group met together for dinner, sharing what they'd seen, what they'd learned, and questions they still had. Afterward, as they had the night before, they walked out to the village green. The area was full of families— young families with toddlers running out the last of their energy and babies lying on blankets. Teenagers grouped together, laughing about something, and then getting up to play with a Frisbee. Where had they found that?

Then there were the older folks—people Max's age. Except he didn't feel that old. He felt more like the goofy teenager leaping to catch a Frisbee, missing it, and falling to the ground with a laugh. He was certain that a core part of himself was still that age. Another part was old enough to care more about catching Shelby's hand than a Frisbee. She allowed it while they were walking, but then she pulled away from him and sat on the far side of their circle.

It felt good to be with others and yet together. They would soon be back on the road, back to depending on each other, and Max understood that they needed to gather their strength now.

"We should talk about tomorrow," Gabe said.

"Specifically?" Patrick stopped rubbing Bianca's shoulders and sat forward, suddenly all attention.

"Routes. I've received a few pass codes, and I think we can make it back more quickly and with fewer mishaps." He pulled out a map and showed them a route that skimmed Oklahoma City to the east, continued down west of Fort Worth and dumped them right back onto Highway 281 north of Abney.

"You think we can get through here?" Max tapped the Dallas–Fort Worth metroplex. "They were nuked. Remember?"

"Which is why the military has been able to go back in and establish a presence. They've transported out the survivors, though there were precious few. Mostly people who had tornado basements, enough food to last them, that sort of thing."

"Why go that way at all?" Shelby asked. "Why not go back the way we came?"

"We could," Gabe admitted. "But reports are that Wichita Falls has expanded their borders. And we definitely can't cross the border on NASA's road."

"They found it?" Bianca reached up and rubbed her shoulder like she had a crick in her neck. Maybe she did. Their cots were good, but they were still cots. She was probably ready to be home in her own bed. But she wouldn't be going

431

there. She'd be going to Patrick's. They were ready to start their life together. She glanced up, seemed to read Max's mind, and smiled.

"They did. We won't be crossing there because there's a new toll booth—group of goons that the government plans to deal with in the next week."

"Too late for us," Shelby noted.

"Our other option is to go farther west, which would be a significant detour."

Max noticed that Carter and Lanh weren't saying much. They were listening, but they weren't offering an opinion, which was completely out of character.

"Do you feel good about the new route?" Patrick asked.

"Yes. The military codes will give us access to I-35 where it crosses the Red River, as well as guarantee safe travel around the Dallas–Fort Worth area."

"I thought the government wasn't branching out." Shelby rubbed her index finger over her thumb—back and forth, back and forth, like a worry stone. "I thought it was going to be years."

Gabe didn't answer immediately. He glanced around to be sure no one was in listening distance, and still he lowered his voice. "We have twelve separate prototypical towns or government centers . . ."

"Twelve?" Shelby asked.

"At least, and they plan to extend to twenty-four by the end of the year." He held up his hand when Bianca started firing questions. "That's all I can tell you. The point is, the central government understands the importance of maintaining corridors of transportation, and they've managed to do that. We can get through this way."

"I don't like coming into Highway 281 through the Glen Rose area." Patrick shook his head. "The road winds through some areas where there is significant elevation gain. It's the perfect spot for an ambush."

Everyone started talking at once then. There was concern because they would be in one vehicle, which could compromise the safety of the supplies they were taking to Abney if that vehicle were attacked. How much ammunition did they still have? Would they approach the area during the day or the night? Even Carter and Lanh were jumping into the discussion now. Max glanced at Shelby. She nodded once, so he raised a hand to get everyone's attention.

"One of Shelby's interviewees was a young woman who is a member of the Remnant."

"Kinsley Storm," Shelby said. "Twenty-four and working with the government's transportation department."

"Transportation?" Bianca asked.

"Specifically, horses." Max motioned for Shelby to continue.

"Kinsley has given us the name and locations

of the Remnant groups in north Texas. One of them was near the Glen Rose area. They'll help us through."

The group was silent as everyone digested the information.

Finally, Max leaned back and said, "So it's settled. We leave at first light, and we take Gabe's route."

Carter glanced at Lanh, who nodded. Then he said, "There's something we need to talk to you about first. Lanh and I . . . we've decided to stay."

SEVENTY-ONE

Max thought he understood on one level what Shelby was going through. On another level, he knew he couldn't begin to fathom what she was feeling. Carter had been a major part of her life for nineteen years. He'd been the main focus of her existence since the flare. Now he was saying he was ready to be on his own. From the expression on her face, that was something she had not foreseen at all.

Carter and Lanh had made their announcement and then laid out their reasons logically and succinctly. It was something they'd obviously given a lot of thought to.

Shelby had been unusually quiet, nodding, not asking questions, reaching out once to squeeze Carter's hand and later to pull him into a hug. They all patted the boys on the back, said they understood, and wished them the best. It felt too casual, even to Max. After all, they weren't leaving them for a semester. It could be years before they saw them again.

She hadn't begun to cry until they were alone. Then only a few tears trailed down her cheeks, which she quickly brushed away.

"In one sense, it means you raised him right." They were walking along the river. After

435

everyone had congratulated Carter and Lanh, Shelby had walked away from the group, and Carter had followed her. They'd spent less than five minutes together, standing shoulder to shoulder. Max had waited until he saw Carter walking back, and then he'd given her a few more minutes alone. Eventually, his heart had propelled him to find her.

"Tell me you're not here to cheer me up."

"Do you need cheering up?"

"I don't know what I need, Max."

They walked in silence for a few more minutes, the nearly full moon lighting their way.

"I knew this day would come."

"Of course you did."

"And I thought I was ready—before the flare."

"But since then . . ."

"Since then it's been day to day. Our entire life has become day to day."

"Maybe that's why he wants to stay."

Shelby turned and looked at him sharply, but she didn't argue with what he'd said, so he pushed on.

"This gives both Carter and Lanh a chance to focus on the future. They won't be consumed with finding enough food each day . . ."

"Or enough medicine."

"That too."

Shelby stopped and plopped down on the riverbank. The sound of the water flowing by was oddly comforting—its persistence, its naturalness. It occurred to Max that life was that way. It kept going regardless.

"How could I want him with me when he would be safe here?"

"Relatively."

"Oh, I understand nowhere is safe, not like we thought we were before. But that was an illusion, Max. This world isn't meant to be our haven. I know that. But I can't help wanting what's best for my son."

"Carter knows how much you care about him."

They were silent a moment, and then she said, "It's about more than safety. Did you notice the way his eyes lit up when he talked about what he'd be doing? Robotics and pharmacology and herbs."

"I did."

"I only understood half of what he said." She sighed and flopped onto her back, staring up at the stars. "He's actually excited about something for the first time in a long time. Maybe for the first time since Kaitlyn died."

That sat between them for a moment, along with the memory of all they'd lost.

"If Carter stays—"

"Oh, he's staying. I wouldn't think for a minute of asking him to give up his dream for me."

"Okay, he's staying. But you're not going to be alone now, Shelby. You'll still have me." He reached for her hand and laced his fingers with hers. More than anything, he wanted to pull her into his arms, wipe the look of concern off her face, and be her strength when she was hurting. He wanted to confess his undying love once more, but something told him that now wasn't the time.

"I could stay too."

A stone dropped into the pit of Max's stomach.

"MacRae brought it up earlier today. They'd let me. They'd let any of us."

Max shook his head. "I have to go home. I have to be there for my parents."

Now she rolled over onto her side. Propped up on one elbow, she studied him in the darkness. "The crazy thing? I want to be there for them too. I want to be back at High Fields. It's where I belong, helping the people we know and love—not out here pioneering the new world. I want to go home."

"Does that . . . could that have anything to do with me?"

He could barely make out her expression in the moonlight, but there was no mistaking the feel of her palm against his cheek or the tenderness of her lips on his. He pushed his fingers through her hair, kissed her eyelids, her cheeks, her lips once more, and suddenly there was nothing between them. The flare and the deaths and the grief and the fear all melted away as she kissed him again. Then she rested her forehead against his. Her breathing was ragged and her skin hot under his hands. She held his face between her hands, kissed him once more, and then instead of saying another word, she stood and walked back to their barracks.

They'd snuggled and hugged and cried and wept together in the last nine months. They'd also fought and hollered and clashed wills. He'd even kissed her a few times, but Max was sure that it was the first time in many, many years that Shelby had allowed her feelings for him to show. Was she finally letting go of the past? Was she ready to move into the future? And if so, what did she want that future to look like?

SEVENTY-TWO

Shelby woke to a sunny, cold spring day. When they walked to the mess hall, grass crunched beneath their feet. A light frost had carpeted the grass, the tops of tents, even the leaves on the trees they walked beneath. It was winter's last hoorah. Summer was on its way. She wasn't looking forward to months of blistering heat and dry weather, but they had survived it once.

They would survive it again.

Before they reached the mess hall, she pulled Carter and Lanh off to the side. The conversation didn't last long.

"You two don't need my permission . . ."

"We don't want to do anything that would hurt the group," Lanh said.

"Or you," Carter added.

"I know you don't, and that thoughtfulness shows how much you've grown in the past year. This is good, though. It's what you boys should be doing . . . oh, what am I saying? You're men now." She hugged Lanh and then Carter. "I'm proud of you both, and I know that what you're going to be doing here will make a difference. It's the right thing for you to do. It's right for all of us."

Lanh grinned, and Carter readjusted his black hat.

She was going to miss both of them so much that it felt like she was leaving a part of herself in New Town. She could tell herself a thousand times that it felt right, that it was right, and that it should happen—but she still struggled with a profound sense of loss. The ache in her heart was like a gaping hole that she couldn't imagine healing, but the relief on their faces? It eased that ache the tiniest bit.

"Promise me you'll write."

"There's no mail," Carter said.

"When there is."

"Oh. Of course."

"Too bad we can't text." Lanh led the way into the mess hall.

"Or Skype. That would be radical." And then the two started talking about abandoned technology and how it could still be integrated into their new world. Just like that, their minds and attention were on the future. Which was as it should be.

They filed into line behind their group. Max had filled his plate with fresh eggs, bacon, and grits. Where had they found grits? "Military storage facilities," Gabe said. The butter was fresh, though, and the coffee strong and hot.

Shelby told herself that she should eat while

she could, but after the second bite, she gave up on that very good intention and focused on consuming two cups of coffee.

Everything had been loaded into the Hummer the night before.

All that was left was saying goodbye.

There were a lot of pats on the back, hugs, promises to be careful, and vows to make it home as soon as the roads opened. Shelby stood back and tried to memorize every aspect of Carter, as if she would ever forget a single detail.

The right side of his mouth rose slightly higher than the left when he smiled.

His voice was lower than it had been six months ago.

He was thin—the word *sinewy* came to mind—but he was also strong.

She was astounded that she could love another person as much as she loved her son. It felt physically painful, like her heart had been cleaved in two and part of it resided in the young man standing in front of her.

When Gabe, Patrick, Bianca, and Max were in the Hummer, she pulled Lanh into a hug and whispered, "Please be careful."

"You know we will be."

Carter stood there awkwardly for a moment before wrapping his arms around her and pulling her into a bear hug. She breathed in the scent of him, this man-child who had been the greatest blessing of her life. He ruffled her hair. She stood on her tiptoes and kissed him on the cheek, and then she climbed into the vehicle, tears streaming down her face.

SEVENTY-THREE

The drive south went smoothly—at first.

Gabe slowed the Hummer as they passed the station where they'd left the Dodge and the Mustang.

"Someone should play taps," Bianca said.

But it occurred to Shelby that if they hadn't had the Hummer, their story might have ended there. No, that wasn't true. They would have walked. They would have somehow made it to New Town. It had been their fate, their destiny, the road that God had prepared for them. How else could she explain finding it? And the fact that they'd reclaimed their vehicles from Hugo, survived the tornado, found the Mars expedition survivors, and outrun the Wild West cast from hell.

The flare, the deaths, the universal devastation might have shaken that particular aspect of her faith somewhat, but the foundation of what she believed was strong. She could see God's hand guiding their path. And yes, she realized that was contradictory, but she was learning to accept that at times life was contradictory. You pushed on, regardless.

They circled Oklahoma City to the east per MacRae's instructions, which brought them closer to the urban center than they had been before. The sight of the city skyline immediately brought back the certainty that they weren't in New Town anymore. Furthermore, there was no doubt that the city was dying. Smoke rose from several of the skyscrapers. Abandoned cars stretched for miles filling both the inbound and outbound lanes. The road they were on, the one MacRae had told them about, seemed to be the only through access, and they were only allowed on it because Gabe had shown a piece of paper to the sentries on the northern end. The military had a presence here, but it was a subtle one. Little more than a conduit from one destination to another. Only two lanes had been cleared. The road contained little traffic.

A few military transports.

One sedan that must have held someone important because there was a military jeep in front of and behind it.

"It's almost as if life is beginning to return to normal," Bianca said.

Shelby was again sitting in the middle of the backseat of the Hummer—Max, then Shelby, then Bianca. Gabe was driving, and Patrick was riding shotgun.

She stared out the front windshield, trying to see what Bianca saw. Trying to find hope in the landscape in front of them. "Except there are no families on this road."

"And then we have the burning buildings to the

west." Patrick turned and smiled back at his wife as he said it.

Max was frowning at something on the horizon.

Patrick noticed and asked, "What were you and MacRae talking about this morning? At breakfast?"

"Their need for a court system."

"A court system?" Patrick snorted. "Maybe in ten years."

"Maybe someone needs to start planning for it now, and maybe it doesn't need to be the last thing on the list."

"Spoken like a lawyer looking for a job," Patrick teased.

"Max is right," Gabe said. "I spoke with the general about that very thing. What they're doing will work in places with a limited population and good people in charge. Once you get too many people, or you get the wrong people in charge, it's going to fall apart."

In the distance, Shelby spotted what Max had been frowning at. A tent community, throngs of people milling about, a river of humanity flowing out of the burning city. Shelby couldn't fathom where they were going. She didn't want to imagine that. She wanted to close her eyes and forget. She wanted to wake up back in High Fields, sequester herself in her little cottage, and sleep for a week.

"You did the right thing," Bianca said.

"I had no choice."

"You did. We both know Carter wouldn't have stayed if you'd asked him to come back."

"I keep wondering . . . what does the future hold for him? What will his life be like?"

"It'll be better, Shelby. You know that. MacRae assured us they have adequate medical supplies for the people in New Town, including insulin."

And that was the deciding point. How could she argue that Carter's future was in High Fields?

Without medication, returning there would be a death sentence. What had Lieutenant Perez said? One to two years before they would branch out to rural towns, and there was no chance that Carter would survive that long on the insulin they had left, even calculating in what the general had given them. She'd made the right decision. Carter had made the right decision, and the fact that Lanh was with him helped.

Shelby squared her shoulders, determined to focus on the best parts of her son's future. "Did you notice how excited he was describing wind turbine trees and solar fields?"

"It's his world." Max rubbed at his right temple as he spoke. "Us old folks might understand and certainly appreciate what they design, but it will be their world to grow up in. What we had? Air-conditioning twenty-four/seven, texting, and Amazon deliveries? Those things will be a distant memory."

She supposed there were things she wouldn't miss, but the thought of the life they'd lived before the flare being a distant memory didn't sit well with her. She pulled out her journal and read over her notes, adding details here and there, correcting spelling, assuring herself that what they'd left behind was real and not a figment of her imagination.

The road stretched out in front of them, and they made good time. Shelby felt herself being pulled in two directions. She resisted the distance stretching between her and Carter, and she longed to be back at High Fields.

She wanted to slow them down and at the same time urge Gabe to drive faster.

Gabe didn't drive any faster. They maintained a safe speed of forty-five miles per hour. Each person watched out the vehicle windows, alert for trouble. But there wasn't any trouble. There was only desolation and emptiness. They all felt it. After the hope and inspiration of New Town, their world seemed all the more shattered.

They had no trouble crossing into north Texas, once Gabe and Patrick exited the Hummer and spoke to the guards.

Rejoining the group, both men looked even grimmer, and Shelby understood that this was the dangerous part. They were back in the fray now.

As Patrick buckled his seat belt, he said, "We'll

be passing far enough west of Dallas that the route should be safe."

"No danger of contamination?"

"Not that far west. The prevailing winds at the time of the blast were to the east. We'll take a wide path to avoid any problems."

"How long?" Shelby asked. "How long until . . . people can go back into the Dallas area?"

"Not in our lifetime." Gabe met Shelby's gaze in the rearview mirror. "Or Carter's."

They stopped outside of Gainesville, well north of the DFW area, and decided to spend the night a half mile off the road in a grove of oak trees. They'd passed an abandoned gas station and motel, but no one wanted to risk being in a high-profile place. Better to camp in a field, where they could see anything that might be coming toward them.

As they were eating dinner, Max sat there, paying no attention to the bag that held his MRE.

"If you're not going to eat that, I will," Patrick said.

Max handed it over without a word, and that was when Shelby realized something was terribly wrong.

SEVENTY-FOUR

"I'm in the early stages of a migraine." Max didn't bother looking around. He knew how this news would be met. He understood that his illness was endangering the entire group. The timing was terrible, but there was nothing he could do about it.

Patrick, Bianca, and Shelby knew about his condition, but Gabe didn't, so Max directed his comments to the doctor.

"I wasn't aware that you had them." Gabe began rummaging through his medical bag, which he kept in his backpack. "Do you know what kind?"

"Basilar."

Gabe looked up, nodded once, and slowly closed the bag. Max knew that he would be all too aware there was nothing they could do.

"You have received a professional diagnosis for basilar migraines?"

"When I was much younger. They have become less frequent over the years. Unfortunately, they tend to hit at the most inopportune times."

He glanced at Shelby and waited for her to tell what had happened a week and a half after the flare.

"He had a bad one when we were leaving

Abney headed for the ranch, Carter and Max and me. It was . . . it was one of the worst I've ever seen. I should have recognized the symptoms—"

"I should have told you. I thought I could . . . I could . . . make it, but I put you and Carter at risk. I won't do that again." Even talking was painful. He closed his eyes and tried to focus on this all-important discussion, but the voices of his friends sounded like they were being blasted through a loudspeaker. He longed to clamp his hands over his ears and shut out the noise.

"You held it together somehow, Max. I still don't understand how you did it, but you managed to keep driving until we were a safe distance from the goons trying to attack us."

Shelby continued to stare at him, and Max saw such compassion there—not blame, but tenderness—that he wanted to put his head down and weep. What had he done to earn the affection of this woman?

"He basically passed out once we made it to the roadblock that had been set up on the south side of the ranching area where High Fields is located." Now she grinned ruefully at him. "I thought those boys were going to shoot us for sure, but then one of them recognized Max, and after that the cavalry arrived."

"I'm yelling too now . . . ." He shook his head and attempted to correct the words coming out of his mouth, "I'm telling noo two."

Patrick tried to hide a snicker, and then they were all laughing. Not that it was a laughing matter, but sometimes stress and strain found a way out regardless of how you tried to hold them in.

When the laughter had subsided, and Shelby had wiped away the tears slipping down her cheeks, Max said. "Leave me."

He knew that the odds were they wouldn't, but he had to try. He had to make them see that getting back to High Fields and Abney was the priority.

"I'll . . . catch up." He shook his head again, but the small movement sent a blinding shaft of light from the sunset through his right eye. It wouldn't be long now. He'd be curled into a ball, and it could be hours or even days before he came around again.

Not that anyone was listening to him.

"We'll build him a shelter, there in the trees," Gabe said.

"I'll find the tarps." Patrick was on his feet, heading toward the Hummer without waiting for Max's response.

He couldn't very well argue when he had trouble speaking coherently. The migraine was progressing more quickly than he'd anticipated. Actually, he'd suspected it in the middle of the night when he woke with a throbbing at the base of his skull. He'd prayed he was wrong.

Max looked over at the Hummer, saw two, closed his eyes, and willed his vision to clear. When he opened them again, there was only one vehicle. His tongue felt thick, and the words continued to jumble together when he tried to speak. He allowed his head to fall into his hands. The inkiness of the night would help if he could survive the pain another hour. He dreaded sunrise and the motion of the vehicle. He recoiled at the thought.

"Shelby and Bianca, get his bedroll and pack, also some water to keep next to him." Gabe stood and helped Max to his feet. "We want to put it all as far back in these trees as possible. Tomorrow's sun will be brutal."

And so Max succumbed to the ministrations of his friends.

His bedroll was tucked in the shelter of the trees.

Shelby helped him to his feet. He made the mistake of looking up, and the early stars and moon began to spin.

"Whoa, cowboy. Easy there." She wrapped her arm around his waist and shuffled him over to where he was supposed to sleep.

A groan escaped his lips as he crawled into the sleeping bag. He quickly backed out, lurched away from his bedroll, and vomited in the bushes.

Gabe checked his pulse. "As I'm sure you know, traditional migraine medications are ineffective and dangerous for you to take. However, I do have morphine if the pain becomes too much."

"Tho nanks."

"All right. If you change your mind, let me know."

Bianca set his pack next to the bedroll along with a bottle of water and his flashlight. Patrick checked his weapon, left it and extra ammo within reach. Shelby formed a pillow out of some clothes, tucked it under his head, and kissed him softly on the forehead.

He'd known deep down that they wouldn't leave him. But after what had happened on that fateful trip to High Fields, he'd felt duty bound to at least warn them. They were a team in every sense of the word, strong because they could and did depend on one another. For the foreseeable future, Max would be helpless, but he at least knew, as unconsciousness claimed him, that he was in good hands.

SEVENTY-FIVE

Shelby understood how hard it had been for Max to admit he could no longer travel. Actually, he might have been able to. Gabe could have sedated him, and they could have tucked him in the back of the Hummer. But that seemed unwise at best and foolish at worst.

The truth was that they needed Max. They needed each person in their group if they were going to make it back to Abney. The devastation of Dallas and the dangers of Glen Rose loomed in her mind—both giant question marks. Her thoughts shied away from imagining what Dallas would look like. Would they be able to see evidence of the fallout? Would there be bodies? Would a black soot cover everything?

And Glen Rose. She'd always loved that portion of the drive from Abney to Dallas, but now it represented another hurdle in their path. There was no doubt that the twisting road running alongside Chalk Mountain would be dangerous. It was too tempting a spot for some group not to have claimed it. They could attempt to go around, which might not be any better. Often predators depended on that, splitting their resources between a vulnerable spot and the backup roads.

Their best hope was to find the Remnant.

But first they had to wait for Max to recover.

"He's going to be all right," Bianca said.

"I know he will."

They were finishing off the coffee, sitting in front of the small fire that was blocked from the wind and hidden from anyone that might pass by. The flames crackled and popped, and the smell of smoke would reach far and wide. But that didn't in and of itself invite trouble. Campfires were the norm now. They were everywhere. She could look out across the night and make out one, then another, and a third.

Other people trying to find their way.

"Might take a day or two."

"Probably two." Shelby stared into the fire. "Do you remember what you said to me? That day in Abney when I was trying to decide whether to go to High Fields?"

"I imagine it was something direct. Subtleness isn't my gift."

"You called me your *hermana.*"

"And you are. We're sisters in the truest sense of the word."

"You reminded me that everything can change—in an instant."

"We could all use that reminder."

"You told me to forgive Max." Shelby swiped at the tears coursing down her cheeks. "And you said—"

"I said you might not get another chance."

456

"I've had a lot of chances, but I've squandered them. Seeing him that way . . . seeing him so helpless . . . I understand how much he means to me, and how much I need him."

Bianca reached for her hand, pulled it into her lap, clasped it as she interlaced her fingers with Shelby's.

"I've been a fool."

"Then stop."

Shelby laughed, a pitiful sound given that it came out as she choked on a sob. Why did her heart have to hurt so much? Why did she keep losing people she cared about? Only Max wasn't lost. He was lying a few feet from her. She only had to figure out how to bridge the distance she had created between them.

"I have to stop being so afraid."

"What, exactly, are you afraid of?"

"Caring too much?"

Bianca stood, leaned down, and kissed her on top of the head. "There's no such thing, *mi hermana*. There's no such thing."

Shelby watched her walk away, walk over to Patrick. She said something, reached down, and touched his face. Patrick rubbed the top of his head, took her hand, and led her toward their bedrolls. Their commitment to one another was evident in so many different ways, from the looks they gave one another to something as simple and ordinary as reaching for one another's hands.

With that image in mind, Shelby stood and made her way toward her guard position. Two of their group stood guard in three-hour shifts while the others slept.

She had duty with Gabe, each of them positioned at opposite ends of their camp.

There was no fear of falling asleep. She felt more awake than she had in years. Her eyes were suddenly opened wide, and she could see everything around her, hear everything, sense everything.

The starlight was brighter. She could make out the sound of a redbird in a nearby tree. A cow lowed softly. Shelby held her rifle at the ready, every fiber of her body attune to the world around her, to the possible danger approaching them. But there was no danger that night. It was a spring night in Texas, the March wind occasionally gusting, the stars big and bright, the moon gracing them with a bit of extra light.

This was their world. She could go through it alone, or she could accept the love that Max continually offered her. She'd always thought of herself as a brave person, but love wasn't for the faint of heart. Did she have that kind of courage? She wiped her palms on her pants, marveled that her body was reacting like she was standing on a precipice. And maybe she was.

When her shift was up, she'd made up her mind.

She gathered up her bedroll, her pack, her weapon, and her flashlight, and moved it all next to Max.

He didn't wake, didn't stir in any way.

His mother had said it was often like that, as if he had to slip away until the pain eased.

It didn't matter that Max wasn't aware of her presence. She knew she was beside him, watching over him, there in case he needed her. She knew she was where she was supposed to be, which is perhaps why she was able to drift off into a deep, dreamless sleep.

SEVENTY-SIX

One day passed, and then two. They continued their rotation, and for Shelby the time became a blur of guard duties, meals, sleep, and monitoring Max. Each time she came off duty, she checked on him to make sure his breathing was steady and his shelter was as dark as possible. They'd hung some of their extra clothing over a tarp to block out the worst of the sun.

The weather grew steadily warmer. An afternoon shower left them dripping wet but cleaner. Gabe, Bianca, and Patrick had sheltered in the Hummer. Shelby stayed with Max. The others offered, but she needed to be there with him. She realized now, more than ever, how much she cared for him.

Perhaps it was seeing him so incapacitated that he was unable to even reach for the bottle of water. Perhaps it was knowing that she couldn't move forward without him, wouldn't even consider doing so.

It was the middle of the third night, as Shelby was coming off a guard shift, that Max reached for her hand and pulled her close to his side. She set the low-light lantern on the ground. It cast a soft glow across the makeshift shelter.

"How are you?"

"Better."

"Can you drink a little?"

He nodded, so she uncapped the bottle, held it for him, supported his head as he sipped from it.

"I'm sorry." His voice was gravelly, soft, tender.

"You have nothing to be sorry for, Max. This isn't something you can help. It's part of who you are."

"And you love me anyway?"

The words were teasing, but she saw the seriousness in his expression, the worry in his eyes. Why would he worry, though? He had to know he'd held her heart in his hands for more than twenty years.

"I do." She reached out and ran the tips of her fingers up and down his face.

"Marry me, Shelby."

"Now? Here?" It was wrong to make light of his words at such a moment, but her heart was thundering so fast that she felt light-headed. It had been almost a year since the flare. Max had spent every day since that terrible event trying to prove his loyalty, striving to show how much he cared, sacrificing for her and Carter and their friends. This was a man that she could trust with her future and with her heart.

"Okay," she whispered. "I'll marry you."

"As soon as we get home."

Shelby glanced at her watch. Twenty minutes

after three in the morning, and they were discussing wedding plans. "Maybe you should focus on getting well."

"I'm better." He struggled to a sitting position, pulled her into his arms, and kissed the top of her head. "We'll be to Glen Rose by noon, Shelby. By sunset we should be home."

She reached up, touched his lips, allowed him to kiss her, and for the first time in many years, she didn't hold a thing back. She yielded her dreams and hopes and fears in the space of that kiss.

True to his word, Max was ready to leave at sunrise. Shelby felt herself grinning when he shared their plans to marry with the group as they ate granola and sipped campfire coffee.

Cheers, hugs, and congratulations, and then they were on their way. But as they passed northeast of Dallas, their mood grew more somber.

Bianca leaned forward and tapped Gabe on the shoulder. "Explain why we're not seeing effects from the blast."

"All indications are that the blast occurred in the downtown area. We don't know why or who was responsible. The destruction there would be complete."

"Vaporized?" Max asked.

"Pretty much. Everything from the blast site out one mile in all directions would be gone. Severe damage another quarter mile—it's doubtful anyone within that radius would have survived."

No one spoke. They stared out the Hummer's windows but couldn't see anything noteworthy. In fact, the entire area was a ghost town.

"Moderate damage up to two miles out, and light damage for three and a half."

"But we're nearly twenty miles away, and everyone is gone." Shelby clutched her journal as though it might hold answers to what they were seeing. "Why?"

"People panic in unknown situations, especially ones that have been portrayed over and over again in movies. My guess is they saw the mushroom cloud, heard the blast wind, and they ran. Maybe they were worried about the weather changing, blowing radioactive fallout their way."

"Such a waste." Patrick practically spat the words. "Things were bad enough. People were dealing with enough, and some maniac had to get his hands on a bomb. But why set it off? What did they hope to accomplish?"

No one spoke for a few moments, honoring with their silence those who had perished. When they'd driven another mile, Gabe cleared his throat and said, "General Massey is of the opinion that it was intentional, not accidental— and before you ask, I can't tell you why. Several groups, both foreign and domestic, have claimed responsibility."

"How do we know that?" Bianca had been staring out the window, but now she leaned forward into the front seat. "How can they know that?"

"Morse code still works. Couriers can travel on foot or on horse or even in a vehicle as we are. His information is solid. That's all I can say."

"Not much information, if you ask me." Max crossed his arms. "Someone did it. We could have told him that."

"He knows more, but I can't share it." Gabe nodded toward a roadside park. "Anyone want a break?"

"No." Shelby knew she was speaking for the entire group, that they all felt the same. "Let's get out of here."

SEVENTY-SEVEN

They stopped to eat lunch in the Hummer, stretching their legs and using the facilities, which basically meant stepping off into a wooded area to go to the bathroom. It went unsaid that no one went anywhere alone. They were on high alert.

Overall they were making good time, and Max should have felt pleased. He *was* pleased.

He was still riding a high that Shelby had agreed to marry him, that she'd finally knocked down the carefully erected emotional wall she'd kept between them. Everything was different—the way she looked at him, her hand on his arm, even the way she wrote in her journal and then pushed it into his hands. At long last, they were a team, and he knew a peace unlike anything he could remember.

But riding beneath all of that was the undercurrent of danger. Like a storm, they could practically smell its approach. They skirted Fort Worth, began to see people again when they dropped south to Cleburne, and then they turned west to Glen Rose. No one was on the roads, but occasionally they would spot a farmer in the distance, working with a team of horses and planting his crops the old way.

465

The sun was dipping toward the western sky by the time they turned north on Highway 144.

"Go north for 7.2 miles," Shelby said.

Patrick turned toward the backseat to study her.

"I thought you weren't mentioning the Remnant in your journal."

"I'm not."

"So how is it that you have a map to their encampment in there?" He nodded toward the journal she was holding.

"It's sort of in a code."

"Yeah. My woman is a code-breaker." Max wriggled his eyebrows, but no one laughed. They were all tense and ready to be through this last part of their journey. In the old days, they would be a mere ninety-minute drive from home. He pushed that thought from his mind.

"I didn't break the code. I wrote it."

"She's modest too."

"I wrote down some details of Kinsley's 'family homestead.' " She put virtual quotation marks around the last two words.

"Nearly there," Gabe said.

"You should see a field with an antique tractor parked near the road, a weathered scarecrow in the seat. Turn west."

Gabe slowed, pulled onto a dirt road, and stopped the vehicle in front of a gate. The lock was an old-fashioned combination one, where you turned seven digits and then yanked on the bottom. Max had been with Shelby when she interviewed Kinsley. He'd reached over and stopped her pen when she'd nearly written down the code. Instead, he'd suggested they both memorize it. Now he climbed out of the Hummer and walked up to the gate.

It opened on the first try, and everyone let out a subdued *hurrah* when Max turned toward them, a grin on his face and the opened lock in his hand. Gabe drove through, Max relocked the gate, and they proceeded up the dirt road.

Their instructions had been to reach the crest of the road and wait. It was a vulnerable position, and they had no way to know that this portion of the Remnant hadn't been infiltrated. Still, it was their best bet. Otherwise, they'd be driving straight through enemy territory. There was no way to know how far around they'd have to go in order to find an open route. So they waited, first ten, then twenty minutes. Just when Max thought that no one was home, they were surrounded by men on horseback.

Bianca was standing to Shelby's right, Max on her left. They were once again in a semicircle, standing a fair distance from the Hummer and with no packs or weapons on their persons.

Gabe had also insisted they leave the doors of the Hummer open. "Otherwise, they might worry we have more guys inside, waiting to jump out."

"Can we help you folks?" This from a woman wearing a tan Stetson, with long, gray hair held back with a leather strap. She was probably Hispanic, or she might have simply been weathered by too much time riding in the Texas sun.

"We were looking for a friend." Gabe had his hands half raised, a show of goodwill and respect.

"Goes by the name of Micah," Patrick said.

"Last time we saw him, he had five friends with him." Shelby felt ridiculous saying it. But that was the code—had been the code from the very beginning—Micah 5.

"We could use his help." Bianca shifted her weight from her right foot to her left. *Queremos llegar a casa a nuestra familia.* Is he here? Is Micah with you?"

Max later would think back on that moment, of the hard-looking men surrounding them and the vulnerable position they'd put themselves in, and he'd think that Bianca's switching from flawless English to her natural language and back again might have been the one thing they could have done to prove which side they were on. She was, after all, a Hispanic woman trying to find her way home.

The woman cocked her head, waited the space of three heartbeats, and then said, "My name's Concetta. Welcome to the Remnant."

The home she led them to was made of stone. Max guessed it to be at least a hundred years old, though from the looks of it, someone had updated everything before the flare. Concetta gave them a brief tour. Solar panels adorned the roof. A cellar adjacent to the house had been expanded and updated with additional shelves, a metal door, and a generator, which ran the lighting.

Beyond the storage room was a room with cots and a small kitchen. "This was Benjamin's fallback position. Not that he ever planned to live down here, but he wanted to have the option."

"Benjamin . . . he's the person who owns all of this?" Gabe stood with his hands on his hips, turning in a slow circle, studying the place.

"Everything you see belongs to the Remnant. Benjamin West is our leader, but he doesn't own any more or any less than another member."

"Where is Benjamin?" Max asked.

"He's moving cattle at the moment. You'll meet him at dinner, assuming you all can stay that long."

"We'd hoped to be home tonight," Max said.

"Maybe by sunrise." Concetta led the way back up the cellar stairs and out into the waning sunlight.

"You've helped people through before?" Shelby asked.

Max understood the urgency behind her words. It seemed they were so close that they could barrel their way through if only these people would point them in the right direction.

"Yes, and it gets harder every time."

"Back roads?" Bianca asked.

"Pastures. The only way through is via other people's property, and we know the people who will allow that."

"Are they part of the Remnant?"

"Some are. Some merely want whatever we're able to pay."

"Which is what?" Patrick asked. "What do you have to pay them with?"

"Seed, at the moment, is what folks need most. The seed we had before the flare is gone. And the crops we had . . ."

"Won't produce seed." Max scuffed the toe of his boot into the dirt. "We had the same problem at High Fields. Heirloom seeds have become quite valuable."

"And will probably remain so for the foreseeable future."

They spent the next hour viewing modifications that had been made to the barn, the fields, water retrieval systems, and even the chicken coops.

"Didn't know you could improve on a chicken coop," Bianca said.

"You'd be surprised what we've been able to

improve on. When you take the wisdom of our grandparents and combine it with the advances in technology—those that are still available to us—what you have is a very workable situation."

Which all sounded a bit too optimistic to Max. But if he'd thought this group of folks who constituted the Remnant had been sheltered since the flare, if he'd worried that they were naive, he was convinced otherwise at the evening meal.

That was when they met Benjamin and learned exactly what the Remnant had sacrificed to remain in existence. He had an artificial leg strapped to his right stump. "Found it in a medical supply store. Fits pretty well, considering."

Less than thirty years old, Caucasian, with a small gold ring in his right ear, Benjamin filled a lot of stereotypes for the millennial generation. And though he'd obviously suffered much, he retained an unfailing optimism about the future.

"You sustained your injury after the flare?" Gabe asked.

"During, actually. I was in a small commuter plane traveling from Dallas to Wichita Falls when the flare hit. We went down in a field." They'd finished eating, and now everyone pushed away their plates, sat back, and were transported back to that fateful day.

Max thought of Gorman Falls, Shelby stumbling into him as they descended the trail leading back to the parking area, looking up to see the lights of the aurora borealis, and the sight of planes falling from the sky. The terror and uncertainty of those first few days was still palpable. He wasn't sure it was something he or any of them would ever forget. He wasn't sure it was something they should forget.

"So how did you end up with the Remnant?" Max asked. "Did they rescue you from the plane?"

"They rescued me from far more than that."

SEVENTY-EIGHT

Shelby generally didn't put much stock in dramatic conversions. Hers was a faith that had grown from her childhood. Certainly, there'd been times during her life when she'd had to fall upon her belief, when she'd grown closer in her walk, but what Benjamin was describing was an entirely different thing.

"My grandfather was the pastor of a small local church," Benjamin said. "My family was in the pew every Sunday morning and most Sunday nights. By the time I was sixteen, I'd stopped attending. I was too busy playing football and studying for my SATs."

"Kinda scrawny for football," Patrick noted, causing everyone to laugh and easing some of the tension in the room. Seated around the table were the five from their group, plus another seven from the Remnant, with Benjamin sitting in the middle.

A baker's dozen. Shelby tried to think of it as a good thing, and pushed the superstition of unlucky thirteen from her mind.

"Running back for the Joshua Owls."

Max choked on the water he'd been about to swallow. "You're making that up."

"Nope. We all teased our teachers about it being a terrible name for a mascot, but we wore our

473

jerseys proudly. Joshua is a small town, so, you know, everyone got to play. I was good, though. I was fast." He reached down and rapped his knuckles against the plastic prosthesis. "Never imagined this. No, I was arrogant. I was certain that the world was mine to grab by the horns."

"You went to college," Bianca said.

"I did. Southern Methodist University School of Business, graduated with a master's and a top-notch job. I was on my way to big things when our plane dropped into a farmer's field not too far east of here."

He nodded to an older man. Shelby remembered his name was George but little else.

George said, "My wife and I, God bless her soul, were standing outside looking at the aurora when Benjamin's plane crashed into our field. We didn't have a lot of neighbors, but the ones we had showed up and helped pull folks from the wreckage. Eighteen people in all, including the pilot and crew. Fourteen of them died on impact. They're still buried there on our place. Evelynne, a young lady who was dressed in military uniform, died a week later."

"Which left me, Nick, and Christian." Benjamin nodded at two other men who were seated around the table. They nodded in acknowledgment but didn't add anything to the story.

"It's amazing that you survived such an injury," Gabe said.

"One of the men who rushed to help was a veterinarian. He knew immediately that amputating my leg was the only way to save my life. He never hesitated, and that was a miraculous thing in and of itself." Benjamin let his gaze travel around the table as he added, "It seems we can be divided into two types of people now . . . those who have adjusted to this new life and those who haven't."

"Of the ones who haven't, some try to hide, hoping they will have enough to survive." Concetta raised a hand in testament to those poor lost souls. "Others try to take what they need, what rightfully belongs to others."

"It was after the amputation that saved my life that I had the vision." There was no apology in Benjamin's voice. He related what had happened as if he were describing a meal he had helped to prepare the day before. No emotion. No doubt. Simply sharing the facts.

"I can't say if it was Jesus or the Father or one of the prophets of old. I'm not a theologian. But I do know that a presence appeared beside my bed and told me to care for the sheep. No explanation, no details, but I knew what I was supposed to do. I also knew then that I would survive the loss of a leg, that in this world there would be much loss. Losing my right leg was not the worst thing that could have happened to me. George lost his wife. Nearly everyone here has lost someone. I eventually traveled home, only to learn that my parents had perished within the first month—one from violence, the other from health complications."

"We have all lost someone," Shelby agreed. "But that doesn't make it any easier."

She glanced over at Bianca, who was watching Benjamin closely.

"You're right. It's not easy, but we must focus on the call rather than the loss. In the months immediately following the flare, we crossed paths with the Remnant three times, and eventually we joined them in their quest to help God's people. This place belonged to Concetta—"

"It belongs to us all now," she said.

It occurred to Shelby that she hadn't mentioned the place was hers. When she'd first shown them around, she'd simply said, "It belongs to the Remnant." Shelby wasn't a Bible scholar, but it reminded her of the early Christians who gave all to the church. Was that how they were supposed to live? It seemed to go against the grain of what it meant to be American, and yet these people were defending their country and standing up for Americans, but doing so in a fundamentally Christian way.

"We made some modifications to the house and barn early on, and those things helped us through the winter."

"You spoke about a quest to help God's

people." Gabe folded his arms on the table and studied their host. "Who is that, exactly? Who do you consider to be God's people?"

"Everyone. And you're wondering if that includes the hoodlums of this world. Yes, it does."

"Maybe you haven't seen what we've seen," Patrick said.

"Perhaps. Or perhaps we've seen worse. But who has sinned so much as to remove himself from the reach of God?" When no one answered, he continued. "If possible, we help all who seek God's path for their life. We do not judge a person by their past but by their works, by the state of their heart at this moment."

"All good and fine until someone pulls a gun on you."

"Yes, we must be discerning." Benjamin allowed his gaze to travel over each member of their group. "It is important to distinguish good from evil because we are also called to protect God's sheep. If that means slaying the wolves, then so be it."

SEVENTY-NINE

Max wasn't completely comfortable with Benjamin's story. Seeing visions? Hearing voices? Perhaps it had been the extreme pain of the amputation or whatever drugs the veterinarian had found to give him. There was no doubt that Benjamin believed he'd seen and heard something, that he believed he'd been called and set apart by God. Regardless of the circumstances for his conversion, Max did believe that the man's heart and commitment were in the right place.

They'd agreed before coming to dinner that they would share everything they'd learned at New Town, everything except the exact location. No one thought it would cause a mass exodus to the Flint Hills of Kansas, but they'd given their word to the general that they would leave out that one specific detail when talking to others. As for the rest of the information, it could provide the hope folks needed to survive the next three to five years.

Benjamin's group had a few questions, but basically each person took the news of the continued existence of the federal government with a shrug and a shake of their head. "No one we know has been sitting around waiting on the cavalry."

They did express interest in the types of power New Town was using.

"We haven't had time to focus on that here," Christian admitted.

"You'd think it would be a priority," Benjamin added. "But it's taken all of our attention to stay safe, have enough to eat, and fulfill our mission to the Remnant."

Gabe, Bianca, and Max took turns explaining about the different types of technology. Shelby had pulled out her notebook and was taking notes, though she assured Benjamin that she wouldn't reveal where they were situated or the code on the gate's lock.

"I'll focus on your conversion and how it resulted in your helping others."

At last the conversation turned to how they would reach Abney.

"You're right to assume that the area around Chalk Mountain is dangerous." Concetta placed her hands in front of her on the table and entwined her fingers together. "The elevation doubles in a relatively short distance—from six hundred and twenty feet to a tad over twelve hundred."

"Hardly a mountain," Gabe noted.

"True enough, but in Texas, any rise in elevation is an opportunity."

No one asked her to explain what she meant. They knew. Max knew. If someone were higher than you were, they could see you coming, see you going, intercept you at any point they chose, and shoot you at any time.

"Gangs?" Patrick asked.

Benjamin shrugged. "Labels aren't so important. Is the place guarded? Yes. Could you travel safely through on the highway? No."

Shelby stopped writing, her pen raised a half inch above the page. "Can you get us through?"

"Shouldn't be a problem," Benjamin said.

Concetta added, "Even with that Hummer of yours, provided we can fit you through some cattle gates."

"And if we can't get through the gates?" Bianca asked.

"Then we'll pull the fence down, put you through, and replace it. God willing, you'll be on the other side of Chalk Mountain before sunrise."

Concetta offered them a place to sleep in the barn. "At least you'll be out of the wind."

And indeed it had picked up again from the north. They pulled the Hummer into the barn in case they were being watched. The plan was for them to leave at three in the morning, which meant that it would be a good idea to get some rest. Gabe had stayed behind and examined Benjamin's amputation site. He returned to the barn and collapsed beside them on the far side of the Hummer.

"How is he?" Max asked.

"Basically, the man is in remarkable shape."

"And mentally? Is he . . ." Max made a circular motion beside his head.

"Ah, Max. I think your lawyer brain wants evidence when a situation can only be interpreted by faith."

"So you believe his vision?"

Gabe shrugged. "Doesn't matter if I believe him or not. The point is that he's willing to help us. But as a matter of fact, I do. My grandparents often spoke of such things. On several occasions, they warned me that the greatest challenge of our generation would be the inability to believe that which can't be proved."

They maintained their watch schedule, though it seemed a bit of overkill. Everyone was too keyed up to sleep. Home was less than one hundred miles to the south.

Max found Shelby sitting with her back against the wall, cleaning her weapon. One of their solar-charged lanterns spread a circle of soft light.

"Patrick's a bad influence on you."

"Think so?"

"Maybe. Or maybe his compulsive ways will save our lives in a few hours."

He removed his rifle and handgun from his pack, cleaned both, and repacked them. Then he pulled Shelby into the circle of his arms. With her back resting against his chest, Max felt as if a hole inside his heart had been filled. "Still plan on marrying me?"

"I do."

"Think of it. By this time tomorrow we could be man and wife."

"I wish Carter could have been there."

"He's the one who suggested I ask you."

"What?" She wiggled around in his arms so she was facing him. He could just make out the look of disbelief on her face.

"You're surprised that Carter knew how we felt about each other?"

"I'm shocked he would speak to you about it."

Max pushed a lock of black curls behind her ear, allowed his fingertips to linger on her face. "His exact words were, 'Go ahead and ask her already.' "

Shelby's eyes widened in astonishment, and then she began to laugh, and he joined her. Perhaps that was how the rest of their lives would be. Terrible trials punctuated by unexpected moments of joy. It wouldn't be such a bad future, he realized. It wasn't so very different from how they'd lived before. Only the particulars had changed. Perhaps life had been filled with danger and uncertainty since the day Adam and Eve were banished, since the day God placed an angel with a flaming sword to guard the east side of the garden, to guard the tree of life.

God created a perfect world, and man spoiled it.

Man was spoiling it again, but they could still

see God's hand. Perhaps proof of his presence wasn't as dramatic as an angel with a sword. Maybe that proof was in the help of a man who'd lost a limb, or the faithfulness in a group of friends, or the beauty of a sunrise. Perhaps proof of God's provision was everywhere, if only they had the eyes and the faith to see it.

He must have nodded off, because he was suddenly aware of the sound of Patrick and Bianca talking in low voices, the smell of Gabe pouring hot water over instant coffee, and the feel of Shelby stretching in his arms.

Dawn was still a few hours away, but their day—their last day on the road—had begun.

EIGHTY

Shelby realized she should be afraid, but she couldn't manage it.

Was this what soldiers experienced? Was this battle fatigue? She glanced at Patrick, but he was teasing Bianca, holding something up high so that she had to jump to reach it. Changing tactics, she landed a light punch to his stomach. He laughed and dropped the granola bar. They didn't look like they were experiencing any type of fatigue, but Shelby had woken with limbs that felt like deadweight, a buzzing in her head, and a heaviness in her heart.

"Count your blessings, Shelby. Counting your troubles won't do a bit of good." Her mother's voice was strong and steady in her memory, and it brought a measure of peace to her anxious soul.

Carter was safe.

They were nearly home.

Max loved her.

Max kissed the top of her head, which caused her to feel remotely like a dog. She didn't mind. She wanted to be treasured, cared for, enjoyed like the family pet. She was ready to start the normal part of her life. And though her heart still ached for Carter, she was coming to terms with the fact that he was where he should be.

She would see him again. She promised herself that. Even if it meant finding another vehicle and driving back to the Flint Hills.

Three of Benjamin's men walked into the barn. Max and Shelby joined the others, including Gabe, who pushed a mug of coffee into Shelby's hands. She sipped the piping hot liquid, willing the caffeine into her system as they huddled over the same map they'd looked at the night before. Nothing had changed. No great revelations from the night watch.

When Benjamin walked into the room, Shelby realized that she did believe his story. He held himself like a man who had nothing to prove, like someone who had seen the future and wasn't afraid of it. How was that possible in their world? But there it was. They could do worse than to follow someone like Benjamin West.

"Three cars. Mine in front of you, and Christian's behind." He nodded to a man with a long beard who had eaten with them the night before, one of the men who had been in the initial plane crash with him. Someone they could trust. "We drive with the lights off and hope the wind will muffle the sound of your Hummer."

"Sorry. The electric cars were all checked out."

It might have been the first joke Shelby had ever heard Gabe make, but if she thought it was because he was nervous, she was sorely mistaken. A close look at his face only showed the eagerness that she felt bubbling up in herself. Was he as excited to be home as she was? Would he even stay in Abney? Of course he wouldn't. He had information to deliver to Governor Reed. That expression on his face? It was a look of satisfaction over a mission nearly completed.

"Gabe, follow close to me, but not so close that you'll ram me if I have to stop suddenly. Christian and Nick will stay a little farther behind to close gates and watch for any trouble coming from our rear."

There didn't seem to be anything else to say, but then Concetta stepped forward, raised her hands, bowed her head, and in a calm and steady voice said, "Bless these your children, Father. Show them your mercy this day. Cover them with your grace. Lead them safely home."

Tears pricked her eyes, but Shelby quickly blinked them away. Now was not the time to become emotional. She could tell, though, from the looks on her friends' faces, that Concetta's prayer had touched their hearts as well. They would go down fighting if they had to, but they'd rather sneak through the properties surrounding Chalk Mountain, pop out the other side, and head home without causing a stir.

Dew-stained grass brushed against her pant legs.

Stars blazed overhead.

Gravel crunched beneath their tires.

Patrick drove. Gabe, who was undoubtedly the best shot in their group, rode shotgun. Shelby sat in the middle of the backseat with Bianca on her right and Max on her left. They rode with the windows down, straining to hear the sound of trouble.

But all they heard was a mockingbird in the brush, a deer snorting as it spooked and darted in the opposite direction, the hoot of an owl. The wind gusted occasionally, though it didn't affect the Hummer at all. It did blow through the vehicle, tossing Shelby's hair until she found a ball cap in a seat pocket and rammed it on her head.

They left Concetta's property, her figure fading in the rearview mirror. Slowly, they maneuvered through another cattle gate and then crossed a pasture, the Hummer rocking up and down, reminding her of when they'd crossed the Flint Hills. There were no lights in the distance this time, though. Whoever owned this property, presumably another member of the Remnant, was tucked in tight for the night. They crossed another cattle guard, ascended a hill, and stopped at the top before they plunged down again along what must have been a cattle trail because it certainly wasn't wide enough for an automobile. Branches scratched against the vehicle, and several times barbed wire ran so close that Shelby could see the barbs in the waning moonlight.

She lost all sense of direction as the Hummer turned and twisted, climbed and plunged back down.

They'd crossed the final pasture, and Christian was closing in behind them when Shelby saw the two-lane highway in front of them.

Could it be so simple as that? Were they home free now? It had been too easy. Hadn't it?

The radio Benjamin had given Gabe crackled.

"We've been spotted," Christian said. "Patrols are coming from the south. They're two clicks out."

"I'll handle them, Gabe." Benjamin's voice was solid, unafraid. "Make a right on the highway, proceed with your headlights off, and travel as fast as that Hummer will go."

"We'll stay and help—"

"These are people I know. We can handle them."

"Roger that. Thank you for your assistance."

As they passed Benjamin's lead vehicle, Patrick passed off the Remnant's radio to the person riding in the passenger seat. Shelby caught a glimpse of Benjamin in the dashboard lights. His eyes were calm, resolute, faithful.

They climbed out of the pasture and onto the paved road, the hum of tires against pavement making a markedly different sound.

Patrick accelerated until the wind rushing through the vehicle was like a relentless hand pushing Shelby back against the seat. No one moved to roll up the window. They were all on alert, straining to hear the sound of gunshots. Worried that despite Benjamin's presence, they would be pursued.

But who was a match for a Hummer, even one with a few nicks and scratches?

They sped through the night, sped south toward High Fields.

Shelby knew she should be worried about crashing into an abandoned car or hitting a deer or being ambushed by some other desperate group. She clutched her rifle between her hands, ready to defend these people she'd grown to love more than her own life, knowing they were doing the same and were ready to die for her.

EIGHTY-ONE

The drive south was uneventful. Max felt the tension inside of him unwind. Every fiber of his being understood how close they were getting to home. He could practically taste it. They hadn't passed a single roadblock, probably because they had Benjamin's specific instructions regarding which roads to avoid. It wasn't a direct path, routing them instead east through Walnut Springs and Meridian, and then southwest through Cranfills Gap. He had expected trouble there because another elevation gain led up to and through the gap, but the road was clear, and they sailed straight through.

West on 22 and then back east to Jonesboro. West again to Ireland, and finally, finally they hit Highway 84, which led them to Langford Cove.

Max fancied that he could practically see High Fields to the south. They could all feel it as the darkness of night began to recede.

Patrick loosened his grip on the wheel.

Gabe engaged the safety on his rifle and laid it across his lap.

Bianca tapped her fingers against the roof of the Hummer.

Shelby reached out and squeezed Max's hand.

A few more miles to go. When they turned

south onto Highway 281, the Hummer's lights revealed an ocean of color. Bluebonnets carpeted the right of way alongside the road, Indian blankets popped up through cracked foundations, paintbrushes scattered through and around and over the destruction.

They drove slowly through the small collection of buildings that comprised Langford Cove. On the east side of the road sat First State Bank, its furniture still scattered across the lawn. Max could practically see that earlier version of themselves—

Patrick and Bianca in the Mustang.

He and Shelby and Lanh and Carter in the Dodge.

Gabe leaning against the Hummer, arms crossed, patiently waiting.

So much had changed since that day. They had experienced things and seen things that he hadn't expected to see in his lifetime. A new government? New Town? Possibly a new world. Hope. That was what they'd seen and experienced, and it colored the way they perceived everything else.

The grocery store was still looted.

The taxidermist remained closed.

An empty lot was all that remained of the feed store that had been in operation since Max was a young boy.

They passed the school, which looked like an abandoned ship, and accelerated out of town.

Certainly devastation was all around them, but hope was on the horizon. Max realized that would have sounded ridiculous coming out of his mouth, but it felt right in his heart.

When they turned west off the state highway, something inside of Max began to unwind. They were nearly home. They'd made it.

They were waved through the roadblock, with several folks shouting, "Welcome back," and "Good to have you home." There was even an "About time you got here," followed by laughter and, of course, a few whistles for the Hummer. No one tried to stop them. Their questions would wait. No doubt each person manning that roadblock understood how tired Max and his friends were, how much he would want to see his parents.

They turned into the lane and started up the hill. The family graveyard sat on a rise, under the shade of a massive live oak tree.

His heart seemed to stop. "There are two more graves."

Gabe's foot came off the gas pedal for a second as they all turned and stared. Wooden crosses had been placed at the head of two freshly dug graves.

"Max, I'm sure they're all right." Shelby covered his hand with hers.

Bianca turned to stare at the graves as they passed. "Someone would have said something.

Someone at the roadblock would have mentioned . . ."

Patrick didn't say a word, but the look that passed between him and Max said enough.

Max felt an ache in his heart that was a physical pain. He reached up to rub at his chest, and then they were at the house. He scrambled out of the vehicle and ran toward the porch.

His father stepped out first.

His mother was right behind him, and she was cradling something in her arms. No, not something. Someone.

EIGHTY-TWO

"Where are the boys?" Georgia asked, a look of alarm on her face.

"They stayed in New Town." Shelby put an arm around the older woman, explaining about Carter and Lanh as they moved into the kitchen and gathered around the old oak table.

Max took a seat next to Shelby. "Tell us about the baby and the two graves."

"Her parents made it to the roadblock, but there was little hope that the mother would survive." Georgia stared down at the tiny girl in her arms. "The woman had an infection of some sort. Doc Lambert did the best he could."

Gabe performed a cursory examination of the child as Roy fetched glasses of water for everyone.

When Gabe finally said, "She seems to be healthy," they all let out a collective sigh.

"What happened to the father?" Patrick asked.

"Shot." Max's dad looked tired, relieved that they were back, but tired from all that had transpired. He'd taken the news about Carter well—they both had.

"Went after baby supplies." Georgia raised the baby to her shoulder and rubbed her back in slow, small circles. "We told him not to. We told him we'd make do."

"He was shot? Around here?"

Roy cleared his throat and pushed on with the story. "Thought he knew a place. He'd heard about a delivery truck, but he was shot before he even found it. Barely made it back, and by the time he did, there was nothing anyone could do."

"What's her name?" Shelby asked, reaching for the child. She cradled the infant to her chest, one hand on the back of the child's head, her eyes closed as she kissed it.

"Grace. Her parents named her Grace. We promised . . . we promised that somehow we would take care of her."

"She's a sweet thing, but I don't mind admitting that Georgia and I are a little old for raising an infant."

Bianca sat forward on the edge of her seat, her eyes locked on the child. "We can find someone in Abney. I'm sure someone will be willing."

"No. We're meant to take care of her—Max and I are."

Georgia gave her a shrewd look. "Max and you?"

Blushing like a schoolgirl, Shelby buried a smile in the soft fuzz of Grace's hair and shot a glance at Max over the baby's head.

"We're getting married," he said.

"Married?" Roy grinned. "When?"

"Tonight? Now? As soon as we can get Jerry over here."

Georgia wrapped one arm around Shelby's shoulders, pressed her curls down, and kissed the top of her head.

"All good things," was all Roy said as he shook his son's hand and then pulled him to his feet and into a hug, which ended with them slapping each other on the back.

When his father released him, Max squatted in front of Shelby, reached out, and touched the child. The look Shelby gave him held such tenderness that he knew what her next words would be.

"Right, Max? We can keep her, raise her, care for her?"

"Of course we will."

Max had the horrid image of the man and woman not making it through the roadblock, of the child dying on the outside beside her parents. But that hadn't happened. Grace was safe now, and she would remain that way if Shelby and Max, Roy and Georgia, Patrick and Bianca, even Gabe had anything to do with it. Because Shelby and Max might raise the child, but she would be a part of the family they had become.

The light of dawn flooded the pastures as they walked back out onto the porch. Sunshine splashed across the landscape, gracing fields, pushing back the shadows, bringing the hope and promise of a new day.

EPILOGUE

High Fields Ranch
Fourteen months later

Grace toddled across the porch, landing beside the beagle pup they'd bartered for the week before.

"Worth every penny of the fish I promised to take them for the next month," Max had said as the pup chewed on his fingers. "Our baby girl deserves a dog to grow up with."

Grace squealed and reached for Dodger's floppy ear, rubbing it between her fingers as Carter had done with his blankie many years ago.

There was so much Shelby wanted to tell her son. Tell him—not write it in a letter that might or might not be delivered: their trip home, Bianca and Patrick's move to Mason to be near Bianca's sister, Gabe's intention of finding a woman named Lenora, her marriage, Grace.

"I can't believe it. I'm afraid to believe it." She held up Carter's letter that had been delivered to Abney via military transport. The mail was running again, but the delivery was unpredictable at best. They'd both read Carter's letter several times. Roy and Georgia had read it too. They'd cried and laughed and cried some more. Carter and Lanh were coming home.

"God is good," Max said, pulling her onto his lap.

"All the time," she whispered, as Grace pushed herself into a standing position, toddled across the porch, and insisted on climbing up with them.

The lights were still out.

Food was scarce.

Life was hard.

But Carter was on his way home, and the federal government was sending out advance parties to establish a presence in rural areas. In Texas that would be in county seats, which meant Abney.

They had all changed since that afternoon they'd been hiking at Colorado Bend State Park, the afternoon that the largest solar flare in recorded history had plunged their world into darkness. Their jobs had changed. Their way of living had changed. The things they did to help and protect one another had changed.

But inside, Shelby felt like the same girl who had gone to the senior prom with Max Berkman. He was the love of her life, and she could trust him with her heart. That was what she had learned. That he was trustworthy, as was God.

In spite of what had happened or would happen in the future, she understood that truth. He was good—all the time.

DISCUSSION QUESTIONS

1. In the second chapter we see that Shelby's attitude toward her son has changed over the course of the last year. She understands that he is a man now, and that she no longer needs to treat him as a child. How does a change in attitude like this affect the way we relate to one another? In the Bible, 1 Corinthians 13:11, we read, "When I was a child, I talked like a child, I thought like a child, I reasoned like a child. When I became a man, I put the ways of childhood behind me." What does this verse mean to you?

2. In chapter 12, Shelby explains to Max that she has changed. She says, "I feel stronger than I've ever been." Can hard times do that to you . . . make you stronger? Why or why not? In Psalm 28:7, David says, "The LORD is my strength and my shield." In what ways is this true in your life?

3. When Shelby and Lanh are discussing his family, Shelby realizes most problems can be overcome, but "not knowing . . . it was something that weighed on you constantly." Do you agree? If all technology were taken

away, would you miss communication—phone calls and emails and texts—the most? Why or why not?

4. In chapter 22, Carter admits to himself that he has an "on-again, off-again" relationship with God. He has no trouble believing when he sees the bounty of God's creation, but he can't understand why bad things happen to good people. Do you know anyone who struggles with this? Where in the Bible can we point them for comfort? (When I'm struggling, the words found in the book of Job, chapters 38–42, have been particularly helpful.)

5. Chapter 29 portrays a difficult scene of vigilante justice. Max is torn by what they are doing. He has dedicated his life to law and order, and yet he feels a need to protect the families that Hugo and his goons would prey on in the future. Are the group's actions justified? Was there a better solution? Explain your answer.

6. After the tornado, Carter has an epiphany of sorts. He realizes that "there were times when their lives teetered in the hands of God." David writes in Psalm 139:16, "Your eyes saw my unformed body; all the days ordained for me were written in your book

before one of them came to be." What does this verse mean to you? And does it bring you comfort or increase your confusion?

7. Shelby wakes in the country church. As she's walking outside, she looks back and sees a rainbow of color slipping across their row of backpacks. She thinks of this as a blessing, a sign that God is still in control. Have you had a similar experience? Do you think God sends us reminders that he cares for us? Why or why not?

8. When Shelby sees the lights of New Town, she covers her face with her hands. Carter "understood his mom's need to put her hands over her face, to hide from the hope that sparkled in front of them." We do that sometimes. We hide from hope. Read Psalm 3:5; 1 Corinthians 15:58; and Psalm 147:11. What does the Bible say about hope?

9. Did you find the technologies in New Town to be believable? At the end of this book, you will find more detailed information as well as sources where you can read about alternative energy technology that already exists. Why do you think we're not incorporating this into our power grid more? What are some ways that we could begin to do so?

10. When the group is stopped, waiting for Max to recover from his migraine, Shelby confesses that she is afraid of caring too much. Bianca's response is, "There's no such thing." Sometimes allowing ourselves to care unreservedly for another person can be frightening. Yet our model is God's love for us, and Paul prays in Ephesians 3:18 that we might have the power "to grasp how wide and long and high and deep is the love of Christ." How can that love embolden us to love others?

AUTHOR'S NOTE

The technology described in New Town does currently exist. In March 2015, Google announced their intention to build a biodome to house their new headquarters. VIT Technical Research Centre of Finland created a prototype for 3D printed trees that harvest solar energy. Wave energy products are in use off the coast of Australia, and the US Department of Energy has invested heavily in the hydrokinetic industry. Wind turbine trees were tested in Paris, France, in 2015. Statistics show that in 2015, 13.44 percent of domestically produced electricity came from renewable energy sources (including solar, wind, hydro, geo, and biomass).

There are, in fact, only three places to cross the Red River between Wichita Falls and Dallas. At many places along the Texas/Oklahoma border, the banks of the Red River are ten feet steep, and while people can descend to the river with four-wheel-drive vehicles, they become stuck when trying to climb back out. For the purposes of this story, I've made the banks steeper and less navigable.

The National Cancer Institute estimates that 1,685,210 new cases of cancer were diagnosed in the US alone in 2016. The top four cancers in order of number of patients affected are non-melanoma skin cancer, lung cancer, breast cancer, and prostate cancer. "The number of people living beyond a cancer diagnosis reached nearly 14.5 million in 2014 and is expected to rise to almost 19 million by 2024." You can find more information at https://www.cancer.gov/about -cancer/understanding/statistics.

The Flint Hills of Kansas is the largest unplowed remnant of tall grass prairie in the world. Located in east-central Kansas, it combines a unique variety of grasslands, wetlands, and woodlands. The area is approximately 157 miles long by 93 miles wide. The hills can be accessed from the Flint Hills Scenic Byway. More information can be found at www.flinthillsdiscovery.org.

Several mock Mars missions have been conducted in recent years. One NASA-financed study took place on a remote site in Hawaii. The yearlong isolation experiment ended on August 29, 2016. The purpose of the study was to evaluate long-term isolation scenarios and how such isolation affected crew members' health and productivity.

Massive solar flares are not fiction. The Carrington Event occurred September 1-2, 1859. Auroras were seen as far south as the Caribbean, and telegraph systems throughout Europe and North America failed. More recently, large solar storms were recorded in 2003, 2011, 2012, 2013, and 2015. Research by NASA scientists indicate there is a 12 percent chance a large storm will happen in the next ten years. This report stresses that while coronal mass ejections and solar flares are not physically harmful, they could blow out transformers in power grids and disrupt satellite/GPS systems. A recent assessment by the Department of Homeland Security reported to Congress that a massive electromagnetic pulse event caused by a solar flare could leave more than 130 million Americans without power for years.

EMERGING
TECHNOLOGIES

Home Solar Panels

Solar panels work by harnessing sunlight, transforming it into energy, and then sending that energy to an inverter, which converts it into electricity. As of October 2015, less than 1 percent of global energy consumption was provided by solar energy, though that percentage is growing exponentially. Germany currently is the leading nation in installed solar energy devices.

The average solar panel size needed to power a home is 600 square feet. According to *Forbes* magazine, installing solar panels on your home will reduce your electric bill by an average of $84 per month. Estimates on the cost to install solar panels on a home vary widely. Some institutes place the cost at approximately $17,000, while others state it will cost more than $50,000. Though the expense is considered by many to be prohibitive, tax incentives of up to 30 percent exist to encourage conversion to solar energy.

3D Printed Trees

Solar trees blend art and scientific advances in the area of renewable energy. As such, they have increased the visibility of existing and emerging solar technology. They are often used to enhance landscape and complement architecture in commercial or public buildings by promoting awareness, understanding, and adoption of renewable energy. They are not used as a primary source of energy, but rather complementary to rooftop solar systems. Although scientists and engineers continue to develop this type of green technology, it is not currently available for purchase in the public sector.

Ocean Wave Energy

Wave energy harnesses the power along coastal regions and can be installed in nearshore, off-shore, and far offshore locations. Advantages of this type of technology include the fact that waves are truly renewable and unlimited, environment friendly, and widely available. There are a variety of methods to harness this kind of energy, including devices that are perpendicular to the direction of the wave, multi-segment floating structures parallel to the direction of the waves, and floating structures. Pilot projects within the United States exist in California, Oregon, and Hawaii. Wave farms also exist in Portugal, the United Kingdom, and Australia. The potential impact on the marine environment is still being studied.

Faraday Cage

A Faraday cage, named after English scientist Michael Faraday, is an enclosure that blocks electric fields. Faraday invented them in 1836. They have the ability to shield whatever is stored inside from external electromagnetic radiation. Common examples of this type of device are MRI machines, microwave ovens, and even suits worn by electrical linemen. They can be small enough to hold a laptop or large enough to protect a tank. As the importance of electromagnetic shielding has grown, Faraday cages have become more widely available. The technology has been applied to the field of electromagnetic compatibility and the design and installation of electromagnetic interference-shielded chambers.

ABOUT THE AUTHOR

Vannetta Chapman writes inspirational fiction full of grace. She is the author of several novels, including the Pebble Creek Amish series and *Anna's Healing*, *Joshua's Mission*, and *Sarah's Orphans*. Vannetta is a Carol Award winner, and she has also received more than two dozen awards from Romance Writers of America chapter groups. She was a teacher for fifteen years and currently resides in the Texas Hill Country. For more information, visit her at www.VannettaChapman.com.

Center Point Large Print
600 Brooks Road / PO Box 1
Thorndike, ME 04986-0001 USA

(207) 568-3717

US & Canada:
1 800 929-9108
www.centerpointlargeprint.com